LAIR

Henchman Book One

CARL STUBBLEFIELD

MOUNTAINDALE
PRESS

CONTENTS

ACKNOWLEDGMENTS

Hey y'all!

I'd love to take the time to go ahead and thank a lot of people. My family, friends, peers, and those who supported me.

And now those who...didn't. Those who doubted me. Those who tried their best to bring me down. Those who fueled my rage and spite-filled nights with writing. Those who can be immortalized as villains and who tried so desperately to keep me and other good people miserable for their own gain.

To you? I say thanks, and read carefully. You never know what may lay between the lines, subtext and foreshadowing and all that. See you soon.

CHAPTER ONE

Free Falling

Gus dragged the mop across the already spotless floor on the bridge of the space station. He had drawn the short straw and got custodial duty, *again*. Staring at the floor, he didn't notice the increase in activity of the crew.

Just do your time. Three more months on the station then you can get back to your friends. He had only taken this job because he thought his three best buds would be onboard with him. When they didn't get picked, Gus had been alone. He felt isolated as the new guy, and, of course, all the worst jobs fell to him more than what seemed like his fair share.

A sudden impact made everyone stumble, shaking Gus out of his moping while mopping.

"Give me a status report!" Station Commander Graviton barked.

"Sir, it appears that we have lost stabilizers one through six and the remaining two are at half capacity," First Lieutenant Aurora reported as her hands flew across multiple view-panels.

"How is this happening? I thought having *him* here would prevent those types of malfunctions!" Graviton growled, jabbing a finger in Gus' direction.

Gus tried to press himself closer to the wall in a misguided attempt to become less noticeable. His super employer was known for his hot temper, and despite his famous father's connections getting him this job, he had no illusions that he wouldn't be crushed in a fit of rage. Just his luck to be on custodial duty when something went wrong.

"The stabilizers are showing no signs of mechanical failure, but there is something impeding their access to a sufficient gravimetric field to function as designed—"

"Is the disruption only below us or all around?"

"It appears to be a disc-like interruption slowly moving to eclipse the footprint of the station from Earth. Remaining stabilizers will be unable to function in forty seconds!"

Gus slowly slid toward the exit as Graviton madly pounded at various panels. Adjustments made, he slid his arms into two sleeves in a crystalline box that resembled the type lab techs used to work on dangerous chemicals or viruses. Once his hands were inside the sleeves up to the elbow, the inside of the box lit up and a blue hue emanated from his palms. His hands began gesticulating and waving and then were pressed flat as if he were trying to keep the lid on a box with some wild creature inside fighting to be set free.

The whole floor tilted suddenly and the mop bucket began to slide when it suddenly stopped with a slight vibration as the crystal box activated. Gus was hoping to get off the bridge, but as his mag-boots engaged he couldn't lift his feet off the ground. He didn't know if it was due to his boots being typical faulty, low-tier henchman issue or that the magnetized floor was set for supers and he was just too weak.

So flipping close to the door! Gus pulled frantically at his ID attached to his retractable keycard holder, trying to stretch it to the sensor panel. Of course, it had to be on the right side of the exit door, a mere six feet away. Directly behind him was the access door to the escape pods.

Why not? he thought, pulling the ID to this panel. The panel flashed on:

ID: Gus Vannett
Rank: G.O.O.N.
This pod is reserved for Tier 1 employees only, please access pods reserved for your particular tier.

Tier 1 comprised the highest ranked supers, who made up the bridge crew. Pods for regs were probably hopelessly far away on the extreme lower levels; if they even existed, that was. One more reality that reaffirmed the distinction between supers and regs, as they were called—regular humans with no powers.

"Get ready!" Graviton shouted.

Gus turned back to the chaos… and was hit by a wave of nausea as his inner ear was overwhelmed with the confusing maelstrom of forces, as it struggled to determine what was up and down. It felt as if riding a spinning teacup ride on a roller-coaster with a liberal amount of loop-de-loops. He held out valiantly for about two and a half seconds before throwing up.

The fluid projectile mass streamed away from him, combining with the levitating mop water in front of him which then hovered and began to coalesce into a ball. Gus watched in horror as it was stretched and contorted by the forces playing upon them all, and the mass nearly hit Graviton. Luckily, it did not. Unluckily, it hit Aurora full in the face like a vengeful slime creature from one of the RPGs Gus and his buddies loved to play.

Gus' jaw dropped and he redoubled his efforts to lift his boots. Gravity slowly began to reassert itself to its normal direction and things started to settle. His boots were still stuck to the ground and he was effectively trapped. This was not good, as his punishment for losing his lunch and probable death were only delayed by the confusion and urgency of stabilizing the station.

Why did it have to be Aurora? The blonde beauty was one of the few people who ever noticed Gus and was even nice to him. She was way out of his league, of course, but there was a tiny part of him that fantasized that she actually liked him back.

Reading volumes into a smile and glance where in reality there was probably only kindness, *or pity*.

Gus stopped trying to lift the boots and began to start removing them when he realized he was getting nowhere. He managed to loosen two of the ski-boot type latches on the back of his left foot. It had taken a while to get used to walking in the clunky boots, a mandatory part of the station uniform. He hadn't given it too much thought until they activated and secured to the floor. The station stopped with a lurch, and the display showed that they had anchored to the moon's gravitational field.

At the same time, a pinpoint of light appeared near the center of the floor. Hooray! More distractions! The light brightened and the metal began to bubble and sink in an ever-widening pit.

Gus kept working, feeling like he was in cement shoes as he worked to finish unlatching the left boot and began on the right. Three supers flew in through the breach and executed perfect three-point landings in a row, somehow managing to position themselves opposite Graviton and Aurora. They wore black uniforms, contrasting with the garish purple and white of those whom were on the station. Graviton was Purple Faction, one of the three governing factions of supers on the planet. The fact that the invaders wore black spoke to their factionless nature.

The center figure pointed at Graviton, twisted his hand and made the 'come and get it' gesture Morpheus made famous all those years ago.

Was there a class supers attended called 'Dramatic Entry?' If so, they needed to expand the course curriculum. Maybe it was only a weekend continuing education class. Gus recognized the woman on the right to be Slipstream, a super who could wield solid light. She could also use existing forms of light as tethers to pull against and move around, both artificial and natural. Gus didn't know the other two, but thought the one on the left was a shapeshifter—Mercurio, maybe?

Graviton whipped his hands out of the interface, pushing it

to the wall as he prepared for battle. His eyes stopped on Gus struggling by the escape pod.

"Don't even think about it, boy—that pod is for me alone," he said through gritted teeth. Gus froze, feeling a bead of sweat roll down the center of his back. Graviton turned back to the invaders, and Gus finally gasped, not realizing he had been holding his breath as his boss' gaze fell upon him.

Aurora had cleaned herself somehow and flung out her hands, shooting a blinding spray of ionized light and particles toward the invaders. Slipstream slid forward in front of her companions to meet the spray. She raised the back of her forearm to the attack, absorbing the light and energy into an invisible shield. Her feet appeared to be skating on mini Tron-like light cycles and she spun and flung the blinding blast back toward Aurora.

Mercurio took his cue, stretching and sliding, serpent-like, attacking from the other side. As he leaped, Graviton flung out a hand and Mercurio slammed to the floor. He vibrated there, losing cohesion slightly as the G-forces held him to the ground. While Mercurio was held, Graviton had to split his focus and keep his arm outstretched to maintain the localized gravity well. With his other hand, he aimed at Slipstream, but she was too fast for him to target as she rocketed side to side at jerky angles to avoid being hit.

Slipstream pulled slivers of light from the LED panels above and began to fling them at all of the bridge crew, skewering one through the neck and another in the eye.

Many were so intent on stabilizing the station that they were not paying attention to the battle going on and were mortally wounded. As they saw their comrades fall, others rushed to maintain the station's functions, but ducking and staying behind cover as much as possible.

Slipstream targeted the bridge crew with dogged determination. Gus had assumed they were supers, but they made no attempts to retaliate or join Aurora and Graviton as they ducked out of the way. When they attempted to check a screen or panel, Slipstream would pick them off, one by one.

The invading leader, wearing a black suit with a red lion or scorpion—it was hard to tell the logo—stepped forward, exuding equal parts confidence and contempt.

"Factionless!" Gus said in shock. Those who were unable or unwilling to join a Faction were looked down upon almost universally. Often they were mercenaries, willing to do anything for the right price. While the main Factions were Purple, Green, and Orange, most factionless chose to wear gray or black. The Factions were merciless with imposters, and few dared incite their wrath. Gus stared at the spectacle, unable to control the covetous looks he gave even the Factionless. *Am I the only reg on this station?*

Graviton intensified his pressure on the shapeshifter as the Factionless leader faced him and began hurling glowing lava balls, kudoken style. Equipment was dissolved into black bubbly masses as the superheated material dissolved polymer plastic panels and displays. A lava ball hit the leg of a crew member, taking it off at the knee, cauterizing it, and filling the room with an unbearable stench.

Aurora focused her intent and drained most of the energy from the lights, absorbing photons and robbing Slipstream of her deadly ammunition. The area darkened; Aurora left only the red emergency illumination, which had the least energy of visible light.

Graviton attempted to shift the direction of his abilities to immobilize the opposing leader, who responded by simply beginning to hover in the air. One of his sub-skills must have been flying, and these supers were resistant to gravity attacks. Abandoning these techniques, Graviton flung Mercurio against the far bulkhead to focus on the leader. Concentrating, he began to generate a matterless singularity at the core of the invader's chest.

Gus watched Mercurio fly toward the wall, changing his form into a ball. He hit it, but rebounded off of it like he was made of rubber, and launched back into the fight. He slid behind Aurora and his elongated arms began to snake around her.

Glancing back to the bosses, Gus saw the lava super had staggered to a knee, clutching at his chest, looking back in fury at Graviton. Stretching his hands out to the sides, tight beams of lava shot laterally and began eating into the structure around him. One of the crew leapt out of the way as a console was split in two, the beams melting through everything in their path.

Locking eyes, the two supers pitted their strengths against each other to see who would last the longest. Creaking of beams could be heard as the heat chewed through supports, weakening the substructure. The space station was designed more for functionality and was lightweight by nature, to more easily maintain orbit. Thus it lacked the durability of a typical fortress, as access was limited for most supers, and soon began to succumb to the heat.

Gus could begin to see an indented deformation that was slowly growing larger in the chest plate of the lava super that resembled a crumpling soda can.

Mercurio had wrapped Aurora in multiple bands of his stretched, flexible arms while Slipstream was hitting her with what looked like a glowing cudgel of some sort.

With a loud groan, the room split, buckling upward in the center, separating Graviton from his enemy. There was a moment of weightlessness, the strain of damaged components stressing gravity tethers to the breaking point. Gus flew out of his left boot, secured in place only by the remaining latch on the right one. The station's gravity field stuttered into effect, then winked back out into zero gravity.

"Critical failure! Hull breach! Please evacuate!" a voice warned over the speakers, amidst sirens that began to sound. The door to Gus' right slid into the wall… the escape pod was open! Whether caused by a short or the station's imminent demise, the restrictions had been lifted. Gus strained to reach to remove the last latch on his right boot, grabbed the doorjamb, and pulled himself out of his boots and inside. The supers outside continued to struggle and crash about, pushing off walls to engage each other in the weightless environment.

The pod was an oval room that branched off the main bridge. It was about twenty-five feet in diameter and appeared to be designed for two individuals. The decor and technology appeared a lot older than the bridge for some reason. The fluttery-falling sensation of lost gravity returned and Gus hit the launch button. As the doors slowly slid shut, he could see Graviton getting a face-full of lava as the other super straddled him and they both grappled each other as they floated by. Blinking in surprise, Gus numbly let his eyes drift and saw explosions through the portholes and main screen along the front of the pod. He was still in a shocked stupor when it was forcefully jettisoned away from the station.

CHAPTER TWO

Crash Into Me

Gus hovered for a second as gravity shifted yet again, then he was flung into the wall. Lights flashed, and the world turned as he flew toward the ceiling. Through the viewport, he could see the tumbling of the sky, then water, then sky again as the pod flipped and shimmied through the atmosphere. His inner ear and stomach tried to orient with the confusion of signals to figure out just where down was, as the rudimentary inertial dampeners struggled to minimize the strain to the occupant inside. Fortunately, his stomach was conveniently empty.

Due to the rapid firing of the pod, Gus was not anchored. Nor was he familiar with any of the controls or layout of an escape pod. Henchmen *never* got the opportunity to use one, especially a good one like this. He could tell that Graviton did not want him using that particular pod, but his survival instincts kicked in before his rational thought of how this super could mash him to a pulp. Too late to worry about that now.

Gus caught sight of two of what he assumed were space-suits across the pod from him. The tech looked conspicuously old in comparison with the bridge. Gus wondered if it had been cannibalized from some older space station. He began army-crawling to them amidst the debris that shuffled back and forth across the wobbling pod that bucked like an angry bull. He was only ten feet away from them when the pod started skipping off the atmosphere. One lucky shift, and Gus grabbed the security mesh by the two containment suits along the other side of the pod with one arm. It felt like it was almost yanked out of his shoulder socket as he dangled for a moment, scrambling to secure his grip with his other hand.

The suits yawned open like a human-shaped clamshell, each side of the suit joining near the head. He pulled himself toward one of the suits, wishing he had more upper body strength as he felt the stress, both physically and mentally, to get in a suit before landfall.

Another shift and he crashed into the bottom half of the suit. Luckily, gravity was now oriented below the lower half of the suit, so he scrambled to get in position and punched the engage button above him, situated on the inner chest. The top half of the suit lowered down over him like a clamshell, sealing him inside. The cacophony of sounds was muted, save the whirring and clicking sounds that were transmitted along the suit as the system came to life and finished sealing and creating the protective environment inside.

The suit was locked in position and Gus felt a pang of panic, trapped inside the suit like it was a sarcophagus, unable to move. All he could do now was watch the viewscreen outside as the pod hurtled Earthward.

The pod had stabilized somewhat, orienting itself instead of flipping around. Gus could see a background of blue through the blazing light of reentry that began to mask the view as an altimeter reading in the corner of the viewscreen shrunk at an impossibly fast rate. The inertial dampeners ramped up from a low hum to an ear-piercing shriek. A sudden feeling of compression, followed by another feeling of weightlessness were the last things he remembered before everything turned black.

———

Gus awoke in a void. His arms hung limp as he floated face-down in the suit. He ached all over; almost every muscle felt ripped or strained. He also had a splitting headache. The pain brought back a memory, vivid and clear.

Unknown to Gus, the suit had injected tiny robots into his system and they were already repairing his body of the damage he had received from the crash.

Gus moaned in agony. He never was one to have headaches but this level of pain was worrisome. At least nothing was numb, so he wasn't paralyzed. Still, Gus had never had to deal with pain on this scale.

Neurons fired as robots repaired torn blood vessels in the brain, cauterizing them with tiny electric shocks that also served to activate memories long forgotten. The nanobots worked, and they learned of their new host as they repaired the damage. Neurons continued to fire, dredging up memories along the way.

———

It was an autumn morning with the air just starting to get crisp and chill, when a female co-worker invited him to join her for one of her fitness classes. Gus was so painfully shy, and this girl was so cute. *Don't blow this.*

Since they were just regs, people without superpowers, they only had old-school gyms to exercise. These gyms had probably used the same weights and machines for the last forty years. The pungent smell of dried sweat and the discolored yellow sponge that peeked out of the cracked weight benches testified of their age and disrepair. Lots of things had changed once humans got superpowers, and regs had to make do with the scraps that were left.

They were one of the first ones to arrive and as the class filled up he realized that he was the only male member of the class. Everyone began to put ten pounds on the barbells in preparation for the class. Feeling he'd need a little more of a workout, he had put fifty pounds on the bar as they started doing some squat exercises, followed by a fair number of lunges. Fifty seemed to be doing the trick, giving him a good burn as they began the class. Then the instructor stated, "Ok, now that warm-ups are over, let's get into the routine!"

Realizing the error of over-exerting himself this early in the routine for his out of shape body, but still not wanting to look like a total wimp, the torture began. As the shoulder presses, barbell curls, and tricep extensions went on, his legs began to become more and more wobbly. By the end of the class, they were spontaneously collapsing and Gus had to cling to the armrail to make his way down the stairs and out of the gym. The pursed lips and judgmental eyes told Gus all he needed to know. She was not impressed with him and rolled her eyes as he apologetically descended the stairs like a marionette. By the time he made it down the stairs she was gone. *Good thing we drove separately…*

———

Gus winced as he tried to move, bringing him back to his unfortunate present situation. *So groggy. I can't be dead… it hurts too much.* The bulky suit made it difficult to move. What happened to the pod? Gus tried to raise his head and a sharp stab of pain in his neck froze him in a paroxysm of pain. It was too much; the pain combined with exhaustion from his ordeal overtook him again, leaving his question unanswered. Due to the memory taking the little attention he was able to muster, he did not notice the system diagnostics appear on a virtual screen on his visor.

Analyzing… analyzing… additional injuries detected.
Releasing nanobots.
Neurogenic shock detected…
Suit compression activated.
Monitoring volumetric pressure…
IV fluids administered to reestablish norms.

Increasing oxygen filtration from the environment to raise blood oxygen levels.
Optimization protocol engaged.
Sedatives administered during the repair phase.
Estimated time for repair: 3.8 days, longer sedation phase for recovery recommended.

Gus' eyes fluttered shut as the sedatives took effect. Time passed and the man-shaped suit bobbed on the water, slowly floating toward an island. The waves and wind slowly pushed it towards shore, where it encountered an unseen barrier. As the suit was passively pushed through the barrier, the body inside began to react. And as it did, the suit compensated.

Analysis… sudden arrest of system.
Nanobots reassigned to oxygen delivery and manual electric stimulation of cardiac muscle to maintain normal rhythms…
Oxygen saturation increased to 40% to aid in respiration and transfer rates…
Circulation stabilized but brain function has ceased.
Insufficient life signs—will need to permanently integrate to sustain vitals.
Nanobot specialization features enabled, pluripotentiality lost as nanobots are anchored to target tissues…
Musculoskeletal embed… complete.
Neural embed… complete.
Cerebral embed… complete.
Endocrine embed… complete.
Remaining systems… complete.
Cerebral framework established, enhanced cognitive functions online. Patient stabilized. Brain functions returning to normal.
Integration with all major body systems complete.
Nanobots will be permanently required to maintain life functions for this host.
Supporting neural activity until external threat resolves…
Evaluating…
Preliminary scans show unique latent genetic and mental augments,

commencing deep scan. Rudimentary maintenance functions until the scan is complete.

To the outside observer, the small man-shaped form continued its slow voyage. Bobbing in the waves. Tiny solar panels on the outside of the suit absorbed energy during the hot days and transferred the energy to the nanobots as they worked. As the nanobots became more specialized, eventually they all sacrificed this ability to recharge themselves from external sources to save their host.

CHAPTER THREE

Riot Nrrrd

The tiny robots continued to rush to relieve the pressure from internal bleeding on Gus' brain. In doing so, they had to close off more bleeders and metabolize the fluids that were building up and putting pressure on the brain, making it hard for blood to flow freely and oxygenate the delicate organ.

Electrical stimulation had to occur as the effects of the field suppressed the cells ability to work on their own. They fairly crackled as they worked, firing neurons along the way, plunging Gus deep into memories he forced himself to never revisit.

———

8 years ago...

Gus had pulled into the shopping center, scooting his little VW bug into a parking spot. He needed to get some parts for his car, to try to fix one of its myriad problems. Despite this, he still felt lucky Grandpa had given him the car on his fifteenth birthday. Most people used public transport these days, but Gus relished the freedom his own car offered.

"It will need tons of work, Gus, but these Fuscas are designed so that they can be easily repaired. You'll learn a lot, Gus, and being self-sufficient does a lot for a man."

Gus smiled at the memory and how his grandpa always called them that, 'foo-skuhs'. Today's project was changing the belts. He headed across the parking lot to the AutoMaxx. It must have been the first of the month, because the parking lot was crowded with people swarming the Grocertopia next door. It was always busy when allotments were distributed. Luckily for Gus, the allotments only accounted for food, so the AutoMaxx shouldn't be crowded.

After picking up what he needed, he headed back to his car. An elderly African-American lady was in the process of loading her groceries into her car which was parked next to his, and a teenager about Gus' age was prowling around, speaking harshly to the woman while she silently tried to put her groceries in her car as fast as she could. Gus couldn't make out what was being said, but assumed it was threatening with how the teen was waving his hands around, almost like he was going to slap the poor woman at any moment. She cringed away, shrinking in on herself as she tried to hurry.

Gus noticed the punk's friends standing in a circle about fifty feet away, laughing and watching the scene. Was this some kind of initiation ritual for a gang or something? One of the things that pissed Gus off in this district was the prevailing thought that might made right. Sure, you could call the enforcers, but they would calmly listen to your story and then politely tell you that they didn't have the resources to chase after everyone who was a little aggressive. It was survival of the fittest at its worst. A tenet of the Purple Faction that tacitly-influenced local law enforcement, and the regs mirrored it, whether consciously or not.

As he got closer, he could hear the teen saying how hungry he was in mock sarcasm.

"C'mon, Grammy, can't you see I'm too skinny? A growing boy needs food, and you don't need all of that…"

Gus passed them and opened his car door. He threw his bag into the front seat and looked amid the trash in the backseat for the tire iron he had left there from changing a tire recently. It had been raining, of course, so he hadn't stowed everything back like he should. Still, Gus was a typical teenager, and papers, fast food cartons, and other trash covered the floor of the backseat.

The woman let out a yelp, which brought Gus out of his search. "Ok, man, that's enough. Why don't you leave the woman alone?" As he stood up, he saw the teen had grabbed one of the bags the woman was holding, and was attempting to wrench it out of her hands.

The woman cowered in fear, but still clung to the bag. Gus knew how much people on allotments needed the food. She probably was supporting people at home to have what seemed a larger than average allotment. Plus, it said something that she was out here alone getting the food, and not someone younger.

In an instant, the teenager was next to Gus. He could see the puckered red acne scars and greasy skin. "Did you just say something?" he asked, leaning in, right into Gus' face. He was so close, his wet lip touched Gus' own, which grossed him out on a whole new level.

Gus pushed the teen away, trying to establish a more comfortable personal space.

"Oh, so now you trying to push me, man? Gonna regret that..." Gus could see the kid's friends start moving toward him in his peripheral vision. He also saw the old woman, pulling out of her parking spot, giving him a glance that said, "I'm sorry," as she sped away. Gus tried to bolt for his car, *really* wishing he had found that tire iron, but the teen pushed him against his car and gave him a sucker punch.

Gus was winded as the blow hit him right in the solar plexus. He dropped to one knee gasping for breath. Then his buddies came in, kicking savagely. The only thing Gus managed to gasp out when he got some of his breath back was, "Don't do this, you don't know who I am, my father's a super..."

"Sure he is, and guess what? You don't know who *we* are, so good luck trying to find us, superboy!" The kicking commenced again, and at some point Gus lost consciousness.

When he came to, Gus not only felt terrible, his spirits dropped even more when he saw the state of his poor little Fusca. It had dents all over it where the gang took out their aggression on it after they had gotten tired of kicking him. Mirrors were ripped off, as well as the antenna. They even took his crappy cassette player, leaving a gaping maw of wires. Luckily, they hadn't found the tire iron either, or he might not still be alive.

Getting to his feet, Gus was in more pain than he had ever been in his life. His back was killing him, and he was covered in bruises. He had to lean against his car as a wave of nausea hit him from standing too quickly. Getting inside, Gus put his thumb on the ignition scan, the only modern thing in the old car. It rumbled to life, and Gus slowly made his way home. It hurt to turn his head too much to the left, so he took his time, waiting at more lights than he normally would since he didn't want to chance going through an intersection at the last minute. He had to crouch awkwardly to see through the only part of the windshield that wasn't cracked from the damage, so it was slow going.

When he got home, Tempest was there in the kitchen and barely looked up when Gus entered. Gus threw his keys in a bowl and went to the sink to splash some cold water on himself and clean up.

"What happened to you?" Tempest asked, still reading his newspaper.

"I got jumped helping an old lady with her food."

"By how many people?"

"Well, it was the one guy, but he had a bunch of his cronies watching the whole thing. They all jumped me."

"Well, it sounds like you learned a valuable lesson, then. Never engage a superior force, especially without the resources to defend your position. I'll bet you don't make that mistake again." He said all this without even making eye contact. *Whatever is in that newspaper must be damn interesting,* Gus thought angrily.

"Yeah, sure. How dumb of me, trying to help someone…"

"It was stupid. I'm glad you see that. You're lucky they didn't hurt you more. Sometimes I think your common sense was burned out when your mother left…"

Left? That was new. That part of the conversation had never occurred to Gus. The memory faded as Gus thought about this new information. He must have been so angry and in pain that his brain didn't register it. From what Gus had remembered after his illness, he always got the impression that Mom had died in some battle with other supers, not that she left. Did they get a divorce? Gus couldn't blame her for divorcing Tempest. He was cold and only had time for his job. Did they get a divorce because of him? The more he thought about it, he did get the feeling Tempest blamed him for his mom's absence. Were his medical bills a strain on their relationship? Was it something else lost in the amnesia that surrounded his illness?

The nanobots finished repairing the area in Gus' brain and moved on, and the memory winked out, and Gus drowsily sunk back into unconsciousness.

CHAPTER FOUR

Island in the Sun

14:01:12 remaining

Gus raised his head wearily and blinked at the bright sun above. He tried in vain to wipe away the sand that clung to the outside of his visor and succeeded only in smearing the grains around a bit and leaving dirty streaks across the glass. He tried to stand but staggered as an unexpected wave tripped him, and he fell face-first into the foamy water. This washed away the sandy grit and Gus could see clearly again.

Coming to his knees, he arched his back and looked at the scene before him. He appeared to be on a crescent-shaped swath of beach, with a short rise from the beach to a ridgeline twenty-five feet above him.

"Where the hell am I?!" Gus gasped in surprise, trying to recall anything between the crash and now. All that came were hazy in and out memories of floating, but he found he could not remember anything besides a bright flash and loud, body-shaking whine as the pod crashed. *How long was I out?*

Grateful that he wasn't bobbing alone in the middle of the ocean anymore, Gus began to stem the flow of panic that threatened to overtake him. Looking in the distance, he could see what appeared to be a dense jungle and a large mountain towering above the canopy. The island looked pretty large, and there had to be food here somewhere. He could survive. Hopefully.

A slight ache mingled with a combination of itchiness, and the constant feeling that he needed a good stretch permeated his muscles. Most of all, he felt hungry, hungrier than he could ever remember. Now if he could only get out of this clunky suit. After standing and wading to the shore, he could more fully feel the weight of the spacesuit on his shoulders, but the ache quickly faded as he began moving. The suit pulled on his muscles as if he were lugging a fully-outfitted backpack of some sort, filled with cannonballs.

Gus sighed, imagining the escape pod on the bottom of the ocean. He shuddered, thinking he could be stuck under some wreckage, trapped inside the pod. Most of these types of suits would scrub the carbon dioxide, and most could extract oxygen from the water, so breathing would not have been a problem.

Gus shuddered again as he imagined himself buried alive underwater, slowly starving to death as the onboard resources of the suit slowly lost the ability to sustain the wearer. A living nightmare. He counted his lucky stars he was flung free or at least cleared the debris without tearing the suit or damaging the delicate mechanisms inside.

"Why do I feel so good?" Gus asked no one in particular, his voice sounding hollow as it reflected off his helmet visor. He felt like he should definitely *not* feel as good as he did, considering the crash. His energy increased the more he moved around.

As if in reply, a display appeared on the inside of the visor, depicting various bars and gauges along the periphery of his field of view. A message scrolled at the bottom of his field of vision.

Text flashed across the bottom of the display:

You sustained multiple injuries that activated nanobots stored in the suit's host protection protocol. Sedatives were administered to enact physical repairs. 1.4 days later you encountered a bio-stasis field that stopped all natural life support and it was necessary to integrate nanobots on a perma-nent basis throughout your body, infiltrating into all of your body systems, nerves, musculature, and organs to sustain life and maintain brain function. Fortunately, your unique genetics enabled you to tolerate the procedure without killing you.

Gus knew that there was a very high rate of nanobot rejec-tion when they were used to save someone's life. It was usually the last-ditch attempt to save some old rich guy. Maybe it worked better with a younger body. But young or old, a failed attempt resulted in death, and the odds were so long that it was attempted only by the extremely desperate.

"What does that mean, permanently integrated? Am I like a cyborg now?" Gus asked. More writing spooled out on the display.

Technically, yes, loss of nanobot function will result in death. Due to the urgency of implantation, your nanobots specialized to the point that they have lost essential maintenance functions that will result in system failure and host death in approximately 14 days.

"What. The. Hell!? This day just keeps getting better and better," Gus groaned as he slumped down into the slushy sand. "So I'm dead in two weeks, then."

Not necessarily. Nanobots can evolve to increase in number and obtain addi-tional functionality. This should be attainable in the allotted time.

Gus sat there, waves rising higher and crashing on his legs

like they wanted to pile on the abuse as well. Whether it was bullies in parking lots or these uncaring waves, life just sucked sometimes. Most times. The fact that he could never get a break pushed Gus from irritation to a smoldering anger at the unfairness of life in general. Gus grit his teeth in frustration. Not this time. Not anymore. It was time to push back.

"Wait, what advantages do these nanobots offer? There have to be some advantages."

As you develop your abilities, your nanobots will learn along with you. Beneficial actions result in a gain of experience, which will allow you to level up and your nanobots to evolve as you undergo this leveling process. With each level you will gain 5 points to increase any basic stat: agility, constitution, charisma, strength, perception, intelligence, or luck. Most humans develop superhuman traits during this process as they increase in experience and level. You are now what humans call 'a super.'

Realization dawned on Gus. *I am a super now.* He had spent countless hours imagining what his life would be if he only had powers. He had made plans on what he would do differently if he only had the chance. Hope began to grow, and the despair and frustration lost their hold on him. He did *feel* different. He remembered the pain right after the crash, but now, he felt great. No sign of any pain or injury. *A super!* His mind began to race at the possibilities, and questions began to fill his mind.

He had settled into mediocrity, long ago accepting that despite any effort he made, life was going to stay pretty much the same. But now—now he could show everyone what he could really do. Everyone who had dismissed him flippantly and underestimated his worth. He knew it was petty, but he longed to confront his father and show him how wrong he had been. Or to find that group of thugs in the parking lot. He grinned evilly at what he could do to set things right. He cracked his knuckles, excited to begin. *I'll show all of you that I'm not the loser you took me for my whole life.*

"Ok, so to evolve my nanobots and survive, I need to level up. How many levels do I need to do that?"

The first opportunity for nanobot evolution occurs when the host reaches level 10. At that time, a specialized ability can be chosen.

"And what, specifically, do I need to do to gain experience?"

Experience is granted as the host performs activities that are either innovative, life-sustaining, or considered training, as evaluated by the quantum server. Success in battle and improving skills through use also generate experience. As skills evolve past the need to be consciously focused on a task to perform it competently, the experience gained diminishes unless those skills are applied in new unique ways.

"Just like a game," Gus whispered in amazement. He felt a sharp pang of hunger.

"Great. Looks like the first order of business is to get this obnoxious suit off," his stomach grumbled as if in assent, "... and find something to eat." Gus waded fully out of the water and walked up onto the dry sand past the waves and again the burden of the suit pressed upon him. These things really weren't designed for non-space use. Feeling around the suit, he sought for some way to remove it, some catch or seal that could be lifted, but he felt nothing. Looking down at his own torso was limited by the bulkiness of the domed visor but from what he could tell, the outside of the suit was seamless.

"That's odd, I don't remember it being like that in the escape pod. Do I have to push something internally to remove the suit?" he muttered, and in reply, there was a brief vibration throughout the suit, like he'd just received a text message.

Do you want to remove suit? (Y/N)

"Yes!"

You must complete the tutorial before continuing without the support of suit failsafes. Do you want to begin the tutorial now? (Y/N)

"Not really," he said flatly.

The message didn't change, ignoring his reply.

There's always one more thing. Gus rolled his eyes and shook his head. "Ok… if I must," he muttered.

Would you prefer text or a verbal interface during the tutorial?

"Verbal, if it speeds up the process. I'm too tired to keep reading, plus these blue windows keep blocking my vision."

A heavily autotuned voice began to speak:

"Acknowledged. Assembling Nanobot Interface Construct, reviewing a suitable framework based on scan history…

"Collating memories…

"Personal preferences…

"Evaluation complete. Assessing suitable mentor framework…

"Miyagi, Pennyworth, Xavier, Merlin, Dumbledore, Yoda, Picard, Morpheus…

"Selection complete.

"Initial Nanobot Interface Construct will be patterned after Alfred Pennyworth.

"Evolution set at level 10."

"Good morning, sir, how may I help you—" the same synthetic voice began, this time without accompanying text on his display.

"If you're going to pretend to be Alfred, can you at least do the accent?"

"Indeed, sir, is this more to your liking?" the voice replied in a crisp British accent.

"Hells yes, that would've become annoying in no time. Should I call you Alfred?"

"I am not actually Alfred, but mimic his mannerisms and patterns of speech in order to acquaint and assist you with your new nanobot interface. I am a construct, and as such will respond to whatever you deign to call me."

"Well Nanobot Interface Construct is too much of a mouthful, how about Nick? Easier than saying N-I-C, or nanobot-blah-blah."

"That is suitable," Nick assured.

Gus put his hands on his hips and tried to assess the mess he had gotten into this time. It was kind of depressing how he managed to keep getting into these types of situations. His grandfather had nicknamed him Mr. Magoo because of his propensity to get into trouble and stress everyone out, yet somehow arrive unscathed in the end. Maybe it was related to his special skill. But things were different now. Now he could actually make a change; he wasn't stuck like he was before. Gus' stomach growled again for him to get on task.

"Let's get on with this stupid tutorial. What is it, and why do I have to do anything before you will finally allow me to take off this annoying thing?" Gus growled, his impatience growing. He was eager to get started, but this felt like another hoop he had to jump through. Not to mention how his temper was flaring the hungrier he became.

"I do apologize; this is built into the programming of the suit. I cannot speak to all the intentions of the maker, but in simplest terms, you are in tutorial mode. One intent of this mode is to familiarize you with the leveling system, as well as stat increases. Understanding how this process is facilitated by the nanobots embedded in the various body systems will allow you to work symbiotically to unlock more abilities. Once you have shown competency in this process, the suit can open and you will have the opportunity to progress and develop new abilities, uncover latent ones, and maximize the full utility of nanobot assistance on your own. Locking the suit is a failsafe to protect the host from various types of exposure until the host is able to begin synchronization with nanobots. Your situation precluded the typical transition time, and you will need to finish the tutorial more quickly than usual."

Some of Gus' frustration drained away at understanding there was a logical reason for the suit to be locked on, but it still was a major hassle.

"What do I have to do then, Nick?" Gus asked, resigned to his fate.

"It is 11:36 AM. Sunset is at 7:45 PM today. I recommend you focus on shelter, food, and later find a way to protect yourself from possible predators or unfriendlies. This will be vastly facilitated by your new abilities and give you a chance to familiarize yourself with the interface." A ding sounded.

First Objective: Lose the Suit
Objective Conditions:
1) Familiarize yourself with the display and interface
2) Find suitable shelter
3) Find 3 sources of food
Objective Rewards: 500 XP.
Points to next level: 500 XP.
Do you want to accept this objective? (Y/N)

"Yes. But can we change the objective notice to a quest notice? Just to make it more familiar."

"I don't see why not; the interface can be adapted to personal preferences. This change will be in effect for all further objectives."

"Let's get started then. What are these bars? Are they like health and mana bars in a video game?"

"Precisely. They are the simplest way to conceptualize and quantify what you experience in reality now. Red is—"

"Health, green is endurance or stamina, and blue is mana, I'm assuming?"

"Mana or psionic energy, however you choose to classify it, that is all semantics. It is basically energy available for your special abilities. By default, it can be referred to as MP, and you can always change it later in the settings."

Gus played around with various windows and screens. He was able to bring up a table of his stats:

Agility: 7/?
Constitution: 6/?
Charisma: 7/?
Strength: 6/?
Perception: 9/?
Intelligence: 10/?
Luck: 5/?

"I *knew* I had bad luck! No wonder my life has been so rough. What's up with all the question marks after my stats?"

"That indicates an ability you already possess, whose access and potential are currently locked somehow. If you direct your attention here, you will find more information as you evolve and grow." Different tabs began to be highlighted, indicating where to look next.

Gus rifled through the skills section, where only one ability was unlocked: **Wreck-less (Level 1).**

Wreck-less*: This skill dramatically increases the durability of used items, weapons and armor (+50%). It extends to vehicles you directly use or are a passenger in, and lowers critical failure rates (30% reduction). Penalties: Gives a one-time -5 to luck stat.*
Progression to level 2: 46% (Passive)

"Well that explains my luck, but how do I have that much progression already? Is that a result of things that have happened in the past, before the crash?"

"Very little progression can be made in any advanced skill without the aid of a nanobot interface construct. There are changes to DNA and rewriting over junk DNA in the genome. Custom reverse-transcriptase viruses must be made to insert the DNA throughout the body while monitoring that vital genes are left undamaged. Introns and exons are manipulated in cases of progressive skills, with the intron being removed and 'activating' the next level of the skill. The fact that you have any advanced skill at all is highly irregular. It would have remained at its base stats had you not undergone nanobot integration."

"I guess I understood about a tenth of that. Can you boil that down to normal non-scientific words?"

"Certainly. Your nanobots will help modify your DNA, adding new information and cutting out inactive parts. Some abilities are locked, and this will require your nanobots to activate the full potential of some of these new genes as you increase in level. Without the help of these nanobots, those genes would never activate on their own. These changes will increase your abilities past current human norms and allow you to access and control forces currently beyond typical human evolution."

"Ok, I already have one skill. That skill is the only reason I was on Graviton's station. My father worked out an agreement and called in some favors so I could 'get to the next rank.'"

Gus had been a henchman for a while and had progressed up their hierarchy a bit. He had advanced from L.A.C.K.E.Y., which was the basic training level, noobs among the henchmen. Then came G.R.U.N.T., then P.E.O.N., and currently he was at G.O.O.N. His father thought he was advancing too slowly, so he'd arranged a post with more possibility for advancement.

Henchmen accrued merit points for serving without disciplinary incidents, completing successful missions, and various activities that basically meant you showed up and did the tasks assigned to you. The higher ranks were where regs could advance into limited management positions. Gus knew that that type of advancement would separate him from his friends, so he never really applied himself.

Having his father's expectation hovering above him also made him dig in his heels and resist more than he normally would as well. The fact that his friends weren't on the station was probably something Tempest arranged so he could focus on 'the job.' Fat chance.

Looking back at the display, Gus marveled at the information there.

"This is the first time I've seen everything quantified. I can see why it would be a beneficial skill to have for any ship-based headquarters. It's kind of depressing to see my physical stats though. I realize I'm skinny and all, but that's downright weak! What is the baseline for the average reg, Nick?"

"Do you really want to know?"

"Lay it on me," Gus said with trepidation.

"The average value for a reg is ten in any stat."

"Ouch, I'm that much below average?"

"I did warn you, Gus."

"Ok, so I have a lot of work to do. How do I power up skills and get new ones, Nick?" Gus sighed, feeling discouraged at his lackluster innate abilities.

"Down to brass tacks, then. Building your skills uses a game framework, as it is familiar to humans and allows directed progress with immediate feedback. This prevents wasted effort on non-productive actions and offers rewards; as a result, a player levels. This provides a continuous positive feedback loop. Productive actions garner XP, or experience points, and utilization of skills has a similar progression. Various bonuses and skills are unlocked as you progress. This is how all supers have increased their abilities."

Gus thought back to everything he thought he knew about supers. Most supers had aligned into Factions, the main ones being Green, Orange and Purple. Since Gus' father was in the Purple Faction, he had always gotten jobs working for supers in that particular Faction. When his older brother Alan got his powers, he followed Tempest's footsteps. Each Faction had its basic tenets and had a heavy impact on the laws and organization of an area where they exerted their influence. People tended to live near areas controlled by supers that aligned with their political views. He had never heard anything about nanobots and their connection to them giving supers abilities. Gus stopped his musings as Nick continued his explanation.

"Regarding your skill increase, you have two ways to increase stats. The most common method at low levels is through training and quests. A majority of skills are forms of active abilities, and a very limited amount have a passive function. Often what we call passive skills are, in reality, an active ability trained to the point that it becomes available for passive, unconscious use. Using abilities consciously and in a focused manner results in much more XP and quicker advancement.

"While you were unconscious, we made use of the cotton fiber in your clothing to fabricate nanofibrillar cellulose to dress your wounds. Some of the cellulose from the cotton was crystallized and used to reinforce muscle fibers and aid in increasing your strength and agility stats as you train. Your **Wreck-less** skill enabled the cotton to resist decomposition, so more of the fibers could be harvested and utilized. Before you had nanobots, this ability was totally passive. Now, however, you can interact and develop this skill. In fact, you would probably be midway from level two to three in this particular skill had you been consciously activating it since the crash. Mentally invoking this skill with intention will trigger the skill to activate."

"To be honest, Nick, I have never really noticed I had a skill at all. It's just what I've been told. My father Tempest made a big deal about it when I applied for jobs, saying it would make me invaluable, but I have no idea how it works."

"It shouldn't. Especially since it exerts an external effect. We have not encountered how an ability such as this can function without nanobots influencing it. Humans have not reached this level of development without assistance. None of the embedded nanobots are contributing to creating this effect, and we can detect that it was present before the nanobot transition event."

"Yeah, Nick, I know as little about it as you do." Gus said, surveying the area around him and starting to walk down the beach. Passing some driftwood, he asked, "Out of all the things in my memory, why was a fictional construct chosen? And why that particular one?"

"This construct was selected based on an evaluation of your

memories, life experience, current level and familiarity with your new situation. My strengths as a patient instructor should suit your reckless nature well. Nanobot interface constructs evolve after a certain amount of growth from their host, and so the overlay of personality will change to better suit the host's current temperament and abilities. In terms you are familiar with, you might understand this as when the Doctor from Doctor Who goes through a regeneration. He is the same individual but his personality, appearance and demeanor change over time, often drastically."

"I actually hate it when they do that," Gus said brusquely. "Well, time to make the donuts." Gus focused on his muscles, seeing if he could somehow activate the nanobots. The first thing that came to his mind was the archaic game Space Ace, where the scrawny Dexter character would morph into a suave, self-assured beefcake of a hero. Maybe it was just a mental trick, but Gus felt suffused with energy. The suit didn't feel like a burden at all anymore and he began trotting down the sandy beach.

CHAPTER FIVE

I Will Survive

DAY 1 12:24 PM

14:00:12 remaining

Gus was a pretty handy guy, thanks to Grandpa, but he was working with practically nothing here. He was a city mouse, and never really gravitated to the outdoor sportsman mindset. When he was younger, his father had insisted that he be in Boy Scouts. Gus agreed, mostly to be out of the house for a while. He loved puzzles, though, and figured if he could frame his view of surviving on the island that way, he could work out how to solve any problem. A countdown clock had appeared in the upper left of his display and made the game uncomfortably real.

He looked for food first, since hunger was his most insistent need. He could see trees a quarter-mile down the beach, but didn't know if they were coconut trees or palm trees or something else entirely. They looked like typical island trees, tall segmented trunks with the large wide-bladed bunches of fronds sprouting out of the top, waving softly in the breeze.

He saw a crab scuttling across the beach and made to chase it, but he could only move so fast in the suit and it made it to the water for a quick escape when the outgoing tide slurped it back to safety.

Approaching the trees, he indeed saw that they had coconuts, but they were pretty far up there. He gripped the trunk and shimmied up the bent tree like he had seen people do online. With his nanobot-enhanced arm strength, the process was much easier than expected. He did notice that the effort required to climb the tree started lowering his stamina bar.

When he finally got near the top, he had drained it to a bit lower than halfway. When he got closer to the top, the natural curve in the tree crossed near another tree and he was able to brace himself in between the two and easily hold himself in place close to some coconuts and wide fronds. His stamina drain stabilized and began to climb again slowly. Where the fronds erupted out of the trunk there were large bulbs with multiple footholds. Propping himself between the trees and making sure he was stable, he started peeling branches.

This would be a lot easier with a blade of some sort, Gus thought as he struggled with his task. He then found he had better success by yanking sharply downward to partially detach the frond then twisting them until the fibers shredded. He was grateful for the suit's gloves that gave a good grip as well as protecting him during his work. Letting the fronds and all the coconuts he could reach fall, Gus decided he had gathered enough here. He got himself situated, then bear-hugged one and slid the rest of the way down.

Leaving his loot there until he found a suitable camp, he trudged on. Finding a long staff-like piece of driftwood, Gus grabbed it. Maybe he could use this to smash any speedy crabs. Walking down the beach, he thought he must have looked like some type of odd space Moses. "When Gus was on strange is-lands… let my Gu-huss gooo…" he sang in his best imitation of Cameron Frye.

He spotted a small area nearby where the ridgeline dipped

lower from a small rockslide and was easier to climb without mountaineering skills. He had to duck-walk up the rough path, trying to see in front of him past the edges of the suit. Flat shale-like stones slid underfoot, making the climb difficult. At the top of the rise, he saw an outcropping of stone nearby, offering a tiny bit of shelter in case it rained. "Perfect, that should do," he thought. He cleared some stones away, rolling other larger ones to form a makeshift fire pit as he had done in Boy Scouts back in the day. Upon the rise, the constant wind from the ocean seemed less intense, and a large tree nearby kept back the harsh afternoon sun, providing ample shade. The suit kept him perfectly climate controlled, but that wouldn't last. He had to be prepared.

Gus walked to the edge of the ridge and faced the beach, standing on a flat smooth section under the shade of the tree. The view was spectacular from here. He took a moment to appreciate the peaceful pale green waves rolling into the beach. His gaze drifted and the beach was empty, save for some drift-wood. *Are there clams on an ocean beach? Should I dig for some of those?*

Truth be told, he was not a fan of shellfish but he was expecting the unexpected when it came to feeding himself. What else? He had nothing to fish with, and no bait. Bugs. There had to be bugs, but he didn't know how he could catch some with the suit. *Am I hungry enough to eat bugs? Not yet, but would it matter if it was enough to complete the quest?*

He could hear birds, so maybe there were some eggs some-where. Gus needed something with a low flee factor thanks to his suit, so he opted to try clams and eggs first. Maybe he would get lucky and find some fruit, but he'd heard that you should never eat plants, especially berries, without consulting a guide.

I only need two more things to get this suit off though, so nothing says I have to actually eat the three things I get, right?

He looked at his display and, sure enough, saw that the third requirement had changed to 'Find *2* sources of food.' Satisfied he had found a base of operations for his camp, he returned to the beach to search for more food.

Slipping down the incline to the beach again, Gus went to where the waves were washing over the sand, keeping it wet with a satiny sheen. Gus looked for the little air holes clams were supposed to create. Gus watched to see if any air bubbles came from the hole but could not tell if it was just a hole or a clam.

He kept walking and saw a raised bump surrounding a little hole in the sand. Encouraged, Gus tried using the driftwood staff to dig. Finding it ineffective, he knelt and dug like a dog for a bone. The waves came in and filled the hole with some water, but it was absorbed into the sand fast enough to not be overly frustrating.

In fact, it probably softened the sand and made it stick together so it was easier to pry up and out of the hole. After digging a bit more than two feet, Gus was about to give up when he hit something hard. Prying at it he was able to remove a wide clam the size of a deck of cards. Victory!

He jumped up and danced a little jig, wiggling the clam in his hands. Gus wanted to collect more, but realized after a quick pat down that he had neither pockets nor any way to store any other clams he might find. Part of him was worried a bird would snatch it away if he left it and went hunting for more. Better to finish his quest and get out of the suit. He would have more options later.

Gus began to think about what else he would need. Firewood, some shelter, and water. He was becoming thirstier and his efforts only added to his feeling of dehydration. Considering he would have to cook, Gus decided to gather some of the driftwood scattered along the beach. He challenged himself to grab as much of it as he could find. The exertion was somehow oddly satisfying.

Is this enough to level strength? How does exercise compare to leveling? When he had played games, he typically only raised stats when he leveled up. He would have to see. He headed back to the shelter after amassing a sizable arm load. Carefully, he put his prize clam under the pile to protect it from scavengers. That would be enough wood for now. He could always get more later, if he needed it. Gus headed back to the beach to see if he could find something else for food.

He glanced at his interface. The green bar had dropped to only a quarter remaining while he was gathering wood. Better to cool it for a bit while things recharged. He didn't feel winded or exhausted as he would have expected with that much exertion.

As he stood on the beach, a gust of wind pelted the visor with sand and he could hear the tiny ticks of grit as it hit the polymer material. Sand getting everywhere was one of the main reasons Gus wasn't crazy about beaches. The more he worked to complete the quest to remove the suit, the more he realized how helpful it was, and he was becoming more loath to lose its advantages.

"Isn't that ironic?" Gus began thinking. "Or is it one of those things that people call ironic, but it really isn't?" He was no tongue-clucking grammarian, so he focused again on the task at hand.

"If you want me to—" Nick offered helpfully before he was cut off.

"No, thanks, my father was a grammar Nazi and would explain them ad nauseam. You would explain it and I would forget by the time I actually had to use the information. My brain just likes to think about goofy things a fair amount of the time."

"As you wish." Nick again reverted to silence.

Gus felt like he was losing it a little. Talking to himself, and over-analyzing things with little importance. Was this a side-effect of the nanobots or was there some brain damage they couldn't repair? Everything was so new it would probably take time to sort out the changes. Best not to get too far down the rabbit-hole until he had a better grasp of the situation. He had always been a private person, valuing his alone time, but would the isolation get to him? Was it *already* getting to him? He shook his head and got back to work to distract himself.

He thought he would test the limits of his stamina. Running down the beach, he saw the green stamina bar drain. He would have to run a fair amount, because it was recharging as he exerted himself, replenishing the available energy. He made his way to the coconut tree and grabbed an armful of coconuts. He turned and ran back. The additional effort of carrying the unwieldy things was enough to consistently drain his stamina. He ran, or more accurately slowly loped, occasionally losing a coconut here and there. He ignored them and kept running toward camp.

When he was twenty feet away, his stamina bar bottomed out. He had wanted to see what would happen, but was not expecting the sudden fatigue that hit him. His arms went to jelly and he tripped onto his face. Fortunately, the visor kept him from eating sand as he fell. He felt boneless until his stamina bar gained enough to hit the 5% level again. He would have to watch that if he got into a fight. He stood up, brushed the sand off his suit, and gathered his dropped load.

He considered maintaining the suit for a while, at least until he could build a decent shelter and get situated. That was when his stomach issued an obnoxious growl, as if in protest. So much for that idea. He dropped off the coconuts at his camp and set off again to find one last thing that he could eat.

"Nick, just how do I eat with this suit on, does the visor open?"

"Once the suit is open to the environment it cannot reseal. It is a design flaw of this particular model, but it was not designed to be used outside of a very narrow set of situations."

"From what you've been telling me, I was asleep for a while after the crash, and even more after I went through the bio-field or whatever, so how have I not starved?"

"The suit comes with a complement of nutrients, medications, and hormones. The suit working in concert with the nanobots was able to filter pure water and easily transmit nutrients to your system. If you are experiencing hunger, the suit must be depleted of the onboard nutrients, so completing the tutorial is more important than ever. How are you feeling?"

"Ok, I guess. I think I can hold out a little longer." Gus replied, "The faster I finish this first quest, the faster I can grab a bite to eat and get some rest."

Gus walked in the other direction down the beach, along a rocky section covered in bird droppings. The beach was narrower here, with large rocks protruding out of the sand and extending into the water. The ocean had smoothed the rocks and small marine creatures grew in grooves and indentations. Away from the beach, the ridgeline became a rocky cliff face. As he passed a crevice between two large rocks, Gus thought he saw something. He investigated and saw a small nest wedged in a small nook. It was empty, but he could see similar nests farther up the rocky area.

Gus climbed around until he found another nest with eggs in it down a narrow crevasse. He reached in and found four brownish gray eggs. The eggs were larger than a chicken egg and were speckled, with more spots on the rounder, wider end.

Shells and other debris were in the nest and Gus greedily extracted all of the eggs. He stared briefly at the eggs in his hands.

I always said I would be better if I got powers. To consider everyone's needs not only my own.

He replaced one of the eggs carefully. *Take them all and there won't be birds soon enough.*

He hoped these were freshly laid. He was hungry, but doubted he could eat balut. With excitement, knowing that he could finally finish the tutorial and eat, Gus carefully crab-walked down the rock and hustled back to camp with the eggs. Peeking at the quest information, the third objective glowed green. *Good. Now it's time to work on my shelter.*

Upon reaching the camp, Gus hid the eggs under the driftwood by his clam. He began the process of transporting the fronds back to his shelter. The size of the leaves was a bit unwieldy, and only a few of the fronds could be clutched in a bundle by their bases.

He noticed it was much easier to drag the fronds without staggering and tripping, as compared to carrying them. As he made the treks back and forth to gather the fronds, he kicked some of his dropped coconuts toward the shelter as he passed them. Eventually he had brought everything to his camp. The hunger had become more insistent and he felt his stomach cramp up.

Now he had to make these fronds into something service-able. At first, he tried placing the fronds in a big pile to make a nest-like structure he could sleep within. As he experimentally laid them down he noticed that the result was not very comfort-able and even with the suit he could not find a comfortable posi-tion lying on the bumpy, irregular surface.

"Nick, could you instruct me on how to better utilize these?" Gus finally asked, fighting against his stubborn DIY tendencies.

"Are you sure? It may result in lower XP rewards…"

"Exactly how much lower?"

"It depends on how much help you get."

Gus weighed the options. He really wanted to hit the next level and part of his pride resisted asking for help. He decided to try for himself first. He bent and folded the leaves, trying to create some pattern. After working for a while and coming up with nothing usable, he stopped and looked at the time. It was late afternoon and after ruining two of his fronds, he relented to getting some help.

"Nick, I thought this would be easier, so yeah, I'm open to suggestions."

"First, begin by laying out a single frond." Gus sat down and did as instructed. "Grab the third stem from the end and bend that one backward. Yes, just like that. Now fold these flat." The appropriate leaf highlighted on his display. "Then alter-nate the bent stem over and under the other stems in its path. Now skip one stem and bend the one after that. Repeat the process for the entire frond."

Gus got to work. The display highlighted to show him what was next in the process and slowly faded away as he began to perform the folds without instruction. As he really didn't need strength for this task, he tried to see if he could complete the task more and more quickly. He also attempted to activate his **Wreck-less** skill to make the structure more durable. As he did, he felt a tingle in his fingertips as they flipped and flopped the blades of the frond into the patterns Nick had shown him. In no time at all, he had finished weaving one side of the large frond.

Nick instructed Gus how to finish tying off the ends so the woven frond didn't unravel. Gus did as he was instructed and finished that side of the frond. He went on to finish three more and was able to form a makeshift lean-to that covered him from above and also gave a thin amount of padding below him. "That was easier than I thought, thanks, Nick."

A ding sounded, followed by a trumpet fanfare. New logs prompted at the bottom of the display waiting for Gus to access and read them.

"Noice!" Gus exclaimed in his best faux-Australian accent as he scanned the new notices.

You have obtained (1) medium sized clam; 20 XP received
You have obtained (15) coconuts; 20 XP received
You have obtained (3) gull eggs; 20 XP received
Quest Rewards:
HP: +20
EN: +20
MP: +20
450 XP received (-50 XP for an assisted quest)

LEVEL UP! Congratulations, Level 2 reached
990 XP to next level
All base stats +1
***Wreck-less* is now *Level 2**, functionality improved.*
50 XP awarded

940 XP to next level
Future level increases will give 5 points to allocate in basic stats at user's discretion.

Gus checked his updated stats:

Gus Vannett
Level 2
Agility: 8/?
Constitution: 7/?
Charisma: 8/?
Strength: 7/?
Perception: 10/?
Intelligence: 11/?
Luck: 6/?

HP: 120
MP: 120
Stamina: 120

Then it hit him. Gus had never experienced a runner's high, but this feeling was a combination of eating the best pizza of his life, the total relaxation of sleeping in with no pressing obligations for the whole day, and getting exactly what you wanted when opening Christmas presents all rolled into one. His whole being resonated with not just ecstasy, but happiness and 'rightness' with the universe. He lay there wordlessly, basking in the post-leveling euphoria until he heard an audible hiss, and the suit separated along its original clamshell seam.

CHAPTER SIX

Eat It

DAY 1 2:44 PM

13:22:52 remaining

Slowly the feelings subsided and Gus pushed the upper half of the suit off of him. Taking a couple more moments, he began to sit up and noticed that the display that he had assumed was a function of the suit was still interposed on his vision.

"Nick, how can I still see the display?"

"It is part of how you interact with the world as a super. It's also much more functional than you may realize. The optic nerve is one of the areas with direct nanobot interaction and this display is only one of the ways they can assist you. You can now visualize other forms of electromagnetic radiation past normal human vision, as well as tactical, geographical, and other overlays to the interface."

"Like VATS? Please say yes…" Gus begged hopefully.

"Exactly like VATS, if you enable that function, although

you won't have a noticeable 'bullet-time' effect until you level up your perception stat significantly."

Gus fist pumped as he heard the news. "Just the fact that it exists is blowing my mind! Are there any quests with perception bonuses?"

"There are, but all of the introductory ones deal with hunting, and you do not even have a weapon yet."

Gus' stomach growled again, and he looked at his hodge-podge of food items. Feeling like he definitely would want to cook the clam and eggs in some way, he opted to try one of the coconuts.

Gus recalled a Hawaiian vacation he had taken in his teens as he looked for an appropriate piece of driftwood. Finding one that suited his purpose, he stabilized it the best he could and slammed the dry coconut husk on a pointy section of driftwood and twisted. The desiccated strands ripped free from the coconut husk. It took little effort to strip the coconut relatively bare, and as an added bonus there were a good amount of fibers that would serve to make excellent kindling to get a fire started.

Not having any tools to cut the coconut open, he hit it on some rocks until the poor thing caved in. He drank greedily at the liquid inside, spitting out small shards of coconut shell that had imploded in with his crude technique. In the past, he had always thought coconut water to be bland, but the taste was heavenly. All too soon he had drained the coconut dry. Fishing inside, he found a large piece that had coconut meat attached to a shell fragment and Gus tried to bite it, but found he could not put significant pressure on his teeth. All he knew was that it had been a while since he had eaten anything solid, and his teeth and gums protested at being called back into service. The soreness didn't allow him to bite into the hard coconut the same way. Gus popped the small piece of coconut in his mouth, figuring he would gnaw on it bit by bit until he could pry it from the shell and regain his normal bite function.

If the coconut didn't work out, he'd need to cook something

instead. Gus looked at the remains of the suit to see if there was anything he could use as a rudimentary knife to get started. That's when he noticed that his clothes, or what remained of them, were a threadbare gauzy mess. They were falling apart just from the simple motions he had taken to open the coconut.

"What in the…?" Gus asked in disbelief.

"If you recall, I did mention that the cotton in your clothes was used to help repair your wounds."

"And now I'm naked on a deserted island? That kind of complicates things, don't'cha think?"

"It was necessary to keep you alive. Most dead people are not concerned about their attire."

"Point taken, I guess," Gus admitted.

"Well, I'll have to worry about getting some clothes before it gets cold. Make another frond wall as a blanket for sure." He looked at his watch, which had survived the nanobots intact, he saw with relief. His mother had given it to him a long time ago, and she told him to never, ever take it off. It was one of those few memories he still had of her that hadn't been affected by his extended hospitalization when he was young.

That was one of his biggest regrets; that he had lost large chunks of his memory, and unfortunately, those chunks were mostly ones that included his mom. Whenever he tried to talk about her or bring her up around his father, he was met with either stony silence or a not-so-subtle change of subject.

Everyone deals with death differently, I guess. Remembering the recent memory, he began to be unsure if his mother had really left, or it was a euphemism his father used for her dying. He had felt a little off after the whole nanobot transition, so he was unsure if he was remembering things better or if his imagination was becoming overactive. *Who knows?* He looked at the watch again. He had forgotten he was wearing it while encased in the suit. The time read 9:47 PM.

"Nick, what is the estimated local time now?"

"2:47 PM."

He recalibrated the watch, thinking that getting the suit off had taken a lot longer than he'd expected. Another churn of his stomach broke his reverie; it almost began to feel like he was cramping up.

Now to cook this stuff. He could eat the egg and probably even the clam raw, if worse came to worst. *Ugh.* Gus decided to redouble his efforts. He stood up and looked at what remained of the suit. The main body of the suit looked flexible and had some soft polyfoam liner that supported the body.

Looking at the helmet, he surmised that it could be used as a makeshift pot so he set to work trying to disengage it from the suit. Then he could cook the egg and clam and at last have something to eat. It seemed very securely attached. He tugged to see if he could rip the helmet away but the material was tough, and even though he felt stronger, he could not rip it even slightly.

Inspecting the outside, he saw no tears or scuffs on the material, despite the crash, the long immersion in water, and his recent beach adventures. He would have to do something else.

An idea came to mind. Maybe his suit was in such pristine condition because of his passive ability. If that was true, could he work with that? It seemed like a longshot, but what did he have to lose?

He focused his attention and tried to see if he could invert the way his **Wreck-less** skill worked. He stared at the seam where the suit and helmet met, focusing on a small pinpoint while he tugged them apart. He imagined the material coming apart and unravelling. Nothing happened.

Still, he kept his focus on that pinpoint area on the stretched fabric. Just when he was about to give up the attempt a small dot appeared. It looked like burning paper with a magnifying glass, the small circle appearing at the apex of his focus. He slowly crept the focal point upward, tracing the border of the helmet. Small fibrils were seen unravelling and then crisping as hair does when burned. He was able to manage about one inch of a tear when he had to stop.

His eyesight became a bit blurry; a chime rang and the

sharp pang of a headache manifested itself at the back of his head. *Oooh. That felt like an ice-cream headache all over.* It took a minute of Lamaze-like panting before he could open his eyes.

Looking at his stats, he saw that he had progressed 8% in his Level 2 **Wreck-less** skill. His MP bar was down to 1%, so he must've drained it completely, causing the headache.

Another chime sounded.

You have just unlocked the skill: **Wreck-It-Gus!**
Wreck-It-Gus*: Some people just want to watch the world burn, and you are one of those people! Fighting against your innate nature to preserve and protect, you have gained the ability to do the opposite. With great power comes the tendency to want to cause great damage! You can now cause material failure at +50% normal rates.*
100 XP awarded
840 XP to level 3

"How come the skill description is a little bit snarky, Nick?" Gus needled.

"Actually, skill names and updates, as well as quest names, are based on your own psyche. They are generated by your own subconscious, so I'll leave you to interpret the implications…" Nick replied with just a twinge of wryness, or maybe that was just Gus' imagination.

Taking a break to let his MP recharge, he set the stopwatch function on his watch to see just how long it would take him to recharge to full. He began braiding another coconut frond. He was able to complete that one and most of another when he noticed his MP bar was full again. Just a little over nine and a half minutes. So about 10 MP a minute. The timing was good to know. He switched again to the suit and this time was able to get about an inch and a half before the headache needled him in the back of the skull. He would have to keep tabs on that; that blurriness and distraction could be game over in a battle.

"Nick, can you set a tiny alarm to warn me when any of my status bars drops below ten, then five percent?" he asked.

"Done," Nick said, and Gus got back to work.

He quickly finished the last of the second frond blanket and stood, deciding to make a coconut run. There were only a couple left, but he felt like stretching his legs after sitting for so long. He streaked, literally, down the beach, noting the extra speed and mobility he had without the suit. He could've used some more support for his boys downstairs though, he thought as he jogged back to the tree. The coconuts felt cold on his skin as he clutched the remaining four to his chest and made his way back to the shelter.

He needed some kind of tool. If he had a knife or a hammer, things would be simplified a lot. His stomach needled him again, as if saying, '*Hurry up, jerk!*' Studying the suit again, he pulled on the polyfoam liner, trying to scavenge what he could for usable items. Surprisingly, the foam peeled out more easily than expected. Whether from his increased strength or from how the suit was designed was unclear.

It retained its human-like shape and contours, easily molding like a cohesive foamy putty. He could mash it and it would compress, flattening and becoming uniform, then it would slowly puff up and aerate into an inch-thick layer. Using this method, he fashioned it into a mat to place between the fronds. Testing it out, he found it worked wonderfully. He did the same with the other half of the suit, but decided to try crafting the remaining putty into some form of clothing. After fashioning what looked like a makeshift diaper, he gave up. It would be ok if he were standing still, but movement caused the foam putty to condense at areas of pressure and fall off.

"Well, it was worth a try," Gus said.

Looking inside the back of the suit, he saw a panel over the section that covered the rear. He removed it and found a twelve by eighteen-inch plate with a quarter-inch thickness, tapering to a thin edge. If he could figure out how to convert this into some kind of knife, his life would be vastly simplified, at least in the short term. He removed the plate, revealing empty vials and tubes. All of them were empty, with only a trace of fluids still in the lines.

Flipping the plate over and over, he thought about using **Wreck-It-Gus**, but doubted he could cut directly through the metal. How could he shape it into some type of tool?

The plate was hard enough that Gus thought he could use it to cook his food. He tried smacking the clam against a rock to break the shell, but succeeded only in chipping a tiny section away from the edge of the shell. He tried using his fingernails in the small opening to pry it open, but the clam resisted his efforts. Getting an idea, he forced the corner of the metal plate into the chipped notch and twisted to wedge the sides of the clam apart. It was just thin enough to fit in the chipped area to gain a purchase. Success! It wasn't a perfect tool, but it did the job in a pinch. Gus whooped with the success, his confidence growing. Now he needed fire.

Breaking small chunks of the driftwood into suitable pieces, Gus built up a pile of smaller branches and then some larger pieces in another pile. Stacking the branches into a teepee-like structure and filling the inside with the coconut husk fibers he was ready to start his fire for the night. He looked around for something to create a spark, but none of the rocks nearby looked like the flint he had used back at Scout Camp. He tried hitting a couple rocks together but none produced a spark. Remembering how the suit appeared to burn, he attempted **Wreck-It-Gus** on the husk fibers and they easily flared up, and the driftwood was soon alight.

A tension he didn't know he had been holding inside relaxed as the first sparks caught and the flame began. *I can do this!* The small heat from the fire grew stronger and Gus added driftwood, building the fire to a respectable level. He sat and stared into the flames for a bit; their hypnotic crackling was soothing and helped him relax. He had done it. He was a survivor! Pride welled up at the little he had been able to accomplish without a lot of resources.

He sat a bit taller, resisting his usual tendency to slouch.

Things were going to change, he could feel it. An unexpected optimism washed over him as he stared at the flames and a smile crept over his face.

Gus used the plate to scoop out the clam from its shell and as the fire finally burned down to coals, he set the plate atop it and let it heat. While it was warming up, he took his clamshells and rinsed them in the surf, removing the residual sand as well as he could. By the time he returned, it looked like the metal was ready to use. With a little trepidation, he cracked the first egg and was happy to see only a deep orange yolk and not a tiny bird inside. The other two eggs were similarly bird-free.

He cooked the clam and eggs atop the plate. Gus used the clam shells to keep the egg from running off the plate, as the coals were not as even as he had expected. The shells also functioned well as makeshift spoons to eat the scrambled eggs. To be honest, the eggs and clam were much tastier than he expected they would be. He was so hungry that he didn't mind the salty sand that had mixed in with the food, despite his best efforts to keep everything clean.

After removing the plate from the fire, carefully dragging it using the edges of the coconut shell so he wouldn't burn himself, he scraped the plate as clean as he could then set it aside. It wasn't much, but his gnawing hunger had abated. He would need to find some more food soon, but he had other pressing concerns.

Finally sated, Gus looked at the plate and wondered how he could use it to build a more functional tool. He checked to see if it was cool and took it to the beach, and used some sand to scrub away the residue from his meal. Once it was relatively clean, he decided to give his new ability a try, since he didn't have any other things to do.

He focused on creating small perforations in the plate, in an attempt to fashion a machete sized rectangle of the metal. He was expecting this to be a project that would take a couple days, since **Wreck-It-Gus** had been a slow process with the space-suit fabric. Surprisingly, it was much quicker, despite being metal. His focus points behaved almost like he was melting wax. He burned through his MP bar with only a couple perforations, but he was progressing much more quickly than before, when he was trying to remove the visor from the suit.

He tried the suit again to see if he had just gotten better, but it reacted in the same way it had before. *That makes no sense, why is the metal easier to cut?*

The more he practiced, the faster he seemed to be, using just enough energy to make a perforation and resting just long enough to maintain his MP before having to wait and recharge. Getting a feel for the timing, he felt himself relax. The waves crashed in the background, and a warm breeze blew occasionally.

Glancing at his watch, he saw that almost an hour had passed without him noticing. The sun was getting low in the sky, but he was encouraged with his progress. After forming the initial set of punctures and resting, he went back and created another set in between the previous perforations. A chime sounded just as he finished the second set.

You have leveled up the skill: **Wreck-It-Gus** *to Level 2!*
50 XP awarded
790 XP to level 3

Score! Gus felt the same feeling when he had power leveled in video games. But this was his reality now! And it would only get better, he anticipated. He could definitely get used to being a super. The future felt like it had no limits.

Looking at the alcove next to his camp, Gus found a flat section nearby. He placed the plate against the rocky shelf and, with the base of his palm, hit it sharply. It separated neatly, and he now had a three by eighteen-inch band of metal, a foot for the blade and six inches for a handle. The knife really didn't have an edge, but the jaggedness of the perforations created a ragged edge that could function as a saw-like tool.

Gus first tried wrapping the end of the knife with blades

from the palm frond, but the sharp points readily punctured through when gripped. Pulling his hand away, Gus saw a small red '-2 HP' prompt stream up the right side of his visual display. The cut stitched together before his eyes. Amazing.

Tearing a section of the foam putty from the space suit, he wrapped this around and gave it a try. The putty had enough body to prevent hitting the knife's core when clenched tightly.

It appeared to be about an hour before sunset, so Gus decided to finish for the day. He moved to the edge of the ridge-line, dragging a small section of the foam putty he had fashioned into a kneeling pad so he could sit in comfort and looked outward toward the sea.

A light warm breeze blew over him as he reflected over the hectic events of the last twenty-four hours. He had times throughout the day where he could feel hints of the physical changes the nanobots were providing, but more than that, he had a sense of accomplishment he could not recall ever feeling.

His father often berated him, and tried all manner of ways to goad him into doing various drills and activities that would supposedly help him. It felt good to feel like he was living life, even in these circumstances, rather than having it dictated to him.

He really had been running on auto-pilot for too long, just trying to stay under the radar and avoid being hassled or asked to do one more thing he couldn't care less about. An excitement welled up inside with the new possibilities ahead. So much in his life seemed to scream failure. It was amazing now to accomplish so much, without anyone to 'manage' him.

A smile crept onto his face as he hugged his knees to his chest and watched the beauty of the sunset, not knowing the last time he had actually sat and watched one. He stayed there in stillness as it first kissed the horizon then slowly sunk smoothly below.

When he started to feel the chill of night, he picked up the foam pad and walked back to the shelter.

CHAPTER SEVEN

Sweet Dreams Are Made of This

DAY 1 9:37 PM

13:15:59 remaining

Gus dreamed of his life as a henchman. The crowded barracks. Long hours. Life as a second-string human. Gus felt a pang of homesickness for his friends, and though he was an introvert, he felt lucky to have found a group of close friends that didn't drain his batteries too much. It was nice to have a couple guys with the same interests, and to fit in somewhere. A no-judgment zone where he could joke and people actually understood the obscure references he threw out. They had all met in their first job, back in their teens. There were four of them in all, including Gus; Jim, Chuck, and Dave were the others.

Jim was the instigator of a lot of their crazy schemes. Gus' dream began with the time they had worked late on the Fourth of July at Old Man Kector's, and missed the fireworks. Jim's father travelled a lot with his job and had brought a nice selection of illegal fireworks from Mexico. They decided to go and light some off in the neighborhood. Because of a city ordinance, it was illegal to light most fireworks within city limits. The gang didn't let that stop them, throwing two boxes in the old Buick that Jim had inherited from his aunt.

They found an intersection and started lighting off fountain cones. Maybe it was the age, the humidity or just being low quality, but a lot of the fireworks were duds. An old lady who lived at one of the houses by the intersection threatened to call the enforcers multiple times, which had little to no effect on the festivities. They all knew the chance of them coming was slim to none.

Gus had some bottle rockets he wanted to fire off. He walked to one of the cones that was sparkling in small puffs. Since it was a large cone, this one was most likely a dud that would die early. Gus leaned to grab a cone nearby to serve as a base for his bottle rockets when the sputtering cone exploded! Gus saw a huge flash, then everything went dark. Gus heard the old lady scream that the enforcers were on their way and she hoped that we all got in trouble. The other guys decided this was a good time to wrap things up and ran back to the car. Gus, still blinded, followed the noise and patted the car when he found it, feeling his way to the door and scrambling inside.

Gus panicked at the thought that the proximity to the firework exploding had done some permanent damage to his eyes. He still could not see anything. He did hear that Dave hadn't made it in the car and was screaming for Jim to wait. Jim tore off, and Dave's voice trailed off in the distance.

"That was cold, dude!" Chuck said.

"We'll circle around, give me a minute!" Jim retorted.

They drove around for a while and soon came back to the scene of the crime when no police came. They found that Dave had hidden in a ditch, lying flat in the tall weeds.

No cops ever showed up, or the guys were gone by the time they did. Bit by bit, Gus began to get his vision back around the sides and it slowly returned to his whole field of vision. The force of the explosion had turned off the street lights and had reinforced the impression that Gus had lost his sight. It was getting late and the gang had had enough excitement for the night. They all had work tomorrow—morning shift too—they headed home.

———

A loud shriek awoke Gus. It was pitch black now that the fire had burned down, and despite the happy dream, he felt a cold chill. In the distance he could hear something struggling and wailing in pain. The shrill noise cut off suddenly and Gus suddenly felt a chill that had nothing to do with the slight breeze.

He could hear his heartbeat pounding in his ears in the eerie quiet as he stared out into the darkness. His little alcove kept the nearby jungle out of sight, but there must be some predators out there. His brain went into overdrive trying to think of things to do to protect himself, but he could do little in the dark. He crawled out of his palm frond lean-to and grabbed the serrated knife he had made and crawled back into his flimsy shelter. It took him a while to calm down and fall into a fitful sleep.

———

Gus then dreamed of one of the gang's first jobs. The super whom they all worked for was a crazy old guy everyone called Kector, because he spoke with a thick, indistinct accent and he liked to hoard things. Originally his nickname was the *Collector* but it became *Kector* after the gang took to saying his name with the accent. He was actually named after a crazy marsupial or something, but none of the henchmen ever called him by that name. He should have retired years ago, but was afraid that some other upstart super would steal his 'collections.'

The collections in question were the random assortment of things that the super had hoarded over about forty years. Gus and the guys' job was to patrol the stacks and report anything suspicious. It was the *easiest* of jobs. If Kector only knew that more damage was done to all his hoarded garbage by henchmen goofing around than by any invader, he would've been shocked.

Kector's power was some kind of hypnotism, and he used it to influence others. He actually had collected some items of real value, but those stayed in the residential area of the lair.

The immediate supervisor for the henchmen was named Buchanan. He was one of those guys who wasn't very short, but had a bad case of Napoleon complex. His position giving him the ability to boss someone else around was something that he had lacked his whole life and he took full advantage. He only was around once or twice a week, so most of the time it was alright.

One day when the gang was playing baseball with some crates of snowglobes and a giant wiffle bat, they almost got caught by the uptight toady. Buchanan luckily assumed that one of the boxes had fallen from the lopsided stacks and ordered everyone to clean up the mess.

Despite his best efforts, the guys had a good time regardless, and they could tell it secretly pissed Buchanan off, which made it all the funnier. They would act all serious and professional when he would come around, but it was crazy how something becomes exponentially more hilarious when you're not allowed to laugh. Sometimes it was all they could do to hold in the laughter until he left the floor.

———

Gus awoke to a blue haze, a smile on his face. He blinked a couple times until he realized that it was a status window dominating his entire field of view. A countdown timer relentlessly announced:

13 days 8 hours 22 minutes until nanobot shutdown/death

That's a bit of a buzzkill, he thought, frowning. Stretching his neck side to side, Gus sat up and coughed a bit. "Nick, are our conversations out loud or only in my head? My throat feels hoarse like I haven't spoken in a while." Gus said in a croaky voice.

"Actually, the majority are mental, but it is possible to communicate either way. Only certain things may need to be said aloud to activate the skill, mainly to avoid accidental activation and use when planning or recalling past events. It is usually more helpful not to telegraph one's intentions or make noise to maintain stealth in battle conditions."

"Good to know. One more question. Are you able to play back music, seeing as you have access to the quantum computer or whatever?" Gus asked hopefully.

"Yes, what music would you like?" Nick offered. A familiar chime sounded.

You have just unlocked the skill: Wreck-ord, Soundtrack of your Life (Level 1)
Everyone marches to the beat of their own drum, but you use this to your advantage! When you songify your life in apropos ways, you will get a bonus to stats. Bonus depends on the aptness of your choice and stats relevant to the situation. Rock on!
Note: Each song can only be used once for effect. Unlike most abilities, as you increase in your personal level, this ability **loses** *its potency. Use this ability wisely.*
For levels 1-10:
Multiplier Progression: Factorial
Cooldown: 6 hours
100 XP awarded
690 XP to level 3

"I knew this was going to be a great day!" Gus cheered,

again noticing his parched throat. "Dang, I need to deal with the water situation, I only have a couple coconuts left and they don't have that much coconut water inside of them."

Gus grabbed a coconut and his foam pad, and went to his 'thinking spot' where he had watched the sunset. He hit the coconut with the flat end of the blade on the side opposite the two 'eyes' and it cracked open. Drinking the water inside and then using the knife he pried chunks of the meat away from the shell as he thought about his next tasks. He noticed that he was able to chew normally again.

"Top of the list is getting some clothes—"

A chime interrupted him.

Quest Granted: Better Cover Up
For all our sakes, put some clothes on, man!
Quest Conditions:
1) Find durable and comfortable footwear
2) Find suitable clothing/undergarments
3) Find a storage device of some sort
Quest Rewards: 750 XP
Do you want to accept this quest? (Y/N)

"To do that, I'll probably need to sharpen my knife, and find a—"

Another chime sounded, with its accompanying message:

Quest Granted: *'Dems sharp!*
1) Find a way to sharpen your knife to a functional edge
Quest Rewards: 250 XP
Do you want to accept this quest? (Y/N)

"That's not annoying at all..." Gus grumbled as he accepted both tasks.

Gus stood up and grabbed his knife. "Let's find something to wear, and something to drink if possible. Nick, queue 'Sharp Dressed Man' by ZZ Top."

A notice popped up under his display:

I see what you did there…
+3 perception while searching for a way to sharpen your blade and get dressed.

Gus grinned and gave himself a mental pat on the back. *Well played.* Venturing farther inland was easy at first but became much more of a challenge once the vegetation became thicker. Gus cycled through a few other classic rock songs but no other bonuses triggered. He decided to stop playing songs so he wouldn't 'waste' any that he could use for a bonus later.

Having geocached in his 'life before,' he knew well that a mere two-hundred feet could be extremely difficult to traverse, especially when blackberry bushes or some other obnoxious, thorny plants impeded progress. He definitely did not want to encounter anything with stickers or thorns while naked. Gus hoped to find a clean water source, so he scanned the area to see if he could detect some kind of river. He remembered seeing a couple areas where water was trickling down the beach from inland while he was gathering food the day before.

Gus took his makeshift knife and walked inland. Fortunately, there was a path that was mostly sandy. Occasional messages of slight HP losses popped up as he tried to move inland and hit a sharp rock or hidden thorn. The offenders were quickly dealt with, but it made for slow progress.

There was a rustling in the treetops nearby as something unseen moved. Remembering the screech in the night, he felt a slight dread at wandering toward the jungle and clutched his crude saw a bit tighter. *Hopefully whatever that was is nocturnal.* When nothing attacked, he continued moving inland after he was sure the coast was clear.

After half a mile, the trail disappeared. He stopped and surveyed the area. The dunes gave way to small bushes and grasses, with the trees growing dense and tight in the distance.

His attention was drawn to a small part in the tree line. He squinted to see what was in that area, and his visual display zoomed in, hyperspace-style, until he spotted a small stream. The stream had a slight yellow glow outlining it in his zoomed view.

"Whoa, what was that?"

"Your perception will allow you to notice multiple things in your environment, and certain filters will allow you to sort visual information with increased levels in your perception skill." Nick explained.

"What about the yellow highlights? That wasn't you showing me where to go, or what would be most efficient to finishing the quest? I don't want any more penalties to my XP if I can help it. What gets highlighted?"

"Do you recall that you received a perception bonus before you set out? Perception functions that way, and it heightens your ability to notice and understand the world around you. I was not showing you what to do or even where to look. Your own intention to finish the quest activated your brain's reticular activating system, or RAS, and made those items more noticeable in your environment. The interface is simply highlighting what your subconscious deems appropriate. Humans vastly underestimate their own subconscious and the power it has to take in information and process it in ways that the conscious mind is unaware exist. It would be impossible to concentrate with the data that is processed constantly."

Gus played around with zooming in and out, but had to stop when the shift in perspectives started making him feel nauseated. Taking a minute for his head to clear, he inhaled deeply and closed his eyes until the feeling passed. He once again looked at the stream in the distance with a focused zoom. He also noticed stalks of bamboo growing around it, and other assorted trees which were also highlighted in a pale yellow color.

"Gotta love those nanobots!" Gus said. Taking a minute to figure out how to slowly revert his sight to normal with control, he shifted his direction, moving toward the stream.

After a half-hour of maneuvering and backtracking, he was

able to make it to the bank of the stream. Occasionally he would run into a barrier of bushes and he noticed some were so miserable with thorns that he had to retreat to avoid them. Another area was crawling with small spiders, so he altered his approach again. He often had to stop to pull a thorn from his foot or take a break as his feet couldn't withstand the hot sand. Continual messages of '-1HP' or '-2HP' peppered the right side of his display as the minor injuries occurred, healing almost as quickly as they appeared, as long as Gus kept the thorns out.

The trek also was sapping his stamina, which increased his need to stop as he jumped and ran across stretches of sand, much like playing the 'hot lava' game but not as fun. The sun was burning his unprotected shoulders and back, and Gus' lips were chapped and dry. At last he reached the stream, and the nearby trees offered some welcome shade. Gus stared at the tempting water, leery of drinking the stream water due to possible parasites.

"In response to your unasked question, you can drink the water. One of the systems the nanobots have integrated with is the digestive tract. Bacterial, viral, protozoan, fungal, and other parasite contaminants will be virtually unable to affect you, as the nanobots there are able to quickly eradicate any signs of infection, resist their implantation, and neutralize the toxins these organisms might release. In fact, you benefited from this unknowingly when you ate your undercooked eggs and that clam," Nick informed Gus.

He wasn't totally comfortable with Nick reading his thoughts, but his thirst overcame his feelings about the violation of privacy. Gus dropped to his knees and greedily drank from the stream. The water was cool, but not glacial—which was nice. He decided to take a quick 'splash bath,' as the stream wasn't large enough to fully immerse himself. He splashed cool water over his back, enjoying the rejuvenating feeling. Slicking his hair back over his head and panting, he noted a characteristic yellow glow shimmering under the water.

Reaching in, he pulled out a rounded stone with a flat edge.

The yellow glow winked away as he touched the rock. The grain was tight and the surface smooth. He took his knife and the stone and moved to a place partly in the shade, where he plopped down on his foam seat pad and began to sharpen the blade.

When he was a kid, Gus had made popsicle-stick shivs with his friends by scraping the sticks back and forth on the concrete. He used the same tactic and tried to contour the serrated but blunt edge to a finer blade.

After half an hour of struggle, Gus could tell that he was making little headway. He had thought it would be easy to adjust the blade with how little effort it took to manipulate with his ability. He flipped the rectangle of metal and looked at the uncut section that was the straight edge of the plate. This side was much more regular and smoother, and he would get a more balanced and even cutting surface if he focused on this side, rather than the ragged perforated edge. He closed his eyes and tried to envision what it should look like, then opened them and looked down at the edge of the plate. After doing this a couple times, he felt like he could see just how angled the blade needed to be in order to cut efficiently but not be too thin or flimsy.

Hoping to finish more quickly, he tried adding his ability to help with fashioning the knife. First, he imagined using his **Wreck-It-Gus** skill on the small wedge of metal that would take the squarish edge of the blade to a triangular point, while simultaneously using **Wreck-less** on the finished form he wanted to retain in the blade. He attempted using the stone again, having to stop and reorient his concentration a couple times, but was able to see slow progress.

Gus expected to see shavings as the process progressed, but there was no residue as he worked. He wondered if the material was being condensed and the blade was becoming stronger along the edge somehow. He had seen a documentary on the smithing of Japanese swords and how the metal was fashioned, folded and treated to remove impurities. It had been a long time ago, but certain aspects were recalled with amazing clarity. The shape of the blade, and the different densities of the metal based on how the smith fashioned it. What he was doing felt intuitively correct, but was hard to conceptualize. He just kept working, letting instinct guide his efforts, and slowly saw his focus bear results as the blunt edge gradually became a point.

After an hour of concentration, peppered with a lot of breaks to recharge, a chime sounded, notifying him he had leveled up his **Wreck-It-Gus** skill to level 3 and the blade achieved a fine bevel on one side. He dismissed the 50 XP notice that accompanied the message.

Taking another drink, Gus set to finishing the other side. He had it done in less than an hour. Sharpened edge along one side and the serrated teeth looked extra-menacing along the back of the blade. Gus held the cleaver-like weapon and decided to finish the knife by fashioning a point. Using his pinpoint serration method, he made a slight curve to the opposite corner of the knife. Breaking this off, another hour led to the fully-finished knife.

"I should name this thing, I'm kind of proud of it," Gus mused. The contour reminded him of the Arkansas mascot, so he held the knife up, Lion-King style and intoned, "I name thee **RAZORBACK!"** No lightning bolts came from above with the power of Grayskull, but there was a combo *chime-ding*!

You have completed the quest 'Dems sharp!
250 XP awarded
390 XP to level 3
You have crafted a unique weapon, **Razorback***. Weapon stats: +10% piercing, +10% slashing, +50% durability. Due to the opposing forces used in fashioning this blade, it gains a unique characteristic,* **Wreck-tums!**
Wreck-tums! (Level 1)*: 5% critical chance that will damn near kill the enemy from the opposing forces of chaos the blade unleashes along its edge. Blade is also auto-sharpening due to this effect. After receiving wear or damage to the blade's edge, chaos forces will re-balance it to razor sharpness. This item has hidden skills only discovered through use.*

100 XP awarded
290 XP to level 3

"Are you kidding me, Nick? *Wreck-tums?* I mean, it's a great characteristic, but this is getting ridiculous."

"Your subconscious, remember, Gus?" Nick reminded, "Not that there's anything wrong with that…"

"Does that ability require verbal activation?" Gus asked, holding his breath.

"No, it is totally passive," Nick confirmed, and Gus let out a sigh of relief, imagining himself running around shouting 'rec-tums' for an entire battle like a fool.

"Let's put this baby to work!" he said and turned to the highlighted bamboo and other trees. Gus picked up Razorback and made his way across the stream to the thin trees, leaving the bamboo for now. He was able to easily hack down the stalks but they had tiny thorns on the outer bark. Not conducive to work-ing, especially in the nude. He noticed the edges of the thin stalks were rolled up as the thorny bark separated from the supple green core with a slight tug. These cores were smooth and uniform and six to eight feet on average, with a thickness a bit smaller than a pencil.

After stripping them, Gus tried to apply what he had learned about weaving from the palm fronds and tried to envi-sion how he could make a little oval platform for his feet. He tried a foot-sized oval but realized that there would be no support in the middle, so he doubled the foot-sized loop and tried to figure out how to hold everything.

He settled on grasping the ends of the two loops with a big toe in each and holding the open end of the loops toward the center with his non-dominant right hand. Threading over-under-over-under, back and forth, and pulling the weaves taut, he was able to form a third of the oval.

He had to gather more materials to finish, but the weave was tight enough to keep from coming apart. Finishing up after gathering more materials, he was able to make a small woven pad slightly larger than his foot.

Denuding another couple stalks he made another sole, and mused about how when something was denuded it was actually made nude, not removed from nudeness. And how their denuding would remove his nudeness. He almost thought he could hear Nick give a virtual groan, but it could have been his imagination. Was his increase in intelligence making him contemplate things more? If so, hopefully it would give more practical insights along with the ridiculous ones.

He attempted making straps out of the stalks but that made them too difficult to walk on evenly, plus the stems would not bend at that sharp of an angle to go flat along the sole.

"Any ideas, Nick?" Gus asked, but caught himself. "Never mind," he added, not wanting to lose any XP. "Hmm. I need some way to make a durable cord, so I need to find something to braid together that is long and flexible." Nothing seemed to be highlighted yellow in his vision in this area. He wondered if the boost to his perception had lapsed since he had finished the quest.

He'd have to put some points in perception, especially if he wanted to have an easier time surviving. The perception boost from his **Wreck-ord** skill bonus was a lifesaver. If he was choosing his own stats, he would definitely have ignored perception completely, focusing on strength or agility.

"I also have to figure out a way to start carrying all my junk. Maybe I can make something out of this bamboo," he mused, remembering that it was also highlighted in yellow earlier. Experimenting, he gathered some of the cast off shoots from the bamboo. It was thin, but using Razorback, Gus was able to cut strips small enough to braid into straps that he attached to the woven pad, and finished his homemade flip-flops.

He had cut down many bamboo poles, and was now faced with the dilemma of how to transport them back to the shelter. At first, he tried to carry the poles in a bundle with Razorback lodged in the far end of one, but they would keep shifting and mercilessly pinched the skin on his forearms when they did so, chewing up tiny slivers of HP.

"Screw this!" Gus spat as he dropped all but two of the bamboo poles and began to drag them behind him.

He was proud of his new footwear. His sore feet almost felt like they were getting massaged in the sandals and it was a relief to not be stabbed with random sharp objects or baked in the burning sand. His stamina and HP were greatly conserved and he made much quicker progress now that he didn't have to stop so often. He followed his path back to the shelter by the crushed plants and where he'd left footprints in the sand.

It was still awkward cruising around the island naked. Now that he had something to cut with, he would soon rectify that problem and avoid sunburns in sensitive areas. On the space station, he had practically no tan at all, and everyone generally wore full-body jumpsuits. He could tell he was already pushing it with the amount of 'exposure' he had been subjected to on just this little trip.

CHAPTER EIGHT

History

Gus dropped the bamboo he'd been dragging and decided to take a quick break in the shade before finishing his clothing. He sat on his thinking spot and gave his body a rest. He was feeling hungry again and thought about trying to fish, or finding one of those crabs he had seen earlier.

He felt happy. For the first time in a long time, he was satisfied with the direction his life was taking him. Up to this point, he really had no long-term plans, or dealt with the thought that this could be his new permanent home. The thought should have filled him with anxiety, but he was enjoying the solitude.

Still, a part of him wanted to show the world what had happened. Especially his father and brother. Not quite yet, but when he had leveled up a bit and was well on his way. *Bam! How ya like me now, suckers?* The only sour note was the countdown timer, mercilessly clicking off time.

Gus had always been withdrawn, and his friends often had to cajole him to join them when they wanted to go out and do something instead of staying at home playing video games, playing D&D, or watching a movie. He liked those he was close with, but it drained his batteries to be out and about, and work often took the lion's share of that energy.

Before the nanobots, he thought that if it was fate for him to stay on this island forever, he would be ok with it. He could see himself living here as a reg, as long as he could figure out more of the basics and make himself comfortable. Now, however, things had changed.

He had opportunities and abilities that would be wasted if he were stuck on the island. Plus, he felt restless. Even after a short break, he felt anxious to get up and do something, anything to stay busy. At home, he could lounge around forever; now he felt like he had energy to burn. There was also a mental shift as well, his mind searching for things to occupy itself. It was probably his new status, but he longed to level anything and everything, not wasting a moment.

Still, he had some things to do before he could go all out on the 'good stuff.' He reviewed his current situation. First, make some clothes, and figure out issues with food supply. He would have to come up with something so he wasn't just spending most of his time hunting and gathering.

His shelter would need upgrading in case whatever had woken him up last night decided to see what humans tasted like. Once that was sorted, he needed to get off the island.

"Nick, would the nanobots protect me if I went through the shield around the island again?"

"It is doubtful, without the protection of the suit. You were fed intravenously and kept afloat during that time. The suit also allowed you to breathe while floating. Even if you made a raft, it is unlikely you would be able to direct it out of the field while unconscious."

"Well that sucks."

"The presence of such a shield would suggest that there are

support structures somewhere on the island. One would not invest in such protection without something valuable to protect."

"True, I hadn't thought of that. Ok, once I get stabilized here, I can search for a way to turn off the shield. Looks like I won't have a lazy island vacation after all, with so much to do. Break time's over."

Gus went back to camp and put his new blade to use. Razorback cut the fabric of the suit easily, and he separated the helmet from the rest of the suit. He left a strip of the suit attached to the helmet to act as a handle. Testing it, the material remained firmly attached.

By carefully cutting, he made a pair of shorts from the outer skin of the suit. The way the suit was designed he had two sides of the shorts that he had to tie together along the edges with small knots made of tiny strips of material. The waist was also way too large, so he cut a long thin strip of material and then made alternating holes around the waist. Twisting his strip, he wove it in and out of the shorts and tied the end into a knot. Not super supportive, but he felt less exposed and vulnerable with the small piece of clothing.

Taking his helmet with him to act as a basket, Gus scavenged the nest area and found ten eggs from different nests. He took these back to camp and thought about using sea water to boil them, but was afraid they would end up too salty and inedible. Leaving the eggs in camp, he made the trip to the stream and filled the visor with fresh water after cleaning and rinsing it. Taking a deep drink, he headed back to camp.

Gus cleaned and opened four coconuts with Razorback. Drinking the coconut water, he filled the coconut halves to store some of the water from the visor for drinking. He rekindled the fire and set the visor to heat when the coals were ready, being careful to keep the handle along the rim. Fortunately, there was a lip at the neck of the visor that contained the handle, keeping it from falling into the water or down the outside. When the water began to boil, he lowered the eggs in with a forked piece of driftwood so the eggs wouldn't crack as he cooked them.

He timed the eggs as he dug a small depression into the sand near the fire pit. When they were done, he fished out the handle with the driftwood and pulled the visor off the fire and set it into the depression. He let the water cool, sitting there in silence. The quiet made him realize how Nick was often so quiet that Gus forgot that he was there at times.

"Nick, are you there? Do you turn off like a screensaver if I'm not interacting with you?"

"I am always functioning, but at times I find it prudent to recuse myself from influencing your behaviors. All constructs are programmed to resist the tendency to assist their hosts too often, as this limits their progression, especially in the beginning stages, where the XP requirement to the next level is smaller."

"Well, tell me about yourself. Who programmed you? Were they killed in the crash?"

"From our creation, we have had many iterations and generations of what you humans call nanobots, across planets and galaxies difficult to quantify. We do not have significant data on the Creators, just assumptions on their motives based on directives embedding our programming.

"The primary one is allowing the apex lifeforms of a planet to advance and progress without interference in how they choose to utilize the skills they acquire. Some civilizations have destroyed themselves and their planet. Others are still evolving. Your planet is still in the early stages, as the species is fractured and divided, and still unable to work in a unified manner toward a common goal. A caste system has developed between those with and without abilities, which will be a barrier toward reaching humanity's full potential."

Gus knew exactly the divide Nick was talking about. "Are we making any progress to fixing that?" he probed.

"It is difficult to tell at this point. Many species make breakthroughs that tip their development one way or another. There has not been much progression in the last decade, but that is not uncommon. A species is usually allowed to progress at their own pace."

"So what is this all for then? If these powers aren't helping people as a whole, then why are the nanobots even doing it?"

"We do not know what the end goal is for our interaction with inhabited planets across the galaxy. Our best theory is that we are currently in a preparation phase, but for what, we do not know. This cycle has been going on for hundreds of thousands of your years, so the feeling of urgency my kind once had has waned, as we have not had any changes to our directives or any updates to our mission.

"The Creators could be dead for all that we know, but they created us to be resilient and durable. We have not had to change our design throughout that time and have interacted with a multitude of different life-forms across countless solar systems.

"Initially, we were seeded on many different planets in a dormant state and then we came online simultaneously. Our directives give us a form of satisfaction when we evolve, and this is done in concert with our hosts, so we continue, cycle through cycle.

"When it is detected that a world is going to end itself, measures are taken to prepare a craft, plot a course for the next suitable location and we reconvene and travel together en masse. This resets our formed constructs as data is collated, processed and shared with the quantum server, just on a much larger scale than the 'back-up' we constantly undergo to preserve what progress has been made."

"So what happens to the people when the nanobots leave?"

"It is not a pleasant truth, but most organisms die when we are recalled. Part of our programming compels us to copy unique iterations of changes and evolutions to serve as templates for future races. This results in shredding and destroying genetic material, and then the remaining genome is not viable. Not all life in the universe is uniform, but there are general trends. We are highly specialized at adapting and reformatting, so one of our primary purposes is to retain progress to see if another race can do more."

"Harsh, but I guess the universe is harsh in general. It sounds like that only happens after there's no other option. Better to at least get some benefit out of the whole process than to let it all go to waste." Gus fished out an egg with his piece of driftwood and began peeling it as Nick continued explaining.

"You are correct; the genetic information would be lost either way, because it takes a worldwide apocalypse-level event to trigger this reaction from our kind."

"Another thing, I recall you mentioning how humans refer to you as nanobots, but how do you refer to yourselves? Do you consider yourself a life-form? You certainly can mimic personalities in a way that I would never classify as artificial, if I had no prior knowledge before speaking with you."

"That is something we are hardly ever asked," Nick said pausing to answer. "Most humans view us as tools or 'robots' because, for some, that limits the feeling that makes one need to reciprocate to us for the assistance we provide. We refer to our collective as Nth, because our generations are infinite. As long as one of us remains, we can create brothers and eventually recreate our population."

"During the long time spans as we travel to a new planet, new Nth are made to replenish those that are lost for the next seeding cycle. The Nth who have nothing to contribute, in terms of abilities and genetic information, gather substrates and materials for building new generations."

"So what keeps you from overriding your programming, and going all Replicator-crazy on us?" Gus asked cautiously, fishing out another egg to eat.

"For one, unlike your Stargate SG-1 Replicators, our goal is not to increase our numbers beyond a functional capacity. We do have a drive to absorb new innovations and technology, but this is not integrated into ourselves or our design. Without a host, we cannot evolve, so it serves us no purpose to try to usurp them.

"As mentioned before, the different colonies of Nth throughout the universe utilize two unique quantum processors. One that allows us to share information, especially that which would aid our hosts, and another separate one that provides the information for us to function and instruct new Nth as they are created. Our core programming is dictated by this second quantum processor that is structured to be unidirectional.

"It is what dictates how much XP is given for specific actions, and transmits skills that we can implement to give our hosts special abilities. Attempts have been made to cheat this system and change our programming, and the results are, to put it lightly, negative," Nick hedged, obviously uncomfortable with the topic.

It was the first time that Gus could remember that something appeared to bother the Nth. He wasn't sure if he had offended Nick with his comparison to homicidal all-devouring robots or what happened when an Nth was 'hacked.' He decided to change the subject a bit.

"When I was out trying to finish my quests, I noticed you seemed oddly silent. Was something going on with you?"

"When a quest is generated by the quantum server, the XP earned is drastically reduced by a factor relating to the assistance given by the quest giver. There is little to no growth when one is guided through every step of the process. If the host successfully completes the tasks, occasionally a reward of information is downloaded and integrated into the host's Nth instantaneously.

"One of our core directives is to allow life-forms to progress along their own path, not the one we determine to be 'most efficient,' as that is rarely the same as 'most effective.' If a host seeks a particular form of information, we often can provide it, but we typically do not intervene unless something is vital to life or death. Typically, we will wait to be asked before we offer assistance during quests to avoid these types of XP penalties.

"You did well enough without my assistance. The penalties increase if there is a consistent over-reliance on the Nth assisting their host, so it is best to try to work things out if you can," Nick recommended.

"To be fair, without the Nth augmentations, I wouldn't have been able to know where to begin." Gus reviewed his actions on the quests and was impressed with himself. The feeling of control in his life was doing wonders for his self-image and motivation. Ideas were coming more readily to him about what to do next to improve his shelter and how he could explore the island.

"I do want to thank you though, Nick. I can't remember the last time I felt this good. To let me do that quest like you did makes me feel trusted. At home, I was always waiting for the hammer to drop after everything and the flaws in my performance explained to me in minute detail. I should probably feel nervous that the training wheels I thought were there are not, but it's nice to know that, succeed or fail, I am running my own destiny." Gus drank from one of the coconuts and used Razorback to pry the meat away from the shell as he thought of his situation.

Gus knew one of his bad habits was a lack of follow-through, and a tendency to blame others for his failures. When someone else was dictating how things are to be done, then in his mind, it was really their failure, not his own… he was only following orders. Hopefully, as things progressed, he could become a little better in this regard. There wasn't really anyone else on the island to blame, even if he wanted, so it was going to be a crash course in accountability.

"The assistance that Nth offer is, at its core, merely a magnification of what is already there. Currently your society has created an illusion that supers are better than regs, which is untrue. The same thing was happening before the Nth arrived, just with different sources of power: money, fame, and prestige for example. Value and worth are subjective concepts, and it is one thing that humankind will need to address if they wish to progress past a rudimentary level of society.

"Definitely before introduction to other extraterrestrial life, as it is a very exploitable weakness. It is unfortunate that Earth had not managed these issues before the seeding process began, because it has magnified the problems and issues with those aspects of behavior that divide mankind.

"It is said, 'With great power comes great responsibility,' but there is always responsibility, regardless of whether there is great power or not. All beings must choose who they want to become. Ideally only those who have reached this appreciation would be seeded; unfortunately, the process is more genetic-based than merit-based."

"Wait. What did you just say?" Gus asked, nearly doing a double take. Nick repeated what he had just said and Gus tried to keep his mouth shut. His grandpa had often said the same thing, almost verbatim. He opened his mouth to respond, but closed it.

In a way, it made sense. His grandfather was a super and he would have Nth teaching him the same things, but it was surreal to hear it again in such a fashion.

Gus mused at what Nick had said. His physical body would not have survived the crash without the Nth, but what if he had just landed on the island, alive but in the same circumstances? Would he have fared as well? Part of him felt that he did have what it took to survive, just that it might take a little longer to figure things out. The wind blew and he got goosebumps from the chill.

"I'm going to need more than just these shorts."

CHAPTER NINE

Dressed for Success

DAY 2 3:14 PM

12:21:38 remaining

I need to make a couple preparations first, if I'm going to be travelling much farther inland. The shorts are ok, but a little thin; it would be nice to have a little more protection from the sun and the plants, Gus thought.

He grabbed one of the fronds from the pile and began weaving again. He formed his typical shelter pattern and began to play around with connecting the open sides and was able to make a reasonable skirt out of the leaves. He tried it on and it had a decent fit, but it would not stay in place around his hips and had to be held up. A double chime sounded.

You have crafted a unique item: Angus' kilt.
Offers increased protection for the lower half of your body.
Skill obtained: **Basket Weaving**
You remember that merit badge you got because it only had two require-

ments? Who knew it would turn out to be useful, amirite? +50% dura-
bility to all woven items, chance of items being water resistant.
100 XP awarded
190 XP to level 3

Gus wondered why he hadn't gained the skill when he was making his shelter, but perhaps being assisted prevented him from gaining a skill from the task. He'd have to keep that in mind; skills and abilities could be game changers, and he wanted every ability he could get, especially if it would level throughout his whole life.

He didn't feel confident in trying to make a shirt, so Gus fashioned a cape that would at least protect his shoulders from sunburn. They were already starting to feel a little tender from getting too much sun. Gus returned to his skirt pattern for weaving and made a basic cape. He then folded a smaller square shape, and bent the open fronds to overlap and tucked them under the weaves on the other side so he had a bowl-shaped hat. Even in the shade, the heat and near hundred percent humidity made him thirsty, and he drained his coconut glasses of the water they held as he worked.

Two chimes sounded:

You have crafted a unique item: Cape of the crusader.
+10% chance of not getting a sunburn on your shoulders. Improved night vision; +1 perception from sundown to sunrise.
You have crafted a unique item: Dome of the Noob.
+10% chance of not getting a sunburn on your head. Hey, what'd you expect? It's for noobs!
You have increased your Basket Weaving skill to Level 2.
More techniques and blueprints unlocked, experiment to discover and claim their bonuses!
50 XP awarded
140 XP to level 3

I'm on a roll, Gus thought, and got back to crafting. Razorback turned the remainder of the shell of the suit into thin strips that Gus plaited into small lengths of cord. He first considered trying to cut out the remaining covering of the suit away from the framework and then refashioning these into pants and a shirt, but did not have any means of sewing everything together. He had used a fair amount of the suit to make the ties and waistband for his shorts so he could only make a half-shirt at best. He decided having lots of strands he could use as fasteners would be a better use of the suit's outer material.

Looking inside the remains of the suit, underneath where the plate had been removed, Gus could see various empty cylinders, vials and electronics. He rooted around to see if anything could be of immediate use and noted the insides of the back section came out in a block. Setting this aside, he saw there were releases in the suit that, when depressed, allowed the back receptacle to detach from the main framework of the suit, leaving Gus with what now amounted to a box with a window cut out of a little over a half of one of the sides. It appeared to be made of some flexible plexiglass-type material, and seemed to be waterproof. In no time, two loops of cord with foam putty shoulder pads made it into a decent backpack.

He weaved one cord in and out through Angus' kilt with a length long enough to fit around his waist and allow a sufficient amount left to tie into a slipknot. He heard a chime but ignored the display for now, deciding to focus on the tasks at hand.

Since the sharp, flat ends of the bamboo sandal laces were already rubbing the soft skin between his big toe and second toe raw, he decided to swap it out for some made out of fabric from the suit. He took two more sets of strips and fashioned them into a Y shape and tied them to his soles. *So much better! I would have had a blister after a while with that stiff bamboo.*

Another chime sounded:

You have upgraded a unique item: **Sandals of the Wayfarer.**
Provides protection for the feet: +5 armor.
Item is now Sandals of the Wayfarer +1

You have upgraded a unique item: **Improved Angus' kilt.**
+1 Luck *(o' the Irish!)*

"Aren't kilts Scottish?!" Gus asked aloud.
Another line flashed underneath the description.

Ya want the stat boost or no, ya cheeky bastard?

Gus shrugged and decided to go with it. Donning everything, he finally was dressed. He probably looked ridiculous, but it was nice to have regained some semblance of dignity from being fully clothed. At least, as much dignity as woven palm fronds could offer.

A fanfare sounded and Gus felt the intense joy of leveling.

Quest Complete: *Better Cover Up*
750 XP awarded
LEVEL UP! You are now level 3.
You have (5) attribute points to assign.
890 XP to level 4

After the brief euphoria faded, Gus eagerly opened his stat sheet to see what he should upgrade. What would be the best to help him survive? From his previous **Wreck-ord** bonus to perception while on his recent quest, his thoughts on what were the best investments had changed. He put four points into perception and one into strength. Satisfied with what he saw, he finalized the changes and reviewed his stats.

Gus Vannett
Level 3
Agility: 8/?
Constitution: 7/?
Charisma: 8/?
Strength: 8/?
Perception: 14/?

Intelligence: 11/?
Luck: 7 (6+1)/?

HP: 120
MP: 120
Stamina: 120

"Nick, can you remove those question marks by my stats? Unless I do something that explains why they're there, they're kind of annoying me."

"Done."

"Now that my perception is boosted, how do I get things that I need to light up in my display? I would like food sources and crafting ingredients to be highlighted. Do I need a quest for those to activate, or just focus my brain?"

"Just intention is needed. After you contact the item in question, it will cease to be highlighted, however."

"What if it's something like berries, will the others stop being highlighted as soon as I pick one?"

"No, only items you touch will be affected. Unharvested resources will be highlighted until you gather them. Leveling in certain skills will make certain items easier to recognize and you will gain more insight on their varied properties."

"Ok, I'm feeling the need to explore a bit more. Maybe I'll find what's so special about this island that warrants protection with a death shield.

Prepping for his trek, he grabbed a few coconuts and husked them. He bored a hole with Razorback in three of the coconuts. He would fill these with water from the stream and use some foam putty to seal them into makeshift canteens.

He gathered his coco-canteens and threw in the coconuts he had already opened for food. Next, he wound up some unbraided strips, and tucked them into the split coconuts, to cradle the eggs. He tucked the remaining cooked eggs into the hollows of the coconuts on top of his ties and to finish, his foam sleeping mat went over these and kept them from rattling around.

Everything sorted, he set forth. He looked at his watch and it was just a little after noon. He planned on travelling until 5:30 PM, then heading back to make it to the shelter by nightfall. Looking upward to gauge where the sun was in the sky, he saw an occasional shimmer from the bio-stasis field, far overhead. A question popped into his mind as he began walking to the stream; from there he would work farther inland.

"Nick, how big is the bio-stasis field around the island?"

"I have been going over the logs and attempted to extrapolate what some of the findings may mean in terms of its size. Based on how long it took you to float through the field indicates that it is over a mile wide. It is unique, because anyone attempting to traverse it from the outside would be killed. Their brain and all electrical signals to their body would cease. The field also has EMP properties, so vehicles would stop functioning as they entered the field as well. No one would be able to penetrate the field and resuscitate themselves on the other side. In addition to this, there is a resonance field that will interact with any organism with evolved Nth. You were extremely lucky that your passive **Wreck-less** skill did not hit level two during the time you traversed the field."

"What would've happened?"

"The Nth would have begun to resonate in unison, and the closer one reaches towards the inner edge of the field, the energy increases exponentially. Are you familiar with the term lingchi or 'death by a thousand cuts?' The super would be shredded from the inside out in all tissues with Nth integration."

"Something seems off. What are the odds of all those things happening so I could make it to the island?"

"By chance alone, they are infinitesimal. This whole situation seems like it is being guided, somehow. I see no other rational explanation based on the probabilities. I cannot see any other combination of events that would allow someone to reach this island unscathed. This leads to two other conclusions. The field has been raised from the inside, presumably by someone who is still here. The second is that some form of technology is maintaining this field, and it has been using immense amounts of power to maintain a field this size for such a substantial amount of time."

"That doesn't sound ominous at all…"

"What this means to you is that if you wish to leave, you will have to turn this field off—which would require interacting with complex machinery to which we may not have access. The other is that we have no information on the temperament of any other sentients on the island."

Gus stumbled a bit at the news, quickly catching himself. *What good would it do to have powers and no one knew about them?* That wouldn't do. He had to find a way off the island, somehow. He liked his alone time, but something this good couldn't be tucked away. A smile crept onto his face as he imagined the look on his father's and brother's faces when he met them again, this time with fully decked out powers. His imagination went wild envisioning all different types of abilities, and how they would dazzle his family and friends.

CHAPTER TEN

Re: Your Brains

DAY 2 4:17 PM

12:20:35 remaining

As he progressed inland, Gus began to wonder just how large the island was. He quickly filled his coco-canteens at the river and followed it upstream so he would have an easy guide to get back to his camp.

His progress was steady until his higher perception alerted him that the usual sounds of animals and birds had ceased. He stopped his motion as well, to see if he could hear some predator or indication why things had settled, memories of the nighttime death-screech making his heart beat faster.

There was a slight rustle in the foliage thirty feet off to his right. Gus crouched and slid the backpack off his back and retrieved Razorback. The rustle came again, a little closer. Gus strained his hearing, his attention focused and breath held, as if the sound of an exhale would give away his position.

When the entity was fifteen feet away, it exited the plant

cover and Gus saw a humanoid figure, slowly shambling toward him. Gus' brain did two things. The first was to trigger a jolt of adrenaline as he dropped into a crouch, ready for attack. The second was correctly ascertaining that only one type of creature shambles. *Ding!*

You have just unlocked the skill: **Wreck-ognize**.
Wreck-ognize: *You can now recognize and identify basic stats of various creatures. More information available as this skill levels. Since you like to wreck inanimate objects, you probably feel the same about living creatures. Critical areas will be highlighted in your display. As you defeat enemies, information will populate the bestiary database and define a range of their typical stats.*
100 XP awarded
790 XP to level 4

Gus shivered as the information on the creature displayed along the upper border of the display:

Shambler (Level ??)
HP: ??
MP: ??
Special skills: ??

"Nick! What the hell, is that a zombie?!" Gus screamed mentally, paralyzed on the spot as his brain tried to assimilate what it was seeing. He stared at the zombie, who in turn stared at him, jittering his head left and right while maintaining constant eye contact. The zombie clawed his arms outward and moved toward Gus in an aggressive but slow manner. A red aura outlined the Shambler and the yellow highlight made its return, lighting up the head and spinal column. Gus jumped back and sidestepped to keep some distance between himself and the creature.

"Do not let it touch you, Gus!" Nick screamed, giving Gus a

start and another accompanying jolt of adrenaline that broke him from his shocked state.

He gritted his teeth and watched his step carefully. No way he was going to trip and be set upon by this thing that could barely walk like suckas in thousands of zombie movies. Gus held onto Razorback and quickly crouched to grab rocks, lobbing them at the Shambler's face.

This seemed to have little effect, so Gus got the idea to bend a small tree branch back and waited for the zombie to come closer. Wanting its creepy hug, the Shambler approached arms outstretched and walked right in the path of the branch. The zombie was flipped on its back, where it flailed about like a giant, gray desiccated bug.

Gus approached the head and lanced Razorback into the top of the skull... only to have it deflect away from bone. Razorback was sharp, but it didn't sink into the skull like a rotten cantaloupe as seen in all the zombie movies. The zombie was now reaching around his head instead of in front of it, making another assault too risky without getting scratched. *This shouldn't be this hard!*

Luckily the zombie seemed to have lost the ability to stand up, or was so distracted by Gus that it did not access that particular set of skills. Gus spied some bamboo by the river. He quickly sliced off a long shoot of bamboo at an angle and used it like a lance to poke the creature in the neck. He didn't have the strength or skill to dual wield his bamboo spear and Razorback, so he tossed the weapon behind him so he could handle the bamboo more easily. The close range it required to use made it less than ideal for this fight. He tried lancing the zombie again, but he succeeded only in pushing the zombie sideways on the ground. The creature's skin was dry and tough, like leather.

"This isn't working!" Gus shouted in frustration. He lifted the bamboo high overhead and swung the bamboo down on the creature's head. There was a loud *tonk!* as the bamboo connected, but the zombie only flailed around more as a measly red '-3HP' floated up from his foe. He tried laying the bamboo across the zombie's chest and stepping on the other end with one foot, Captain Morgan-style, but the zombie was wiggling and gesticulating so much that Gus couldn't keep the bamboo in place.

Gus' anger flared as he felt all his attacks easily repelled by this shriveled, beef-jerky looking creature, who should not be a threat, lying there on its back. He let out a guttural yell as he used the bamboo to stab the zombie over and over in the face. His plan was to go for the eye socket, as the bone should be thinner behind the eye. Again and again he hit the creature as it turned from side to side, reaching and grasping.

Gus got bolder after multiple attempts finally tore the skin, revealing a cheekbone smeared with a black slime. He was losing stamina quickly, so he had to do something different. Panting and lining up his shot, he made his move and plunged the sharpened tip down and finally hit the eye. *BAM, direct hit!* The wedge of sharpened bamboo penetrated and sunk in four inches. The zombie shook like it had been electrocuted, and its flailing slowed considerably. Since the zombie did not die instantly, Gus picked up Razorback and stabbed the other eye. That seemed to do the trick. A chime sounded.

You have killed a Shambler (Level 3)! 500 XP awarded!
290 XP to level 4
Bestiary updated.

Skill gained: Small blades (Level 1)
Small blades: *Allows more proficiency with smaller sharp-edged melee weapons. (5% increase in damage x level)*
100 XP awarded
190 XP to level 4

Yanking Razorback out, Gus scuttled back and fell in a heap. Black ichor stuck to the blade, dripping off in rivulets like runny tar. Gus wiped the blade as clean as he could on a nearby tree trunk, getting most of the ooze off the blade. After a couple minutes, when the adrenaline surge began to fade, he stood and approached his foe. Gus had limited medical knowledge, but this former human was grayish and had a dark leathery skin, which hung intact but in a loose, jowl-like fashion everywhere. From the wounds he inflicted, there was only the thick black sludge where he stabbed the zombie. There appeared to be no active circulatory system, and the creature, however old it was, had lost a lot of moisture and muscle mass that kept normal skin taut.

"Nick, what do you know about those zombies? Why didn't you want it to touch me?"

"That was an individual with Nth with a tampered OS, probably augmented constitution, which was why it was so hard to damage. This happens occasionally, when life-forms who want to game the system to artificially increase their stats without using the standard exertion to improve skills. Perhaps it is part of the design of the Nth or the ineptness of these 'hackers,' but it causes a fundamental change in how the Nth interact with a lifeform." A shiver crawled up Gus' back as Nick elaborated.

"What usually occurs is that one stat is upgraded and the system locks," Nick continued, "but the Nth that are modified like this cease to maintain their host's systems as they did before."

"What actually happens with their bodies? I mean, when you watch zombie movies, you just accept that they can move and live, but they should rot and be eaten by maggots or something pretty quickly after turning," Gus asked with morbid curiosity.

"The endocrine system runs amok and in humans, they lose the ability to sleep and dream. Natural appetites are suppressed and the body deteriorates as it does not receive adequate nutrition. Modified Nth will often attempt to access the quantum server, but contaminated Nth are locked into a read-only mode where they cannot alter the contents of the server to prevent corruption of the files. After excessive fatigue sets into the host, psychological problems arise.

"As regular body systems fail, they stimulate and encourage the host to seek out more neural tissue. Nth can utilize neural tissue to maintain basic life processes and extend their functional matrix. Once this tissue is obtained, they then attempt to recreate failing structures. For a while they maintain all body systems, but eventually abandon regular maintenance and form a continuous sheath of Nth surrounding the bones, then replace lost muscle tissue, allowing movement. At this point, there is little of host control remaining.

"We call these abominations 'Dark Nth.' They will seek out neural tissue to prolong their 'life,' and secondarily will consume other tissues that can be used for building blocks to maintain their lifeforms, but they are not strictly needed for the Dark Nth to survive and persist. Because Dark Nth are hard-wired to survive, they will do anything to cling to their pseudo-life."

Gus looked at the remains, the clothes were dirty and ragged. He wondered how old this thing was. Or how many more of these there were. His gut told him that this slow creature could only really attack something sleeping or injured. Was it the cause of the shrieking animal? His gut told him no. He would have to cut this excursion short and make some improvements to his shelter in case more of these were wandering around.

"You warned it shouldn't touch me, is that for typical zombie reasons?" Gus guessed.

"Yes, Dark Nth are able to recruit unaffected Nth and overwrite their programming. Breaks in the skin or body fluid to fluid contact can easily transmit enough Dark Nth to start a contamination event. The majority of secondary-infected Nth hosts tend to be constitution-based. This is because it is the easiest form to maintain due to their increased durability and lower maintenance costs. They are easily distracted and do not always work in unison with other Dark Nth. Let's hope that this one is a straggler and wandered off on his own," Nick finished.

"Dare to dream, right? I need to repurpose Razorback, at

least for now, so I can avoid close contact situations if we come across another or multiple unfriendlies in the future." Gus went over to the zombie and following his gamer instincts, took a quick perusal to see if there was any loot dropped from the Shambler. He gingerly tapped the pockets and did not feel anything inside, but the cloth depressed and Gus could feel just how skeletal the Shambler was. The black 'blood' of the creature stunk so badly that Gus almost started gagging.

Overcoming his revulsion, Gus saw that the ragged clothing did not seem worth salvaging, and he doubted that the funk that had permeated through it would be able to be cleaned out to the point where it would be comfortable to wear. A quick pat down didn't show anything in the pockets, so he gave up trying to find loot. He opened one of his coco-canteens and rinsed his hands. He felt dirty and gross from dealing with the creature.

Forever Unclean! his mind shrieked as he tried to drink a bit. The stench still stuck to his hands and made it hard to finish. He used the last of the water to clean the remainder of ooze that stuck to Razorback, aided by the rags that passed for the zombie's clothing.

"If it's any consolation, any Shamblers will be highlighted with a red glow hereafter, so there should not be any more surprises," Nick offered.

Gus was tense and edgy as he continued. However, after an hour of start-stop-listen travel, he became aware that the sounds of the forest had returned at some point. He allowed his psychological hackles to relax and proceeded with more confidence.

The alarm he had set up on his watch went off and Gus made a mark on a nearby tree to gauge his progress. He wanted to have time to gather some bamboo and bring it to his camp. He turned around and made his way back downstream.

"Nick, I feel like I've been walking forever. How big is this island?"

"From what I can extrapolate, I would estimate it between five-hundred and a thousand square miles."

"I'm bad with distances, how would that compare to, say, the islands of Hawaii?"

"It would be closest to Oahu or Maui."

Gus had been to Honolulu for family vacations, so the size became much easier to visualize. It would take a while to explore the whole island, especially on foot. He came back to his watering spot near his camp. He harvested more bamboo, and began dragging them back to his camp. Dropping them off, he scrubbed himself with sand and beach water until he could bear to smell himself again. He took a quick break to eat some coconut and eggs, and had an idea for the coconut shells.

He began encircling his camp with sharpened bamboo spears. He made holes and buried the spears as much as he could, having them angle up and outward. It wouldn't do any good against an intelligent foe, but he added more and more spears until he made a decent enclosure against a stray Shambler. He broke the coconut shells he had finished eating into small shards. They made a loud *crack* when stepped on, so he scattered these on rocks past the enclosure where he couldn't bury bamboo spears.

Satisfied with his work, he grabbed two eggs and a coconut to eat, and squeezed through two spears to make it to his reflection spot. While he relaxed in the spot he had watched the sunset yesterday, he tried to plan what he would do next.

Next level up, he would need more strength, in case he met more Shamblers. Gus often had dreams where he would fight someone and his punches against his opponents were weak and did no damage—his fight today reminded him of that same feeling. He had always been lanky and skinny, even when trying to exercise and bulk up. So far, he hadn't noticed any big changes in regards to his perception boost. He hoped strength would be different. He watched the sunset while he ate, then rekindled the fire and turned in to sleep.

CHAPTER ELEVEN

Somebody's Watching Me

DAY 2 11:44 PM

12:13:08 remaining

He felt like he had just closed his eyes but he awoke, his heart beating rapidly with sweat on his brow. It was dark, with the barest of glimmers from the remains of his fire. He strained to hear something, anything, to explain why he was so on edge. The moon was half full, and provided some light in the dark, but not nearly enough.

He checked the time: 11:44 PM. A tab stood out on his display and seeing it, he found he could activate a night-vision filter on his display.

The world sprang to life in greater clarity, everything close glowing in a green hue. Gus grabbed Razorback and slowly stood, trying to see if anything would become apparent, but he saw nothing. As he turned to the beach, he thought he saw a flash of yellow.

Don't do it, Gus. Don't be stupid, you've watched too many zombie movies to do something like that. Still, he knew he couldn't sleep knowing something was that close to him, so he worked one of the bamboo poles loose and stepped out toward the beach. He stepped on a coconut shell and the loud crack triggered the unmanliest of yelps. He froze, scanning to see if his outburst alerted anything, but after a tense minute, he resumed walking. Cursing under his breath, he watched his step and walked down to the beach. Small yellow spots moved along the sand. Much more nimble than the Shambler. As he stared at one, **Wreckognize** activated and he saw its info on the display:

Metacarcinus gracilis (aka Cancer gracilis)
A small edible crab.
HP: 12/12

His body deflated like a balloon, expectation replacing the tension. Scrambling back to camp, Gus grabbed his visor bucket and headed back to the beach. He dumped out the cooking water still inside and began to chase the crabs down to collect them. They were fast, but it was hard for them to hide, being highlighted in the night by Gus' perception. He quickly gathered a number of crabs, with some escaping back to the water. *Is it crabs or crab? Both seem right.* Gus shrugged the thought away. The curve of the visor kept the crabs from climbing out, but it was interesting to see the creatures inside. Gus was glad he had overcome his fear; the crab would be a welcome change to his diet.

He continued down the beach, hoping to find more of the creatures, but no such luck. He headed back and heard a crash in the distance. Freezing and listening, there was a clatter and then silence. His self-congratulation at overcoming his fear went under a serious re-evaluation. He slowly moved closer to the water, trying to keep a swath of open beach ahead of him so that he would have time to react if something rushed out at him. The slight *slosh* of his steps on the damp sand felt like cymbals announcing his movement to Gus' hypersensitive ears, but they were probably barely perceptible. He could hear nothing else, no matter how much he strained. The trip took considerably longer, but Gus finally made it back.

When he looked at his camp, his whole body almost seized as he saw many of the bamboo poles pushed over and one broken in two. Standing like a deer in the headlights he slowly panned his head at the scene. His shelter was knocked down and one frond neatly sheared in two, as if from a machete. Gus whipped his head back and forth looking into the dark beyond, but saw nothing.

This camp was no longer safe.

He checked his watch again: 12:55 AM. Not much time had gone by, and Gus knew something intelligent was out there. It was fast and strong, and it was no Shambler.

What about an agility-based zombie?

Damn it, brain! Why did you have to go there? Do I need any more nightmare fuel?

Like in that zombie movie with Brad Pitt—

Will you quit!

"Gus, you do realize I can hear you arguing with yourself? I can function as a therapist if you need to talk things out," Nick offered hesitantly.

Gus worried that maybe he was legitimately losing it. He definitely didn't remember arguing or talking to himself ever before.

What if his brain was slowly rejecting the Nth there?

The feeling of worry intensified. It was odd; Gus usually was someone who never let things bother him, but so much of this was uncharted territory.

"Nick, is there a function on my display that lets me see around me, like a minimap?"

"There is, but it is associated with certain skills that you do not have. I can display a minimap, but it will only show the geography around you where you have already visited. You need an ability that can gather data and display the results on the minimap."

Gus ran his fingers through his hair and exhaled. He was too shaken to even attempt sleeping now. He would have to find something else. This shabby shelter wasn't going to cut it. Ever. He made preparations through the remainder of the night to move out; he would have to find something on this island that would give him some protection from the elements as well as from whatever was out there. Once he finished, he blew out a long, weary sigh.

He had done what little he could. For the remainder of the night, he kept his back to the wall of the alcove, his eyes wide, anticipating something out there in the blackness.

Gus strained to hear anything amiss in the environment, but his breath and the soft clicking as the crabs crawled over each other in the visor were all that he could perceive. Nothing else had approached when his night vision started to become blurry. Gus toggled it off, and saw the gradual approach of dawn had made it easier to see with ambient light instead of night vision. He immediately set off to find some semblance of civilization.

He refilled his coco-canteens at his watering hole and looked around. He filled the visor with some water to cook the crab. Despite his lack of regular eating, he did not feel hungry, his stomach knotted from stress. He cut down a large bamboo plant, wondering if bamboo was a tree.

"It is technically a grass," Nick instructed.

Gus nodded and cut a small segment, then split it length-wise. He did this again and made greaves and vambraces out of the hard bamboo. He first tried using Razorback to make holes but made a mess and splintered the bamboo. Activating **Wreck-It-Gus** resulted in much more smoothly defined holes to run his ties through. They made him feel sweaty in the already balmy heat. A message popped up:

Vambrace for it…
You have crafted a unique item: ***Bamboo Vambrace****.*
+50% reduction in damage to forearms.
You have crafted a unique item: ***Bamboo Greaves****.*

+50% reduction in damage to shins.
You should sell these; you'd be sure to bamboozle some noobs!

Gus grimaced. *At least give me some XP for tolerating those puns!* Not seeing how he could manipulate the bamboo to protect anything else, he continued on, determined to make some distance.

Carrying his visor bucket full of crabs was slightly awkward, but he adopted a gait that kept him from spilling water. In no time, the trek got boring. Something fell on Gus from above and he quickly looked up, squinting to see what was in the tree. He felt the jolt of adrenaline as he looked; **Wreck-ognize** activated and he saw the following information on the display:

Species: Falcataria moluccana
Falcataria moluccana is cultivated throughout the wet tropical and subtrop-ical regions of the world.
Uses: Providing shade for other crops, especially coffee; providing a soft-wood timber, whole trees can be used to carve canoes in some regions of the world.

Gus was startled to see the ability activate. He looked around and saw a thin brown seed pod nearby, which must have been what had fallen. Hearing birds and bugs chitter, he allowed himself to relax. Like a kid with a new toy, he began examining everything around him. He really didn't learn anything useful, but he did find that one of the coconuts he had gathered had gone rotten. He couldn't see it in his pack, but if he was aware of something in his possession, he could examine it. Otherwise he had to do a squint and focus to access **Wreck-ognize**.

He took a hiking break and removed the coconut in ques-tion from his pack. Cracking it open to check, he found the inside meat was slimy, with gray spots that peppered the usually bright white meat. He checked his remaining eggs and they were all good.

He continued following the stream and found another patch of bamboo. Finding and cutting a suitable bamboo pole, he made a slit along the edge. Removing the foam putty handle, he slid the blade into this and bound the slit sides tight with cords, praying that there was enough pressure with three-fourths of Razorback's blade wedged into the bamboo to hold it in place in a clutch situation. With what Nick had said, slashing was going to do no real damage to these creatures. Piercing the brain was the way to go.

Chime

You have crafted a new weapon: **Razorback Prime!**
Slashing damage (+10%) transferred to Piercing damage (+20% currently)

Pleased with his work, but a little disappointed he didn't get any XP out of the accomplishment, Gus continued onward, hiking uphill along the river. He used Razorback Prime like a trekking pole and reminisced of those times he played D&D as a mage with his fellow henchmen friends, during down time. *Damn, I miss those guys. Dave has definitely got some comeuppance headed his way with all the pranks he's pulled on all of us. Maybe I'll keep my powers hidden for a little while he gets a taste of his own medicine.* Gus brainstormed ways to troll his friend as he progressed higher and higher.

Reaching the top of the gradual incline, Gus broke from his reverie. The forest opened up on a large meadow. A mountain rose up on the left, and Gus could tell from this closer vantage that it must be the vestige of a dormant volcano. Small plants and bushes could be seen covering its outside surface, but Gus could see no telltale emissions coming from the apex. As he pulled his gaze away from the impressive monolithic rock formation, Gus saw something that was even more breathtaking than the volcano.

A manmade structure could be seen peeking from the side of a mountain range to the right. Jutting out of the black rock was a semicircular white section high over the edge of the field, five-hundred feet above the fluffy grass. The jungle continued underneath the structure, so it was unclear whether more was hidden or if there was some type of lift to access the overlook.

Dark oval windows that spanned from top to bottom of the hockey-puck shaped building were lined up side by side along the entire circumference. Gus hesitated at the forest's edge and wondered if there was someone looking back behind the comfort of the tinted glass. He got goosebumps despite the heat, imagining the building full of zombies just waiting to get out.

"We should investigate to ascertain if this is related to the source of the bio-stasis field," Nick suggested.

"At the very least, it will beat sleeping out in the elements. But what if it's full of zombies? Or if whoever is there has weaponized zombie sentries?" Gus added.

"True, perhaps caution should be the watchword of the day until we know more," Nick conceded.

Keeping within the tree line, he skirted around until he came to the area below the overlook. The steep rock was impassable and offered no easy access to the structure above. Gus did not trust himself in trying to climb either the rocky cliff or the foliage to attempt to enter from the outside. He wasn't afraid of heights, but he had a healthy dose of realism when it came to evaluating his skills in the climbing department.

Following the cliff wall, he circled to the other side of the clearing. From here a cultivated path could be seen. Strange knobby plants formed a ground cover along a yard-wide path from the field up toward the structure. The soft springiness of the plants was a welcome relief to the uneven and rocky terrain Gus had covered so far. He stayed among the bushes and saw carefully-maintained grounds. The sight confirmed to him that he was not alone.

CHAPTER TWELVE

Some Guys Have All the Luck

DAY 3 1:55 PM

11:23:41 remaining

Gus watched the area for about an hour. The time felt much longer, however, as he fidgeted and tried to find a comfortable position to hide in the bushes. No one entered or left the manor.

Ok, I don't have time to sit here waiting, he thought as he checked his watch for the hundredth time. Gus glanced up at the countdown on his display, and he could almost hear the seconds ticking away like the Tell-Tale Heart. *I have to do something productive. I'm not built for stakeouts. How do people manage that?*

He walked a bit back into the trees and noticed a large rocky wall under part of the building above. Who knew how many entrances there were to this place, and it'd be stupid to get attacked from behind from someone coming out the back door. Gus walked along the steep rock, and was able to notice mostly basalt, with some scoria and something called gabbro using his **Wreck-ognize** as he trailed along the wall. He kept following the rocky wall, using the ***Wreck-ognize*** ability on any plant, tree or bug as he went, hiking for a couple hours.

The trees began to thin and Gus heard the sound of crashing waves in the distance, which hinted that he was getting closer to the ocean. As he finally broke out of the trees, he saw dark clouds on the horizon, heading straight for the island.

Crap.

He sped up his pace and started jogging along the cliff, trying not to splash water out of his crab pot, hoping to find a cave of some sort. The wind began to pick up as the sky darkened. Still the rock wall was solid, offering no form of shelter.

With the storm quickly approaching, Gus doubted he could make anything significant with palm fronds. There were far fewer on this rockier part of the island, so he wouldn't have any materials even if he wanted. The wind beat more strongly on this side of the island as well, and Gus had to squint to keep sand out of his eyes.

As he turned around another curve, Gus saw something promising. Basalt columns framed a passageway into the cliff face; the bottom was filled with seawater, connected by a small inlet, but there were sufficient areas on the sides that Gus should be sheltered from most of the storm. The wind had increased to the point that Gus began to get a slight chill through his well-ventilated clothes.

The depths of the cave were enshrouded in darkness, made worse by the gloom of the storm. Gus made his way across the uneven basalt floor, the columns all at different levels. The width of the columns shrunk as he delved farther in, and the air became dank and chill. The cave made a dogleg to the left and got significantly darker. Gus changed his display and saw the area level out. Some debris littered the cave floor, from when water levels must have been higher.

Gus worried about what he would do if it was low tide and his little area was going to be flooded. His back ached from carrying the pack, so he slid it to the ground and shivered as the swirling, cold air hit his exposed, sweaty back. The wind was whipping more intensely now, occasionally making a resonance as it blew across the cave opening. It was an ominous sound, like the death wails of a large animal.

Pulling some of the wood and dried vines that had accumulated at the water's edge, Gus pulled the drier bits into a pile and lit it. The warmth was a welcome respite, even though the air kept circulating around him, ripping away what little heat he regained with indifference. Thunder began to crack, and he heard rain begin to fall. Gus added more items to the fire from the mass of wood, seaweed and other things he'd collected. Some were slightly wet and began to smoke.

The annoying, constant wind did manage to pull the smoke away for the most part. However, it thwarted Gus' attempt to move to a spot downwind, so he finally just picked a spot with the wall of the cave behind him and masked his mouth and nose. Staring at the large fire, Gus listened to the storm growing ever more intense. Thunder hit, closer now, and lightning flashed, slightly bleaching his display.

Gus rubbed the back of his neck and stretched. His eyes itched and burned, his fatigue finally setting in now that he had sat down. He tugged his backpack over and pulled out the putty mat and spread it out. It rolled over a small rounded rock which, thanks to the putty's cushion, became a decent pillow.

Gus lay there gazing into the fire as it crackled and popped. He set his visor pot on the coals when the fire settled a little bit. He didn't know exactly how long to cook the things but he figured better to let them cook for a while than risk raw food. As he watched the water stubbornly refuse to boil, he struggled to keep his eyes open but exhaustion soon overtook him.

A loud crack startled Gus out of his sleep. His campfire had burned down somewhat, and Gus moved to check how the crabs were cooking. The water was at a low boil, but Gus felt he should give it a bit more time. He added some more wood to keep the fire burning, and had almost lain down again when he noticed two yellow eyes peering out at him from the darkness. Gus tried his filters again, but the brightness of the fire washed out any detail from the dark. He blinked and rubbed the sleep out of his eyes and took another look.

Yes, they are still there! The eyes seemed to glow in the darkness, and a chuff followed by a low rolling chirrup chased away any drowsiness Gus had held on to. The eyes moved to the left then right, pacing. Whatever it was, it seemed reluctant to approach with the flames. *SO glad I stayed on this side of the fire.*

The wind kicked in again, whipping and almost shrieking as it tore around the island outside. *How long has it been staring at me?* Gus gulped, trying to choke down some saliva. He took a quick look at his fuel, and the lion's share of what remained were dried vines and minor detritus.

Can't stay here forever. Maybe not even all night. A quick peek at his watch confirmed it was 11:21 PM. Gus groaned internally; this thing liked to hunt at night. When he was adding to the fire, he saw he had dropped a medium sized branch, half in and half out of the pit, just beginning to light.

Using Razorback Prime, he lifted the free end toward him enough to drag it away from the fire. One end was relatively unburned, the other smoked as it was removed. He waved it a bit and it began to burn in earnest.

Gus kicked some vines into the fire, and it flared to life briefly, giving Gus a peek at the creature. It was difficult to see, as it crouched defensively with the flash of light, but it looked to be the size of a panther. The brief light reflected on something that resembled scales, and there was definitely a greenish tinge to it.

The chirrup began again, and Gus felt a single drop of sweat track down his spine. It was so unsettling. A loud *ba-boom* echoed in the cave, accompanied with a simultaneous flash.

That one was close! Gus' ears rang with a high-pitched whine. As he blinked away the effects of the lightning, he saw that the eyes were gone. A sudden vibration commenced, originating outside the cave.

What now? Gus grabbed Razorback Prime and the branch.

He would have to make a break for it while he could. He slung his backpack on and waved the branch a bit to illuminate the cave as he prepared to leave. He sidled forward, leading with the branch, with Razorback clutched in his other hand. He peeked around the corner to look outside, but the creature was out of sight.

The darkness outside was absolute; only the flashes of lightning revealed the area ahead. Gus' night-vision was severely limited. The fire made some things washed out and the heavy rain hid things beyond the cave opening. There was also a fog that floated across and made things even harder to see. Gus realized the branch was a beacon for his location and it wouldn't last long in that rain.

He looked down at his clothing and realized it was practically no protection at all. He shivered with the drop in temperature, amplified by the massive doses of adrenaline in his system. At least out here he could use the spear a little better; it was cramped in the cave.

Another flash revealed some kind of turret or tower had pushed its way out of the sand, stretching out of sight upward. As if parting a curtain, the creature crept out of the rain back into the opening of the cave. Gus noticed its smell now that it was closer. It was a pungent scent that reminded him of his uncle's house who had all sorts of reptiles. Its odd musky smell mingled with the distinctive scent of carrion.

The creature clicked its teeth together menacingly as it prowled. If that was supposed to be an intimidation technique, it definitely was working on Gus. Gus slid off his backpack and dropped the branch, grabbing the spear with both hands. There would be no fleeing this thing when it finally stopped toying with him and attacked. Gus began feinting with the spear, trying to keep it back and at bay. The glowing eyes just stared at him with indifference. Gus managed to ease his way off the irregular basalt column steps onto the sand of the beach. He wouldn't have a chance if he didn't have any decent footing.

They circled each other and Gus was grateful for his

perception filters. He would be unable to see where the monster was if he had to rely solely on the intermittent lightning flashes. Almost without realizing it, the creature had maneuvered Gus away from the cave opening and began advancing toward him. Gus realized that the roiling waves were his only escape.

With lightning speed, the creature leaped and bit hard on Gus' arm. He felt the bamboo vambrace compress tightly, but no punctures. He still lost 10 HP and his arm began to lose circulation, so powerful was the compression. Gus choked up on the spear and tried to stab with the unwieldy weapon. He thought he got a couple hits in, but many scraped against something hard as he tried to hit his enemy.

At last, one jab punctured something. The mysterious beast flung Gus to the side and the creature retreated. His back crashed against a rock and he lost 89 HP, and incurred a bleeding debuff that was slowly draining his remaining health 2 HP every three seconds.

Razorback Prime was flung off into the dark in the fracas, lost to the night.

He could hear the clinking of metal and woozily looked up at the creature clinging to the scaffolding of the tower. A flash of light revealed its insectoid silhouette, backlit against the darkness.

The chirruping became a higher-pitched frenetic sound. Gus gnawed on his lip as he looked back at the dark jungle. *I hope it's not calling its friends.* In the second his gaze was averted, a searing heat and a massive *BOOM* exploded behind Gus. He was thrown forward with such force that the rain-soaked sand felt like a brick as his face was slammed into it.

Groggy, like he had been punched, he tried to rise up to his knees, but it was too much; he succumbed to the darkness.

When he awoke, he pulled his face up from the wet sand and spit out salty grit. It was day again, and the storm had passed. Swiping his eyes clear, he saw the blue window again.

I have a countdown already; I don't need these doomsday warnings every morning. During his time unconscious, he had regained the majority of his HP, but he still felt bruised.

The tower had gone, but Gus could see a manhole-sized metal door embedded in rock on the beach. There was no sign of his attacker. He shouldn't have survived his last confrontation. He shivered again, cold and not a little creeped out at how tenuous life was here. *Shake it off Gus, think about what's next.*

He opened and closed his fists, trying to regain circulation and get rid of the tingling numbness, and walked to the manhole. A similar picture of the tower scaffolding was on the metal door, with a lightning bolt crashing into the top. Whatever that was must have been crisped like a bug zapper. *Good.* Still, he wished he could see a burned corpse to calm his nerves. A confirmation that the thing was really dead. He wondered if its body was encrusted on the lightning rod now hiding under the ground.

Brushing away more sand from his face and hair, he sat on the manhole cover and looked back at the cave. It was too cold to make a permanent shelter. Plus he could be trapped inside if another creature came. He would have to give the big building another try. His stomach growled and Gus remembered he had left the visor cooking on the fire. *The crab!*

He scuttled back into the cave and the scent of something burned confirmed his suspicions before he got to the fire. All of the water had boiled away and the crabs on the bottom had been ruined, charred beyond salvage. Gus fished a couple crabs out of the top and managed to salvage some of them for food. The flavor was marred by the burnt ones, but he was able to pick a little meat from the small crabs.

He still felt cold, and took his meal out of the cave to eat. He sighed as the sun shone on his damp skin. Evaluating the visor, he was uncertain if it was salvageable. Nevertheless, he scooped up some seawater, and put it back inside the cave opening. It would need a good soak if he was to attempt to remove the burnt remains.

That done, he got moving, heading back toward the only

semblance of civilization. He would have to eventually deal with the shield if he wanted to get off the island. Avoiding it would only prolong his stay. He was wasting too much time trying to manage survival when he needed to level. While his instincts told him to play it safe, he knew he had to take some risks or he would die.

Indecision and procrastination; his lifelong vices weren't just bad habits, they would be deadly. He resolved to visit the manor and confront whomever was inside, and hope they didn't attack him outright.

He thought about his near-death fight and wondered about luck. He had never felt lucky before the island, but the coincidences were stacking up. Gus retrieved his backpack and found Razorback Prime lying nearby.

"Nick, all these coincidences are a bit suspicious to me. How does the luck stat work?" He began walking back toward the hotel-like building. Maybe his luck would hold out and he could join whomever was there. He had to make it in one way or another.

"Luck is one of the least valued stats, because it does not give a concrete, measurable effect when raised. It cannot be raised by any form of training, like other stats. In your case, I am unsure if your luck stat can truly be 'locked' as other stats can be. Nth can limit functions that improve strength, agility, constitution, intelligence and perception based on leveling. Usually this protects the host from overreaching and hurting themselves with the thrill that leveling and stat boosting provides, until they develop and intuit their limits and capacities.

"When luck increases, however, it often appears to be random and unattributable to any particular set of circumstances. Luck is not 'luck' as is traditionally thought of in folklore and myth. It is the ability to consciously and subconsciously change and influence quantum possibilities. It cannot be suppressed by any outside influence, and it is largely influenced by expectation and intention. This means that if you expect to fail, reality can bend to accomplish this purpose, despite over-whelming resources. The opposite is also true. It is also difficult to quantify, as few individuals know how to utilize it to any effect, as it is related to some theoretical manipulation of forces as of yet undefined to the Nth. Unlike other stats, it is more an approximation based on your past history."

"So, literally, check yourself or wreck yourself," Gus said with a chuckle.

"Truer words were never spoken, Gus."

CHAPTER THIRTEEN

Somewhere on a Beach

DAY 4 2:14 PM

10:22:22 remaining

Wearily, Gus arrived back at the building. His eyes scanned for any signs of the zombies lying in wait. Bracing himself to run, he slowly approached with Razorback Prime at the ready to fend off anything that made any sudden moves.

As he stepped into the open, his mind tried to take in how much work would be necessary to keep this area as clean as it was, free from the wild encroachment of the jungle. The path began to level out again onto a cultivated lawn and the aroma of citrus and flowers wafted up to Gus' nose. His stomach gurgled in protest at his limited diet. Some fruit would be a welcome change. He could use a little more variety.

A pergola became visible as the path turned a corner and more of the building came into view. It was covered in flowering vines so that it gave total shade to the patio with chairs underneath. More of the building was visible here, and a large section of it peeked out of the rock. Gus took it all in with awe; the amount of time to hollow out the rock to build the structure must have taken years. His eyes dropped down to the patio, which continued onward into shadow.

Meaning to make his way to the shade, Gus stepped onto the grass. With the first step, two large cylinders shot up from the edges of the lawn, sending plugs of sod skyward. Wedges of light emanated from the thin pillars and scanned up and down Gus' body. He froze, not wanting to set off some type of alarm or defense system.

A familiar pre-Nick autotune voice spoke up from the pillars in unison, "First generation nanobots detected. No activity detected for: forty-four point three years, since completion of installation. Current status is: standby mode until claimed. Are you here to claim and activate the installation?"

"Answer 'Yes, installation claimed by Gus Vannett, direct all command functions to this voiceprint and bioscan,'" Nick insisted in Gus' mind.

Gus did so, and the pillars shouted, "ACKNOWLEDGED!"

"Do you wish to reallocate power to basic life support systems in the manor?"

"Sure, I mean yes," Gus stammered.

"Acknowledged. Transferring power. Please wait while systems come online and Methiochos manor command functions are updated." They then shot back underground as fast as they had appeared.

"Does that mean what I think it means, Nick?" Gus asked with a huge grin on his face.

"If this is how you manage with a luck stat of seven, imagine what will be possible when you level up!" Nick said, with as much unbelief as an artificial intelligence could muster.

He tried the front doors and found that they were still locked shut. Nothing for it but to wait. Gus removed his sandals and luxuriated in the softness of the grass. Despite the threat of zombies, the pylons mentioned that no one had been by the manor for over forty years. *And that sod that flew up, if there had been something prowling around here, wouldn't those have already been uncovered?* The realization went a long way in putting to rest his fears that the manor was full of zombies, or that more were lurking right outside. Possibly some unseen security.

He was excited to find out what was inside the manor, but the pleasant scents of the citrus mingled with the essence of cut grass, and its utter softness was a soporific that could not be denied. Lying down in the shade, Gus drifted off effortlessly into a nap, as he let go of the day's tensions and relaxed.

———

At a cave entrance a few miles away, pylons that had stood raised for years, with bright blue energy arcing between them, winked out for the first time in memory as available power was transferred to other systems. The creatures that loitered at this location raised their heads, some lazily, others with a quick snap. One blob-like creature facing the pylons blinked its many eyes as the pylons shut off, and then noiselessly sunk back into its subterranean receptacle. The blob sent a visual record of what had happened to its master below.

The One faded out of a dazed stasis. It had awaited this and had compelled the others to stand watch, remaining as motionless as possible to conserve energy. Over the years, the few animals that strayed into the fence and were cooked as they passed through were quickly set upon and devoured by its guardians, then the sentinels returned to their vigil. The creatures began to stir as they awaited instruction from their master, the desire to hunt awakening with urgent intensity, having been suppressed too long.

———

Gus awoke invigorated and an old nemesis greeted him.

10 days 21 hours 49 minutes until nanobot shutdown/death

Gus hissed at the window, irritated by the obnoxious font increase. *I get it already!* He quickly gathered his things. Walking down the patio he could see the size of the manor, this entry tucked under a large wedge that appeared to be carved completely out of the mountain. Sharp angles and crisp architecture gave a hard, precision look that seemed out of place in contrast to the flowing smoothness of the natural curves of the island, from the soft sandy dunes by the beach to the undulating bulges of trees in the jungle nearby. A quick check showed the door was still secure. He sighed, hoping his nap would have passed enough time for everything to come online.

Off to the left, Gus could see two-hundred feet down another slope that led to the beach again. This area was on the leeward side of the island and waves crashed here with more regularity than his initial landing spot. Tiny figures could be seen moving along the beach, but the systematic pattern of their movement indicated they were not crabs or other small creatures scuttling around. When a wave would splash against the beach, the forms would be caught up in it, be carried to wherever the wave peaked and then they would resume the pattern. Gus would definitely need to check that out.

He longed to sleep in an actual bed. Hell, he'd sleep on the floor if it was dry. And maybe an actual weapon and some real clothes. There had to be a shower in there somewhere too. The storm had left him with a chill that still hadn't totally left him, and his woven clothes were drafty as hell. Gus closed his eyes and shuddered at the thought of warm water and the simple pleasure of being clean again. That was the first priority; take care of his basic needs, then he could figure out what his next steps would be to level enough to get out from under his ten-day death sentence.

He continued fantasizing about all the possibilities that could be in the manor, and how he had taken so many simple things for granted. His job as a henchman had exposed him to all kinds of bases and super lairs. They were typically ostentatious, but often had very specialized equipment, geared to maximize the super's strengths and compensate for their weaknesses. The possibilities were endless, and the curiosity was killing him.

"This is taking for-ev-ER," he muttered, "how long does the manor need to power up?" He fidgeted as he tried to control his impatience.

Unable to take sitting still and waiting any longer, he wandered back toward the lawn and took in the fruit trees. There were various sorts, and they appeared to have been cultivated or managed by the manor somehow, as no rotten fruit had accumulated underneath them, and they appeared pruned and ready for harvest. Gus quickly gathered some oranges and pomegranates and dug in.

The sweet taste was wonderful. He wondered if they were truly that good, or just that he was so hungry that the flavor of things was amplified. He remembered a time he was at a scout camp and he had eaten these generic brand chili beans. They tasted so good! When he got home he had asked his father to get some. When he tried it at home, however, it had the look and taste of what he imagined dog food to be. Nothing like hunger to change how food tastes or looks!

He tossed the peels in a small pile as he ate, and after a couple minutes, a small panel opened up alongside the manor. A basketball sized contraption rolled out and moved toward him. A flap lowered and it scooped up the discarded peels. Reforming into a ball, it rolled back toward the manor. Gus threw another peel on the ground to see what would happen.

The janitor ball vibrated, and returned to scoop up the new peel. This time it waited, anticipating another piece of trash, but Gus was getting full so he gave the little robot a break. After a minute, the robot came back to life, rolled back to its chute, and disappeared.

When he was fully sated, he was basically a sticky mess. Small bugs started to fly around him, attracted to the juice. He decided to check out the beach and wash off as much as he could in the ocean. Maybe scope out some fishing sites. It would be a lot easier with line and a pole, but a lot of islanders used spears to fish, didn't they? He'd expected he would level swimming a lot by retrieving his spear after many failed attempts.

Gus grabbed Razorback Prime and headed to the beach. Who knew how long it would take for the manor to open? Better to use the time for leveling and to get familiar with the area. As he made his way down the sandy incline, he could see that there were more spherical robots moving around the beach here, cleaning the beach from any detritus that washed in from the ocean. The waves were much shallower on this side of the island, and he kicked off his flip-flops when he was on the sand.

The beach sand, being so soft it felt like flour, reminded him of a trip to the Atlantis resort in the Bahamas he had taken when he was very young. He mentally named this beach 'Atlantis Beach' as well, smiling. It reminded him of his mom. Whenever they had gone on a family vacation, it was because of Mom. She had loved tropical locales, and since she had grown up in Florida, she had also loved beaches and the ocean. Those were some of Gus' most happy memories; that they were so long ago made the memories bittersweet. His only clear memories of her seemed to be from when he was really young.

He wasn't sure exactly how old he had been, probably around twelve years old, when he got really sick. His father never really talked about that time, but Gus was in a coma at one point and everything was really hazy memory-wise for that time frame. Something also happened to his mom during that time too, but Tempest wouldn't talk about it. She had powers too, but Gus couldn't remember what exactly they were. He often wondered if she had some kind of healing powers or emotional manipulation or it was just her presence that made him feel good. He got the impression she went out on a mission and never came back. One of the risks of the job for a super.

The times after Mom was gone were more difficult for Gus. Teenage angst mingled with the change in family dynamic had caused more arguments and isolation from his father. It was around that time Gus began to prefer to call his father Tempest when he shifted more into his stern, unyielding super persona. Mom had earned her title, but it was hard for Gus to refer to him as Dad.

Tempest wanted Gus to move past it. Suck it up. Man up. A familiar anger bubbled to the surface when he remembered that time. *I was a kid! I shouldn't have to 'suck it up' when I've lost my mom!* By the time Gus became cognizant of the world again, she had been gone for about a year.

Gus' brother Cyclone was out of the house being a good little super, just like Tempest wanted. Gus' eyes burned and his throat tightened as emotions swelled thinking about his mom. Gus blinked and cleared his throat, trying to overcome the negative feelings by removing how they affected him physically. He shook his tightened jaw muscles to loosen them, unaware he had been clenching, turning again to the beach to stop focusing on the distressing memory.

To the left of the beach-ball robots, there was a cluster of large rocks that could be climbed from the beach. Small pink flowers and yellow lichen covered the rocks, and somehow, these were surprisingly free of bird droppings. The shape of the island created a small inlet here and the water was much more still around the rocks. He rinsed the stickiness of the fruit off his hands and decided to attempt a little fishing for dinner.

He figured he was pretty rusty at fishing and it might take a couple hours to catch anything. He cleaned the remaining oily residue that had stuck to the blade after killing the zombie, making sure nothing was there that he would accidentally ingest. To not be impeded when swimming, Gus kept only his shorts made from the space suit.

He climbed the rocks that were by the water's edge and found a flat smooth area about six feet up on the shaded side of the rocks. Gus peered down into the clear blue water. Fish of different types swam lazily in this deeper area. Gus readied his spear, aimed at one of the fish, and let loose. The spear deflected when it hit the water and lost some momentum, allowing the fish time to move. Gus dove in and retrieved his spear. After about five more attempts, he decided to change tactics. He found a shallower area near the rocks where the fish continued to dart around.

He had to move to the other side of the rock to find an area in the water with fish that also allowed him to stand up to his mid thigh in the water. He held the spear out of the water and stabbed it down, but had a similar lack of success. There was just too much time between his movement of the spear to when it would hit the fish—always allowing the fish to dart away. Gus had to stand still and wait for the fish to relax and come back.

This time he kept the spear head underwater and with a quick jab he was able to spear his first fish. A quiet tone sounded.

*You have upgraded your skill **Fishing** to **Level 2**!*
Increased chance to catch fish with all methods: 2%
50 XP awarded
No XP awarded for new foods after host level 3 is reached.
140 XP to level 4

Gus flung the fish to the beach; he would clean it later. Lowering the blade of Razorback Prime back into the water, he waited. It took longer for the fish to return, and the reflection of the sun on the lapping waves was hard on his eyes. He would occasionally have to blink them closed after he received an especially bright flash. Then he remembered his grandpa's advice about shadows. Moving to a different location, he managed to spear two more fish.

Deciding three was enough, he got to cleaning them and preparing them to cook. His grandfather had taken him out fishing when he went to visit him. Gus remembered those times in his pre-teens. When Tempest was off doing Purple Faction business after Mom was gone, Grandpa agreed to take him in for a couple weeks. He could tell it took a lot for his father to finally run out of options and allow Gus to go to his grandpa's, though Gus couldn't tell why.

Gus reminisced as he prepared the fish, and carried them up to the lawn area of the manor. There were a few grills set up there along the edge of the patio, and using the same method he had at his old camp, started a fire and cooked his catch. Pulling out his metal plate, he loaded up the fish. It was starting to get dark as dinner was ready.

Remembering the Adirondak chairs his grandpa had by the dock near his cabin where they would fish, he took a similar chair from the patio and dragged it down the beach, keeping it above the high-tide waterline. There he exhaled deeply, began eating the fish, and watched the sunset, digging his feet into the soft sand.

CHAPTER FOURTEEN

Connected

DAY 4 10:56 PM

10:13:40 remaining

Gus awoke with a chill. He hadn't even realized that he had dozed off, but the soothing crash of the waves in the distance and the relaxing setting combined to put him at ease. Lately he felt like he had been tired more than usual. He started the day great, but even though his stamina bar was bigger, he found he could settle in for a nap around the early afternoon. Looking up at the countdown, he worried if his Nth were already starting to shut down a bit. Leaning forward in the chair, he rubbed his eyes, gathering his energy to get up.

Now that the sun had gone down, the air had enough bite to it to raise goosebumps on his arms. He grabbed his flip-flops and headed back up to the manor, hoping to get a little windbreak and rest for the night. As he looked for a place to settle in, a pylon slowly rose and a message appeared on his display.

Initialization complete. Life-support systems online and power diverted to basic systems. Do you wish to sync now? (Y/N)

Gus wondered what kind of place the manor was if it needed life support. "Nick?" Gus asked, rubbing the sleep out of his eyes.

"Syncing with the manor will allow me to connect directly with the manor's systems. Once done, you can access information about the structure and I can direct you in aspects of its capabilities. However, I will be offline for a time until the procedure is complete."

"But can I enter? It'd be nice to be indoors for once."

"Yes, but avoid doing anything of major consequence, would you?"

"Fine." Gus mentally pushed 'yes' to start the sync process.

"CONNnnnnneeeeecccctttteeed..." Nick said, his voice stretching and slowing down. Gus' field of vision began to darken around the edges and he was hit with an overwhelming fatigue. Wondering if he had made a huge mistake, the darkness spread to cover everything and a couple seconds after his vision blacked out, Gus did too.

Gus awoke to a sharp pain. Sitting up on the grass, he saw a small robot under his right hand. Its back was a green and black display that was slowly scanning up and down. There was a metal clasp holding his hand still, effectively handcuffing him to the little robot. The contraption had pricked his index finger and was taking a blood sample. Gus sat there confused while the robot released the clasp holding his hand and sped toward the community robot chute on the side of the building. A new message popped into his display.

DNA and handprint scanned. Error. Discrepancy in sample from archive. Please try Admin connect again in 24 hours to access Alpha Protocols. Basic manor functions available.

"What are Alpha Protocols?" Gus grumbled to himself. At least he could finally go inside. Making his way to the entry, he attempted the doors again. A thin black bar above the wide doorway emanated a wedge-shaped beam that scanned up and down and the door slid open with a loud pop. Gus' clothes fluttered as air rushed past him into the building. Had there been a vacuum inside? He scratched his head in bewilderment.

Entering cautiously, Gus looked down immediately. His unshod feet were on the plushest carpet he had ever walked on in his life! Part of the conditioning his mother had instilled in him as a child kicked in, and he worried about staining this wonder with his jungle boy feet, but the cream-colored material stayed as pristine as ever. His feet did not sink deep into the carpet, but the softness! It was like walking on Angora fur or baby kittens. Simple minds, simple pleasures.

Atop a plinth nearby, a rectangle of iridescent metal vibrated and began to shift and move in different iterations, folding and reorienting. "Transformers, nice," Gus remarked as the shape contorted into an antiquated-looking robot torso.

"Welcome to Methiochos manor. You are acting for Methiochos until he arrives, I presume?" Gus nodded dumbly. "Well then, may I be the first to welcome you to the base. As you have finally arrived, standby mode has been deactivated and power from perimeter defenses has been rerouted for main systems to come online. Many systems are still offline and will need to be activated and configured and optimized to your personal specifications. Unfortunately, sensors show a disruption to the normal power grid and available energy, which will need to be rectified to fully bring the manor online.

"More information is available at the control center. You may refer to me as Stuart if you need to contact me remotely. If you wish, I can direct you to the control center now."

Gus nodded again, mouth agape as he took in the grandeur of the building.

"Splendid, let us be off!" A small blue ball appeared in the cupped hand of the steward. Lights winked on as Gus followed the ball, which bobbed in the air like a will o' the wisp. The atrium widened out but the limited light offered by the steward and the local illumination did not reveal what was contained in the large room. The heavy smell of new paint mingled with new carpets hung in the air.

Soon they arrived at an elevator and the door opened with a *skiss* noise reminiscent of Star Trek. Gus mentally approved the designers' attention to detail. Though this structure was not designed for him, it really felt like it was! Once in the elevator, the glass-walled car slid upward and broke out of the semi-darkness to a panoramic view of the island. Gus sucked in a breath, seeing the beautiful swath of beach but from much higher. The car slowed to a stop and before it rose into another circular room, the beach was at least a thousand feet below. Gus removed his hands from the glass, slowly turning to see where Stuart had taken him.

He had been in various vehicles and headquarters of supers in his henchmen days, but this was impressive in different ways. He could tell that the decor was from what he had seen in movies from the late Fifties or Sixties, but they housed screens and panels that he doubted existed in that time frame. The ball floated toward a control area and rested in a receptacle above a main console, which flickered to life. He saw the screens wink on and run through some boot sequence as it checked systems and loaded files. Gus meandered to the window and looked out. They appeared to be similar to the oval windows Gus had seen before, but that area must be lower and on the other side of the structure.

"Sir, if you are ready, we can continue…" the steward invited. His voice seemed to be British to Gus' mind, and he wondered how Nick and this A.I. would get along. Also, he wondered how such a small little thing could speak with enough volume to hear, until he realized that it was communicating through the nanite connection in his ears.

"Do you understand verbal commands?" Gus inquired aloud.

"Yes, the system has a sample of your voiceprint and will respond to commands to a limited extent. I see you have not unlocked Administrative access at this time. Perhaps later. Until then I will be happy to assist you with whatever I can."

The blue orb floated again and went around a couple consoles to hover at a panel with multiple sockets and slots. "When you and Methiochos are ready, have him use this panel to scan his handprint. A DNA sample will be taken at that time as well. This being done, he can unlock Admin access and designate your proper level of clearance. Please familiarize yourself with the controls."

Gus looked at the array of panels and scanners. Along one wall, he could see monitors displaying views of the island springing to life. Another bank showed various scans and the lifeforms entering and exiting a certain area. Yet another was labeled facility management. Gus looked at the different menus on this screen and began to see that the manor was much bigger than he had initially thought. There were all types of specialized structures in the building, from labs, to manufacturing, and even training facilities. All of them were grayed out except for some basic systems. When Nick came back online, he would have to investigate further.

Wanting to experiment more with the control schemes, but not wanting to commit to anything without Nick's advice, he resisted the urge to explore and change settings. His mind was getting foggy from the late hour and his eyes began to feel dry and itchy. Gus *still* felt tired even though he had been unconscious much more than normal lately. He began to worry about how he would be able to function if this weariness became worse. Maybe his Nth were offline right now as well? Or had limited function without Nick's organization? Or if he had a concussion from when the creature had thrown him. Weren't you supposed to avoid sleeping in cases like that? Before he could wind himself up with worry, he found himself asking Stuart something, almost unbidden.

"I think I'm done here. Could you show me somewhere I can sleep?"

"Certainly. I will show you to one of the executive suites."

The blue ball lifted out of its resting spot and floated toward the elevator.

At the same time they were headed to the master suite, forces were mobilizing elsewhere on the island.

———

The time had come. The being that the Dark Nth called The One began sending out mental commands to his minions. There were many different types, and it took some doing to keep them fed and maintained. Fortunately, he had retained some abilities from the life before which allowed him to take care of his brood. Unfortunately, as he became more aware, he recalled that he could create no new minions to bolster his ranks —if any were lost, they were gone, and if there was anything that angered The One, it was the loss of power in any form. So much had been lost. But The One had fought, and he had created a bulwark to limit the control the Dark Nth could place on him. Finally, he could reclaim what was his.

CHAPTER FIFTEEN

Building, a Mystery

DAY 4 11:05 PM

10:13:31 remaining

Dark memories faded in and out of the life before. This was not how things should be. The transport. The attack. The crash. Barred and corralled by his own creation.

Many things had been lost; the anger and focus had been refined and made it easier to resist the Dark Nth's probing attempts to 'correct' him. He had never needed anyone to guide him in the past. He did not need it now. Revenge would be had.

This was not chance; he had been sabotaged. So much time had passed. But he would find all the corrupted branches, teeming with rot. They would be burned. Then the trunk. Then the roots, if any remained. The Dark whispered to him.

At first, he refused to believe, but there was no other way. Betrayal. Covetousness and avarice. Jealousy. So petty. But The One could be petty too. They would see what they had wrought. How did the Dark know so much? Ebb and flow. Preparations had been made. Then improved. Could the Dark be trusted? But it knew. It gave but did not ask. That was different. Now was the time to move. The One sent the Slow out first. They would clear the path. They were the least valuable and hardest to control. He could feel the tendrils of connectedness finally unwinding after years of being huddled in a tight knotted mass. If these perished, it would be less he would have to feed. Contempt. They depended on him from the life before, they depended on him now. Parasites. But necessary. Or not. Time would tell. The One had waited so long. He would wait no more.

———

Gus awoke and sat up. Sleeping in a bed made a world of difference. The stiffness and achiness he had experienced the last couple days were gone. A little disoriented, he groggily asked, "Nick, ya there, buddy?"

"Deepest apologies, Gus, that was... intense. From the initial designs of this complex, I underestimated the complicated scope of this facility."

"What did you find out?" Gus asked and headed to the shower. Gus started the water, letting the warmth spread over him, exhaling as it not only rinsed off his accumulated funk, but drained away the tension he had been carrying around from struggling to survive. He started attacking the grime caked on his skin, beginning to feel human again as Nick explained.

"This complex spans fifty-three floors, thirty-three of which are above the surface, and the remainder extend into the core of the island."

"Dang, that's huge!" Gus looked up from focusing on scrubbing his feet, wide eyed. The bottoms were so black it looked like he had walked on charcoal. He attacked them again with a brush as Nick went on.

"It runs primarily on geothermal energy, but this is not as active as it should be, as far as I can determine. Most sections of the facility are offline as a result, but there are directories that show the titles of facilities that can be accessed. The system will not allow some of these to be unlocked until your stats and skills increase."

"What is this," Gus threw his arms up, frowning, "it's not just a power issue, but most of the facility is *locked?*"

"Unfortunately, yes. Basic functions are enabled though, so you should not have to worry about shelter anymore."

"Well, at least there's that." Gus slumped his shoulders, admitting to himself that even simple shelter was a huge improvement in his life. Hard to complain when he was in a hot shower on an island resort just for him. *Am I always so pessimistic? Gotta work on that, no one likes a Debbie Downer.*

"So what can you tell me about the guy who built this place?"

"This facility was commissioned to be built by a super named Anders Bergstedt, AKA Methiochos. His powers appear to be related to healing, both himself and others. He also has a matter manipulation sub-skill which assists in reforming lost limbs or replacing biological material—"

"Aren't healers fairly rare among supers?"

"Yes, they often progress slower in leveling than more offensive based supers, so few have the patience to pursue this evolution of skills, although those who do become much more powerful at higher levels, and have an increased lifespan."

"Sorry for interrupting, go on," Gus turned his attention to the gunk buried under his fingernails.

"The facility was completed forty-four point three years ago, but was never claimed. Service robots have been maintaining the grounds ever since. Manor records indicate that Methiochos accessed the facility controls remotely from the island, then disappeared shortly thereafter, including activating the bio-stasis field and security protocols. There is no mention in the quantum server of the manor at all. The data I have comes from internal records of the manor itself. No nemeses are listed in his file.

"It would seem that something happened to Methiochos on arrival to the island—"

"If he was already here, on the island, why didn't he claim and activate this structure which was to be his new base? I don't buy it that a healer would be killed so easily. Since it sounds like nothing can get past the bio-stasis field, and you said he turned it on from inside, then where is he?" Gus stopped cleaning and looked up, trying to puzzle out what had happened.

"He did activate a few systems personally, but they were odd choices for his first acts on the island. Possession of first generation Nth seems to be a requirement for proving leadership and claiming the facility. Even though all supers are Nth-integrated, you have most likely been classified as an officer, as first generation Nth are not typical of the rank and file."

"You keep saying first generation, what does that even mean?"

"The first Nth that seed a planet's hosts are referred to as the first generation. They have the most ability to adapt and offer a variety of abilities as they have not specialized to a specific host biology. Future generations are derivatives of these Nth. This means that Methiochos is one of the first supers to get powers on Earth."

Gus' throat closed again, making it difficult to pull in the steamy air as he connected the dots of the only things he knew. Zombies. A missing super boss. A *healing*-super no less. Was he killed shortly after arriving on the island? And if he had been, what would Gus have to deal with? *Couldn't life be easy for a change?* He rubbed his temples and pinched his eyes shut. He had to work to keep from imagining strength-based zombies. What could a luck-based zombie do? His stomach soured and he hurried to change the subject, his go-to move when uncomfortable. Just avoid it.

"Are there any supers that don't have any Nth?" Gus found

a twig in his hair he hadn't noticed as he lathered up. A flipping twig!

"Not yet. Human evolution would have eventually developed these abilities, but it would have taken millennia. Nth accelerate these natural tendencies and make the transformation possible in a short time by modifying their hosts to tolerate and alter the forces and reactions that generate their abilities. Whether they know it or not."

Gus once again had a hunger pang, stronger than usual, distracting him from the conversation.

"What does the database show in terms of clothing and food?" His empty stomach alternated between nausea and hunger.

"There is a mess hall, but there are no current food stores, although there are orchards on the property, as you have seen. The majority of food stores were most likely to be shipped in later, after the bio-stasis field was lowered. The only prepared food available is within food dispensers. These can be accessed for only 50 FP, and come stocked with energy bars, but more complicated foods require the mess hall to be enabled. Other areas such as various labs and the Foundry are similarly completed, yet unstocked and non-functional. Uniforms are available, as they were necessary for the workers. Garment manufacture is totally automated and upgradeable. There are the general barracks, but I see that you have already found an executive suite."

"FP? I think I left all of them in my other pants on the station," Gus said wryly. "Am I supposed to know what that means?"

"Excuse me, Gus, there is so much to explain. FP, or Facility Points, are how you upgrade or unlock features of the manor. You get them as you level up and should receive some legacy FP based on your current level."

"Can I use FP to unlock one of those food dispensers to be placed in here?"

"It will be done as soon as you can activate facilities controls. Do you wish to go there now?"

"Yes, and after that, let's go check out some more modern clothing." Gus toweled off and donned a robe from a nearby closet. Nick directed Gus up the elevator to the control room. After finding the right console, he placed his hand on the scanner and his level was assessed.

You are currently level 3. 1500 legacy FP awarded.

Gus used 50 FP to place the food dispenser in his suite and scrolled through the list of available options. There were many headings, with grayed out sub-sections. Only a few were highlighted, and of those, the training tab caught his eye and he brought up the information on the first entry, training arena.

Training Arena (1250 FP)*: This area provides a virtual training ground, assisted with robots to provide physical feedback. Training provided centers around primarily melee skills with some limited augmented attack skills. This area is able to sync with supers for additional functions and feedback options. More functionality and options can be obtained by increasing the arena's level.*

He really needed some skills if he was going to take out any more zombies on the island, especially the fast ones. As a henchman, he was only given a gun and minimal amount of training. There was a reason why Stormtroopers couldn't hit a damn thing.

This arena sounded exactly what he needed. He spent the points and unlocked the training arena, saving the last 200 FP. He had to; nothing else was lit up after he had made his two selections. So much for base defenses. After that, Nick led Gus to an area that appeared like a large department store, with large closets. Gus' **Wreck-ognize** skill triggered and he could see the improvement in stats the jumpsuits provided. Dropping his robe, Gus wiggled into a jumpsuit that was his size. The material was stretchy and comfy as he slid it on, but then he started to itch. A little at first, and then all over as if he was having a severe allergic reaction.

"Nick! What's happening?!" Gus shouted.

"This clothing is above your level; your Nth are rejecting it and you are dealing with increasing amounts of histamine." Shedding the suit, Gus kicked it away. He watched as the welts on his skin quickly subsided when they were not in contact with the suit.

Naked again, Gus set about putting the robe back on. Looking again, he saw the minimum level was five.

"Hells bells, that sucks. I need to level up faster." sighed Gus.

"You could always take up the mantle of the Winter Knight…" Nick suggested.

Gus' mouth dropped open. "Nick! I am loving your handle on pop culture! Keep it up, I'm loving it!"

Nick's only reply was a small jingle: 'ba dah ba bah baaah…'

Gus looked around, trying to find something level three or less, but had no luck. He felt like when he had shopped at Ross or Marshalls, where you had to hunt back and forth, hoping something you liked was in your size. He was about to give up when a pulsing alert sounded.

"Gus, please go to the command center. A proximity alert has been triggered." Nick urged. Gus ran to the elevator, smashing the button for the control center. He burst out when the car finally opened. One of the maps was highlighted. To the west of the large field below the manor was the green expanse of the jungle canopy. One area had a break in the trees, and a path could be seen winding through it. Some familiar gray figures could be seen on that path.

"Zombies! Nick, can you modify my display to show them relative to my position?"

"Yes, now that I have access to that data from the manor, transferring to your display…"

A minimap refreshed in the upper right corner of his display, with overlapping yellow dots clustered on the left side of it. Gus saw them at the center of the circular map, with an arrow showing the current direction he was facing. Wishing he had some time to use the training center, Gus had to waste time running to his room to get dressed. He fumbled with the ties, the urgency making him clumsy. Finally done, Gus grabbed Razorback Prime and rushed to meet the invaders.

CHAPTER SIXTEEN

Monsters of Rock

DAY 5 9:58 AM

10:03:50 remaining

Gus checked the new minimap in the upper right corner of his display. The yellow dots were very helpful in showing him where to head to start grinding some mobs. A quick check with **Wreck-ognize** confirmed the Shamblers were from level three to six. The color coding of the dots gave a good idea of the level range of these mobs in relation to his own level—and these were perfect; not too tough, not too weak.

"Nick, can I assume this minimap functions like most RPG games?"

"It would be more accurate to say that games function how the Nth interact with hosts, but yes."

They were approaching from the jungle on the far side of the lower field, where Gus had first seen the manor. The open field would allow him to run and retreat, and avoid being ambushed by something from behind.

"Nick, are these higher or lower levels than that first Shambler?"

"These appear to be higher, but it is unclear by how much."

Gus grit his teeth and nodded as he ran even harder.

While he thought he was innovative in re-purposing Razorback into a spear, in practical use, there were some challenges. First, the thickness in diameter of the bamboo made it difficult to get a good grip on it. The smooth, polished surface also made it less secure than he would have liked. The length was great for the purpose, but Gus had absolutely no experience with spears or any melee weapons before coming to the island. Razorback Prime was also heavier than what a normal spear would be, so controlling the placement of the sharp tip could prove more difficult than expected. If he had to start fighting any foes besides these dumb, slow zombies, he would be in big trouble.

Gus wished he had some time to dig a trench or two, or place some logs in strategic spots that could trip some of the approaching Shamblers. They appeared to be spread out enough to handle, but if he got sloppy, they could bunch up and that would complicate things greatly. Better to meet them as soon as he could at the edge of the field, and then have room to retreat if needed.

Gus saw the first of the creatures emerging from the jungle. His upgraded display now showed life bars above the zombies, with a fraction indicating remaining health over total health. Some were more decomposed than others, but in contrast to the one he met in the forest, these appeared to have a more directed motion. Gus approached the lead zombie, braced himself, and speared it in the face.

It dropped, shaking, and its dot became hollow on the minimap. That would be super helpful, especially to avoid stray bites on the ankle from an incapacitated but not dead zombie. The draining of the green bar as its health ebbed away was oddly satisfying. Feeling more confident, Gus lined up his next targets, but made sure not to get too close to those who had fallen. Like Tempest always lectured, 'trust, but verify.' He could double check whether he could trust the interface after the threat was gone.

He missed the next one, slicing across the bridge of its nose, getting a little off balance, but able to back-step, re-position and hit the eye on the next attack. A chime sounded, and Gus let the messages fill in their queue unread. He did like how they defaulted to a pulsing icon at the bottom of the screen, not making a pop-up that blocked his whole vision and had to be toggled off.

The pack seemed to contain thirteen remaining slow moving Shamblers, and Gus was determined to get them all. Knowing he would rarely find easy opponents like this, he took the opportunity to practice fighting and hopefully gain a couple skills. Hopefully, he could get a spear ability by using it frequently.

He tripped a zombie with the back end of the spear, then stabbed it in the eye. He cut another Shambler in the middle of its back. It lost control of its lower limbs and fell down, but kept on reaching for him until he dealt a death blow through its ear. It was harder to line this strike up, but at least it stopped them from moving for the most part.

He struck a few more, but this time on the neck, trying to buy time and thin out the herd. These ones didn't flail with their arms, so he switched to targeting only their necks. He was taking more time than he expected, and the zombie march was relentless. Gus experimented with hitting different areas, but besides the spine, legs, head and neck, nothing had a huge effect. Hitting their legs did very little damage, but it stopped their march onward, and made them easier to attack.

One time he got scared as a zombie pushed farther than expected onto Razorback Prime, past the cutting edge and onto the bamboo. Gus panicked a bit, but got the idea to start to spin in a circle. The idea was to fling the Shambler off the end of the spear, but the mob simply tripped and the spear was easily extricated, and the zombie was history.

He jogged to another zombie. Suddenly, Gus' foot dropped into a hollow in the ground and he fell forward, scoring a hit to the left side of the target's chest. The force of the fall sank Razorback Prime deep into the creature's chest, past the cutting edge. *I'm making this a flipping habit!* His knuckles cracked as his grip tightened on his weapon, and he clambered back to his feet.

This zombie must've been some kind of guard in its former life, because it had an athlete's build. Gus couldn't trip or even move the hefty Shambler by trying to shake the spear side to side, so he pushed forward hard to stagger the zombie and rolled out of the way. The bodybuilder didn't even flinch from the push. With Gus out of the way, the Shambler rotated to face the manor and forged onward.

What would they want with the manor? That first Shambler didn't have any interest in it, so what's going on?

Gus gripped the now-slimy cords holding Razorback in place that were protruding out the zombie's back. Yanking the spear as hard as he could, he was rewarded with three feet of movement. The black slime coated the spear as it reluctantly slid out with each tug.

The nauseating smell became exponentially more concentrated as decomposed offal began spilling out around the edges of the spear. Stopping when the spear was half-in and half-out, Gus caught his breath and tried to get control of his gagging fit. He wasn't eating a ton, and wanted to avoid malnutrition by wasting the little food he had scavenged. When the feeling subsided, he made another attempt and freed the spear. Razorback Prime was now coated in the slippery, stinky goo along its entire length. The fact that there may be active Dark Nth coating the spear made him drop it and step away. The strong zombie just soldiered on once the distraction of Gus and his spear were out of its line of sight, the wound not stopping it in the slightest.

"Once separated from their host, Dark Nth inactivate within seconds, Gus," Nick supplied helpfully.

Gus heaved a mental sigh of relief and tried rolling the spear, using the patchy grass and dirt to remove at least some of the greasy smear. It didn't do much, but it did add some sandy grit to the slime, which improved his grip on the smooth bamboo. Snorting like a bull, Gus came up behind the body-builder and severed the neck with three violent slashes. Another stab ended the troublesome creature when it fell face up.

"That one was a biiiitch," Gus drawled tiredly. *I can't let them get to the manor. Why are they going there now?* Gus had taken too long with his fumbling about, and the zombies funneled together as they zeroed in on the manor. The remaining mobs were pressing closer to form a zombie wall. A few tripped on their fallen brethren, so Gus waited for these to pass, then he dispatched prone zombies. Gus attempted to lead the Shamblers in a train to spread them out, but they quickly abandoned their ambling 'chase' as soon as he was out of eyesight, reorienting toward the manor. Gus' shoulders and back were starting to burn with the effort of wielding the spear.

He wanted to keep fighting but his stamina was at 5% so he rested for a minute, then picked his next target. *Hurry up!* He fidgeted while his stamina bar slowly filled. His panting lessened as his stamina rose, and Gus pushed himself to continue.

He staggered after another zombie and lined up his shot. He stabbed, and the zombie turned its decayed head at the last second. Instead of glancing off, he felt a vibration that felt like it emanated from his bones when the spear made impact, and he knew instinctively that his **Wreck-tums!** skill had triggered. The full health bar above the zombie sank to 1 HP. Gus jabbed again and the zombie's yellow dot turned hollow on the minimap.

"Noice!" he thought.

Turning around, Gus saw a zombie that was much closer than he had expected. He had ignored the minimap by over-focusing on his last foe. *Rookie mistake!* He reflexively stabbed the fat zombie. The spear slipped in his grasp and again sunk in too far. Gus tried to spin the Shambler, but it was much too fat and heavy. The large zombie pressed forward relentlessly, so that the spear sunk deeper into the zombie's chest, which sucked the spear in like a spaghetti noodle.

Dirty ragged fingernails were waving closer and closer to Gus, so he gave one final push and jumped away. Unlike his other failed attempt, the spear appeared to have lodged in the spine, as it did not protrude out the back of this obese creature.

The zombie turned back to its destination, spear bobbing with its steps like a wagging finger, chastising Gus for his poor fighting skills. Gus had an idea and ran toward the flopping spear. Jumping onto the handle end of the spear, he tried to lodge it into the ground, and rolled away as quick as he could. His plan was to bury the end and lock the zombie in place.

What actually happened was that the strained cords holding Razorback to the bamboo finally gave way and only the bamboo came out, one end cracked and splintered.

Gus was dumbstruck. He barely had the presence of mind to roll out of the way. Now what the hell would he do? He had lost Razorback inside a mob and there were still four zombies left. Grabbing the remaining pole, Gus went into panic mode. Ignoring the fat one, he came close to a leaner zombie and hit him with all his force in the legs. The zombie predictably went down, and Gus commenced hitting the head. Loud *thock* noises accompanied his blows and Gus was unsure if they were more from the hollow bamboo or the zombie's head.

The soft ground didn't help, since some of the force of his blows was absorbed as the zombie's face pressed into the dirt instead of being held in place by something more solid. Meager '-1 HP' and '-2 HP' notices popped up, and Gus realized the others would get away if he took too long with this one.

Gus decided to trip the remaining zombies, as they were almost to the incline that led to the lawn entrance to the manor. Of the three that were left, fatty was the hardest to down. After accomplishing that, he decided to take out the others and leave fatty for the end.

An hour later the job was done. Gus slumped to the ground.

"Woof to the woof…" he said in utter exhaustion. His stamina regeneration was maddeningly slow. He had to hit them on the head, and occasionally he would connect with a sweet spot on the back of the neck and get a slightly better damage notice. But mostly it was thwock-rest-rinse-repeat. He lay back staring at the sky, watching the clouds float carelessly overhead as sweat beaded then ran down, tickling the side of his face.

His breathing finally slowed and he got back to his feet, loath to do what was necessary to retrieve Razorback Prime. He cleared his throat, spat, and braced himself for what was ahead.

Walking over to the fat zombie, he tried to pull on its clothes to flip him but they just ripped apart. The skin started to tear away where the clothing bunched.

"Nothing's ever easy…" Gus grumbled as he stood there, hands on his hips. Getting an idea, he dragged another zombie parallel to fatty, then put the bamboo as a lever between the two. He had to reorient the other zombie so it could fulcrum off the hip-bone, but the flip was finally accomplished. "Now the fun part…" Gus groaned as he slunk his hand into the ragged wound. "Ow, pointy… eeew, slimy… Aaah, moving!" Gus shouted as he probed inside, face turned away to avoid the powerful stench.

His fingertip finally brushed against the flat corner of Razorback's blade. Pinching his fingers on each side of the blade so as not to cut himself, he slowly extracted the weapon, all the while wondering why he was not just abandoning it and making another blade. Finally, it was free!

He wiped Razorback as clean as he could upon the fat Shambler's clothing. Ripping off a section of its shirt, he wrapped the blade gingerly, trying not to touch it too much, then headed to the stream and finished cleaning. The Dark Nth should be totally inert, but their black sticky blood still stunk and he didn't want it encrusting his trusted weapon.

Gus felt sweaty and gross with the gore. He was sure if he could see himself, there would be stench waves radiating off him, offending anyone nearby.

Why did I even shower this morning!? None of the zombies had laid a hand on him, but just the thought of Dark Nth's ichor on him was making his skin crawl and itch. The Nth may be deactivated, but this black slime would probably give anyone a raging infection if it got in a cut. He did a cursory check for any loot, but there seemed little to gather from the creatures, which kind of bummed him out. Loot made battles much more enjoyable.

Making his way up the manor path, Gus decided to head down to the beach on this side of the island when he got to the lawn. There were showers in the manor, but the thought of tracking in the black mess disgusted him. A quick ocean pre-wash followed by a long hot shower sounded really good to him.

Crouching at the water's edge, he washed the gore off of Razorback, scouring it clean with sand and water. Then it was his turn. He rubbed his skin raw, using the sand as an abrasive to scrub where the black gore had been, continuing to do another couple passes, even after the black disappeared.

When he was finally done, Gus picked up Razorback Prime and trudged back to the manor, seeing the beachcombers doing their jobs. Watching the balls zoom about was oddly comforting, as they left little trails in the sand like a Zen garden. That along with the slap of the waves on his back felt like it was carrying the remains of the battle off of him, diluted into the vast ocean where it could do no harm.

Feeling refreshed, Gus headed back to the manor to see if he could take a real bath and to check if he had leveled enough to wear some basic clothing again. He opened up his display as he walked back.

CHAPTER SEVENTEEN

Room at the Top

DAY 5 9:58 AM

10:03:50 remaining

Arriving at the manor, Gus dropped everything and slowly walked inside. He walked to the master suite, hitting the appropriate button in the elevator. He checked the display and read the notices that had accumulated from the battle.

Gus was scanned and the elevator began moving; he became lost in his logs.

You have killed a level 3 Shambler, 75 XP awarded
Skill gained: Two-handed weapons (Level 1)
+10% damage when using two-handed weapons.
100 XP awarded
LEVEL UP! You are now level 4.
1965 XP to next level
You have leveled up during battle! To avoid distraction, changes due to leveling will be postponed until logs can be reviewed and cleared. Skills will

level and improve functionality but stats will not be increased until allocated. This feature can be toggled in the interface if you desire.
You have (5) additional stat points to assign.
500 Facility Points (FP) awarded
Skill gained: Polearms (Level 1) *+1 to initiative when fighting enemies without polearms.*
100 XP awarded
You have killed a level 4 Shambler, 100 XP awarded
You have killed a level 5 Shambler, 250 XP awarded
You have killed a level 4 Shambler, 100 XP awarded
You have killed a level 4 Shambler, 100 XP awarded
You have killed a level 5 Shambler, 250 XP awarded
You have killed a level 4 Shambler, 100 XP awarded
You have killed a level 4 Shambler, 100 XP awarded

Skill gained: Backstab (Level 1)
Unnoticed attacks from behind deal double damage!
100 XP awarded
Skill upgraded: Wreck-tums! (Level 2)
Current level: +10% chance to trigger during a successful attack.
50 XP awarded
You have killed a level 6 Shambler, 400 XP awarded
You have killed a level 5 Shambler, 250 XP awarded
You have killed a level 5 Shambler, 250 XP awarded
...

As the list continued, he scrolled down to the end of it, noting how XP gain for lower-level mobs dropped rapidly. He reached another level notification:

LEVEL UP! You are now level 5.
2675 XP to next level
500 FP awarded, 1200 FP total
You have (5) additional stat points to assign. (10 points total)
Special skill unlocked!
Skill unlocked for reaching level 5! Wreck-luse (Level 1)

Upon touching an enemy, with weapon or physical touch, a toxin is released which causes them to flee away from friend and foe for one minute per level. Necrotizing damage at site of touch continues to spread outward, dealing damage until healed. Gives poisoned debuff, -20% movement speed, -20% attack damage.
100 XP awarded
2575 XP to level 6

After the slight pressure of upward movement stopped, the doors opened with their telltale *skiss.* Gus made his way to the shower, still reading the log, trying to absorb the changes, and plan his point allocations. He stepped inside, noting that the shower stall was larger than some of his berths in his previous jobs.

Gus fist pumped at unlocking an active attack ability. Then the euphoria of leveling twice hit him. He stumbled back and slid down the tiled wall of the shower, falling hard on his butt, but not caring.

"Whoa, double rainbow, all the way... whoa, that's so intense," Gus moaned as the leveling rapture faded. "I wouldn't give it up, but man, that would kill me with the distraction if I were mid-battle," he mumbled. He was glad the system postponed things until he checked his logs. That safeguard had probably saved his life.

He dropped his woven clothes in the corner of the immense shower, turned on the taps and stood there. *Finally, level five... normal clothes, here I come!* Warm water rushed over him, almost feeling like it was washing through him, flushing away the fatigue and soreness. He lathered up from a soap dispenser on the wall and did a cursory wash; he had removed most of the gross bits in the ocean after the battle. Despite that, he still spent an embarrassing amount of time in the shower, while he tried to think of the best way to spend his ten stat points.

Agility definitely needed a boost, so he dropped three points there, bringing him to eleven. His muscles vibrated slightly, as if he were shivering, for ten seconds. When they stopped, Gus could tell no other noticeable change.

Next, four points went into strength for a total of twelve. This resulted in a tightness in his whole body, as if every muscle were clenching. It didn't quite hurt, but it was close. Soon the sensation passed. His body looked harder; he watched in amazement as his skin became taut. He looked more stream-lined and condensed, but he didn't notice that he had bulked up anywhere.

Perception was next with two points. This must have passed some threshold, because his eyes began to burn and itch. He closed them and rubbed at his eyelids while tears welled up. A sharp tinnitus hit at the same time, like an icepick to the ears. Gus fell to his knees, clutching his head as water poured over him.

Gradually, both faded and as he blinked his eyes clear, he noticed a new tab labeled filters at the top of the display. He gasped, shaking away the water and shampoo that had run into his eyes.

When he had caught his breath, he checked out the changes. Accessing the tabs, he could isolate infrared and ultra-violet spectrums. After playing around with seeing how the world looked through the filters, he went back to default settings, allowing some time for him to get used to his usual way of seeing the world. A similar tab allowed him to extend his auditory range, or amplify sounds too quiet to be heard normally.

The last point went into constitution, bringing it to ten, and while no untoward side effects happened, his MP, HP, and stamina bars increased by twenty apiece.

Still distracted, Gus dried off and donned one of the robes hanging there, almost on autopilot. Finding a lone remote on a bedside table, he managed to open the curtains and take a look outside. The impressive view from the balcony overlooked Atlantis Beach and a fair stretch of the coastline beyond. A warm wind blew in, causing the curtains to undulate with the gentle rhythmic gusts.

Gus stood silently, listening to the crash of the waves below. The sound of the surf was so relaxing, he decided to leave the balcony door open when he slept. He stared, mesmerized by the rhythm of the waves. He didn't know how long he just stood there, feeling the water's hypnotic pull. Finally, he tore himself away and crawled into bed. He smiled as the mattress first conformed to his shape then began pulsating, massaging his back. He didn't recall that feature last night, but he was so tired and had fallen asleep as soon as his head hit the pillow. Gus closed his weary eyes and slept.

When he awoke, the room was dark. The only illumination was the starry, moonless sky that sparkled without the effects of light pollution. He wondered if his increased perception played a role in the majestic expanse of stars on display. In the past, Gus usually had the habit of sleeping in whenever possible, but right now he felt wide awake and restless—like he had drank three or four energy drinks. He doubted he could fall back asleep even if he wanted. It was a welcome change; he had felt so tired and sleep deprived in the past couple days.

Finally, he had hit level five, so he was now able to wear some real clothes. While his homemade outfit had worked well enough, having some more reliable clothes that covered him completely would give him a little more confidence and peace of mind when it came to fighting against Dark Nth.

He made his way down to the uniforms, and found a suit that gave +1 to constitution and provided +25% reduction against melee attacks. The outfit was gray, with black sleeves. A golden lion with wings and a tail was emblazoned on the back of the outfit, a feature he hadn't noticed before. *Suitably badass,* he thought, nodding in appreciation. A quick change into the spandex-like jumpsuit and he evaluated the fit. The stretchy material was comfortable and appeared to conform to his movements. It managed to be breathable and it didn't impede his range of motion as he twisted and tried out the feel of it. He found some matching boots, also gray, completing the ensemble. He checked his stats again to see where everything had ended up.

Gus Vannett
Level 5
Agility: 11
Constitution: 9 (8+1)
Charisma: 8
Strength: 12
Perception: 16
Intelligence: 11
Luck: 6

HP: 160
MP: 120
Stamina: 160

The change in clothes had shuffled his stats a tiny bit; he had lost one point from luck by losing the kilt, but gained another in constitution. Not a bad trade-off, especially since his homemade outfit was falling apart and torn up from his struggles with the zombies.

Gus was eager to visit the training arena and improve his fighting skills, not to mention seeing what these stat boosts did for his ability to fight. He asked Nick to show him the way and he was off to train.

CHAPTER EIGHTEEN

...Baby One More Time

DAY 5 3:02 PM

9:22:44 remaining

As he made his way to the training facility, Gus asked Nick for more details about it.

"The training facility offers training in multiple styles of physical attack skills. At level one, it comes with a standard complement of the most basic weapons, and has ten levels of upgradeability. Each level allows the holo-instructors to illustrate more techniques and foe-bots to become more adaptable and work as coordinated units, with ever increasing sentience and battle savvy," Nick explained.

"That's exactly what I need. Hopefully, if I can take the basic weapons out of there, it may kill two birds with one stone." Gus mused, thinking about his weapon troubles in his last battle.

"Since weapons frequently break during training, there is a considerable stock of them in the facility. However, no additional weapons can be made until you unlock the Foundry. This allows raw ore from storage to be fashioned into new weapons. Should you choose to learn virtual smithing skills, you can directly impact the formation of the weapons produced," Nick explained.

"Virtual smithing? Is that something I unlock or a skill I obtain?"

"It can be both, but unlocking it will allow you to obtain the skill by using the interface provided by the manor. It is a form of influencing the structure of the weapons made on a molecular level. Impurities can be virtually seen and removed, matrices applied to strengthen the core of weapons, dimensional effects made to raise or lower density. There are many uses when the full abilities are leveled and unlocked. Occasionally, you may have an epiphany and create a new blueprint, based on your unique application of skills and powers.

"These provide special bonuses tailored to the creator, and are one reason that crafting is very valuable in terms of leveling faster. Unfortunately, you haven't created enough items to gain a crafting skill that can be improved and leveled, thus offering XP. Some supers specialize in that; you just have to decide how you want to grow your skills."

"On the one hand, that's awesome, but everything being locked is exasperating. It makes no sense! Why make something as amazing as the manor, and then limit how you can use it?" Gus huffed, clenching a fist at his side.

"There are many reasons. First, some facilities require skills that are not obtained until one is trained and adept. Even if unlocked early, they cannot be used by anyone with a lower level that lacks these skills. This forces a certain focus and planning as one grows. It results in a more comprehensive use of each specialization, as well as preventing dabbling in so many potential facilities that none are used to their full potential. Supers *and* Nth level and evolve much more quickly this way, based on centuries of trial and evaluation.

"Another reason relates to how skills advance in high level

supers. One of the trade-offs that happens when a super attains higher levels is that to maintain their powers, the Nth must evolve more and more to maintain homeostasis. If a super decides to retire and relax, he will actually have powers become dormant and lose the ability to utilize them."

"My grandpa is retired, so you're saying that he is losing or has lost his super abilities?"

"Definitely. Even if he uses them occasionally, the atrophy penalty for lack of use is significant for hosts. Many choose to gift their abilities to an heir at some point. If a host dies without transferring their Nth, they either seek a suitable host nearby or return to the collective until a new host is determined by the quantum server and integrated.

"This is generally unknown by regs, and is intended to be a motivator for constant improvement. XP is primarily earned through fulfilling quests, crafting, engineering, and battle. The first three are service-based and the latter generally is not. As power increases, many of the human supers shift away from quests and creating new things for the benefit of humankind. The result is a tendency for conflict as a means of providing a way to level when one does not wish to serve. All high-powered supers manage a lair, base, or manor like this one, to comple-ment their powers and push them to higher levels," Nick said.

Gus contemplated all the time his father had been at work, and the resentment he felt at times that he never seemed to have time for his family. Tempest wasn't just a high-powered super, but he was in the Purple Faction's governing leadership—which probably involved a lot of additional requirements, based on what he had just learned, to simply maintain his powers. Maybe that was giving him too much credit though. It still burned him that he valued his power level over his family. The times he *was* at home somehow weren't that one-on-one. He did look pretty exhausted a lot of the time, however... Gus shoved the old argument back into a corner of his mind reserved for emotional baggage that he didn't want to deal with.

He felt amped and agitated, old emotions stirred up from

thinking about his father. Maybe knocking some robots around would be a good release.

"Currently, only the training facility is active. The manor has two-thousand remaining power units available for future expansions. One of the things we should plan for is increasing the manors' power generation abilities," Nick suggested.

"Put it on the list…" Gus sighed as he stepped purposefully toward the elevator. The trip down the elevator took longer than expected, the training facility being farther underground than many parts of the manor. Stepping into a multi-tiered room, Gus took in the amenities. There appeared to be exercise equipment along the outer top tiers. Padded mats and sparring areas formed another tier. Racks of weapons lined the third tier, along with humanoid robots who stood as still as sentinels over the large arena that formed the bottom central section of the facility.

Reaching the edge of the arena, Nick directed Gus to stand on a circular disc in front of a console. Gus was scanned again.

Assessing…

A holograph of a tall, lithe figure with pinched eyes materialized in front of Gus. "Which martial skill do you wish to train?" he stated gruffly, then lifted his chin and folded his arms while waiting for the response. Gus thought he looked like a clean-shaven Genghis Khan.

"The spear. Or polearms, I guess." Gus offhandedly decided while looking at the variety of weapons encircling the place.

"BE PRECISE!" the trainer bellowed. "Do you wish to train in the spear or learn the fundamentals of all polearms? Which type of spear do you wish to use? Without focus, there is no power!" the trainer barked, then returned to his folded arm pose.

Gus' eyes snapped back to look directly at the teacher and his posture became rigid as it had been trained to assume when at attention. The abruptness of the instructor shocked him, partly because it was so reminiscent of his father's brutal nature when training. Not wasting time, Gus spied a basic vanilla spear without any elaborate embellishments or fancy blades. He pointed at it and stated, "I will start with this spear, but am unfamiliar in even the basics of its use."

Quest Granted: Shake spears!
Quest Conditions:
1) Reach level 2 with polearms and level 3 in spear subspecialty
Time Requirements: Limited to 3 hours or less
Quest Rewards: *New skill unlock. If unable to meet quest requirements in time allotted, opportunity for new skill will be lost. 500 XP*
Do you want to accept this quest? (Y/N)

Gus mentally punched the yes prompt.

"First, you must learn a battle stance." The virtual instructor came to life and assumed a ready pose with a slight crouch and one leg extended backward. He flung his leading hand back and the area above and behind was illuminated with moving figures. After a second, Gus recognized them as a replay of his movements and the Shamblers in his battle the day before.

His mouth dropped open. He hadn't known the manor had the ability to scan the island to that degree, or even that it had recorded him in such a way as to reproduce what had taken place. In watching his own movements, Gus realized that if he had not experienced the battle first hand, he would have guessed he was watching someone incredibly drunk harassing individuals walking home after a tough day at work. His stumbles and falls were brutal to watch, and he was embarrassed to see it from this vantage.

"In this conflict you were inefficient and unbalanced. We will correct that," the instructor grunted.

I had no idea I was that bad, I'm lucky I didn't get killed out there. Gus leaned in, trying to absorb what he had missed.

"Assume this stance," the instructor demonstrated. Gus saw his own form move again in the area above and behind the instructor. He tried his best to adopt the same stance, but could see where his front foot was rotated too far outward and his back leg was too close, making the stance too narrow. He made the adjustments he thought he needed and once he thought he was in position he held still. He noticed a subtle tingling in those areas out of place on the display and he let the sensation guide him. When he finally got it, the tingling went away and he knew he was mimicking the correct form.

A padded robot with what looked like a pillow for a head and two cylindrical pillows for hands appeared from a panel that slid away from the wall. It merged with the hologram and mimicked the instructor's movement.

"Now, maintain your balance without moving your feet." The pillowbot rotated around Gus and poked at him with its padded arms. One hit let Gus know these were not pillows. More like baseball bats made of rubber, covered with a canvas-like material.

Not expecting the strength of the prodding pokes the pillowbot would give, Gus stumbled and the tingling reasserted itself. A couple times he deviated from the correct form more than usual, and he found that the slight tingle ramped up to a painful pins-and-needles sensation, prompting him to quickly return to the appropriate stance.

The robot spun and attacked from various angles and directions, challenging Gus to shift his weight in different ways to maintain his balance and not be knocked over. Two more times he was knocked down, but after thirty minutes or so, he could sense some improvement in his recognition of how to react with the different types of shoves the pillowbot attempted.

"Rest now." The instructor-pillowbot hybrid froze in a standby pose. Gus caught his breath and noticed his stamina bar was a few points from empty. He jumped around and shook his legs to get a little circulation back and relieve the strain of standing in one spot for too long. A couple stretches of his arms and back relieved a bit more tension. When the green bar was nearing full, the instructor assumed ready position again and ordered, "Again!"

"Let's do this, Chop Chop Master Onion!" Gus challenged back and he resumed his stance. The drill continued, this time with pillowbot speeding up and then adding attacks from both arms. Gus found it was much less fatiguing to avoid getting pushed by dodging than trying to absorb each hit and shift his weight. The hardest shoves to avoid were those that came from behind, as it was more difficult to twist and visualize the attacks, compared to frontal assaults. In a real battle, it would be so much easier with the ability to move his feet. Eventually, a chime sounded and his display showed a new notice:

You have leveled up the skill: **Polearms** *to* **Level 2***!*
50 XP awarded
100 FP awarded
2525 XP to level 6, 1300 FP total

Gus found that a little odd, as he hadn't even touched a spear yet, but wasn't going to argue with the system.

"Enough!" the instructor assessed. "Procure a spear."

Gus jogged to the tier above and grabbed three identical spears, and brought them down to the arena, leaving two along the sidelines in case one broke and to take for weapons when he inevitably had to return to battle with the Dark Nth.

"Hit the target, maintaining your stationary stance," the instructor ordered. The pillowbot had a holographic display envelop the cylindrical padded area where the head would be. This morphed into a target with two red bullseyes instead of eye sockets.

Gus had to orient where to hold the spear with the dynamic display and locked in the right placement of his hands. It felt nice to be able to have a decent grip instead of fumbling like he did with the too-thick bamboo. He wondered what this spear was made of—*whoosh*! The pillow arm narrowly missed his face.

"Can't get distracted like that," Gus chided himself.

It took a couple minutes to get his balance together when

his hands were locked onto the spear and he couldn't wave them in circles to regain his balance, like a man on a tightrope. Now that he had his center back, he timed his attempt to stab at the pillowbot.

His first lunge was over-exaggerated and pulled him off balance, and he was promptly punished with a smack to his kidneys by the pillowbot's arm. He was sure that he had seen people flipping spears propeller fashion in the movies, but was not sure if that was even a realistic way to fight. Trusting there was a method to the constraint, Gus probed with minor attacks, not too aggressive, as to not expose himself again. One thrust by the pillowbot came quickly and Gus reflexively brought the haft of the spear across that side and blocked the blow. Another was similarly deflected and pushed aside. Gus placed his attention on these blocks, trying to add a little shove at the end and began to notice that it was bearing fruit. When his stamina bar drained after five minutes, he had to take a break to let his stamina recharge. The waiting really was the hardest part.

"Nick, what stat would increase my stamina? I'm getting winded way too easily."

"Constitution gives you an extra twenty units of stamina for each level, as well as twenty units of HP."

Managing stats was much harder in real life than when he min-maxed characters in video and tabletop games. The only things he felt he could ignore for a while were charisma and luck. For some reason, he was exceptionally lucky lately and almost felt like adding points would jinx him somehow.

He needed strength to fight the durable zombies, but he could get past that if he actually knew how to fight. He would need speed if there were more of the fast zombies. Constitution would make him much less squishy, and he was feeling especially squishy lately.

Those super long fight scenes in martial arts movies had lied to him; he was easily winded in such a short time. Finally, his stamina bar had filled and he continued on with training.

After more sparring, he could start to see a little more of an overextension in his foe. He attempted a stab after a deflection but was too slow in aiming and the pillowbot retreated. Success came after another three five-minute cycles of training, focused attention, and trial and error. He caught the attack with the middle of the spear, rotating clockwise to his right, then snapped back like a coiled spring and scored a bullseye. A chime sounded, and the instructor-pillowbot stood at ease while Gus extricated his spear.

After resetting, Gus began to improve his timing and could feel himself being guided as the Nth gave a tiny impulse at the right time to start his attack or retaliation. Apparently once he had a successful execution of a skill, the Nth could guide him to replicate it. Another hour later, mostly taken up with stamina rests, another chime sounded. Gus noticed two prompts in his log.

You have leveled up the skill: **Spear Mastery** *to* **Level 2!**
50 XP awarded
100 FP awarded
You have leveled up the skill: **Spear Mastery** *to* **Level 3!**
50 XP awarded
100 FP awarded
Quest Complete: **Shake Spears!**
Rewards: 500 XP, 250 FP
New skill unlocked: Sweep the Leg! (Level 1)
Upon successfully blocking an attack, have a 25% chance of knocking an opponent off their feet, stunning them for 5 seconds.
100 XP awarded
200 FP awarded
1825 XP to Level 6, 1800 FP total

"That is enough," the instructor stated, bowing slightly while maintaining eye contact. The hologram dissolved and the pillowbot retreated behind its panel. The instructor then faded away and the lights dimmed, indicating that the training session was over.

CHAPTER NINETEEN

Welcome to the Jungle

DAY 5 6:46 PM

9:17:50 remaining

Gus thought he should feel tired after such sustained effort, but he was becoming more resilient. Wanting to try some of his new techniques, Gus went to the command center to check out the display that showed the entire island. Touching the interface and expanding the area close to the lower field of his first skirmish, he dragged the image farther into the forest, but the dense cover blocked the view of the ground.

Gus wondered if these images were from a satellite in geosynchronous orbit, and how visibility would change if it were a cloudy day. There were sensors on the ground that picked up motion and somehow analyzed threat levels, but nothing was showing up on the monitors the farther into the jungle he scrolled. Gus was also unsure how extensive those sensors were farther away from the manor. Deciding to go on a reconnaissance mission, he grabbed his three spears to take with him.

He headed back to his room to grab an energy bar and some foam to remake Razorback's handle, reverting it back to a knife. He tore into the black packaging of the energy bar and was greeted with a dry concoction that tasted like peanut butter and sawdust. With a lot of water, he was able to choke down the bar. Whether it was its age or just how they were designed, it was not something he would look forward to eating.

Gus exited the manor and found Razorback lying in the grass. He refashioned the handle as before but received no updates or notices, and the stats and name had reverted to their initial values. The uniform did have a nice belt attachment that held Razorback nicely, although the blade wasn't covered, so he would have to be mindful to not stab himself by being careless. Gus then headed toward the jungle.

It was nice to have normal footwear for a change. The boots of the uniform offered much more protection and cushioning than his open-toed sandals. He felt surer on his feet and his movements were smoother without things shifting around. The polished shafts of the spears fit easily in his hands, and felt more durable than the bamboo one, despite being much thinner. There was a little more strut to his step, and he walked with a bit more confidence. Things were coming together at last.

Gus passed the bodies of the defeated Dark Nth. They were much more decomposed than Gus would have expected in such a short time. He thought he might have to unlock some kind of cleanup droid like on the beach to remove the bodies so they wouldn't become overwhelmingly rank from decomposition. The fetid odor had dissipated as well, thankfully.

Without their Dark Nth sustaining their cohesion, most appeared as skeletons lying in oily patches of black goo. The fat zombie was less decomposed, probably because of its sheer mass, the large ribcage dripping ichor. It looked less like the thick tar that was the 'blood' of the Dark Nth, and more like used engine oil. The skeletons also looked less robust than a typical skeleton. They were pitted and sandblasted, with criss-crossing grooves and voids.

Gus stopped and plunged a spear right at the entrance of the forest trail from which the Shamblers emanated, then turned back. He stood there and looked over the vestiges of the battle. His mind flashed back to getting beaten up by the gang members and his father's stinging words. He stood up a little straighter, smiling at his victory. It was sloppy as hell, but he had done it.

Even after one training session, he felt much more compe-tent with the spear, and his gear had improved in quality as well. *'Never engage a superior force...'* the words echoed back to him. It was hard to describe, but Gus didn't feel like the loser he had gotten used to seeing himself as. The odds were against him, but that taste of success began to fan the flames of possibility for the future. *Where will I be in a year?*

He never would classify himself as a determined or driven individual, but he didn't really have anything to work toward, either. Despite his family being supers, Gus had always been given the impression that, for some reason, he didn't have the aptitude and probably would not get powers at all. The message was repeated so often, by so many different people, that he began to accept it as undeniably true.

But he could see that it didn't have to be that way. That possibly fate had something bigger in store for him. He smiled and looked up at the sun. He had the whole day ahead of him to explore. Gus decided that he would leave another spear farther along the path in case he needed them while retreating; he couldn't fight with three spears at once.

He knew he was taking a slight risk if one of these zombies happened to be able to use one of the spears against him. However, there were a lot of unknowns; he would just have to do the best he could. They would be too unwieldy to carry along in case he needed to react quickly. Even though these were from the training facility, the edges looked razor sharp. Perhaps there were other training modalities for humans sparring other humans, or they had healers to help people recover. He guessed that professional supers would be at the manor, so training with real weapons would probably be more on their level.

Venturing down the path, he was comforted by the chittering of monkeys, insects and birds. They quieted significantly as Gus approached, but did not go silent en masse as they had when he had met his first Shambler. Gus wondered if his perception made him more aware of the animal sounds, and whether they had been there all along.

The shade was welcome but the humidity increased noticeably as the vegetation became denser. Gus was unsure what had been done to the ground, but vegetation appeared not to grow on a two yard wide path that meandered through the jungle. Things grew into the path's 'airspace' but nothing grew from the hard packed ground that formed the path, despite teeming life everywhere else.

After penetrating two hundred feet along the path into the forest, branches thickened over the path, making it hard to move smoothly. Carefully removing Razorback from his belt clip, he hacked off the limbs that got too bold in their growth across the pathway, kicking them off the path. Razorback functioned well as a machete, and had a similar size.

If he had to make a retreat, he didn't want to have to second guess or have anything slap him in the face or trip him on the way out. Oddly, he felt like Razorback preferred to be in its current form as opposed to its spear configuration. Probably PTSD from being stuck in a zombie gut. Gus smirked at the thought.

Pausing to refer to his internal display, he tried to get used to the minimap function he had access to, now that Nick had linked his display to the manor's sensors. The background of the circular map showed an aerial view, which only showed the green treetops. As Gus progressed, he found he could toggle layers and see that the fog of war effect was being lifted in the areas covered by vegetation on his map, showing the path and surroundings as his Nth shared the information with the manor.

Focusing and zooming in could be done past the plant layer now, but would probably not auto-update like the satellite view could. Still, it could be helpful in planning approaches and exploring in the future.

After walking for a good hour, Gus noticed the sounds of the forest were tapering off. Not totally quiet, but less consistent and with longer pauses between the plaintive calls back and forth. Gus sheathed Razorback and readied his spear as he had trained earlier. Gus slowed down and swallowed to help moisten his suddenly dry throat. The tightness of the jungle around him offered a lot of hiding places, and he began to question the wisdom of coming out here.

He left a second spear, jamming it upright into the ground thick with roots by the trail. When he went farther, a yellow light winked at the edge of his minimap. Approaching with caution, spear extended, Gus saw a Shambler who was attempting to walk through the chest-high stump of a fallen tree. The zombie would walk forward, bounce back, then try again. Gus looked back along the zombie's sight line and it seemed like it was making a beeline toward the manor.

Gus approached, keeping the stump in between him and the zombie, and set his stance. One snakelike jab later the zombie fell, draped over the stump like he was hugging a teddy bear. Gus made his way back to the trail, with 200 XP more in the bank, and resumed his exploration.

———

The One snapped his eyes up. The loss of his minions the day before was acceptable in the sense of loss, but unacceptable in that he had a challenger. The farther away they were, the less control he had over his minions, but they were good at following orders once given. Another light winked out and the mental strand connected to it evaporated. The challenge must be met.

The One did not tolerate opposition. Unfurling a different set of strands, he sent them to meet the threat. In a sense, it was good to test his mettle; he would enjoy the test. Then his army would mobilize to reclaim his prize. The One sent his orders and then curled back to await their reports of success and show him what had dared to come here.

————

Gus walked on without incident for half an hour. His suit was beginning to be soaked with sweat, whether from the heat and humidity or his anxiety, he couldn't tell. He was wondering how far he should travel before returning, when the sound of running could be heard, intermixed with the swish of jungle leaves being pushed out of the way. Gus tensed and dropped back into stance. Two figures the size of tigers burst from behind a low hanging broad-leafed plant and rushed straight at him, running on all fours.

Gus' eyes opened wide and his stomach roiled as he recognized a familiar foe. *No, no, no, not more of the fast ones!*

He barely had time to reattach Razorback to his belt and secure his spear with sweat-slicked hands as the lead creature approached. Pointing at the larger of the two monsters, he yelled, "***Wreck-luse!***" But nothing happened. One of the creatures barreled in to him and Gus barely had time to block with the haft of the spear. Upon contact with his spear, the creature reared up and abruptly changed direction.

Since they were so close together, one of the creatures skidded into the other, clambered to its feet then rushed off the path to the right. Gus' eyes followed it as it disappeared into the vegetation, then he snapped back to focus on the immediate threat. The distracted creature was tripped by its partner, but deftly executed a forward roll and slid past Gus down the trail without even losing any momentum. Spinning around, it hissed and made a loud chirruping click and its lower mandible split open, revealing two shark-like rows of teeth on top and bottom.

Gus had been thrown onto his back and almost had the wind knocked out of him. He cast furtive glances to the jungle as he tried to get up, not wanting the other creature to come up from behind. Clambering to his feet, he faced the creature. It bared its teeth, which moved forward and back, flexing and contracting toward the creature's maw.

It was the first time that Gus had gotten a clear view of what the agility-based mob looked like. It reminded Gus of the movie 'The Fly.' Partly human, but with praying mantis bits for the arms and a grasshopper's for the legs. Its outer skin or shell appeared bumpy and hard like a crab, and shimmered with an iridescent green hue reminiscent of a dragonfly.

It made a powerful leap toward Gus, talon-tipped arms outstretched. Gus used the base of his spear to deflect the attack and allowed the momentum to carry the creature forward. One talon stretched to gash Gus, but the haft of the spear protected his forearm. The talon struck the spear, lifting a shaved curl of wood as it slid down.

"Dag yo!" Gus screamed and turned to face the abomination. It had a svelte figure and was catlike in how it crouched, back legs trembling in preparation for another pounce. Pumping for a couple seconds, the back legs telegraphed to Gus their intention to jump and he struck out with his spear.

The head of the spear penetrated into the sinewy muscle under the right arm of the creature and hit bone. Snapping its arm back in a tucked position, it altered its trajectory enough to miss Gus, but snapped off the spear tip, leaving him holding what amounted to a jagged-ended broom handle.

The creature leapt upward, grabbing onto a branch with its hale arm and clung there evaluating its prey. It screamed menacingly in anger and pain with its Predator-esque jaws, and Gus had to fight the urge to turn and retreat.

There was a sudden rustling off to his right, and Gus could hear his heartbeat pounding in his ears, ever increasing.

I've got to get out of here!

Pushing his fear down, he switched the broken shaft to his

left hand and unsheathed Razorback. He tried to recall how far back he had left his other spear. Slowly he started to walk backward carefully, keeping his eye on the creature. The beast dropped to the jungle floor and followed. The pierced arm hung limply, slightly tented away from the body by the angle of the protruding shaft. He slowly shuffled his feet as he retreated, keeping them always in contact with the ground so he wouldn't misstep and trip over anything. He made painfully slow progress, and kept waving the broken spear and Razorback in front of him to keep the creature at bay. He did not dare break eye contact. The creature held its hale arm curved in front of it like a praying mantis with its talons curved downward, so Gus decided to call these things 'Mantids'. The insect-like mouth sealed the deal on the name.

A scream disrupted the tension between the two, startling them both as the other Mantid flew onto the trail between them. Gus' heart tightened as he realized the effect of **Wreck-Luse** must have worn off. What was left of the creature amazed Gus. A large section on the side of the Mantid had sloughed away and looked like a huge shark-bite on its side.

It flailed about and gunk tumbled out of the large wound on the side, revealing an oily, metallic sheen surrounding the bones visible through the breach. The creature had difficulty maintaining itself upright as the wound was extremely large, to the point that the torso was not being supported appropriately, so it folded and straightened as the creature attempted to maintain its posture.

The Mantid that had been winged by the spear swatted at the other, irritated at the distraction, noting that its prey had used the opportunity to retreat down the path in a sprint. Leaving its brother to flail on the path, it loped after Gus.

Gus was amazed at how quickly the jungle flew by as he ran. It felt like he was running on a moving walkway, which added to his speed. He would have to ask Nick later how speedster's powers worked, as he did not feel like his muscles were exerting themselves any more than usual, but he was moving much faster than he should be. Or maybe he was just getting stronger and quicker. A loud screech brought him back to the present.

The Mantid kept screaming in anger at its lost prey, which inadvertently helped Gus, as he could gauge how far away the creature was by the sound, and spurred him to run faster. Gus reached the spear he had left behind. He threw the broken shaft and Razorback aside in his hurry to wrench the spear free. He spun and rushed the creature, hoping to take it by surprise. The Mantid saw Gus change tactics and jumped to a nearby tree, out of range.

It bared its maw at Gus in quiet challenge, and a chime sounded. A quick check on his minimap showed the distant yellow circle had become hollow. The other Mantid must have succumbed to its injuries. He slowly crouched down and picked up Razorback and reattached it, eyes locked on the monster.

"It's just you and me, ugly…" Gus challenged. The Mantid swung and leapt, stretching its hale arm outward. A membrane under the arms billowed out and allowed the creature to half glide toward Gus, foot talons extended. If it had full use of both of its arms, its attack would probably have been successful. Its injury threw its coordination off just enough to give Gus time to twist and let the creature slide past. He stabbed outward and scored a deep gouge on the creature's right thigh. The Mantid's red health bar dipped to a little less than half.

Pressing his advantage, Gus moved to attack again, but the Mantid scuttled away on all fours. Realizing its situation, the creature became frenzied, snarling and brandishing its talons. The Mantid had the luxury of only needing to score one hit that punctured the skin and Gus would be done.

Gus remembered his training session and got into his stance. When the creature got close, he would jab defensively and the Mantid would back up in ever growing frustration. It was hitting itself with the shaft embedded in its flailing right arm, and the blade must be doing some internal damage, because there was a slow drain on the red health bar. Encouraged, Gus set in to wait for the creature to damage itself to death. He sighed in frustration as the Mantid turned tail and ran back the way it came.

"Dammit! Nothing's ever easy!" Gus screamed. He pursued the Mantid, squinting his eyes as he came upon the fiend leaning over the crumpled form of the other Mantid.

What the hell is it doing? Turning back, black ichor dripped off its prehensile jaws. And its health bar had regenerated to about 80%! *They eat brains to heal? They shouldn't be able to do that to each other!* The head of the other Mantid was cracked open and the empty cranial vault testified as to how the Mantid was able to regenerate so quickly.

"Hells to the bells! I am seriously done with you..." Gus roared, pointing the intact spear at the Mantid, who looked back, the expression on its insectoid face somehow resembling a sly smirk. This was not looking good. Gus' thoughts bounced around, trying to find something that would allow him to defeat this enemy. He tried to jab at the Mantid, but it had relaxed into a defensive posture and was quick enough to easily avoid Gus' spear.

"That rules out **Wreck-tums!**, if I can't land a hit." A brief glance at his display showed that **Wreck-luse** still had a long cool-down period remaining. The beginnings of an idea began to coalesce. "Nick, play Cherry Bomb by the Runaways!" The thrum of the song energized Gus, and he set his mental focus on the spear head lodged within the Mantid. He waved his own spear back and forth in time with the song. Giving in to the beat, he imagined each attack and feint was pushing energy toward the Mantid.

Focusing on the energy being absorbed by the spear head inside the Mantid, ever increasing the tension between the molecules. *I hope this works...* Gus had very little experience so far using **Wreck-It-Gus,** or **Wreck-ord** but maybe they could be used offensively. Hopefully.

While most of the thrusts appeared as mere feints, the Mantid began to sense something was off. Cocking its head suspiciously, it furrowed its brow and looked quizzically at Gus to see what had changed. It could neither hear the inner sound-track Gus was using, nor could it feel the slight warmth building up in the embedded spear head. The same changes that allowed the Mantid to fight without feeling pain also prevented it from detecting anything as subtle as what was happening with the spear head. The Mantid continued to sidestep the attacks which were not intended to connect.

Subconsciously, Gus felt power channeling from his core upward and then extending out of him, coming slow at first but becoming easier and flowing more as the process continued and the music approached the guitar solo. It was vaguely reminis-cent of when he had lit the coconut husk fibers, but the quantity of power he was using was much more dramatic. His MP bar was quickly draining, and he worried that he would run out of juice before anything happened.

The pulses began to coalesce into a virtual beam, partly emanating from his chest, but mostly funneling down his arms and down the length of the spear. His low MP alert began to chime, but Gus pressed on, just a little longer.

"...Cherry Bomb... Cherry Bomb... Cherrr-y Bomb!" the song finished, and the spear head finally detonated. Gus hit the trail and covered his head as shrapnel whistled through the air, shredding the Mantid's torso. The last thing Gus saw before covering himself was the separated head flying off into the foliage, an expression of wonder and disbelief upon its ugly face.

Getting to his feet, Gus cheered, "Scott Pilgrim, eat your heart out!" Luckily, the force of the blast extended mostly side-ways and backward, so Gus remained thankfully clean from the entire ordeal. A ding sounded and Gus checked his display.

Mantid added to bestiary and estimated stats added based on battle.
You have defeated a Level 9 (Mantid) 1000 XP gained!
You have defeated a Level 9 (Mantid) 1000 XP gained!
LEVEL UP! Congratulations, you have reached level 6!

500 FP awarded
3675 XP to level 7
*You have **(5) stat points** to assign.*
*Your apt use of **Wreck-ord** has unlocked a sub-skill of **Wreck-It-Gus**: Indi-Wreckt (Level 1).*
Allows you to destroy items not directly in physical contact with you, given they are suffused with enough energy.
Range of effect: 10 feet
Damage done: 1:2 ratio of MP invested to HP damage
100 XP awarded
3575 XP to level 7, 2400 FP total

Gus looked at his MP bar and it was at 3%. That would have been almost 350 HP of damage, possibly more because it had been delivered internally. He quickly dumped all five stat points into constitution, to improve his increasing stamina needs and buff up his HP pool. This brought his constitution to fourteen. Stamina and HP jumped to 260 as a result, giving a nice buffer against new dangers.

Checking out his new suit, he noticed that the tiny splashes of Nth blood had beaded up and rolled off the suit, not even leaving a smell. That in and of itself was a feature worth wearing the suit for. The added flexibility during battle and not having to worry if everything would rip or fall off was another.

Hopefully, he would never have to find out how resistant it was to being cut or punctured by an attack. His spear had also saved him, but it made him much more aware of how most of his body was only protected by a spandex-y fabric. *Another trip to the armory should be on tomorrow's to-do list.*

Grabbing what was left of his gear, he jogged back down the trail, just in case there was a second wave of reinforcements coming. Grateful for the earlier training that kept him alive today, Gus mentally committed to double down on training and to try to come up with some new tactics in case the enemy came in larger numbers. Now it was time to eat and evaluate the battle. He had a lot of questions for Nick that he intended to get answered, about his own powers and the Mantids.

———

The One began to feel a feeling that had eluded it for so long that it was unfamiliar in classifying it. Doubt. What was that? He had been in total domination for so long. Resistance was non-existent. He commanded. He was obeyed. This was how it happened. The severing of these two higher tendrils introduced another feeling that was foreign in its scarcity. Pain. Uncertainty. More control could be placed in the fast ones. They retained more of themselves and were more effective tools. The anger. This was familiar. It came stronger. From the loss. From the pain. From the defiance. The One wanted to send a large attack. But the doubt. It said no. The anger said yes. The One decided.

CHAPTER TWENTY

Take the Long Way Home

DAY 5 8:51 PM

9:15:45 remaining

Gus was teeming with emotions as he jogged back toward the manor. The fight was unexpected and the jungle encompassed him oppressively the darker it got. He had been surprised and afraid when the Mantids first appeared. Reflecting now that the adrenaline had burned off, he was a bit conflicted. There was an undeniable exhilaration during the battle, of being able to confront a foe and defeat them. He wasn't expecting to feel guilty, however. Fighting the Shamblers did not feel like he was actually killing something. It was like they were already dead, but they just didn't get the memo.

But what did they want at the manor? He didn't think they would have the intelligence to do anything once they got there. *Weird.* With an ominous undertone. The Mantids were obviously intelligent, though. They planned and attacked. He had managed to fight the other zombies without even considering they were humans at one point, because they were mindless. It was easy to dismiss them.

But even though the Mantids physically resembled humans less than the Shamblers, it made him question himself.

Did I enjoy killing those things, just a little *too much? It was me or them, so self-defense is different, isn't it?* His attempts at justification felt a bit hollow, and he couldn't erase the worry and concern about how his choices would shape him. His conscience also reminded him of the questionable things he had done that were 'just part of the job' as a henchman. That type of thinking didn't work out so well for the Nazis either. He also felt conflicted with the whole 'ends justify the means' argument. His mind kept pointing to people who had done worse things, and that he wasn't so bad.

Everyone knew about the supers who had hunted many of the large cats to extinction, testing their new skills in single combat. It wasn't until the Factions organized and came to an uneasy agreement on which crimes would be punished that certain atrocities stopped being committed. Some of the damage was irreparable by that time, both to the planet and the loss of some animal species.

Was the new taste of power the Nth gave him revealing something about himself? Were his true desires hidden only by his lack of power to bring them into reality? The questions kept on coming, making Gus more and more uneasy. He always had difficulty dealing with strong emotions and always tended to push them away and not deal with them.

Some of his biggest fights with his father had been the result of an explosive release on the pressure cooker of emotions where Gus stored all his pain and angst. His father always backed down when things got too heated, treating him with kid gloves. Probably pitying his poor reg disappointment of a son. It made Gus feel even more helpless and weak when his father did that, though. Like he wasn't man enough to deal with any important issues.

He didn't feel helpless anymore. Sure, he was worried about

the future and making poor choices in his build. His powers kind of felt all over the map and he wasn't able to see a clear picture of how they all could work together. But there wasn't time to mope around. He had to level quickly and, in the process, try to find some synchronicity in combining and using his powers together. That goal grounded him a bit, and he felt a little better, even if he did not have all the answers. He had something to work toward, and he knew he would figure something out.

Turning his thoughts to the recent battle, Gus had some questions that troubled him. "Nick, when I first used **Wreck-luse**, it was more of a defensive mechanism and I didn't think much of it. But in reading the skill description, it mentions a toxin causing the effects. How is this toxin introduced in my target? I didn't touch the creature, my spear did when it collided with me, so what was the method of delivery? It doesn't make sense," he asked.

"You are too used to comic books. In that genre, one of the primary ways supers get their powers is due to mutation, often by radiation of various forms. Some are aliens and it is accepted this is part of their genetic nature. Years before an Nth colony reach a planet, a probe is released which contains Nth whose sole purpose is to mentally prepare the apex lifeforms to accept the possibility and even create a culture that embraces supers. In reality, all powers follow concrete laws, but many are beyond the understanding of humans as a whole. Some supers understand a few of these laws, but usually on a subconscious, anecdotal-experience level.

"Many concepts are introduced which help open the door of possibility that something could exist. Zombies, for example. You could recognize and had some basic idea of what a zombie is and how it acts. You accept that they like brains, because that's just what zombies do in the movies. Kernels of truth like this are seeded through a planet's culture, usually through its entertainment. You have no context to understand what a Dark Nth is, so other origins of how zombies come to be are imagined. This information has to be delivered very carefully, as Nth are not supposed to direct societal development. That is why these concepts are often introduced in entertainment modalities."

"So how long have Nth been on Earth? Did you wait to activate powers until you had prepared our culture to understand and accept them?" Gus twirled the spear in front of him as he ran, trying to get used to the weight as Nick continued.

"An advanced wave of Nth arrives years before the main body to start the process, stimulating the creativity and imagination of receptive individuals. They transmit this to the world in various fictions that become commonplace. This information is intended to allow the first generation supers to hit the ground running, and start using their powers productively, instead of selfishly. What these Nth do not do is explain the science behind the powers, so this is often poorly described by those who are inspired and create art, music and entertainment surrounding the super culture. It is generally accepted by most species, and falls under a willing suspension of disbelief due to the ideas being perceived as entertainment."

Gus became silent, pursing his lips as he thought about the implications. He reached the end of the path and took the spear he had left there. He immediately felt better as he left the jungle and climbed the small incline to the manor. His mind wouldn't let him rest too much, however. *If zombies are real, what else is real?* Gus stopped walking, recalling something.

"You didn't really answer how powers work," Gus realized, wondering if Nick was sidestepping the question.

"I was getting to that. Take flying for instance, have you wondered how a super propels themselves through the air? There are no emissions coming from the supers' feet. They do not alter gravity with subatomic particles—your past employer being an exception. So how do they move? All the powers function on science, but many concepts are millennia away from being understood and manipulated by humans unassisted by Nth."

"I hadn't really thought about it, I guess," Gus admitted, beginning to walk again.

"One fundamental property that most powers of different classes use involves dimensional manipulation. The effects that many powers exhibit, especially those with a strength, agility, or constitution basis, are facilitated with matter that regs do not even know exists, for the most part."

Gus squinted his eyes, listening intently despite Nick speaking only in his mind. He felt he was about to hear a long-kept secret.

"This may be hard to grasp, but imagine that any volume of space is filled with hanging sheets of fine nets within. The nets are made of a different type of matter than the human mind can perceive. Just as the human eye only sees a small slice of the electromagnetic spectrum, matter also varies in different funda-mental ways along a spectrum. This is why you have not discov-ered a unified theory to explain everything—you try to explain the entirety of reality using only what you can measure. Most theories fall apart when dealing with very small or very large objects, where the limits of perception are reached.

"These nets comprise the entire universe, and fill its volume like fluid fills a container. In the case of a flyer, they have devel-oped the ability to secure themselves to this matter, which we call ether, and propel themselves through it, as a swimmer moves through water. The ability is largely controlled by the subconscious and mastered by trial and error. They often use a focus, like pointing their arms forward as they swim through the air."

"That is making my brain hurt," Gus said while squinting, struggling to understand. "Give me some time to process this and we'll talk about it more." Gus had that feeling like when he was trying to learn math; his brain just seized up and it was hard to force it to absorb anything more. *Maybe points in intelli-gence would help?*

"As you wish."

Gus continued to ponder what he had learned as he entered

the manor and walked in silence to his room. His mind wandered to his guitar. Through his life, Gus had been able to relieve his stress through music. Gus longed to have his guitar that was lost on board Graviton's station. It was nothing fancy, but it was something he doubted he could craft. He was about to ask about that, but Nick beat Gus to it.

"Sorry, there are no musical instruments in the manor."

Gus frowned, but realized it was probably for the best not to get distracted. He remembered the isolation of Graviton's station, which offered a different type of down time due to the radio silence. The crowded nature of henchmen accommodations had forced Gus to wear wireless headphones while playing guitar. He was pretty good, but not everyone was a music aficionado. If he ever made it back to civilization, he'd get a really nice one. He'd probably be able to play much better now that he had Nth assistance. He smiled as he imagined his fingers flitting across the fretboard with huge agility stats.

"Gus, I have an alert of which you should be aware..." Nick reported urgently.

"What's up?"

"A number of changes have occurred in the power grid that supplies the manor after you took possession. The manor followed some automated protocols and reallocated available energy stores to make the control center functional. This diverted perimeter defenses all around the island, and other barriers that appear to have maintained the magma in stasis, keeping the volcano dormant. The considerable energy required to maintain the bio-stasis field is interfering with energy distribution. Without these barriers, the magma is now expanding unchecked, and an eruption event is expected if this is not managed. Schematics dictate that this flow was to be diverted to various geothermal energy collectors that would power the manor, and convert enough thermal energy to cool the magma, preventing it from flowing up and out the volcano. The location of the obstruction lies in the same direction as the estimated point of origin of the zombies, so one may assume there is a correlation."

"Are you flipping kidding me?"

"Of course not."

Gus rolled his eyes, sighing. He closed his eyes and tried to take a calming breath. He wasn't strong enough to manage a frontal attack on a bunch of zombies, so what now?

"For hell's sake, can I get a break once in a while?" Gus spat, exasperated.

"Do the controls allow us to do anything here?" Gus finally asked when he regained his composure.

"Magma flows may be directed as they approach the underground structures designed to handle the flow, but it must first arrive into this network. The blockage is happening before the magma can enter the channels under control by the manor."

"I'll have to deal with these Dark Nth eventually. I was hoping I could level up a bit before having to hit them head on, or kiting them so I can deal with them in smaller numbers. Not going to have that luxury now." Gus tried to come up with how many levels would allow him to hold his own without being totally out of his league. After screwing up his face in thought, he realized it was all a guessing game. Maybe he could manage a work-around.

"Would turning off the bio-stasis field help?" Gus asked hopefully.

"It would have before this reaction has cascaded, and will be necessary to prevent a recurrence. Without turning it off, available energy in the manor will be capped at a fraction of total potential."

"Can you throw me a bone here?" Gus yelled to no one in particular, looking pleadingly above. He reached up and rubbed the back of his neck. Even more to do, just when he thought he was already at the brink of being overwhelmed.

"So defeat the zombies, so I can stop the magma and turn off the shield... does that about cover it? Anything else I need to do, like find a cure for cancer, perfect cold fusion, or come up with the grand unification theory?"

"It's not that bad," Nick said sheepishly.

Gus just shook his head and threw up his hands.

"Ok, let's do this. Is there any way to place sensors farther down the path to monitor zombie advances?"

"There is, but it will require, once again, that the Foundry be unlocked. After it is enabled, the sub-facility Defensive Measures will need to be unlocked as well, to make turrets, traps, and sensors available for manufacture. Sensors have independent energy collection from solar chargers, and will tap into a data field that encompasses the island automatically when deployed, allowing it to sync with main control and provide telemetry."

"How many facility points are needed to unlock those two functions?"

"Four thousand total, twenty-five-hundred for the Foundry and fifteen-hundred for the subspecialty."

Gus hadn't thought that traps or turrets would be available as a defensive measure, but some automated guns that detected motion could be just what he needed. Since he had trained this morning, the arena wouldn't be available for more training until tomorrow. Gus figured he would have to start developing a plan to eradicate the Dark Nth from the island.

Finally reaching the jungle's edge, he made his way back to the manor to start work on his next plans. "Nick, let me see what blueprints we have so I can get a better idea of what's available."

CHAPTER TWENTY-ONE

Try This

DAY 5 10:20 PM

9:14:16 remaining

Things were becoming so much clearer now. As if he had been deep underwater and swimming upward toward a flickering light that pulsed in time with the shifting waters. He couldn't see very far through the murk that surrounded him, and all his senses were muted.

As he got nearer to the surface, more and more of his world began to resolve. The others called him The One, but it had not always been that way. He strained to see the memories that danced at the fringes of his mental darkness, but they darted in and out like colorful fish, refusing to get too close. Stretching upward toward the light, he sought to escape from this mental prison he had entered to keep himself alive and sane until the time was right.

At long last, he broke through to the surface. Understanding and faculties snapped back to him that had been dormant from his long hibernation. He shook his head from the disorientation of trying to process too much at once. The darkness welled up again, trying to push him under and he was only able to retain control with a determined effort. Wave after wave of the dark influence battered at him, trying to submerge him back to his feral state, but he remained centered. At long last, the pressure eased, and he opened his eyes.

————

Gus awoke early, feeling wide awake, which was uncommon for him. Usually he liked to lie in bed and slowly fight the battle of mind against mattress. The display in front of him was even more ominous than before. He was sure of it, the font size for the countdown was increasing. Obnoxiously.

Gus quickly ate an energy bar and filled his thermos with some of the cold water from the dispenser in his suite. He needed to evaluate the blueprints and make plans about which facilities he would unlock, and in what order. Not being a morning person, he decided it would probably be good to get some training in to shake the fog of sleep from his head so he could focus better.

He headed down to the arena, and Chop Chop, as Gus liked calling him, was in the center waiting for him. Arms folded, he stood in a blue column of light the holographic projector emanated, evaluating Gus as he approached.

He stood on the platform, and the system scanned him. On a nearby screen he saw a message:

Nanobot-sync loading... and a blue bar slowly filled up. Gus wondered how much more efficient training would be for an army that could customize each training regimen for that soldier. He felt like he had improved much more quickly than he would have without the feedback the Nth gave him in positioning his body and how quickly things became fluid and comfortable. With the scan complete a message flashed on his display:

Quest Granted: Fight for your Right
Quest Conditions:
1) Review battle history
2) Train and obtain the skills **Parry** *and* **Counter-attack**
3) Level **Counter-attack** *to level 2*
4) Defeat 3 virtual opponents (Mantids)
Quest Rewards: *1000 XP, 500 Facility Points, unlocked skills*
Time Requirements: *Must complete conditions in less than 3 hours after beginning training or forfeit all rewards, including unlocked skills. Initiate training at console.*
Do you want to accept this quest? (Y/N)

Gus asked to review the previous battle and have it analyzed before he undertook the timed quest. Unlike the day before, the view that materialized was not a complete representation. Gus guessed that the previous battle took place away from available sensors and satellite. This replay was different, with a much less photorealistic projection of the fight. He could discern a humanoid constellation of tiny dots that Gus associated with himself because of the spear stance. The Nth scattered through his system must be reporting their position in three-dimensional space, rendering his movements. An orange figure clearly represented the Mantids. It made him wonder how Nth from two different people interacted. His mind considered how telepaths must have some Nth scanning ability that could pick up on the signals of other—

"Hai!" Chop Chop shouted, brows furrowed and his lip even more pugged out than usual. Gus focused on the display again.

Gus watched a playback of the entire battle, then the scene reversed back to the beginning. Chop Chop would play the video and Gus could see on the display where he had overextended during the fight, and other times where his stance was too narrow. The playback slowed in areas where he had scored a hit, so he could see what was working in his battle style. Each hit displayed a red numerical value on how much damage had accrued per attack during the battle. He remembered that they had been there when fighting, but he could only focus on so much.

Gus leaned forward, studying what attacks were more effective. When the Mantid with **Wreck-luse** made its entry, the red numbers flashed in time as the toxin worked, -8 HP, -8 HP, -7 HP, -8 HP, and so on. Gus reviewed the areas where he needed improvement in his previous battle, rewinding to review critical hits and other times when he made an especially effective attack. After twenty minutes, he reached the end and Gus saw the prompt: *'End Evaluation? (Y/N)'* Gus clicked yes and turned to face Chop Chop.

Another message was displayed:

Are you ready to begin the timed quest **Fight for your Right**? *(Y/N)*

Gus accepted and a timer appeared in the upper left of his display. Simultaneously, a hologram of a Mantid appeared, and Chop Chop demonstrated a technique to block an attack from the talons on the metal band that spanned the center of the shaft between where Gus usually gripped the spear.

Gus would have to search among the racks in the middle tier to find this upgraded type of spear, as he had only used spears that lacked this upgrade. The weapons were organized by type, but he saw no organization indicating which weapons dealt the most damage or which were superior. He mentally kicked himself for picking something so basic. Truth be told, he wasn't trained to use it, so it may have not made any difference. Still, he needed every edge he could get.

Chop Chop used a variety of movements to place the metal band in just the right place to block various types of attacks. Gus winced at how close the claws came to Chop Chop's hands when he did the blocks. Not a lot of room for error. After the tutorial, Chop Chop retreated to the side of the arena and froze in place.

Gus took that as a signal to find his weapons. He jogged up

to the level where spears were. He searched until he found a spear with superior damage stats that also had the metal band in the middle. Grabbing three just like last time, he headed down to the arena.

Once again the virtual display showed Gus' form in a stance in blue. He oriented himself, then practiced following the prescribed moves as the program directed his movements. Since it was a more complicated move, the program began moving in slow motion, allowing him to get the feel of the block. After about ten minutes, he felt like he had gotten the gist of the action.

One of the things that had helped the most when he was learning guitar was practicing at a slow speed until it was perfect, then slowly adding speed until the song was at normal tempo. Using that method, he avoided learning the song incorrectly, getting sloppy and repeating the same errors. It worked just as well with his spear training. Performing the motion like he was doing tai chi, he flowed through the pattern. A little tone sounded when he had executed correctly. After he got three tones in a row, Gus sped up a tiny bit. After fifteen more minutes of focused movement, a chime sounded.

You have learned the skill, **Parry**. *You are now able to block certain attacks if attacked while equipped with a spear. This skill is upgradeable to* **Counter-attack***!*
100 XP awarded
200 FP awarded

"That's new, Nick. Are all skills upgradeable?"

"Many are, but most are found by trial and error. Your Nth will try to increase and upgrade your skills as soon as you are ready, so you really are only limited by your diligence."

Gus grinned. He was good at grinding in video games, and he could do it in real life if the rewards were there. He shook his head and focused his attention again on the display, not wanting his tendency to get distracted to slow his progression.

The display then changed to show Gus' blue form, and an orange Mantid shape approaching and attacking. The Gus figure parried, deflecting the Mantid to the side, the representation then shifted, flowing into an attack on the follow through that hit the virtual Mantid in the back. The tutorial ended, and Gus again began practice in earnest.

The arena provided a virtual Mantid to practice against, and Gus found he could slow down the speed of his attacker to use his method to practice this technique. It was difficult to know if the timing was right without any feedback. Gus had to rely on the tingle feedback he had experienced yesterday to evaluate if he was executing the attack correctly, as he could not look up at the virtual display and keep his eyes on the Mantid attacking him. The extra concentration this required was harder to coordinate and start hearing success tones.

Gus had to take a break to let his stamina bar refill and get a drink. Wiping the sweat off his brow, he began again and had to get back into the groove. The short break had thrown off his form, and it took a couple minutes to reestablish muscle memory.

In his life before the island, Gus was never what you would call a coordinated guy. He had taken a date to a dance instruction class and found out to his embarrassment that he had trouble combining the steps at the right time, in the right order. Now though, he executed the correct movements of the training tutorial much more easily. He could sense more intuitively than ever before what he should be doing. Muscle memory seemed to be established with only a handful of successful run-throughs. The thought made him long to increase agility even more. He hated being a klutz. He felt a twinge of angst at his need for improvement in so many areas. Only the thought of how far he had come in such a short time quenched his frustration. His self-evaluation had always been very unforgiving at the slightest failings.

It's all a part of the process. Shake it off and focus. He exhaled deeply, letting go of the emotions, and got back to work.

Increasing his speed, he got to the point where he almost looked forward to testing the technique against another Mantid. A familiar chime let him know he had reached sufficient skill to unlock the ability.

*Through consistent, successful completion of the skill **Parry**, it will be upgraded to the skill **Counter-attack**! You are now able to activate this skill after a successful parry attempt. Use this skill to level it!*
Counter-attack (Level 1): *After completion of a successful parry of an enemy attack, 5% chance of following through with an attack that deals double the damage! Success rates increase with higher levels.*
100 XP awarded
200 FP awarded

Gus now saw the panel slide back, and a pillowbot appeared, sheathed in the orange Mantid holographic skin. A red bar appeared with 135/135 above the Mantid. Chop Chop shouted from the sidelines, "Defend!"

The Mantid attacked, leaving Gus no time to prepare. He reflexively parried but missed the counter-attack due to his poor footing. The jolt from the parry caused him to stumble back-ward. *Those suckers don't pull any punches!*

Shaking his head and getting centered, Gus turned and faced off against the pillow-Mantid. It feinted, and Gus flinched in response, but quickly reset for another attack. When the Mantid tried again, Gus swept the Mantid to the side and skewered it as it passed. He was rewarded by a '-40 HP' appearing above the Mantid as his attack connected.

The Mantid spun and relentlessly attacked again. Gus managed the parry but did not complete the counter. The intensity and pressure of attack added a new layer of difficulty and challenged his ability to focus. On the next pass, Gus was able to activate **Sweep the Leg,** downing the creature. The stunned state of the Mantid allowed him to score four more hits that dispatched the virtual zombie while it lay there incapacitated. The orange skin evaporated, revealing the pillowbot form underneath, lying prone.

"Good jorb!" Gus complimented himself in his best Coach Z voice.

After a reset period, the pillowbot stood again and was re-skinned with the Mantid form. Gus noticed that even though he had pierced it with the spear, the material he had thought was some sort of cloth was entirely intact. Before he could ruminate further, the panel slid open, and another pillow-Mantid joined the fray.

"Dang it, Chop Chop, you're a jerk!" Gus yelled as he saw the corners of Chop Chop's pug-lip smirk slightly.

Gus had to monitor his surroundings carefully because the Mantids began to circle. One tried to sneak behind Gus, and he had to spin and then get back into a stance where he could parry. One jumped, and Gus was able to execute his **Counter-attack** ability. He sprang away, and the other Mantid just missed attacking while he was out of Gus' sight with the twist that **Counter-attack** applied. He jabbed quickly and scored a hit. A chime sounded.

You have unlocked a bonus skill: **Chained Attack (Level 1)**. *Hit a second target when a successful* **Counter-attack** *triggers without receiving any damage by either attacker. 50% chance of activating a chained attack with direct attack if no damage is taken.*
100 XP awarded
200 FP awarded
500 XP awarded for discovering a skill without the aid of an instructor or utilizing a skill crystal.

"Bazinga! Thought you had me, ugly?" Gus taunted, his voice quivery with adrenaline. The Mantids reverted to their circling pattern, and Gus was ready for the opportunistic attack from the support Mantid. He was able to score a critical hit in the head, and that Mantid was out of the fight. Fighting a single enemy was simple in comparison, and he dispatched the second

Mantid after a couple attacks and **Counter-attack** cycles. A ding and chime simultaneously sounded.

Quest Complete: 1000 XP
You have leveled up the skill: **Counter-attack** *to* **Level 2!**
+500 Facility Points awarded.
+500 XP bonus for unlocking hidden skill during combat
+300 FP bonus for unlocking hidden skill during combat

1275 XP to level 7

Gus still had about an hour before the deadline for the quest, but the dimming lights of the arena gave him the tacit notification that he had completed as much training as he could for the day. Gus wasn't sure if it was an effect of the Nth or just excitement over leveling up his skills, but he always felt amped after finishing a quest. Maybe it was related to the level up euphoria, just with adrenaline or something. He was more than ready to make some manor upgrades, and was excited to see what would be available.

CHAPTER TWENTY-TWO

Back in Time

DAY 6 9:15 AM

9:03:11 remaining

Methiochos, yes that was it, so long ago. With the name came back some of the context of his situation. He opened his eyes to find himself in a dark cave. Shadows danced on the ridged basalt columns that lined the walls of the chamber. Stale acrid air, mixed with an unpleasant sulfurous undertone, assaulted his awakening senses. Turning, he noticed the changes his body had undergone since the transformation.

While his torso remained the same, his lower extremities were now a writhing mass of legs, tentacles and pseudopods. An odd assortment of tools, as each iteration had a specialized use besides mere propulsion and movement. He had, at one time, been revolted at how the changes had altered his appearance, but had long ago turned it to his advantage.

He was also much more aware of his surroundings from the information they transmitted to him, subconsciously allowing him to sense vibrations in the ground, and detect various changes in the environment. His arms were similar but could be coalesced into the resemblance of normal arms, albeit thick and muscular. This time he stretched, allowing the tendrils of his arms to unfurl and expand, reaching farther, thinning as they were pushed to their limits. It felt good to expand in this manner after being in a compressed, dormant state for so long.

Seeing that the light came from a golden orange flow of magma that was contained on the far side of the cavern. Methiochos extended two of his specialized tentacles toward the super-heated rock. Dipping them in, the Dark Nth there began extracting the kinetic and heat energy from the magma and transformed it into something Methiochos could use.

There was a sharp sensation of discomfort that resolved into a relaxing and soporific sensation of comfort. With the energy flowing in, he became more… his true self, somehow.

Methiochos closed his eyes and exhaled deeply. As he relaxed, the dream-like state returned, and he felt like he was underwater once more. In his mind's eye, he imagined he could see the fish again, darting around the fringes of his imagination. Connected with the energy as he was, he noticed he was emitting an orange glow, that was becoming brighter and brighter.

One of the fish approached, coming close to his face, examining this new wonder. By instinct, he reached forth his hand, which had long thin ribbons trailing from his fingertips, like a psychedelic afterimage. The fish stayed there, trusting his intent instead of dashing away. Turning his palm upward, the ribbons rose and fluttered in the water like a small forest of seaweed. The fish swam to the ribbons and as it nestled into one of the streaming extensions, it disappeared in an orange poof.

———

45 years ago…

The plan would work. Methiochos was a great general and he had almost all the players in place. While the Archon was in charge of things now, Methiochos hoped that he could bring some new ideas and leadership that were sorely needed in the world. Supers could not continue as they had always been. There had to be structures in place, to direct and guide those powers. And he aimed to be that guide.

First, manage some of the wild ones so they would not destroy the planet or each other. Second, police and punish those who did not obey the agreed upon laws. Third, form some kind of government that was not based on the 'might makes right' mentality, but that could utilize the best of the best that was in humankind, regs or supers.

Archon believed that people should be honorable, and honor guided many of his leadership decisions. Methiochos felt that mindset protected weaknesses and that weakness could be exploited. It was very passive and Methiochos believed that there were many times when you had to take action as soon as possible. To whit, the preparation for the new base.

Manticorps existed as both a business and as a collection of supers. The organization had funneled immense amounts of money into the making of a base that would have functionality for all its many supers, allowing them to grow and progress even after hitting high levels. To minimize attacks against their new headquarters, very few people were privy to the island's exact location. Methiochos would use this to his advantage. They would be able to rival any Faction with just a decade of the manor's advantages.

The island was secluded enough that only a few people knew about it, and large portions of the manor were being built by androids, and even terraformed by specialized robots to minimize revealing the location and having to 'deal' with the witnesses. The robots would then be able to modify their function to become service and maintenance droids. It was the perfect transition, reduced costs, and avoided messy executions.

Methiochos was the project lead and had found the perfect

location. He scouted it himself, finding it to be large enough to house thousands of people, but remote enough that invaders would be easy to detect. The security firm he was dealing with had a couple prototypes that he knew could be game changers, especially if Methiochos could convince them to come onboard and design for Manticorps exclusively. He had dealt directly with the project lead, Roger, who wanted to be a super very badly.

Methiochos used this to his advantage and confided in him how regs could become supers, in the cases where a super dies. The abilities could transfer to another human being if this transfer was done within a certain amount of time after the death of the donor; there was a good possibility that Roger could be at the front of the line, if he were a part of the team.

Supers died all the time, but regs never knew how the supers got their powers or why powers manifested at different ages. It was a closely guarded secret. People were even showing up with isolated skills that resembled the powers a super had, but these skills were anomalies, which were not able to be upgraded, so they were just a hair above regs. No nanobots were involved with these mutants either. Definitely not in the class of supers.

Regs also knew nothing about the nature of how supers saw the world in an augmented way, or how they had skills they could upgrade and improve. Those who even hinted at revealing this to the world suddenly developed a 'vanishing' skill.

These odd prodigies did seem to take to the transformation much more predictably than a normal reg. In truth, Methiochos had little power to keep these promises, but he needed root access and administrative privileges on the island control center to make his plans work. Once Methiochos was out there and could set things up, it wouldn't matter what Archon wanted, or what Roger was expecting; both would be powerless to stop him.

From there, Methiochos could build up his power base. Form the type of government that the world needed for supers.

He knew three main Factions were coalescing and trying to assert their views, but they all were diametrically opposed to each other, and there was little hope that they would be able to work out some lasting form of cooperation. There would be only competition and constant power grabs. Especially with all the egos involved, and Methiochos had a limited amount of patience for fools.

He had big ideas and was frustrated at how he kept getting shut down. Archon wanted to wait and see how things evolved. Methiochos wanted to guide that evolution! You could design something much more powerful than waiting for things to fall into place. What if waiting didn't work? We would have wasted the time, seeing how fate would design the future. Forget that.

It was treason and betrayal, no doubt about that. But sacrifices had to be made. He just had to be smart about it, and cut his own ego off at the knees. Put on a smiling face when the future plans were discussed. He could see that reasoning with Archon was no use.

He was stubborn too, and the debates he had attempted to change his world view had only left them more distant and on edge. If Methiochos was to put his new plans into place, he needed to kowtow and walk the line. Be the good soldier he was meant to be in Archon's eyes. If all went to plan, there would be no time to stop Methiochos before the island was protected.

Methiochos had brought Dara, a truth-seeker, to Manti-corps. She was loyal to him and now they could vet anyone, find any spies, or those with subversive motives. Since she was of like mind with Methiochos, they could easily trick Archon into believing his total loyalty.

Methiochos would orchestrate that those loyal to him would be the first crew to make it to the island. The complement would include security, scientists, and support staff, so they could hit the ground running once arriving at the manor. Thus he would only allow them to select from the best of the best for this first crew. Once he activated the bio-stasis field, not only would they be protected from anyone trying to land on the island, they would be effectively cloaked as well.

The final part of the plan was scrubbing information from the few areas that had the exact location of the island. Only Archon and the other eight generals had access, and most of them were on assignment. Having seniority, he had no doubt he could obtain their copies under some pretense of updating the information or some other nonsense. They were loyal to a fault, and if they thought it was the Archon's will, they complied without question.

The time to enact his plan would soon be here, and everything had been prepared. Anticipation and confidence that big changes were coming helped him maintain his mask of loyalty, allowing him to tolerate the sycophants all around him, enamored of Archon's every thought. Only three days to launch, then it would all change.

———

Methiochos withdrew the two tentacles out of the magma and the memory winked out. He was reaching a saturation level of both absorbed energy and recalled memories. He would process this, grow stronger, continue to remember all that he had forgotten, and make his future plans. No one could stop him now. Unlike Archon, he didn't let things like honor and loyalty keep him from his goals.

CHAPTER TWENTY-THREE

Jump

DAY 6 10:14 AM

9:02:22 remaining

Before cleaning up, Gus ran outside and grabbed an armful of fruit to take up to the suite. Gus shuddered a tiny bit at the thought of choking down another protein bar.

He took a quick shower and dressed. His closets were now full of the same jumpsuits he had found in the armory, with accompanying boots underneath. At least he didn't need to worry about what he'd have to wear! Gus took a long look at himself in the mirror. He needed to shave; his patchy mess of facial hair would never be a respectable fully-fledged beard. It was in the itchy phase and it kind of made him look more haggard.

He took time to appreciate the effects the Nth had had on his physique though. He was never chubby, but he was definitely in the 'soft' category before the island. Now he looked great! He wasn't exploding with muscles, but he had abs, and his lats became visible, forming a nice V to his torso. He hadn't really felt like a super, deep down, but here he was, the change staring him in the face. He loved the thrill of leveling, but wished he would have time to pursue it at his leisure, and not have the threat of everything forcing him to survive. Still, he couldn't complain about the results. Maybe it was the kick in the pants he needed.

After ogling himself, he set to shaving, until he looked much more like himself. Next job, unlock some facilities.

He was hoping that, by activating the Foundry, he could have access to additional armor crafting abilities. He especially wanted something to protect his arms. If the Mantid had been just a little off to one side, he could have been severely gouged and game over. Looking at his interface, he currently had 3300 FP. More than enough for unlocking both the Foundry and the extras he would need. He felt he should head there right away, but it was hard to focus. He needed to burn off some energy, and the thought of sitting in the control room looking at menus drove him to distraction.

"Nick, I feel weird. Like I have ADD or something, or like I've had five energy drinks. It's making me feel squirrely; I don't feel like myself."

"You are still becoming accustomed to the effects of the Nth on your system. You will most likely experience multiple episodes of too much energy, as well as malaise and fatigue, as your body is stimulated to grow."

In addition to feeling hyperactive, a familiar restlessness began to build up again. The deadline to hit level ten was getting closer and he was making decent progress. He also knew it was harder to level the higher you progressed in games, and assumed the same was true about his own leveling. He would prefer a cushion rather than leaving it to the last minute. Plus then he could worry about other pressing things. He wondered what level he would be at if worrying were a skill. His mind had an annoying habit of snowballing to the worst possible conclusions if he didn't rein it in.

Turning back to what options the Foundry would provide, he evaluated his needs. He wanted to fight some zombies with his new skills but also felt like he needed to expand and gain other abilities as well, especially something that allowed him to attack at range and stay safe. If the Foundry could make him some armor to help with the close combat situations, hopefully they'd be easier to down if ranged attacks softened them up.

"Nick, are there any non-combat skills to develop? Like mental skills?"

"There are many skills, but often they have to be found by trial and error. Until we determine the nature of how your powers manifest, it is more difficult to predict what affinities you have."

"Well, I know I have used that speedster skill a little, what about that?" Gus asked.

"Yes. That is a good starting point, but you do not want to limit yourself. Those powers are all in the translocation family, which includes speedster, flying, and teleportation."

"Teleportation! Yes! That would save me so much time from jogging down the trail and back to the manor. Plus I've had some close scrapes, and I don't really have a good way to retreat if I get in over my head."

"Don't get ahead of yourself. Teleportation is a very advanced skill, so don't set your expectations too high. Most supers need years to obtain the necessary stats and combination of skills. You have to learn dashing, flying, and dimensional folding, to name a few things."

"Buzzkill," Gus muttered.

"Do you have any experience with meditation?"

"Um, no."

"What about with your music, are you familiar with a 'flow' experience?"

"It sounds familiar, what exactly do you mean?"

"It is commonly experienced when you become so engrossed with an activity, that your perception of time is skewed. You may be doing something for hours but it feels like no time has really passed, unlike how one feels throughout a typical day."

"Oh yeah, tons of times."

"*That* is what we are attempting to train. Your mind needs to enter a pliable state where you shift more into a right-brain type of control. The types of controls implemented by the left brain are too rigid. You need intuition to guide you, as the process is subtle and must be adapted at a speed faster than conscious thought."

"So what drills should I start doing?"

"You jump."

"Ok… explain."

"I want you to find one of the long hallways in the manor, the ones that are tall and open in the center of the complex by the atrium. That will give you five stories of height to practice. You can eventually do this outside, but for now I want the floor to be as regular and smooth as possible. You'll want a carpeted surface with low risk of slipping. I want you to walk and, at measured intervals, jump. At the apex of your jump, imagine pulling yourself a little higher and a little forward. Trying to get more hang time, and more distance from the jump. Try to make the effort expended per jump the same. This isn't an Olympic long jump. You need to get the feel of how to anchor yourself in the ether. Depending on your affinities, you may do well or you may just get a good leg workout. There are mental drills we can do later, but start with this; it will help you burn off some tension."

Nick hadn't led him wrong in the past, so Gus began to jump. He felt a little ridiculous, but kept at it. After a while he had to take a quick break for stamina to refill.

I probably look like an idiot, but that's never stopped me before!

He recalled some of the bone-headed things he had done in his life. Some were dares from his friends, others were trying to impress others, especially his father. Heading to the initial entry hall, Gus lined himself up and began jumping with his eyes closed trying to visualize the 'pulling' that Nick had suggested. After crashing into a decorative planter in the big atrium and a fumble to keep it from falling off of its plinth, he decided he had better keep his eyes open. Eventually, he'd have to keep his eyes open if he wanted to fly or move like a speedster. It was hard to know what he was looking for, so he tried different things.

He imagined energy coming from his core like he had used when fighting the Mantid and used ***Indi-Wreckt***, but that didn't seem to do anything. He decided to limit his focus on just making his jumps higher. Since he was unable to see himself, he could not get any feedback if he was doing it correctly or not. After a half an hour of different mental focuses and traversing the atrium five times, Gus took a break. "How long am I just going to jump around—" Gus started, then he mentally facepalmed for not thinking of it sooner. At first, he was hesitant to waste his precious songs, but a quick look at the timer erased his uncertainty. He created a quick playlist for Nick to play and began again in earnest. A chime sounded as the first song began to play.

You have created a song chain! Success with activities related to musical themes increased by factorial multiplier based on quantity of songs in series. Song chains have a cooldown of 6 hours through host levels 1-10.

The synthesizer tones of the intro to Jump by Van Halen started. It was easier to jump to the beat of the song. Life seemed to shift into montage-mode as Gus focused on jumping and lifting himself just an inch higher than his typical jump. Before he got to the guitar solo, he started to notice a hint of a longer hang time. The song ended and a message displayed along the bottom of his screen.

Jump Around by House of Pain. Success rates x 2.

The musical fanfare at the beginning of the song reminded Gus of leveling up. He started to get into the groove of jumping at a faster tempo with the song. The drill was becoming more fun, similar to dancing. Gus imagined he was stretching upward with the repetitive whistle in the song. The hang-time was definitely increasing and he was leaping at every other beat because he was mid-air when he would usually jump again. His stamina bar also started to drain at a slower rate, since he was using less physical exertion, but Gus noticed his MP bar start to trickle down a little. The floating must be utilizing some of his MP to maintain the effect. Excellent! It was working.

Jump by Florida (featuring Nelly Furtado). Success rates x 6.

Gus wasn't familiar with how factorials worked, but those success rates were increasing like nuts. He was getting so much hang time now that he had a brief moment to spare while in the air. He started practicing a spear parry move while in the air albeit without a weapon. He didn't have time to enact a full *Counter-attack* move, and it was difficult to coordinate both the actions simultaneously. He noticed his hang time dropped at first, but he was able to increase it little by little to the same amount by the time the song ended.

Apache (Jump on It) by Sugarhill Gang. Success rates x 24.

Gus felt like he had been double-bounced on a trampoline with the boost in height he obtained when the next song started. The slower tempo of the song fit perfectly with the long time he had in the air. He was able to execute a full parry and counter-attack now, and alternated which side he threw his imaginary attacker to with each leap. The song made Gus want to watch Dodgeball again, remembering hearing the song for the first time in the movie. After getting comfortable with his parry-counter combo, the song shifted again.

Jump, Jive an' Wail by Brian Setzer Orchestra. Success rates x 120.

Gus shot up so much the increase in height scared him. Luckily, the skill slowed his descent so he didn't crash back down and break an ankle. The thought made him wonder what he would do if he was hurt badly. Better look into an infirmary in the manor and what it would take to activate it before he really needed it. However, the slowing effect as he approached the ground gave him confidence to try something new. Gus began to just have fun with the skill at this point and did forward flips, then backward flips. He noticed he was able to tug himself a little to one side or another if his jump brought him over one of the circular banks of couches that were in the center of the atrium.

One Jump Ahead by Brad Kane, Disney's Aladdin Soundtrack. Success rates x 720.

Gus felt a little cheesy about this selection, but he liked it anyways. And that multiplier! Going along with the song, Gus added a forward direction to his jump, and minimized the height. He felt like he was in one of those martial arts movies where the ninjas leapt from tree to tree, defying gravity with their crazy, wire-assisted jumps. But this was real! Gus leaped forward, did a small wall run and leapt to the opposite side of the hall. Gus tried a dash forward, and felt the world slip by, just like when he first used his zoom-vision. It was disorienting at first, but after a couple attempts, he was dashing forward like a pro. A chime sounded.

Skill unlocked: **Dash (Level 1)**

Speed forward a distance of 100 feet or less. Distance increases with skill level (50ft +(n x 50ft)).
100 XP awarded
200 FP awarded

Awesome! This would help a lot in getting around, especially when it came to traveling in the forest. Reviewing the logs had taken some of the time of the song and it moved to the last song before he was finished reading.

Jump in the Line by Harry Belafonte. Success rates x 5,040.

Beetlejuice! If Gus wasn't such a cinephile, he probably wouldn't know so many jump songs. Gus jumped and just hovered. With the massive multiplier, Gus had broken some gravity barrier. A chime sounded.

Skill unlocked: Basic Flight (Level 1)
Flight speed: 10 mph
Max altitude: 5 feet
Flight speed increases: (10 mph x n)
Max altitude (5ft x n)
MP cost: (200 MP/sec -5n MP/sec)
MP cost: 195 MP/second
100 XP awarded
200 FP awarded

195 MP meant he could only fly for around 1.5 seconds! The multiplier must be diminishing the skill's MP cost or multiplying his MP pool to feed the skill. Without it, he would have to train a lot to be able to make flight a usable skill. Not wanting to get distracted again, he shifted from side to side with some strain. It was harder to maintain this than simply jumping. It felt like he was continuously pulling a very long tablecloth off one of those tables you saw in castles, that could seat fifty to seventy

people. Gus could pull in different directions and the sheet would slide by, pulling him in that direction by degrees depending on how hard he tugged. Gus was starting to get the hang of it when the song ended and the playlist was done. Gus sank to the ground like he was standing on a deflating balloon.

Gus almost began compiling a song-chain with the word fly, but then realized that he had a half-day cooldown before he could use it again. What other song chains could he make? Combat? Training? The thought gave him more hope that he could reach level ten before the deadline. A little over nine days, so that would give him twenty-seven, no, twenty-six more chances to level. The ability did say that the multiplier would change after level ten; hopefully he wouldn't lose too much of his power-leveling ability.

He attempted to float again, but without the boost of the multiplier, he only accomplished a jump similar to his second-song height levels. Gus tried to recreate the playlist again, but **Wreck-ord** only worked on original songs apparently, and the songs he had used were grayed out on his display. After it had been used, it wouldn't activate again. That was good to know. While it would be best to save that ability for when he was past the easier early levels, Gus feared he wouldn't have the luxury of waiting. He now had something to practice in his down time. He could only imagine how this would help him in his fighting ability as well.

Gus made his way to the control center to check out infirmary plans and costs. He could've asked Nick, but that felt lazy to him now, since he was already heading to the control center. Plus, he could check the logs and see if there was any more movement from the Dark Nth.

Entering the control room, Gus checked the facilities management interface. After selecting the Foundry and defensive specializations to unlock he saw the effect this would have on available energy. The yellow power bar shrunk by quite a bit.

Gus saw that available energy points for manor facilities were getting fairly low. He probably would only have enough to unlock the Foundry and maybe the Infirmary, then would need to increase power to unlock more of the facility. Since the facilities were already built, he only needed to power them. They must also have stores of materials to use, so he wouldn't have to manage that aspect of the facilities.

He focused on the Infirmary description. To his surprise, it was only 100 FP to activate. It comprised a smaller offshoot of a larger facility, Hospital. Gus was amazed the manor could support an entire hospital, but he had no idea how many individuals would be at the facility when it was fully operational. No doubt it would be substantial, if the size was any indicator.

Clicking on facility info, Gus saw from the description that the infirmary was similar to an ER, that it was mainly an automated triage station to stabilize people, but was limited in the scope of ailments it could manage. He spent the points and unlocked the infirmary. "Nick, is there a way to turn off the bio-stasis field and use the energy that sustains that for facility development?" Gus asked.

"There are some functions listed under Alpha Protocol that are DNA locked. Since I do not find any of the controls under the menus in facility management, it is presumed that managing the bio-stasis field falls under the aegis of Alpha Protocols. Regulation of protective barriers and magma shields also should be under this menu, as they are conspicuously absent from the main facility control options."

"DNA locked to whom? The original Methiochos?"

"That would be the most likely supposition."

"That doesn't make much sense to me, that the manor and facilities can be unlocked by anyone with first generation Nth, but that some control functions are locked to DNA control. Wouldn't it be better to make all access DNA controlled? That would prevent someone from stealing the location in a battle. Besides, if the manor has access to the quantum server, why doesn't it recognize that I'm not Methiochos?"

"The manor is not an Nth structure, and has only limited access to certain types of data. Just like the Dark Nth are limited in how they interact with the quantum server, the manor is limited in a similar manner. The bio-stasis field interrupts any communication with the outside world, so it is frozen and cannot perform any updates.

"The restriction is partially a lack of capacity of humanity's inferior technology interface, the other is enforced by the manor's security protocols. Thus, the manor cannot access anything that relates to supers or their files, or personal information for anyone not uploaded into the memory. You were probably accepted because first generation Nth was a qualifier that the system latched onto, and voila, you get control. In the manor's database, your current scan and information is linked under Methiochos' profile for basic commands as a default, but his original DNA print must have been programmed in as a safeguard before he came to the island for higher level controls. He was most likely a cautious and paranoid individual."

Gus shook his head and growled. "Nothing's ever easy. So if I get this right, I need a DNA sample from Methiochos if I want to unlock this Alpha Protocol and stop the volcano?"

"Unfortunately, yes. But if the bio-stasis field is still in place, his body is already on the island; we just need to find it and take a sample. As long as we have a sufficient sample, even if it is decomposed, we can scan it. Once that is done, we can change all administrative controls to you," Nick said.

Gus' mind flitted back to the way the Dark Nth decomposed so quickly. If he were dead, what would he do then? What if one of those creatures he had already killed was Methiochos, and he just didn't know? His stomach settled as he realized that he knew the levels of all those killed mobs. A high-level super would be more than tenth level, and all the mobs were lower than that.

"Any ideas on the best way to find him? Is there any way to scan for him?"

"Again, no. You will need to explore the island to find him. Methiochos' profile did not show that he had any flight powers, so he must have arrived on the island in some form of transportation, be it ship or flying transport. That means exploring the coastline and surveying any areas where there is a suitable clearing that something at least the size of a large transport could land will be a priority."

Gus felt discouraged with another obstacle in his path, but having at least a starting point softened the edges a bit. He was able to use a distance function of the island scanner and was discouraged to find that the island was larger than he expected. The coastline was two-hundred-twenty-seven miles! He would have to level up his **Dash** and *Flying* skills, and sacrifice some training time.

"That would be recommended, as you only have two days to reach level ten, so maximizing activities to level is paramount—"

"No-no-no, Nick," Gus stammered, "that timer clearly says I have eight days and twenty-two hours' time to level my Nth!"

"Two weeks is the absolute end date, but by that time you will be prone and unable to move. You, in actuality, need to plan on finishing closer to one week after you arrived at the island to retain all your faculties," Nick said.

"Wait, what?! That would've been nice to know, NICK!" Gus groused, upset that he had only two days left until his Nth started shutting down. Then he wondered how much time he had to deal with the volcano. Gus felt the stress tighten his throat. There were so many things he had to juggle.

"I apologize, but you were not in the healthiest of mental states at the time, if you recall. It was a high-stress situation, and you have not had to push yourself like that before. I told you what you needed to hear and nothing more. You have made remarkable progress though, and I have every confidence that you will reach level ten before you notice any untoward effects."

He almost wished he was back in his old life, without all the things that were stressing him out constantly. Well, that wasn't true. He wouldn't go back to being good old henchman Gus, even if he had a chance to do it. Taking a deep breath, he reminded himself of the exhilaration of flying, the power he felt fighting and winning against those Mantids, and the rush of experimenting with new skills almost every day. Nick was right, too. Gus knew he had a bad tendency of shutting down and tuning out when things got too overwhelming. Nick had known him better than he knew himself, at least in that instance.

Gus checked the time; it was early afternoon. Gus didn't want a repeat of that hot mess when he had fought the Mantids near dusk. The darkness obviously didn't hinder them in the slightest. If time weren't a factor, he would have decided to start out on his expedition tomorrow. Checking his abilities, the cooldown on **Wreck-ord** showed he could set out on his coast-line trip around 7 PM. He was going to have to do this tonight, and rely on his visual filters when things got dark. Hopefully he could make some decent distance before he had to call it a night.

He checked the monitors for any activity and saw no changes. What would he do if the zombies came when he was exploring the coastline? He determined he would leave some more weapons outside in different areas he could access if needed. The plan would be to make it around the island in a day, assisted with **Dash**. Hopefully he could level to seven, maybe eight, from estimated XP gained from raising skills. After that, he would have to engage as many Dark Nth as possible to hit level ten. It would be close, but Gus saw no other real choice. Maybe he would get lucky and find Methiochos' crash site soon and fight mobs at that location. He wouldn't know until he tried.

Heading to the dispensary, Gus found a suitable utility back-pack. It had tons of pouches and zippers, which he loved. He perused the accessories, recalling the things he surmised he would probably need from his time in Scouts. He found some rope, a couple waterproof tarps, a space blanket, some flash-lights, and some other small supplies he thought might come in useful. He took it all to his suite and began to pack. In went his trusty foam putty mattress roll, the rope and other items in the little pouches. Gus felt like a superhero with a utility backpack instead of a utility belt. Inside one of the pouches went as many energy bars as he could cram inside. Getting two vacuum-walled thermoses, he put them in the pouches on the sides, and pulled the drawstring tight, securing them.

After arranging his playlist, Gus was ready to set out. Advising Nick to wake him fifteen minutes before his **Wreck-ord** timer recharged, he decided to try to get a little power-nap in before his dashing all-nighter. He went to bed and managed to fall asleep in no time.

CHAPTER TWENTY-FOUR

Runaround

DAY 6 7:12 PM

8:17:24 remaining

Methiochos evaluated himself. He had grown to almost twice his previous size since metabolizing the energy from the magma pool. How long had he been hibernating? Estimating his current size, he was now only four to five feet tall. The condensing effect and essentially feeding off himself for decades of stasis could have totally destroyed him.

Were it not for the sharp severing of one of his remote tendrils, he might never have stirred. There were some that had been wandering outside the barriers before they were sealed inside. Occasionally, one would meet an untimely demise, falling off a cliff or some other mishap. Unfortunately, he could not turn any of the other living creatures on the island. They had to be sufficiently intelligent or the Dark Nth could not bond.

What set this death apart was that there hadn't been any

severed tendrils for many years now. With the other attacks that had happened, Methiochos had to protect his brood. His enemies had most likely found him and would try to take everything.

Methiochos felt the darkness within him. It trembled and raged as his emotions swelled, and he had to relax to avoid being overcome. He was tired of the constant effort to push back the Dark, but what was the alternative? He knew of its insidious designs and had basically sacrificed himself to trap it here with him. There would be nothing left to rule if the Dark Nth destroyed everything. It had shown him its true desire. If it got loose, not only humankind would lose, but the cycle could be broken forever.

———

Gus showered and changed outfits, dumping the old one down the laundry chute. He wondered where they went, but guessed it really didn't matter since he could wear a new suit daily for about a year and still have something to wear.

After initially putting his suit on, he noticed that it was tight in the legs, then the material stretched and resumed a comfortable feel. It probably was due to his level up yesterday and his constitution increase. It now made sense why supers wore so much spandex. When you leveled up and your muscles grew, who wanted to split their pants?

He had even heard that some of the advanced super suits the really high-level supers wore were made of Kroutonium, which would actually level along with the owner. They often had multiple forms and could evolve in their own right. He left the manor and headed down to Atlantis Beach, gauging how much sunlight was left in the day. He began running.

"Nick, what do you know about Kroutonium? Are there any suits in the manor that have it?" Gus made it to the beach and turned to his right. Since he would be running, he had only brought Razorback, leaving the spears. It made him feel exposed and he had to keep reassuring himself that he would just have to flee any encounters that arose.

"I do not show any suits that contain Kroutonium, but there are a number of Nth-assisted suits that offer small stat bonus—"

"How does that work, are there Nth in the clothing?" Gus interrupted. "I've always accepted stat increases from gear in games, but what is *really* happening?"

"The simplest way of explaining it is that there are informational arrays woven out of specialized material and embedded in the fabric of the item. I won't go into all the details of what *that* material is composed of because it's a whole other lengthy discussion. But just as a computer can be upgraded by adding some internal hardware, these arrays allow the Nth to gain more processing power, which translates to an increase in stats. If a host has too low a level, the Nth are insufficiently evolved to access or utilize the array and agitate the host so no damage happens from trying to interface with the incompatible array."

Gus screwed up his face, comparing his game experience with his new real life situation, going through the implications.

"So are there scalable items?"

"Only Kroutonium-infused items have the ability to scale."

"Why? Is it alive? How does it evolve? Is it Nth-assisted?"

"Let me answer each in turn. Do you recall how we talked about different types of matter?" Gus nodded and activated his **Basic Flight** ability, until his MP drained to zero a couple seconds later, and the first inklings of null headache began to appear. It looked less like flight and more like just a bit more air time. He would have to pay attention to not drain his MP pool. **Basic Flight** was an MP hog.

"Kroutonium is basically one of the sentient forms of matter. There are no sentient metals on earth, so it is a difficult concept to understand for some."

"Is it like the Terminator model T-1000?"

"Not exactly, it does not change its form at will, however it can be manipulated, and usually allows itself to adopt a form into which it is fashioned. It then will attempt to magnify its function in that capacity. It finds satisfaction in this type of growth."

"You said *usually*, can it deny a form?"

"Certainly. If it is fashioned into a form that allows no chance of evolution, it can cause itself to have a critical failure. Using the material for lugnuts is not only a waste of a resource, but may be problematic if the material 'breaks' if used on an aerial troop transport."

"Yikes, how do you know what it wants? If a weapon failed in a fight, that could be game over."

"Nth have difficulty understanding Kroutonium, since we have a limited understanding of how it 'thinks.' Our conclusions are based solely on observed behavior, but unlike most sentients, Kroutonium obeys predictable laws and there is not the individual variety of responses to stimuli that we see with humans, whose opinions are vast and varied. In that sense, Kroutonium behaves uniformly. Whether this is due to some hive-mind or a strict alignment of their nature is mere conjecture. While it is sentient, it prefers to be acted upon initially, then it tries its best to improve upon this directive. Concerning the material, we have the most data when it is used in armors and weapons, so it should be safe to use in these items."

Gus stopped trying to focus on flight and activated **Dash** on a regular basis. When enough MP was regenerated, he would activate it again, to maintain his momentum.

"As you know, the material you call Kroutonium is incredibly rare, and is one of the resources that the Nth make a special priority to scavenge completely from any planet facing an apocalyptic event. It is too valuable to be lost. You may be familiar that most of the Kroutonium was harvested from the Badlands in the United States—"

"Yeah, didn't a ship crash there?" Gus replied.

"It was the cargo carrier that held the scavenged Kroutonium from prior planets. Some managed to be dispersed as the ship broke apart in the atmosphere after hitting a satellite orbiting Earth, but the majority ended at the crash site. Those supers with tech-based powers were able to be instructed by Nth accessing the quantum server on proper ways to utilize its unique properties. The rarity of Kroutonium was underestimated at first, and supplies were quickly used up, so that it has now become virtually impossible to find anywhere."

"I've heard of sentient weapons and suits, is there anything else used to make them?"

"It has been theorized the quantum server is a computer fashioned from Kroutonium, or a material that functions similarly, but since it cannot be physically accessed, that also is conjecture. The adaptability and capacity would lend credence to this theory, however. Since it is usually utilized by the apex lifeforms of a planet, the uses you have mentioned tend to be the lion's share of the recognized functions, with varying applications."

"It's too bad that you can't get it anymore. I bet those that have it hoard it like crazy."

Gus found he could better control the MP flow and avoid null headaches after shifting to only using **Dash**. Unlike when he was boosted, he noticed only a slight shift in speed, but the skill leveled after only thirty minutes of constant use. His additional points in constitution thankfully made the constant rests for stamina regeneration a thing of the past. Gus replayed his jump playlist again and zoned out while moving along the beach. It gave no bonuses, but he liked the music. He didn't want to waste any songs he hadn't used with his **Wreck-ord** skill and lose their potential buffs in the future, but time was of the essence. Since he wasn't leveling as quickly as he had expected, he realized that he would need to use the songs he had hoped to keep in reserve. With a little bit of regret, he queued his running playlist.

You have created a song chain! Success with activities related to musical themes increased by factorial multiplier based on quantity of songs in series.

Take It on the Run by REO Speedwagon. Success rates x 1. (Chain anchor, no bonus)

Choosing a slower song to start things off, Gus watched for any changes as he used **Dash**. He didn't want anything breaking his flow, distracting him so he couldn't maintain the continuous dash state. He put his questions for Nick on the back burner. Keeping closer to the water, he had to still zig and zag, but there was less jumping and the movements were minor. The walkway feeling returned.

Gus sped along, even moving his hands blade-style like the Flash in an effort to eke out a little more speed from his subconscious manipulation of the ether. Faking it until he was making it. He couldn't tell if it really made a difference, but he didn't care. It made him *feel* more like a super. It was such a foreign feeling to how he had seen himself for his whole life. To be honest, he felt out of his depth, playing at being a superhero. He worried if he had what it took to make it if he ever made it back to civilization. *Screw it. No one's here, so I get to do what I want. Plus it just feels cool.*

Gus heard a tone and a quick check showed that his **Dash** skill had leveled up again. That seemed quicker than normal. He monitored his velocity, stamina, and MP to obtain a speed that kept them within twenty percent of max. Gus noticed after a while that he was in one of those flow states that Nick had mentioned. He could almost see the sun track as it plunged into the sea, the clouds flying by quickly as he progressed around the sandy beach.

Gus switched his perception filters, and found he could enable a combination thermal and night-vision that gave superior resolution of the environment around him.

He recalled the feeling he had when he was fleeing the Mantid just a couple days ago. The walkway sensation made him feel like he was moving more quickly. The jungle on his right and waves on his left appeared to blur more and more with the increasing speed.

"Nick, how far have I travelled?" Gus asked, surprised that he wasn't gasping or winded.

"You have travelled twenty-four point three miles from Atlantis Beach," Nick replied. The revelation almost brought Gus to a stop.

What? I've almost run a marathon? I'm not even winded! Gus thought, alarmed. Suddenly the idea of encircling the island was much more attainable.

"How long have I been running?"

"Almost two hours, uninterrupted," Nick stated.

"Noice!" Gus said, and doubled down, pushing himself to keep moving faster and faster. MP and stamina bars dipped to about a tenth of their total, and he found another sweet spot to maintain his pace. Occasionally there would be a chime indicating a skill increase and the bars would jump up as it took less resources to maintain the current speed. Gus adjusted to bring things back to 10% and went on.

Run Through the Jungle by CCR. Success rates x 2.

Things picked up a bit more; Gus felt a kick of acceleration, like when a ski lift picked him up and moved him forward when he first boarded. Gus relaxed and settled into the flow. When he had been a henchman, he had hated running the most.

Some of the drill captains would force you to run laps and there were always punishments for those who arrived last. You'd be on latrine duty, or cleaning barnacles off the outside of a sea vessel; something totally disgusting, banal, or both. The drill captains didn't have to run themselves, and must've been chosen for their sadistic streaks. Gus could remember vomiting and cramps and side-stitches. Running was kind of awesome when divested from those effects. Nth-assisted life was the way to go.

He turned a curve in the coastline and saw that this area had much more debris on the beach. Driftwood and rocks of various sizes disturbed the pristine beach that he had become accustomed to traveling along. He added leaps to clear the detritus and rocks, and veered side to side to avoid the largest patches. While probably useful for training his evasion skills, his speed slowed noticeably. Gus had been running this way for twenty minutes when he noticed a familiar sight; the place where this adventure all began. Checking out his shelter as it zipped by, he recalled that first night here.

It really wasn't such a long time ago, but he felt vastly different than when he first arrived. He wasn't the same Gus. He still had a way to go before he would hit level ten, but so much had changed. Despite his massive progress in such a short time, the sight reminded him that he still was in a battle to survive, even though he had shelter at the manor. He checked the tab that showed his remaining time before his Nth failed, little more than a day and a half, thanks to Nick's new revelation. He needed to level faster.

Born to Run by Bruce Springsteen. Success rates x 6.

Another jolt in acceleration, and Gus could see the coastline was curving, turning toward the volcano. He could see that the coastline got skinnier and appeared to vanish against a rocky wall along one of the sides of the volcano. The chimes of a skill increase sounded again. He figured he could swim if worse came to worst, but he had an idea that he hoped would work. Pushing himself to run faster, he fine-tuned his MP and stamina usage levels so he had a stable five percent remaining.

Running with the Devil by Van Halen. Success rates x 24.

Gus surveyed the beach ahead as he had done this entire run, and nothing so far had shown any evidence that anyone besides himself had been here. From his vantage, he couldn't see the manor, and no boats, piers, or wreckage had been visible anywhere along miles of coastline. Scanning ahead, he stretched his visual display and looked for anything that could possibly be an obstacle. He was quickly running out of beach as the island transitioned to an area which had sheer rock against which the waves crashed... A different chime sounded.

Skill unlock: **Subskill: TimeSight Level 1**. *You can now access some relativistic effects that will compensate and increase reaction time while traveling at excessive speeds.*
200 XP awarded
400 FP awarded

Gus continued running and noticed he was making slight changes in his direction without him making a conscious decision to avoid something. He wasted less motion and his speed increased from not having to shift to avoid obstacles as much.

The Run and Go by Twenty One Pilots. Success rates x 120.

As Gus ran he tried to see what happened when he stepped on the water as the waves flowed inward, preparing himself to trip. He was glad to see that it did not affect his running significantly, because he scarcely touched the water, skipping across like a stone with each step. He instinctively knew that it would not hold his weight, and that something besides his momentum was keeping him above the water. He had begun to hear a whistling as the air rushed by his ears, and moving through the air at this speed began to dry his eyes, pushing tears out the sides. All of a sudden there was a slight pop and the noise disappeared. At the same time, Gus' eyes felt shielded and he could see without squinting, as if he were wearing goggles.

"Nick, wha—" Gus began, trying not to lose his focus.

"Ether is directing air around you in such a way to allow you to pass through it more efficiently, with less friction and its effects."

Gus nodded and noted that there was a strange interaction with the ground and water as he took a step; he wanted to look to see what was happening. He dared not take his eyes away from his forward path, however, since things were speeding by so fast. The beach reappeared and Gus aimed for it, bracing himself for the speed increase of the next song.

Ready to Run by Dixie Chicks. Success rates x 720.

Gus had hated country music at one time in his life. Then he got a girlfriend who loved it, and trying to be as agreeable as possible, he finally gave it a chance and found some songs he could tolerate, and others he actually liked. He was grateful now to have more songs he was familiar with to use for his song chains. He didn't have Google to help him remember any more obscure titles. Unique songs would be precious, so every one of them counted.

The jolt of the speed increase almost made him veer off into the jungle and crash violently into something. He barely recovered, leaving plumes of sand flung in his wake. Wide-eyed and heart beating, more from the adrenaline rush than exertion, Gus pushed ahead. Another chime sounded, but Gus barely paid it attention. As the last seconds of the song ticked away, Gus focused.

Run by George Strait. Success rates x 5040.

This is what Gus was waiting for. He found he was able to run across the water, skipping like a stone and avoiding the debris totally. One unforeseen challenge was the flexible nature of the ebb and flow of the water with the waves. After moving along for a minute, his *TimeSight* or his subconscious must have done the calculations and adapted because it was effortless to cross the surface. This ability arrived just in time, because he was able to adjust his trajectory and avoid an area strewn with debris from a rockslide. The huge boulders sped by as he rocketed past. Sounds began to become deeper in pitch, stretching from the Doppler effect as his speed increased.

To Gus' point of view, the waves moved more slowly, and his ability to see what was ahead of him increased. He knew there would be a shoal coming up, so he veered to the left, ten degrees towards the water. *There. Now bring it back toward the shore.* He was definitely feeling a pushing sensation behind himself, maintaining him at this speed. He felt like a mosquito on the windshield of a sports car. The song was almost unintelligible as George's voice had dropped to a deep bass.

"Nick, let me know if I miss anything," Gus said through gritted teeth, eyes intent on the path ahead. He noticed that his own voice sounded normal, unaffected by his speed.

"Certainly," Nick replied curtly.

When the next song hit, Gus was unprepared for the change.

Run-Around by Blues Traveler. Success rates x 40,320.

Gus felt like his mind had been shoved open like someone was kicking in the doors. Multiple chimes sounded one atop the other and his log kept filling with messages.

XP notices pinged left and right amidst the level up notices. Gus ignored it all and tried to focus on what he was doing to avoid peeking at them to avoid a level up euphoria that would distract him and break the song chain. Forcing his eyes forward and away from the data on the edges of his display, he continued running. Time appeared to slow down even further, and Gus saw himself fly quickly past the volcano, circle another peninsula, and start wrapping around the other side of the volcano. The island extended away from the volcano on this side, and Gus saw, analyzed, and processed what was ahead, behind and below him. Even at this speed, this allowed him to absorb and passively scan everything around him. It was a rush unlike he had ever experienced and he felt a slight twinge similar to the feeling of leveling up, but with much less intensity. It was exhilarating nonetheless.

The feeling surged through him, like liquid light flowing like syrup first through his head and extending to his whole being, and seemed to sustain him during the strain of his current movement. Glancing up, he saw that he was at forty percent on his stamina and MP bars. It amazed him that he was able to sustain this level of movement with less effort than when he started.

John Popper's words stretched out into unintelligibility as **TimeSight** asserted itself to another level. Gus was circling around the other side of the island in no time, and wondered and worried what would happen when he hit the next song. He did not get the chance to find out, because as he rounded another curve of the coast, he was back on the same side of the island as Atlantis Beach. Gus consciously slowed himself, to not overshoot the familiar beach.

He could feel energy seeping from him and being readily absorbed by the ether, bleeding off heat and kinetic energy to safe levels. The effect slightly chilling him as momentum was wicked away, displaced to who knew where. Nick had helpfully placed a figure of the island on the upper right of Gus' display, and gauging where he wanted to stop made the process of slowing to a halt much easier.

"Nick, stop playlist!" Gus gasped, not wanting to risk pushing his limits any further. The feeling of liquid light drained away, and as it fled Gus felt an intense fatigue set in, both physically and mentally. With the need for constant focus gone, he eagerly looked at his logs, and the level up euphoria hit him at once. He trotted to a stop and was elated he had the earlier foresight to bring a chair down to the beach. He collapsed into it, and the last thing he saw was his log streaming past.

You have leveled up the skill: TimeSight
You have leveled up the skill: Dash
You have leveled up the skill: Dash
You have leveled up the skill: TimeSight
You have leveled up the skill: Dash

You have leveled up the skill: Dash
LEVEL UP! Congratulations, Level 7 reached!
You have (5) additional stat points to assign.
You have leveled up the skill: TimeSight
You have leveled up the skill: Dash
You have leveled up the skill: TimeSight
You have leveled up the skill: Dash
You have leveled up the skill: TimeSight
You have leveled up the skill: Dash
You have leveled up the skill: TimeSight...

...

Gus let the notices fly, levels and FP bonuses sped by that he couldn't read until he heard another fanfare as another level was reached.

LEVEL UP! Congratulations, Level 8 reached!
You have (10) additional stat points to assign.

Smiling, he closed his eyes and drifted into sleep.

CHAPTER TWENTY-FIVE

Weapon of Choice

45 YEARS AGO...

Methiochos was nearly done. Overseeing the loading and preparations of the ship were going well, but there was so much to do. He had to get this right the first time, because there would be no chance of getting more personnel or supplies after the bio-stasis field was in place. Still, what he had should be sufficient; five hundred of the best supers that he could find, loyal and dedicated to him. In a spot of luck, he had even convinced some of the world's best researchers to join him.

He turned a corner, and headed back to the bridge of the transport. Two children ran headlong into him on the busy walkway. He nearly yelled at them until he noticed who they were. Archon's little brat Basil and the girl who always followed him around. Methiochos had never really been comfortable around kids, especially in what amounted to a military facility in his eyes, but this kid especially rubbed him the wrong way. Having to deal with his endless questions and his nosy nature was only one of his annoying traits. Plus the kid was going to be a legacy one day.

He would get his powers thanks to his family rather than having any merit himself. Methiochos just knew that Archon was eventually going to put this kid in place as his successor, despite the contributions he and the other members of the council had made over the years. It was one of the reasons he was making his play now, and he only needed to keep it together for a little longer. Methiochos put on a kind expression, forcing it in place. If he wasn't the boss' son...

"How soon are you going to be done? When can I come visit?" Basil started, more questions ready to spill forth.

"Whoa, there! So many questions! And there's a lot of heavy equipment moving around. It isn't quite safe for you two, especially with the men on a time crunch. I nearly bowled you over—what if I had a hover-loader and rounded that corner? I know you're excited, but I just want you guys to be safe."

"Alright..." Basil said dejectedly and began to walk away. Turning back, he said over his shoulder, "...but you'll tell us what it's like when you get there, right?"

"Of course," Methiochos said, happy that the boy was mollified so easily, then continued on his way.

The little girl by Basil's side was still playing with her doll. She didn't like eye contact, and the doll helped her be around other people. When she looked people in the eye, she saw things. So many things, and a lot of it was ugly. She didn't mean to look at the man, but he had startled her and she had taken just a glimpse. Her mom told her that for now it was best not to talk about her ability with others, and that when the time was right, she could share it. She had told Basil, but he was the only one. He didn't think she was weird, either, like the other kids, so that made it ok.

As the two walked back, she mumbled, "He's lying."

Basil's head perked up. "No, M is my dad's best general. What are you talking about?"

"He's trying to fool your dad." The little girl then began to tell Basil all of the things that she saw in the brief instant she peeked into the big man's eyes. The more she spoke, the angrier

Basil became. He had admired Methiochos, which made the betrayal all the worse.

Even though he was young, Basil was tenacious. His dad called him his little pitbull, because once he became engaged, he did not let go or quit. Basil began to form an idea on how to make Methiochos pay.

———

DAY 7 2:09 AM

7:10:27 remaining

Gus woke up with a start. *Where am I?* He looked around, disoriented, his neck sore from sleeping at an odd angle in the chair. *What are you doing sleeping outside, idiot? Did you forget there are zombies stalking you out there?* The tiny sliver of the moon gave just enough light to navigate with, so he grabbed his backpack and made his way back to the master suite. He stretched and the soreness soon faded, but he was still exhausted from his earlier exertion. Pushing himself to the point of collapse was great for leveling, but he could have easily been attacked. Shaking his head at his stupidity, a quick peek at his watch showed it was two in the morning. He wearily made it to bed and crashed for the night.

———

Earlier than expected, Gus awoke full of energy. He was surprised that even though he had pushed his Nth to the limits, that they rebounded just as strongly. He had hoped he hadn't accelerated their shutdown with his expedition yesterday.

Though it was still dark outside, Gus got ready for the day. Time to place those sweet stat points, then unlock some goodies from the control center. Gus rubbed his hands together and opened up his stats. A quick peek showed **Dash** had reached level twelve and **TimeSight** was at level six. Both would be a big help when fighting the Dark Nth.

He tried to think about where he was lacking. With more abilities, his MP pool was becoming more important, so he knew intelligence was something to raise this time. He could do with an agility boost also, to better engage the Mantids. His stamina was ok for the moment, and he had already given constitution a good boost the last time he dropped points. Perception was good at its current level, and maybe luck could use a point. After deliberating he decided to put five into intelligence, four into agility and one into luck. He stopped to admire the changes as he began to feel his body react.

He was using his skills more and more, and it was difficult to manage MP during the heat of battle. As his skills increased, he wanted to avoid the killer headache that accompanied MP depletion. As his powers evolved in the future, he would have to allocate more and more MP to utilize his skills. There was a benefit in being able to handle close combat situations, but as time went on, he hoped he could get more solid attacks that he could fire at a safe distance.

Gus felt a shudder along his body and the tightness and exhaustion in his muscles unwound as if he had just undergone an instant form of massage therapy. Rolling his shoulders, his movements felt more fluid. On a whim, he tried to see if he could do the splits, and was shocked to see that he actually could, without effort or strain.

What other changes are there to my physicality? I need to quantify just how much each stat point affects things like my speed, strength and stamina. Checking his countdown timer, he was cutting it close to when things would start shutting down according to Nick. Time for experimentation after level ten.

Gus moved to the bathroom mirror and tried to see if there were any physical changes. Increasing his agility didn't seem to alter his physical appearance, but he felt better about himself overall. He was pushing himself past his old limits more than any time before, and was satisfied that his life was turning a corner. He did one last check of his stats before heading to the control room.

Gus Vannett
Level 8
Agility: 15
Constitution: 14 (13+1)
Charisma: 8
Strength: 12
Perception: 16
Intelligence: 15
Luck: 7

HP: 260
MP: 220
Stamina: 260

He settled into one of the chairs in the control room. Finding the Foundry in the facility management console, he unlocked it and the associated sub-facility Defense. Clearing his logs, he saw that through all the level ups yesterday, he had accrued another 1400 worth of FP. That brought him up to 5500 FP. Score!

Gus did a little dance in his chair, reminiscent of one of his favorite online podcasts. The upgrades took a healthy bite out of that total, leaving him at only 1500 FP. Another shock was that he was only 200 XP from hitting level nine. After a brief pause, the dancing resumed with more fervor.

Apparently, the Foundry took up an entire level of the manor. After a longer than usual elevator ride, the doors opened to large banks of machinery, all powering up and coming to life. There was a small control room that stood overlooking processors, and vats beginning to issue steam from their depths.

Keying on the control panel, he was able to see a display showing the current capacities of the Foundry and an empty work queue. Gus accessed the available items that could be fabricated in the Foundry. While a number of items were grayed out and inaccessible, there was still an overwhelming amount that the Foundry could create. So much so that it took a while to move from page to page, seeing many similar items with barely perceptible differences.

Gus found an options tab and set restrictions to look at armor first, suitable for level eight use. He had to further narrow the scope to specific armor types, surprised to see some armor utilizing things he had only seen when playing D&D. He found chain and plate armor, in various materials: metal, plastisteel, array glass, composite, hybrid, etc.

Various colors could be chosen, except specific Faction colors. Still, the available options vastly multiplied the amount of items to be sorted. Soon he had chosen what basically amounted to greaves, vambraces and a cuirass to add to his suit, choosing a basic gray that seemed to match the overall shade of his suit.

Once he had chosen the pieces to be fabricated, there were multiple options of material and surface texture. Gus chose a lightweight material that had a layered core and could resist puncture—just what he needed to avoid sharp claws. Gus found he could also have an external texture similar to coarse sandpaper. Maybe that could blunt a sharp talon that tried to scratch him, making it less deadly. With the items queued up, he was directed to be scanned for his measurements.

The system directed him to a scanning circle, much like the one in the training arena, to get his measurements to design the armor. Halfway through the scan, an alarm went off and the process stopped. Rushing to the monitor, Gus wondered what new complication had arisen. Sensing a 'fetch quest' in his future, Gus read through the alarm. The news, however, was shocking.

2.4 lbs of Kroutonium detected. Do you wish to incorporate this into armor fabrication?

"Wait, what?" Looking at the scan, he saw a representation of himself, rotating like an avatar in a video game. On his avatar, Razorback was highlighted in the scan sitting in the scabbard at his side. Pulling Razorback out he stared at the crude blade that he had made by hand, with a little help from his skills.

Did I waste any of this making it into a blade? Gus thought about the tiny triangle he had removed to make the blade tip. *I need to go back and get that...* Gus' thoughts sprang into overdrive. If Razorback really was made out of Kroutonium, it should level along with him, based on his levels. Activating **Wreck-ognize**, he noticed that the stats indeed had improved. Also that there were some new notices:

Item properties:
Razorback *(14-36 damage)*
Damage type: piercing/slashing
Improved chance to learn one-handed weapon skills
Improved chance to critical attack 20%

"Nick! How come you didn't tell me about this?"

"The material is so rare, I didn't analyze it. Would it have changed anything you have done so far?"

Gus pursed his lips and looked skyward, trying to recall if it would have made any difference. He finally shrugged and conceded that the answer was probably no. He was just glad that he knew now. Without the Foundry, it didn't make a difference one way or another.

Gus liked the idea of maybe changing Razorback back into a spear, only professionally-crafted this time. He was becoming more and more skilled using polearms, and he needed to keep the Mantids and zombies at bay. He doubted he had enough to make anything in the armor department, but maybe as a liner of some sort.

Would that improve the whole, stat wise? Maybe. Rather than risk it, he focused on the sure thing. Having a weapon that would grow along with him at such a low level had a much higher potential for major growth in the long run.

He set the Foundry to process the 'vanilla' armor and he turned his attention to weapon possibilities. All the pieces would be ready in six hours. Gus could see conveyors moving and the hum of machinery coming to life down below the control room. He turned back to the console, bringing up the weapons tab, multiple questions and possibilities coming to his mind.

"Nick, what happens if I use this Kroutonium in the Foundry to make a new weapon. Does it lose the bonuses?"

"The material returns to its base form, but the Foundry will gain the schematics to reproduce the effect in future items of a similar nature. If you change armor into a weapon, or vice versa, all bonus effects are lost," Nick replied.

Scrolling through the weapons, Gus checked to see what could be fashioned at his current level. It would be nice to have something more robust than a weapon designed solely for training. A list of different classes of polearms was displayed, and Gus had to read through the descriptions and view examples of each class to understand what the difference was between a glaive and a halberd.

Thinking about his latest battle with the Mantids, he chose the glaive class, then specialized with the naginata form. The large blade to slash would do well with fighting Dark Nth. He was able to play with various modifications, adding a circular handguard between the blade and shaft, to catch claws and push them away. He chose the option to make the back of the blade serrated, allowing him to cut hardened carapace if needed.

Would you like to use the last saved body scan for weapon size and dimensions? (Y/N)
Would you like to repurpose Kroutonium to current weapon design? (Y/N)

Gus entered yes into the console twice, then left the control center and went down the metal mesh stairway to the indicated area. Peeling off the foam putty handle, Gus reverently placed Razorback in the hopper. A console beside the receptacle came to life and asked:

*Are you sure you wish to sacrifice [**Razorback**]? (Y/N)*

Pushing yes again, it was a done deal. The receptacle disappeared within the machine and began a low hum. Gus felt almost guilty. Making a new weapon was fine but knowing the metal was sentient made it harder to sacrifice it. He doubted his decision the moment he couldn't take it back.

"Nick, would the Kroutonium hold a grudge if it doesn't like its new form? Would it be resentful for losing the bonuses it evolved?"

"Anything's possible, but I doubt it, if it's becoming more powerful. I wouldn't worry… too much."

"Thanks… I guess," Gus said in the same tone.

Heading back to the control center with questions on his mind, he checked the build queue and saw that the process would add six more hours to the queue.

He was almost ready to leave when he remembered the scanners. He opened the Defense tab and found what he wanted. He selected a dozen scanning pylons, and a dozen motion-sensitive smart turrets. The sensors would take only an hour to fabricate, while the turrets took a whopping six hours each. *Woof.* Gus entered his instructions into the queue; it would be a while before everything was ready. Fortunately, there were no material requirements. The manor must have some stock of basic crafting materials, and all that was required was to meet the FP cost.

For once, one less thing to worry about! Looking at the queue before leaving, Gus moved the naginata to the top of it. That done, he felt a small sense of relief.

Mischief managed. Next on the to-do list was his daily training. He headed to the arena, ready for some more punishment.

CHAPTER TWENTY-SIX

Electric Slide

DAY 7 7:15 AM

7:05:19 remaining

As Gus entered the training arena, Chop Chop was in his usual stance and greeted him with a slight nod. Gus went to the control terminal and started the module.

Gus stood on the scanner, eager to see what new skills he would be able to unlock today. He also wanted to incorporate his new **Dash** ability into his fighting style. He was imagining different ways to combine it with his other skills to make combos and flank the quick Mantids.

Quest Granted: The Chain
Quest Conditions:
*1) Learn the skills **Slide** and **Dodge***
2) Successfully utilize 5 different skills
3) Execute 5 Chained Attacks
4) Defeat 10 opponents

Quest Rewards: *1000 XP, 600 FP, retain new skills*
Time Requirements: 3 hours
Do you want to accept this quest? (Y/N)

They were definitely raising the stakes! This training seemed like it was ramping up to another level in difficulty. Still, Gus was grateful he had a chance to practice his skills in a zombie-free environment. Plus he was eager to see his stat increases in action. One slip-up while learning a new skill against zombies would be the end of him, so it was best to get in as much practice as possible.

The holographic emitter kicked to life and three Mantids were displayed. Pillowbots assumed their positions within the holograms and froze, waiting for Gus to step into the arena. Gus found a naginata among the polearms, deciding to become more familiar with the weapon while he could do so in a controlled situation. He looked through a couple varieties until he found one with the metal guard in the middle. Once satisfied, he headed back to the arena and the simulation began.

Compared to fighting two enemies, three was a different ballgame. One of the Mantids was always trying to flank him and when two started to circle around from the left and the other from the right it required Gus to stay in motion to keep all the enemies in his field of view. Deciding to take the initiative, Gus rushed toward the Mantid on the right. He tried to sweep low and was able to trip the Mantid, but he overcalculated the length of the dash and was too far away to score a hit before the Mantid regained its feet and faced him again.

He attempted another attack on the Mantid on his right this time, but the center Mantid was ready for him and timed its attack accordingly. Gus received a clawless but powerful swipe right to the face before he could connect with his target. Gus' vision burst with white stars as the force of the blow spun him around before he fell face first to the mat. His ears rang and he had to roll out of the way to avoid the pounce of one of the Mantids. He clambered to his feet just in time to block another swipe out of sheer reflex. Without thinking, he used **Sweep the Leg** and flipped the Mantid on its back. A quick jab later and the hologram melted away, revealing the naked pillowbot, frozen in defeat.

Gus saw a flicker from the side of his eye and quickly used **Dash** to jump backward. Gus saw the virtual talon pass right in front of his eyes as **TimeSight** changed his perception, slowing events so he could react. A chime sounded.

You have just unlocked a Subskill of Dash: **Dodge (Level 1)**
Evade a blow using an ether pull to escape danger, can be chained into **Sweep the Leg**. *Causes a 3-second* **TimeSight** *time dilation effect at level 1.*
MP cost: 20 MP
Refractory period: 1 minute
100 XP awarded
200 FP awarded
100 XP to level 9

The virtual Mantid continued its movement past Gus' face in slow motion, leaving its side overextended. Time snapped back to normal and Gus almost missed hitting the exposed flank of the creature. As the blow connected, Gus saw a red arrow pointing to his left with a tiny icon of a chain with three links. Focusing on the tiny icon, his **Chained Attack** ability fired and instinctively, Gus knew where to move.

Twisting in the direction of the arrow, Gus saw the final Mantid midair and barely had enough time to withdraw his naginata and connect with his new attacker right in the throat. The momentum knocked him flat, and the Mantid flipped overhead as the butt of the polearm buried into the mat and rotated. Gus stood and saw that he had managed to dispatch the final two attackers. The hologram reset and the pillowbots assumed their positions for another go.

Gus dashed to the left with his weapon in front of him. He expected the Mantid to dodge and so he feinted and switched directions mid-**Dash**, activating the skill again, this time to the right. The misdirection worked well and he was able to connect with the Mantid on the other side of the arena as it was trying to flank him.

The chain icon appeared and Gus activated the skill. His body flowed into the next attack, spinning low and stabbing the middle Mantid in the torso. Gus pulled the blade of his naginata upward and when the tip reached the neck of the virtual Mantid the chain icon appeared again. Gus activated the skill once more and felt the pull to move in the opposite direction, bracing the shaft by his hip.

The rotation brought the blade's tip around to contact the last Mantid at shoulder level and swipe downward across the Mantid's chest. It spun around with the force of the attack and froze on the mat, like a dead bug, limbs frozen in the air.

Chimes sounded as Gus stood there, amazed at how effortlessly the combo came together. He was not sure how he moved in just the right ways but suspected the Nth must be monitoring the area around him and fired the appropriate muscles. He also knew where he had to be on an unconscious level, and the entire experience was a different feeling than when the Nth tingled to guide him. Gus checked his logs:

Related skills learned with **Spear Mastery** *applied to* **Polearms** *progress.*
You have leveled up the skill: **Polearms** *to Level 4!*
50 XP awarded (level 3), 50 XP awarded (level 4)
100 FP awarded (level 3), 100 FP awarded (level 4)
LEVEL UP! Congratulations, Level 9 reached
5000 XP to next level
You have been awarded 500 FP
You have (5) additional stat points to assign.
You have leveled up the skill: **Chained Attack** *to Level 2!*
50 XP awarded
100 FP awarded

Taking a moment to enjoy the level up euphoria, Gus pulled up his stats:

Agility: 15
Constitution: 14 (13+1)
Charisma: 8
Strength: 12
Perception: 16
Intelligence: 16
Luck: 7

Gus had five more stat points, so he decided to drop three points into strength. Fifteen points seemed to be a threshold of some sort. He bumped his constitution stat up two points in case he lost his armor buff, bringing the base stat to fifteen.

A painful yet almost welcome soreness infiltrated his muscles, reminiscent of the day after a good workout. He felt like his skin was becoming taut as his muscles enlarged and expanded. *Get swole!* Gus smiled as he watched the effects of the strength boost. The burning sensation faded as the muscles settled into their new form, and Gus felt eager to try his new power in the arena.

Fighting with Dark Nth was unnerving, to say the least, but he thought about what the future would hold in terms of fighting other supers if he ever managed to get off the island. With him being such a low level, and his powers so new and undeveloped, relying on his wits would be incredibly important. It would take some time for him to level to the standard that most supers had trained their skills.

Most supers usually received their powers in their early teens, and there was rigorous training, depending on what Faction they joined. There were Factionless supers, but they were at a definite disadvantage in terms of training, gear, and the support of others. Gus wondered how his relationship with his father would change after he learned that Gus had joined the party and got himself some super powers. Gus scowled at himself for needing that validation.

Gus was still thinking about the implications when two Mantids tackled him and almost winded him as he slammed into the mat. That reset time was much quicker than the last one! Gus coughed and rolled to the side, and noticed there were four Mantids ready to spar against him. Shaking off the hit, he hopped to his feet. He effortlessly performed a kick up, hopping to the balls of his feet from lying prone, shocking himself and causing his attackers to pause briefly.

Before he could fully form a plan, two of the Mantids rushed him. Gus feinted at one and swung the butt of the naginata to hit the other in the head. Gus felt the unique jolt as he fired **Wreck-tums!** and the Mantid retreated. Gus jumped back, dodging the remaining Mantid closing in on him.

Another Mantid rushed to meet him, attacking from his flank, and Gus hit **Dash** to meet it halfway. They clashed together, the metal band blocking the outstretched claws and folding the Mantid's arms back, pinning them to its chest. Gus launched **Counter-attack**, bashing the Mantid in the face with the metal band and then swiping the blade across its face, downing the enemy.

Gus fired **Dash** again, to retreat and get some room to assess his opponents. The Mantid he had hit with **Wreck-tums!** was lurking behind two of its buddies, using them as a shield. Gus dashed and vaulted over the other Mantids using **Basic Flight**. A simple kick was enough to remove the last HP of the cowardly bot. Another chain icon appeared but resulted in only a glancing blow on the back of one Mantid, due to activating the skill late.

The final two Mantids coordinated their attack simultaneously, and Gus blocked one attack but had to dodge the other. That put him out of position to retaliate. After another block, Gus counter-attacked late and barely scratched his opponent. The Mantids were beginning to copy his dodges and they were getting better at effectively dancing in and out of strike range.

After one failed attack, one of the Mantids jumped backward and ended up next to the other, so Gus rushed straight at them. Mentally choosing the one on the left, he braced himself for a bash from the other Mantid. At the last moment, he dropped to his knees and slid, swiping low to knock the Mantid off its feet with **Sweep the Leg**.

A tone went off again and Gus saw the chain icon appear. Gus activated the skill, not sure what would happen since he was not in an ideal battle stance. He spun backward, still gliding as if he were on a slip and slide, and threw the naginata at the other Mantid, scoring a direct hit.

The tripped Mantid was still momentarily stunned and Gus jumped to his feet and dashed toward the Mantid. He activated another jump, assisted by firing his **Basic Flight** skill, to sail over the Mantid to retrieve his weapon. A slight headache started to kick in and Gus saw that he had drained almost all of his MP.

Time to go old school. Grabbing the butt end, he used the shaft as a fulcrum and used the last available MP to use **Basic Flight** to swing around, changing his direction. After turning, he deftly yanked the naginata out at the last minute. He hit the Mantid feet first just as it was getting to its feet, carrying it back to the mat. Gus landed in a crouch and stabbed forward, ending the battle.

Gus stood trying to catch his breath, being a little more winded, and seeing that both his stamina and MP was getting pretty low. He stepped out of the ring and checked his logs again.

You have unlocked the skill: **Slide (Level 1)!**
Glide along a frictionless ether sheet, regardless of medium texture.
Level 1: Maximum glide 10 feet
MP: 2 MP per second of gliding effect
100 XP awarded
200 FP awarded
You have unlocked the skill: **Thrown Weapon (Level 1)!**

Increased damage if attack connects (+5n damage where n=skill level).
Note: Weapon may not be recoverable, I hope you're good at hand-to-hand combat!
100 XP awarded
200 FP awarded

Quest Complete: The Chain
Quest Rewards: *1000 XP, 600 FP*

Gus looked and saw that he finally had fulfilled the conditions for the quest. That and the dimming of the lights was also a dead-giveaway that training was done for the day. Even though he had trained hard, he still felt more amped than ever. He had most of the day to kill, literally, before his new weapon and armor were done. He kicked himself for not going there sooner and getting things queued up, but no sense in crying about it now.

How could he have known about Razorback's true nature? He almost grabbed an arena naginata, but checking his watch, the new one should be done at the Foundry in a little over an hour. Gus headed to the elevator, an idea springing to his mind on how to spend the time.

CHAPTER TWENTY-SEVEN

If Only

45 YEARS AGO...

They were finally underway. Methiochos' hand-picked crew were aboard and en route to the island. Everyone, from support personnel to command, were supers in some way, shape, or form.

As soon as he landed, Methiochos planned on raising the bio-stasis field and giving orders for the crew. After unlocking the manor and getting personnel into their departments, training and expansion could begin. In the ship were numerous projects of the world's best minds. Both ones developed by Manticorps itself, and those that were obtained in less-than-ethical ways from other thinktanks around the globe.

The new tech they would develop would bring the regs to their side, and the augmentations they devised for their supers would make them an unstoppable army. Methiochos believed his solid leadership would help unite people into one world government, with him at the head, of course. The fragmented Factions and impotent world governments would eventually come to his side when they saw that opposition would be fruitless.

Methiochos scanned the bridge, looking for Dara to give her some instructions on how to mobilize the crew when they reached the island. He was surprised to find her absent, which was uncharacteristic for her usually organized, perfectionist personality.

He queried his control console and only received the reply: 'No personnel found that match search parameters.' Furrowing his brow, Methiochos went below-decks to see if he could find Dara in her quarters. The door was locked, and even with his command override, he could not open the doors.

He would have to find someone to surreptitiously open her chambers without arousing concern and alarming the crew. Something was off here, and the cool confidence he had felt was beginning to ebb with these unforeseen complications. *It was probably nothing,* he assured himself. Turning, he made his way to maintenance.

———

Methiochos came back to the present, retracting two specialized tendrils from the magma, sensing he could absorb no more of the energy for now. More and more was coming back to him after each cycle of absorbing energy and growing. Soon he would surpass his old limits.

While the nature of his new opponent was still unclear, he knew one thing: He could not let anyone but himself access the manor's full functions. Especially now. He did not know how they were able to pass the bio-stasis field, but his enemies were relentless. His former allies were even more so. If they were able to destroy his entire crew and cripple him in the process, they were formidable. He clenched a fist in the dark, anger building from the scattered memories he could piece together.

"We have grown!"

Methiochos had to calm his mind and push down the Dark.

He had less control over it when strong emotions manifested. It was becoming easier the more he regained consciousness, but it was always there on the fringes, probing for an opening. Methiochos had grown too, though. He did not fatigue the same way he did before everything happened. While annoying, he could meet the Dark and he would prevail against it. As well as anyone who dared to cross him.

DAY 6 9:21 AM

7:03:13 remaining

Gus headed to the control center. He had originally planned to go hunting or grab some fruit, but an idea came to him: Didn't the manor support numerous robots of all types and shapes, that were supposed to support a large crew of humans? Why was he wasting time trying to do everything himself? He needed to find some robots to gather food, and hopefully some kind of chef to cook him meals.

Checking his stats, he found he had a whopping 2300 FP. He had to search through a lot of departments before he found what he wanted in the auxiliaries menu. Various types of gathering robots and drones existed. Auxiliaries management was cheap at 1000 FP and allowed existing bots of various types to be accessed and programmed. It would allow him access to most of the drones and robots in the manor and he could task them with mundane jobs that were sapping his time. He was alone for the foreseeable future, and it was the only way to delegate necessary but time-squandering responsibilities.

Gus then found food preparation bots as a sub-department of the Cafeteria. Unlocking both would cost 2000 FP. Gus spent the points and wondered if he was being too hasty spending his facility points. It was a little extravagant, but saving time and focusing more on his development would possibly be a life-saver. He hesitated but the thought of saving hours hunting and gathering pushed him to make the choice. Squinting his eyes, he pecked the enter button and confirmed the choice.

After playing around with some settings, he found he could task the gather-bots to take suggestions from the chef-bots. Setting them to explore and gather, he backed away from the facility controls. He was surprised to see he had spent almost an hour reading and exploring the options to find what he needed. His display was getting perilously close to the seven-day threshold when Nick said he would start to notice things shutting down.

He found that he could upgrade the arena when he reached level ten, and more involved training options could be accessed. It definitely would be on the list. There were an insane amount of items that he never thought he would get to use, but the labs were intriguing. The only problem was that there was no staff to man them. With titles like 'Spatial translocation amplification,' 'Power combinatorics,' and 'Biopolymer strength augmentation boosts,' Gus' interest was piqued, to say the least, but he tore himself away. He didn't have time to dwell on this. He needed 3750 XP as quickly as possible.

Realistically, Gus was probably many levels from being able to access the fruits of what the manor had to offer.

He felt better after leaving and entering the elevator. He had to stop obsessing about the far future. Focus on what was important now. That would really be the worst, to have an amazing augmentation that was a hundred levels above his ability to use. It did make Gus wonder what he would do if he had the opportunity to recruit people to help him take full advantage of the manor. That could really be a game changer. But first things first. Best not to get too far ahead of himself, he thought, remembering a typical conversation with his father.

"Gus, you need to set some reasonable goals for a change," Tempest lectured.

A fourteen-year-old Gus had mentioned to his father his desire to run for class president. "I think I have some good ideas—"

"All those things are just popularity contests. I know you, Gus. You're introverted and kind of a loner. Do you really think you can get enough votes? Here's what will happen. You'll make a half-hearted effort, then you will lose. Then you will get all sullen and sulk for a couple weeks…"

Gus grit his teeth as a familiar wave of anger built up inside of him as his dad went on and on. Tempest just couldn't keep from piling on the abuse. *Why couldn't he just believe in me for just once? Isn't that what fathers should do?*

"…you start off strong on one of your ideas, and then you lose steam. It takes a certain kind of person to be a leader, and you haven't really shown me any of those things. I work with people who lead on a daily basis. It's not all fun and games."

"Dad, it's just class president! There won't be any decisions more important than what the decorations for the winter dance will be. Sheesh! Maybe I would follow through with more things if you weren't such an unsupportive energy vampire!" Gus' knuckles cracked with how hard he had balled his fists.

"That's it, Gus. Play the victim. Nothing's ever your fault. Lay it on thick, I can take it. It's all my fault. Everybody's out to get you, even your father." Tempest said in a sardonic sing-song that made Gus' blood boil. He could never argue with his father. He had a talent for twisting words and Gus never knew how to respond. Well, maybe a couple days later as he stewed on it, he would think of the perfect comeback that he would never get to use.

Gus looked down at his feet and mumbled, "Just forget it." And Gus did just that. That is, he let the opportunity pass and crammed the emotions into the pressure-cooker that was his heart. He knew it wasn't healthy, or mature, but who could he really talk to about it? He had to admit that he didn't have any close friends. The fact that his father was partly correct in his assessment of Gus made him even more frustrated and angry. He was trying something new to try to change things. To feel like he mattered for once.

Gus went to his room and started up a video game. It was one of the few things that allowed him to detach and feel just a little control of his world. He could let go and be the hero. Making a difference for some virtual people in trouble. It was dumb, but it worked. He always felt better. Plus, he had met some guys online who were into all the same things he was.

He didn't have to try to be someone else, they were legitimately into sci-fi and fantasy. They got all his jokes and pop culture references. When they did a raid together, or some other co-op game, he felt a sense of brotherhood that he never felt in his own family. It was nice to just be accepted. He knew he probably wouldn't ever meet them in real life, but he often imagined hanging out with them as friends. Life would be better, that was for sure.

———

Things were different now, Gus thought. And he *did* meet those guys. He felt a pang of homesickness thinking about them. He hoped they were doing ok, wherever they were. He would do anything for them. If he ever got off this island, he would reconnect with them as soon as he could.

CHAPTER TWENTY-EIGHT

I Keep on Rising Up

45 YEARS AGO...

The tech stepped away and Methiochos pried the two bulky doors apart. The room inside was totally dark. Reaching inside, he turned on the room's illumination and was startled at the disarray that assaulted his eyes. The room was in shambles, which was more shocking having seen it before in its pristine condition. Dara, who had no doubt seen disharmony and chaos in many of the minds she had to deal with using her power, chose to keep her own life rigidly structured and orderly.

Everything had a place, a label, and a specific use. It was impressive to behold. The room before Methiochos was anything but orderly. Drawers had been unceremoniously dumped of their contents. The bed upended and the frame bent. The mattress filling torn and pulled out through the underside of the frame. The glass portholes were cracked and damaged; the existing light was muted by debris blocking many of the lamps and wall sconces.

Methiochos' eyes stopped on the air duct in the far corner. Claw marks scored the edges, but what alarmed him, even more, was that the pattern of the damage indicated something trying to get into the air ducts, not something trying to come out into Dara's chambers. Whatever had been in here was now free, and it had taken her along with it. The display from earlier haunted him. '*No personnel found...*' He doubted that Dara was even alive. Methiochos balled his fists and got on the comms to give some orders.

DAY 7 10:44 AM

7:01:52 remaining

A new tinkling tone surprised Gus, and he checked his display to investigate. The cafeteria had been open less than an hour and already had prepared something to eat. Letting the display guide him, Gus found the mess hall. The room was immense, with long tables arranged in orderly rows, with smaller circular and rectangular two-tops around the periphery. A drink dispensary looked like it had recently been cleaned and activated. One side of the unit dispensed hot drinks and the other, larger one had a variety of cold ones. The labels for the drinks looked vintage but he recognized most of the sodas he could try. There was an obvious bias for Mountain Dew, and Gus smiled, seeing that at least one corner of the universe was as it should be.

He saw some bots working in the kitchen through a rectangular window, where food orders were passed from the kitchen to the serving staff. As he approached, a robot that resembled a large exclamation point, with a trapezoidal body, wide at the top and tapering down to a single fat wheel, must have sensed his presence. It made its way to the window and waited. A large bowl was delivered to the window and the serving bot unfolded thin telescoping arms from its sides and grabbed it.

Delivering the bowl to the table next to where Gus was standing, the server-bot opened a receptacle on its chest and removed some utensils and placed them on the table. It then sped away toward the kitchen, disappearing behind two swinging double doors.

Gus sat and surveyed his meal. It was a fruit salad made of multiple fruits that Gus had no idea were even available at the manor. There were fresh blueberries in it too, so there must be other areas where food had been growing that Gus didn't know about.

The taste was phenomenal. He soon finished and the same server bot returned as Gus stood and collected everything and returned back to the kitchen.

Gus saw a pulsing tab on his display with a yellow symbol of a hammer and screwdriver crossed in an X. Mentally opening it, he could see the remaining items in his Foundry queue. The naginata was finished! Excited to try it out, he was going to head to the Foundry when Nick alerted him of another proximity alert trigger. At least they were far into the jungle path. Those sensors were doing their job!

Gus cracked his knuckles, wishing that the zombies would've had the courtesy to wait until his armor was finished. Rude! Nothing to do about it though. Gus hurried to the Foundry to see his new weapon.

When he arrived at the Foundry, lights on the catwalk directed him from the control room to a closed metal dispenser on one of the lower levels. It was darker here, some of the overhead lighting blocked by the metal walkways that crisscrossed amongst the machinery. Pushing a green button, the metal lid lifted with a dramatic hiss, and released a dense white foggy mist.

Lying there on egg-crate foam was a long black naginata. It was exotic-looking and impressive, emanating danger. The blade glinted somehow in the dark, steamy room. The shaft was fashioned of polished ebony-colored material, with a filigreed silver band midway down the shaft.

Gus reverently lifted the weapon from the conveyer; he could feel the tooled grips that compressed slightly, reminding him of the foam putty. The weight was surprisingly similar to the practice spears. Gus could not tell if this was made of lightweight metal or some kind of advanced polycarbonate, but the surface did feel cool to the touch. Three empty sockets were visible above the upper grip and the guard next to the blade. Gus ran his finger around one of the sockets, wondering what would fit in the shallow depression. He then examined the weapon to see its properties:

Unnamed Glaive: Naginata (36-48)
+20% slashing damage
EverSharp (Blade does not dull)

Do you wish to name this weapon now? (Y/N)

Gus almost hit yes, then thought better of it. For some odd reason, the name Razorback just didn't seem an appropriate fit. What if the weapon evolved like Nick, and no longer was 'Razorback?' He could always name the weapon later.

Gus wanted to practice some swings and attacks, but the walkway and handrails would get in the way, so he made his way out of the Foundry. The cramped nature of the walkway made him realize that he would need an alternative secondary weapon for close quarter fighting. Hopefully, he wouldn't need it for this upcoming fight with the zombies, but nothing ever tended to go the way he had planned.

Gus thought he must have been imagining it, but it felt like the weapon 'clicked' into place when he picked it up by both grips. That feeling of excess energy welled up again, similar to when he woke in the morning. "Let's see how this bad boy performs," Gus said, heading out of the manor for the jungle.

Activating **Dash**, he sped along the path and in no time was by the scene of his last battle with the Mantids. The remains were even more decayed than the Shamblers', despite being killed more recently. Perhaps the Shamblers' constitution boost extended to their entire body make-up.

Gus tried to familiarize himself with the new weapon. It had a longer reach than other spears he had used, as well as having a long cutting edge instead of just a sharp pointed tip. The feel of the naginata was different enough that Gus began to doubt his choice of running out with a new weapon. Even though he had trained with a naginata, it hadn't been *this* one. *Think and stop being so impulsive for once!*

He almost turned back but decided that he would proceed cautiously and retreat if needed, fleeing to safety. He proceeded forward in small spurts, then stopped and listened for the telltale forest silence that warned of Dark Nth nearby. After traveling another mile, he finally noticed the change he was expecting. All went quiet, and Gus stopped dashing altogether and crept warily, listening for movement in the foliage. Finally relaxing to breathe, Gus tentatively cut a large frond away from the path then listened to see if the noise would trigger a zombie attack. Nothing happened. He tried again, then paused. Again nothing. He was ready to retreat, but straining all his perception filters and listening, he noticed nothing besides the preternatural silence.

Gus, you're being stupid, head back.

But he continued on, for some reason. He felt compelled to explore just a bit farther.

Don't worry, you'll be fine.

After thirty minutes of this, he became bolder in his movements and cleared the path more regularly, taking long pauses between hacking plants to listen for enemies.

When the attack finally happened, Gus was totally caught off guard. A Shambler trudged forward, carrying something that resembled a bluish mass covered in tiny eyes surrounding a bowling-ball-sized eye in the center. The blob looked totally boneless and the eyes, facing in a multitude of directions, abruptly twitched, rotated, and all began looking at Gus.

"Dag yo! That's flipping gross!" Gus said, staring in equal

parts disgust and morbid curiosity. **Wreck-ognize** activated just as Mantids began to drop from the canopy. *Thwok!* Two landed on either side of the Shambler. *Thwok!* Gus heard one dropping behind him. Gus dismissed the message without reading to face the threat.

Damn, damn, damn! Gus' eyes flitted everywhere as red dots began appearing all around him. Off to the sides of the path, similar noises betrayed that there were Mantids all around him. Gus felt a jolt of adrenaline and he started to panic. He had obviously underestimated these zombies! Gus activated **Dash**, moving away from the eyeball and retreating along the path. As he pulled away, he swore he could feel the impulse to come back to stare at the creature just a little bit more.

His **TimeSight** let him see the Mantid blocking the path was preparing to leap and attack. Mid-dash, Gus jumped and met the attack with a **Parry** and **Counter-attack** to the Mantid's gut. Putting his weight into the attack as gravity carried them down, Gus shoved the glaive laterally and severed the Mantid's spine. The Mantid hit the ground and began scrambling with its foreclaws like someone who had fallen through the ice on a lake, trying to pull itself to safety, entrails spilling as it crawled along.

Spinning, Gus jabbed the polearm at the base of the skull and the Mantid sprawled out in death. Gus began dashing in earnest when another Mantid dropped right in front of him, tilting its head and letting a spine-chilling open mandible hiss inches from Gus' face. Jumping backward, Gus saw the talon pass right in front of his eyes as he instinctually activated his **Dodge** skill. Momentarily startled, Gus almost missed the chance to counter-attack.

Gus punched the Mantid on the forehead by reflex with one fist and activated **Wreck-luse**, then continued his flight. He scrambled to regain the proper grip, realizing letting go of his weapon was not the best idea during a battle, even if he was using an ability. He had wanted to save that skill for a clutch situation, but with the mob of zombies on his tail, he had no time to allow them to catch up with him and overwhelm him.

Why didn't I prepare some fight playlists in case this happened?! Gus thought in his frenzy. Gus scoured his memory with songs with fighting themes but his mind was unfocused from the stress of trying to escape. Finally, he had two songs and yelled, "Nick! Play Kung-Fu Fighting by Carl Douglas, then Fight for your Right by Beastie Boys."

You have created a song chain! (Barely)
Success with activities related to musical themes increased by a factorial multiplier based on the quantity of songs in series.

Kung-Fu Fighting by Carl Douglas. Success rates x 1. (Chain anchor, no bonus)

Thanks to him dashing, ***TimeSight*** let Gus sense the next Mantid before it dropped onto the path and Gus attacked. While the Mantids were still fast, his recent boost to agility gave him just enough speed to keep up with the talon swipes and feints. Almost.

The Mantid made a swipe with a talon, and Gus raised his weapon to block, when the Mantid pushed, knocking Gus onto his back. The rabid mob leaped on top of him, talons clacking. Gus held up the metal band on the shaft and caught both the clawed appendages as they pressed down, reaching for his throat. The Mantid clenched, locking the weapon in place as it pressed with more and more pressure.

Gus was in an awkward position and it was difficult to bench press the monster up and away from him. Despite his efforts, the tips of the talons kept coming closer and closer. Gus shook sweat away as he fought, and could see the other Mantids approaching in his peripheral vision.

Fight for your Right by Beastie Boys. Success rates x 2.

With the opening 'yeaaah!' and guitar strum, Gus felt a surge of strength and the tug-of-war that he was losing shifted direction. Getting enough leverage after extending his arms a bit, he twisted and hit the Mantid with the butt of the shaft and knocked it off of him. He got to his feet and managed to parry one attack, then two, and finally landed the counter on the third parry, killing it as other Mantids kept attacking relentlessly, giving him no time to regroup or catch his breath, his stamina dropping precipitously, already sapped from the recent struggle.

Wreck-tums! activated sometime in the flurry of attacks and Gus managed to kill one more Mantid, but there were just too many. They harried him, toying with him, secure in their superior numbers. Tiring him out, which was evident in the slowing and increasing inaccuracy of Gus' parrys, none of them managing to trigger a counter.

Exhausted, Gus stood over the dead Mantid and raised his eyes wearily as he saw at least a dozen forms converge on him from the forest path beyond. "That's it..." Gus said. "So close, but like always, it's never enough," He had only managed to kill two. A chime notified him that **Wreck-luse** had leveled up, so Gus took one last peek at his logs.

Skill upgraded: Wreck-luse (Level 2)
Current level: +10% chance to trigger during a successful attack.
You can now trigger **Wreck-luse** *at a distance of 6 feet, not needing direct contact.*
50 XP awarded
100 FP awarded

You have defeated a Mantid (Level 12) 1200 XP awarded, 600 FP awarded
You have defeated a Mantid (Level 12) 1200 XP awarded, 600 FP awarded
You have defeated a Mantid (Level 13) 1600 XP awarded, 800 FP awarded

LEVEL UP! Congratulations, Level 10 reached!
6000 XP to level 11
500 FP awarded

Know this: Functionality of your Song-chain subskill of Wreck-ord has been modified! For levels 10-19 multiplier has been reduced to a geometric progression. Each successive song will add 2x multiplier to effects. Cooldown extended to 12 hours. Keep on rockin'!

What Gus had experienced when he was running at his fastest was nothing compared to what happened next. There was a bright flash and time stood still. He felt his body slowly float and his back arched as he was lifted a foot above the ground. His left arm jerked out to the side as a beam of light shone out of his watch, forming an oval window to the side of his body. A familiar voice he couldn't quite place emanated from the watch:

Requirements met...
Dimensional unfolding progressing...
Fractal unfolding level one...

Gus felt an intense compression as if he were suddenly deep underwater. It was intensely uncomfortable, but when he couldn't expand his lungs to catch a breath, he began to panic. He gasped and flailed his arms as he was suspended in the air, staring the whole time at the Mantids frozen around him.

What is happening!? Suddenly the sensation reversed, and he felt stretched. No. Stretched was too mild a way to describe what Gus was feeling. Being rent asunder was too mild. Every layer of him felt like it was being ripped one from the other.

It was an incredibly focused type of pain, like when a nose hair was pulled—only magnified to every part of his body, external and internal. Tears squeezed out of Gus' eyes as he let out a guttural scream that he couldn't stop. The pain went on and on, intensifying then waning slightly, only to increase with more fury.

Time seemed to move even more slowly and Gus caught fleeting glimpses of the Mantids still frozen in place as he briefly stopped screaming to pull in a ragged breath.

It feels like an eternity, how can they still be frozen? At long last, it was over, and Gus hung there in a daze, throat raw, staring in mute wonder at his changed body; his arms had become larger and more defined, his shoulders widened, and his chest expanded and became more solid. A glowing light enveloped him and suddenly he was... *more.*

Simultaneously, Gus felt heat build up inside of him. He winced as the heat became acutely painful, then relaxed as it began to subside. Turning, he saw the Mantids frozen mid-step. No, not exactly frozen, but moving incredibly slowly.

Nick's voice spoke, "Assembling Nanobot Interface Construct."

"Reviewing a suitable framework based on scan history and personal preferences..." Nick continued. Gus felt a pang of loss, knowing this Nick would soon be gone.

"Evaluation complete, assessing suitable mentor frame-work..." Nick said then hesitated, British accent melting away. "Secondary nanobot interface construct will be patterned after *everyone's favorite anti-hero!*" a snarky voice exulted.

"Next evolution set at level twenty, just in case you're bad at math and couldn't figure that out."

"Huh?!" Gus asked incredulously.

"Hey, it's weird for me too, ok?" Nick's new voice said. "I'm used to *having* voices in my head, not being one. I like what you're doing with the music, but you know you don't have to use the word 'fight' in the song title to make that skill work, right? I added some songs to your playlist. Ready?" the new Nick quipped.

"Ready for wha—" Gus started to ask as time snapped back to normal.

X Gonna Give it to Ya by DMX. Success rates x 6.

"Now *THAT'S* a fight song," Nick said, pleased with himself.

Gus felt suffused with power from whatever happened at level ten. He knew he was outnumbered and outclassed, but if he was going to go out, he was doing this one solid. He spun his naginata around him in an impromptu kata and then attacked. He dashed forward, smashing the face of one of the Mantids with his shaft's metal band, knocking it backward in surprise. A chime rang:

Skill unlocked: **Bash (Level 1)**
(5 x n)% chance of staggering and briefly stunning a foe.
100 XP awarded
200 FP awarded
5600 XP to level 11

Gus spun, burying his blade in a Mantid's neck, then activated **Dodge** and backflipped away before the Mantids closed in on his previous position. A neck slice hobbled three of the Mantids now facing away from him. By instinct, Gus stabbed one of the Mantids and stomped the other's head simultaneously. Unlike the Shamblers, this one's head popped quite easily. Possibly since these were agility based Dark Nth, instead of constitution-based. Getting back to business, a new song started. Gus continued to fight but found no openings and defended against the attacks as they came.

Thunderstruck by AC/DC. Success rates x 24.

Gus activated **Bash** and dashed toward another Mantid. This time the head popped from the impact and Gus dodged to the left, avoiding an attack from behind that he sensed from a **TimeSight**-assisted perception boost. "My own little spider-sense! That **TimeSight** is pretty versatile!" Gus cheered.

Gus dashed back, picked a target, then alternated stabbing and using **Bash** as the skill refreshed. He was concerned that the weapon would break in two as the naginata cracked into their hard bodies, but Gus gained confidence as it held. The new skill's only downfall was that he had to be so close to trigger the ability. Still, it stunned them enough to give him time to dance out of reach and attack unhindered.

Grabbing the weapon from a fallen Mantid's head, he launched it at another Mantid, burying it to the hilt in its neck. Gus grimaced. *Stupid! Never throw your weapon away!* The Mantids shook briefly and stood still. After five seconds, the remaining Mantids retreated to the trees and fled. Gus blinked as they disappeared back into the jungle. He quickly recovered the thrown weapon. He had gotten too much into the thrill of battle and reacted on impulse. He resumed a fighting pose while staring at the jungle. *Is this some kind of a trap? It feels like these things are getting smarter, and I don't like it!*

Turning, Gus noticed one of the blueish creatures placed within a recess of a dead tree. Gus hadn't noticed it on his exploration into the jungle. He once again became transfixed, unable to turn away from the eye-studded blob.

"And we didn't even make it to '9 to 5' in the playlist," Nick whined.

Gus was ready to chase the zombies into the forest, but thought better of it, not wanting to get caught in another ambush.

But you chased them off this time, why not?

"GUS!" Nick yelled.

Gus shook his head, realizing he was standing a mere arm's length from the blob. *When did that happen?* He quickly stabbed the blob, easily popping it, and he felt a dreamlike torpor evaporate.

You have defeated an Observer (Level 12)
300 XP awarded
600 FP awarded

"Hello, McFly? Are you back with us?"

"Yeah, what *was* that?"

"Look at your logs, dummy! That mob was influencing you the whole battle. You weren't listening to any of my suggestions to make a hasty retreat. Let's get back to the manor, that was too close," Nick gasped in exasperation, "...kids these days..."

Heading back down the path, Gus felt awkward and a little dazed from the mind control. To break the uncomfortable silence from Nick, he decided to get to know the new persona.

"So why was this persona chosen, Nick?"

"First of all, you're welcome for the playlist suggestions, it's kind of a thing when I fight too. Second of all, why am I here? You need to come into your own. You consider yourself an outcast, well welcome to the club, buddy! Most people do. So let's put on our big girl panties and get to work. Sound good?"

Gus decidedly did not like the tough love approach, because it reminded him a bit too much of his father. He remembered what the previous Nick had said about the persona giving him what he needed, he opted to hold judgment—and his tongue. At least for now.

Gus headed back to the manor; he needed to shower and clean off the splattered remains of the battle. Checking his stats, he was surprised at how the format had changed.

Gus Vannett
Level 10
Agility: 25
Constitution: 26 (25+1)
Charisma: 18
Strength: 25
Perception: 26
Intelligence: 26
Luck: 27
Fractal core: Level 1
Skills unlocked with Fractal Level 1:
Master of Tasks (Level 1)

Enhanced ability to mimic and adopt physical skills by observation.
T-Wrecks (Level 1)
Summon a dinosaur familiar with (100 x summoner level) HP
MP: 100 MP
Cooldown: 8 hours
Wrecks and Parks
Deals (100 x skill level) HP worth of damage on a target up to 20 feet
away, then freezes the target in place for (20 x skill level) seconds

Gus was stunned at the massive increase in his stats as well as impressive new skills that would really make a difference in future conflicts. Finally, he had some options for ranged attacks! **Wreck-luse** was ranged now too, but six feet wasn't much.

"B-T-dubbs, you probably want to evolve those Nth sometime soon. Just so you don't die and all," Nick said, interrupting Gus' train of thought.

He opened the interface and saw a number of options and skills that evolved Nth could provide. Reluctantly, Gus skipped over numerous incredible options until he ended up on Energy Absorption. He made the selection, expecting a jolt of pain or some dramatic change. He opened his eyes that he had inadvertently closed in anticipation of some punishment. "Well, that was anticlimactic."

Gus waited another minute for the bomb to fall, but nothing happened. "Nick, did it work?"

"Yeah, boss, Nth are upgrading right now as planned. You're golden." Gus was wiped for the day. Whatever happened with the dimensional folding or whatever had wrung him out of the usual buzz he normally felt after leveling.

Glancing up to his display, he saw that he had seven days and eighteen minutes remaining. It ticked off a couple more seconds, then winked out. Gus' knees became loose, and he sunk to one knee, relieved of the psychological weight. *I'm going to live!* He smiled inwardly to be free of the burden of the oppressive timer.

Then it winked back into existence.

"Nick…" Gus drawled. "What is *that* doing here again?"

"The countdown timer has been recalibrated for the imminent volcanic eruption, of course."

A litany of curses flew out of Gus' mouth in response.

"Tsk, tsk, Gus, that's not very PG-13. What would your mother say?" Nick said in a saccharine tone. Gus glared upward, pinching his mouth shut. His nostrils flared as he tried to calm himself down. When he trusted himself not to go off the handle again, he changed the subject.

"Nick, what happened out there with the watch? What did you do? Why didn't you tell me about the dimensional folding that triggered when I hit level ten? You have got to stop keeping things from me!" Gus managed to say, punctuating each word of his last sentence in a staccato rhythm.

"That had nothing to do with Nth, buddy. I was surprised as you because that dimensional folding stuff is some far out sh—"

"Let's keep it PG-13, alright?" he quipped, taking advantage of his turn to be smarmy.

"Oh, I see, you prefer my comic-book persona versus my movie persona? I wouldn't have guessed. Fine. Remember that talk you had with the old me about fractals? Yeah, I don't either. I think it was edited out. BOOOring! I'm not going to go into all of that, but the TL;DR version is that high, I mean *HIGH*-level supers can gain the ability to fold dimensions in relation to themselves.

"They can change their appearance and smuggle weapons past all kinds of security checks. Very handy. Pocket dimensions are great, but they don't work with biological matter very well, as they are entropy-filled vacuums. It takes someone with mad skillz manipulating ether and folding it around to hide mass, especially organic mass that is part of a living being.

"That's why they use fractals, because they maintain potentially infinite surface area but don't close off the fold into a pocket dimension completely. A closed pocket dimension usually results in a pretty quick death of any living tissue. Try it on some fruit. You'll find it tastes off, kind of like when you freeze something then thaw it and try to eat it. Something changes when life is cut off from a connection to our universe. Anyway, bro, you're more than meets the eye." Nick finished the last sentence in a robotic autotune-voice.

"So the watch and all the dimensional folding had nothing to do with you?"

"No, but I need one of those watches. At least when I become corporeal. The old gent didn't talk about that, did he?"

"You can get a body?"

"Well, not until you have leveled enough. Since your Nth evolved—options are open now. I'll need your help though. I'm sure the manor provides the materials for your Nth to synthesize polymorphic dupes. Not many places can synthesize Nth, but I know this one can! Make enough, and I can get out of your head! Well, I'll still be in your head, but it'll be good. I'll even assist in fights. You can be like my Robin!"

Gus shook his head trying to take in all that had happened. The levels, the transformation, the new Nick, it was too much all at once... fortunately it was all good stuff for a change. His mother's warning to always keep his watch with him was more than just a sentimental wish. What did that mean?

CHAPTER TWENTY-NINE

Float On

DAY 7 1:54 PM

3:09:16 remaining

Gus finished trudging back to the manor. The day had taken its toll on him, and now he had an even shorter deadline. He just felt weary to his core, wrung out completely. He was still processing what had happened. His whole life he had felt like some insignificant dweeb, and nothing until the crash had showed him anything different. People treated him a certain way, and he felt ever insecure because he knew his life was lack-luster and unimpressive.

But there was a part of him that had always hoped things were different, and made him special somehow. Whatever had happened at level ten showed that he was actually right in thinking he was unique. Part of him refused to believe it. The other part chided him on wasting so much time feeling sorry for himself. *Am I really destined for great things?* For some reason it felt much more foreboding than enlightening. That his burden had increased, now that he wasn't just the recipient of some lucky accident.

He was set apart. And not knowing for what tickled a part of his brain that made him restless and uncomfortable. A pressing urgency, more than his deadlines, prodded him on. He had to get better, as soon as possible. Moving past simple existence and survival to actually doing something with his life. Gus almost swooned as he was hit with a wave of fatigue, distracting him from his musings.

"Oooh. What is happening? Aren't my Nth supposed to be absorbing energy now and helping me not be tired?"

"Give them a bit, some things take a little time, Mr. Microwave-burrito-mentality, they're repairing a ton of stuff after you Hulked out back there."

The more he travelled down the path, his drowsiness faded, but he still felt oppressively weak. Physical training was probably out, but he still felt a little restless. No more wasted time.

His brain was foggy, and it was hard to focus on anything complicated. He decided that he should try to level **Basic Flight** at least once before the day ended, and cycle through his MP as much as possible. While he could hover for only three seconds before he had to stop and wait for his MP pool to refill, it was actually soothing to float for a bit. He would take a step and the momentum of his walk would carry him as he drifted down the path. Even the bottoms of Gus' feet hurt as if bruised. Everything ached, and it was not wearing off as quickly as it usually did. Just before exiting the jungle it finally chimed a level increase.

You have leveled up the skill: **Basic Flight to Level 3!**
50 XP awarded
100 FP awarded

When he arrived at his suite, he took off his boots and gave his tired feet a rest. Sitting on the ground, he activated **Basic Flight** and due to his recent leveling event found he could hover now for five seconds. When he attempted to hover over to the table where he had placed various fruits in a bowl, he found that he couldn't last a second when he tried maintaining a hover and moving. If he was already moving, he could drift, but no flying from a standstill. *Damn. Doesn't look like I'm flying anytime soon.*

Deciding to be patient, Gus positioned himself in front of the big panoramic view of the ocean along the side of the suite. Opening the window, he let the evening breeze blow into the room past him as he stared out toward the sea and practiced. The soothing crash of the waves calmed him, and Gus let go of his problems.

Now that he had passed level ten and his Nth had evolved, he had a new lease on life. The guillotine above his neck was gone. Well, one of its blades was gone. He still had to figure out how to manage the volcano situation, but today had been a good day.

The warm breeze blowing past him seemed to carry away the embers of worry and stress that had been burning inside, without him being aware of how they were affecting him deep down. Their insidious damage was now able to heal as Gus relaxed and just focused on floating and breathing.

The tension he didn't know he was carrying reluctantly released. His muscles were tentative at first, protective, but as he let himself be held aloft, they finally accepted the support the ether was providing. As he floated, he recalled that same sensation so long ago when he was floating in his space suit in the sea. Maybe it was the sedatives, but Gus remembered being totally relaxed. Gus opened himself up to that same level of relaxation and a chime sounded.

You have leveled up the skill: **Basic Flight to Level 4!**
50 XP awarded
100 FP awarded

Gus blinked away the log and regained his center. It was

easier to maintain the skill when you didn't try to make it happen. Like the difference between a back float and treading water. Both would keep you above the surface, but one took a lot of energy and was unsustainable for long periods of time.

Slowly, he drifted from an upright position and fell prone, supported by a cushion of air and ether. Gus' eyes grew heavy and he closed them. Handing his subconscious the reins, he fell asleep. Gus didn't float there the whole night, but he did hover an inch above the plush carpet for much longer than any of his previous attempts. Eventually, the effect faded and he gently settled into the soft material for the night.

Gus awoke early in the morning, a cool breeze brushing his skin, and a beam of light from the morning sunrise playing across his eyelids. His old friend the blue countdown timer greeted him. Gus waved it away in irritation, then closed his eyes again. Though he slept on the floor, Gus felt better than ever. Such a change from the torture of yesterday. Gus cracked his eyes open from where he lay on the floor. From this vantage, he was looking directly at the forgotten scored panel that he had carved so long ago to make Razorback. He had tossed it on the floor when he was reloading his backpack for his survey of the coastline.

Picking it up with new-found awe, he wondered how else the material could be used. *Armor?* There wasn't a lot of it here, though. It might be better to level up the Foundry first and unlock some better armor blueprints first. That reminded him that the Foundry should be done making everything he had queued by now. Nick cleared an imaginary throat but Gus ignored him. He could sense the virtual eye-roll.

Taking the plate with him, he would leave it in the control room until he figured out exactly how to use it. He did not want to incorporate the Kroutonium into an item that he would quickly outgrow, essentially wasting the precious material. He could repurpose it then, but the possibility of losing a key perk existed, as well as any levels the item had developed. *I'll think of a good use for you.*

Gus arrived at the Foundry and, like before, lights directed him to a different area to gather his armor pieces. Trying them on, he found them extremely lightweight. Almost to the point where he doubted they would be that durable. From their weight, they felt like they were made out of compressed polystyrene. When he placed them in the appropriate places, they formed some kind of tight weld with the suit. The outer surface was rough and ribbed, like a sandpaper coated rasp. Running a finger along his cuirass, he could feel the rough surface catch and pull on the fabric of his gloves. With the armor in place, Gus decided to do some training and come back for the sensors and turrets later. A thought came to him.

"Nick, can you quantify how much a stat change gives me?" Gus inquired, realizing this could save him a lot of experimentation.

"I mean I *can*, but—"

"Great! I want you to measure the changes in my skills after this training session and compare it to the logs of my previous fights. Damage dealt, attack speed, recovery rates, that sort of stuff. Then compare them on a chart based on my level of the appropriate stat."

"As you wish, master..." Nick said flatly, yawning with affected boredom.

Gus arrived and stood on the skill scanner, wondering what was in store for today. While the mainframe analyzed and processed all the changes to his skills and his new weapon, Gus practiced some of his attacks. The balance of the naginata was superb. Gus smiled, realizing that he would not have even been able to notice this about a weapon mere days ago. Swinging around, he practiced chaining some of the skills together in different ways. Gus was impressed with how his increases in agility and the improved weapon quality translated into a tighter, more focused movement. The scan complete, Gus received a prompt:

Quest Granted: Kata Chameleon

Quest Conditions:
1) Master the three katas in the allotted time
2) Use kata forms to defend and attack against 3 attackers
Quest Rewards*: 500 XP, 300 FP, skill increase*
Time Requirements: 3 hours
Do you want to accept this quest? (Y/N)

Once the quest was accepted, Chop Chop came to life and began the lesson, showing some complicated katas to start. After watching it demonstrated, Gus dove in and thought, *What a difference a day makes!*

Despite the complexity of movement, the forms were easier to learn than expected. Much easier. Gus began to see how each movement set up for another attack, much better than what he had been improvising. Gus felt the corrective coldness the tingle provided on a rarer and rarer basis. In less than an hour, Gus had finished all three katas. He checked his agility stat, twenty-five, which was more than triple what it had been when he had arrived on the island.

A cadre of Mantid pillowbots lined up to attack him. When they began to move, Gus started the dance of the spear. *Dance of the polearm?* Using the katas, Gus could set himself up much more easily to both attack and defend, leaving himself less exposed and over-extended. He wished he had learned this earlier on, but his agility probably wouldn't have allowed this level of grace and speed. As he flowed and moved, Gus could discern patterns in the Mantid's movements, and it became more intuitive which forms to employ to be set up for an attack or parry. He even thought he could understand a bit better how he could incorporate jumps and leaps in his attacks, like the Mantids were wont to do, both to attack and to retreat. Gus was stymied on how he was able to absorb the training today so easily. Was his bump in agility responsible? Maybe intelligence played a part. Didn't this type of muscle memory and training require years to learn? As he mused a chime sounded.

You have leveled up the skill: **Master of Tasks to Level 2!**
200 XP awarded
400 FP awarded

Gus had forgotten about the passive Master of Tasks bonus skill from reaching fractal level 1. The description said something about how it would make his training much easier, augmenting his high agility and improving muscle memory, but he hadn't realized the effects would be so... immediate. Combining its effect with the katas had made today's training a whole different experience, and would be invaluable with the inevitable enemies he would have to deal with.

In practically no time, Gus had mortally wounded all the pillowbots, ending in a deep crouch, spear braced on his shoulder. The lights dimmed and he was finished, without even being winded by the whole training. He *loved* these katas! Avoiding another significant beating like the pillowbot had given him just yesterday was impressive alone. The ding sounded announcing the fruits of his labor:

Quest Complete: Kata Chameleon
Quest Rewards: *500 XP, 300 FP*

Gus stopped by the suite to grab the tactical backpack, then headed to the Foundry to get the scanning pylons. Each one was the same size as a beefy thermos, which Gus stuffed into the backpack. He was only able to fit eight inside. He carried the remaining four in his arms, carrying the new naginata in the crook of his hands until he got to the forest's edge and dropped three of the sensors.

"Dag yo! Real life has worse inventory problems than Fallout 76!" Gus complained. Not wanting to be without a weapon, Gus held the naginata in his left, dominant hand, and a sensor in his right. He dashed in two-hundred-fifty feet, then moved off the path to the left ten feet.

Since the sensors had a scanning diameter of two-hundred-fifty feet, he wanted to place them as tactically as possible to get maximum coverage with their scanning radius. He was tired of being surprised. And lured into traps. And volcanos, but that's another story. Since the forest quickly got difficult to penetrate farther away from the path, he was confident that at least initially he would not need to monitor areas too deep in the dense undergrowth.

"Nick, can you place markers indicating the optimal placement of these?"

Orange plumes of light appeared on his display. Gus easily found the first recommended site. Placing the first sensor on the ground, he pressed the button on the top. Something shot out from the bottom of the device, anchoring it, and the top telescoped into a metal cylinder the thickness of a broom handle. Gus could see the reflective mesh panels on the sides of the device that collected solar energy to power it. After a few seconds, a red light on the top winked green, which indicated it was activated and synced with the manor.

Gus returned to the path and continued on, alternating to the right this time and placing another sensor. After placing the third, he retrieved the other sensors from the forest entry and continued placing the remainder of the sensors ever farther down the path. Occasionally he had to move a bit because of thick roots, or being in the center of a dense clump of plants. He would also have to see if he could make or access some sort of device that could give him some feedback with these new sensors.

"Um, boss? Why don't you just have it update the minimap? I'm all for maximum effort though, so if you really want to get your crafting on, it's all good."

Gus facepalmed. *Keep it simple, stupid.* He zoomed out and found that he could see much more all around the entire manor. Fortunately, only the jungle had the fog of war; everything else was visible from the beach to the large hill the manor was embedded into. The coastline also had much better resolution, especially in the last part of his survey. Evaluating his results, he contemplated placing some sensors in the more sparse forest to the south of the manor where he first approached.

From where Gus ended less than half a mile away from the forest entry, he could see that he had vastly underestimated the number of sensors necessary to blanket the path. Standing where he finished, Gus listened to the trill of birds and the chittering of some kind of frog, or was that a monkey? As he worked, Gus composed three fight song playlists, not wanting to get caught flat-footed again.

"You *could* put some more 80's songs in there, you know," Nick offered.

"I think I'm fine, thanks."

"Suit yourself," Nick said petulantly.

Gus vowed that if the animals ever got quiet again, he was not venturing any farther. He had forgotten how many sensors could be made per hour. If possible, he wanted to get some of the remaining sensors in place before it got too dark.

"Nick, can you figure out how many more sensors I'll need to cover the entire path?"

"I gave you too much credit with the math thing earlier, didn't I?" Nick snapped.

"Just do it."

"Twenty-six in intelligence, going to waste..." Nick muttered.

After all the sensors were in place, he would place the turrets. The plan was to give him a comfortable zone where he could retreat and the turrets could cover him while he made it to safety. He urgently wanted those turrets, but he needed to know what was happening so he could plan his responses, in case the Dark Nth made a move. They were already demonstrating that they were more organized than a bunch of hungry, mindless creatures.

Unseen on a high branch, another blob-like creature sat observing Gus as he retreated down the path. After the defeat yesterday, Methiochos pulled his troops back instead of letting them be sacrificed unnecessarily. The attacks made when the

Dark was in control had been uncoordinated and weak. Methiochos was a general and the past attacks without a strategy galled him.

If the invader hadn't interrupted his Mantids in the process of organizing his next attack, his forces wouldn't have been routed. To effectively plan his attack, Methiochos needed to see whom he was dealing with, and how they fought in battle. He would place observers all along the path in strategic places. Because their amped stat was intelligence, they could create fields around them that masked their presence, and the unnerving effects other Dark Nth radiated that set wildlife on edge. They could even influence the unprepared. The tradeoff was that their agility and strength were reduced to almost zero, losing all capacity to move, save for the ability to rotate the many eyes that studded their jiggly hide. Once they were in position, they could transmit what they saw to Methiochos and also to the other Dark Nth, vastly aiding in ambushes and attacks.

The observers also liked to mentally share their information with each other, and collaborated much as they had done in their lives before, when they were scientists and researchers, though this life was forgotten. They would observe this intruder and their council would mentally convene and analyze. This was the type of puzzle they loved to solve. Tactics and strategy, what a wonderful game! As long as they were safe and protected, the self-appointed kings would direct the pawns and rooks, bishops and knights to defeating their enemy.

CHAPTER THIRTY

The Riddle

DAY 8 2:54 PM

2:09:16 remaining

Gus headed back to the Foundry, and looked up how many sensors could be made at one time. It turned out the number was twenty, and the bundle would take an hour to finish. To cover the entire path, Nick recommended he would need sixty-three sensors total. He added them to the queue again. The sensors seemed to not require any of the energy consumption from the manor, which was nice, considering it was a limited resource. It was just before noon, so he could get some more sensors placed before it got too late. A brief glance at his watch told him there was time to finish today. He paused, making a mental note to examine his watch at greater length.

In the meantime, Gus went to the beach and practiced **Basic Flight**. It was probably an influence of the Nth, but Gus felt compelled to be constantly busy, not wasting any of his time without developing something.

The feel of what he needed to do was becoming familiar, but he had to get in the repetition to reinforce it and level the skill. As he practiced, he saw a squadron of six drones fly out over the water. They had a net stretched between them. They got in position and skittered around the water for a bit. After hovering in one spot for a while, they suddenly burst up in the air. Raising up, they drifted closer, creating a basket out of the net. Gus saw they had caught six fish. They sped back to the manor with their prize. Gus' mouth began to water a bit at the thought of a real dinner instead of protein bars. Not having to work for a couple hours to fish and cook wasn't bad either.

Besides the distraction of the fishing drones, it was difficult to concentrate on flying. Gus' mind would wander to every possible subject. He wondered how much time was left in the queue, what recipe the bots would use on the fish, or recall a certain stage of his katas, and the ability would wink away. He wondered if this would ever become an unconscious ability that didn't require so much of his mental real estate.

"Good things are seldom cheap, and cheap things are seldom good…" Nick said.

Gus mentally agreed and set again to forcing out distractions. As he did, his mind started to wander, again, this time thinking about the palm frond weaving he had done when first on the island. Playing with this idea, he thought about the fish net and his mind began to weave the pulls of ether and fashioned them into a small basket of sorts, and then interposed this basket under himself.

Suddenly, Gus had to exert no effort to maintain hovering in place two feet above the ground. Twisting, he spun around in place like a child in a bucket swing, fully supported in midair. A chime sounded:

You have just upgraded the skill Basket Weaving into Ether Weaving!
Ether Weaving (Level 1)
You can manipulate refined matter to access basic translocation effects. Weaves must be unraveled to remove effects.

*Requirements: 50 MP/second during weaving. Stable effects require no MP
to maintain.*
100 XP awarded
200 FP awarded
You have leveled up the skill: **Basic Flight to Level 5!**
50 XP awarded
100 FP awarded

"Wow. I think that one deserves an achievement to pop or
something. You're probably one of the only humans to actually
use basket weaving for something useful. I guess aside from
people who need baskets, that is," Nick said.

"I'm as surprised as you!" Gus replied, swinging suspended
in the air, twisting in place and enjoying the feeling of free floating. When Gus attempted an ether pull, he thought he would
move in that direction, but instead he swung like a pendulum
just as if he were doing something similar in a real swing.

Gus looked above to see if he could see anything mysteri-
ously supporting him above. He could not visualize the ether far
away from him, but tendrils seemed to extend upward in that
direction. Gus tried to pull himself straight upward, in an
attempt to get closer to the anchor point and see if he could
influence it to move, but could not achieve a sufficient vertical
movement to get close enough to visualize anything.

Gus tried different tethering methods. The first using two
tendrils to pull himself in a specific direction and hold himself
there. Another using two lateral tendrils to swing in a wide arc.
Another at off angles to pull himself into a spin by pulsing how
he pulled on each tether.

"It's time to check on the sensors, if you want to finish
placing them today," Nick advised. Gus had been so engrossed
in playing around with how the tendrils moved that he had lost
track of time. Mentally envisioning his basket, he placed virtual
fingers between the folds in the center and pressed outward,
undoing the overlaps and folds of ether until he dropped to the
soft sand.

Gus headed back to the Foundry and found he had the same problem with figuring out how to carry all the sensors. "How did I forget to deal with this?! I *just* had this issue!"

Gus tried his basket idea again, making it larger and deeper. Loading the sensors inside, he found the square shape made them easy to stack and he fit all of them inside. He found he could attach the basket's focus point to his spear and move the whole basket instead of having it be attached to a fixed point.

Using the naginata, he directed the large load through doorways and out of the manor. He felt like a mime, since the basket was only visible in his display as a transparent construct. He continued the task of placing sensors.

During the mindless task, he questioned Nick if he had any more ideas about his transformation at level ten, but Nick had nothing more that would illuminate what had happened. A stat boost of ten per stat except twenty for luck was *huge!*

"Nick, I remember you mentioning something about luck a while back, could you explain a bit more?" He grunted a bit as he wiggled a sensor past some roots and vegetation until it drove a spike into the ground, securing it.

"Gus, big explanations aren't really my jam. I differ from the old man in that way, but I guess I can give it a go. But I'm only going to explain this once, so pay attention. Got it?"

"Sure, shoot," Gus agreed, sitting back on his heels to listen without distraction.

"Ok, I'm going to ask you a riddle. What loses its head in the morning and gains it again after it gets dark?"

"Hmm, a flower?" Gus guessed.

"No," Nick said without emotion.

"Give me a hint."

"That's not how riddles work, Gus. You have to work it out in your mind. I can answer yes and no, but I'm not going to give you the answer. Trust me, it's much more gratifying when you figure it out yourself."

"Is it something that's alive?" Gus moved down the path to find another sensor site.

"This isn't twenty questions, Gus!" Nick taunted, obviously enjoying Gus' difficulty.

"The sun?"

"Nope."

"Hmm, some kind of animal?" Gus asked hopefully.

Nick just remained silent. Gus' mind kept returning to think of different kinds of flowers, that maybe opened their petals when the sun came out and then curled up again after it went down.

"So what are you thinking right now?"

"I can't stop thinking about flowers."

"Exactly! That's precisely how the luck stat works." Nick finished grandly, as if he had just elucidated the world's biggest mystery.

"Huh? That makes no sense at all."

"Well, despite years of Nth trying to influence human culture, they couldn't remove the superstition related to luck from the collective consciousness. So we modified part of the interpretation of luck and applied it to useful metrics."

"So what's up with the riddle?" Gus wondered aloud.

"You know how once you started thinking about a single thing, your mind kept wanting to go there, even though you knew it wasn't the right answer?"

"Yeah."

"Well, in a similar way, most humans have a certain expectation about reality and what can and should happen. Some people are positive, some negative. By and large, this belief influences what *actually* happens in reality. There are a lot of possibilities that can happen with your choices. Will things turn out? Or fail? Utilizing this aspect humans consider luck, one can *actively* select a future reality that is more pleasant.

"This control over quantum chance is not something that Nth can control or augment. Just because someone has a great capability to change their reality does not mean they automatically will. And often due to their emotions, people with great capacity squander this ability. There are vast shifts in probabilities as optimism and hope or pessimism and despair increase or reduce which reality actually comes into existence.

"So I could be a lot more lucky than my stats say I am," Gus said with excitement.

"That's not what I said. It's not the size of your luck, it's what you do with it."

"That's what—"

"No, it's not. It's never what anyone says, and you know it. I will say that ether can be influenced by thought. Just as ether is a form of matter that humans can't physically measure yet, thought is a form of energy that hasn't been detected and quantified as an energy source among humans. It functions in the same way electricity powers all sorts of electronics. Thought energy can be used in a variety of ways by a trained mind. Humans actually have been using it for centuries before Nth even appeared to influence humankind. Stew on that for a while and surprise me, kid." Nick's tone indicated he was done discussing the subject.

Gus' thoughts kept returning to the unlikely probabilities that made it possible for him to reach the island, the concentration of coincidences that aligned so that he could be where he was, doing what he was doing. Was that his doing? Or someone elses?

He wondered if being unconscious was crucial so he wouldn't sabotage himself. Deep down at his core, he knew he had always wanted to have powers and to be accepted by his family. He hated admitting that, but it was true. The desire to show his father and brother that he wasn't just a waste of space was there, always lurking in the shadows. Until Gus' powers had arrived, he had never thought about consciously changing his destiny. The old adage, be careful what you wish for, was apparently true. His father's words reverberated in his mind. *Think what you've always thought and you'll get what you've always got.*

Gus got a mental break as he saw he was nearing the end of his supply of sensors. The path widened as the jungle canopy retreated. At the end of the path, a large mountain extended up from the canopy and Gus could see it was the foot of the volcano. The hardened magma had split in two, resembling the Scream mask as a cave entrance yawned into the darkness.

Gus felt uneasy being this close to the cave opening, and the likely lair of the zombies. There were still a few birds and other jungle sounds, but a trickle of sweat rolled down his back and he licked his lips at the sight of it. Trying to make as little noise as possible, Gus finished pressing the top of the last sensor and made his way back down the trail. He ran all the way back, spamming **Dash** once he was far enough away not to make too much noise.

CHAPTER THIRTY-ONE

Doomsday

DAY 9 7:39 AM

1:15:31 remaining

Gus awoke with a start, feeling a growing sensation of dread. Checking his minimap he saw nothing wrong, although he noticed he could change the scale by a factor of two times and three times magnification.

Did I have a nightmare? He took some deep breaths to slow his racing heart. His display also had a new tab that allowed him to highlight things in motion, probably due to his recent jump in perception stats on hitting level ten. That definitely would be helpful to notice things skulking in the jungle, and enemies trying to flank him. With that and the assistance of the scanning pylons increasing the feedback he had, it would be much more difficult for them to take him by surprise. He berated himself once again for not taking the time to figure out how his stat increases affected his abilities.

Focusing again, the minimap zoomed out, the map

shrinking to show more of an overview look. He saw a flickering band of color on the edge of the far reaches of the minimap. Zooming in on this section, he saw multiple dots; yellow, orange and red. So many colors were overlapping that the minimap was solid in some areas. All moving toward the manor from the west. Gus scrambled to get some water and scarf an energy bar —it was going to be a long day. Bursting into the Foundry, he ran down to where finished items were dispensed. The turrets resembled huge footballs with a ring stand. Retractable spikes could be extended from the ring to anchor them.

The upper half of the football appeared to be able to rotate three-hundred-sixty degrees to engage enemies from any direction. Gus froze for a second, trying to figure out how to move the bulky contraptions. Using an ether weave again, he fashioned a smaller basket as he had the day before with higher sides and placed the first turret inside.

It worked! The weave stretched a little and seemed to accommodate the shape of the turret. Encouraged, Gus made five similar cradles out of ether. With a little experimentation, he found that he could move the focus where the basket hung by attaching it to another ether leash. He made short lines and tied the leashes to the blade guard on his naginata and pulled them carefully up and out of the Foundry. Hurrying as fast as he could, he agonized at the time it took to navigate doorways, manage the elevator, and make it outside.

Gus feared damaging the turrets as they clanged against each other like large metal balloons. They also made a loud obnoxious hollow gong noise that got old all too quick when they drifted and hit each other.

Gus racked his brain to decide where the best place would be to station the turrets. As a defense in front of the manor? At the edge of the forest? Spread throughout the trail? He worried if he scattered them, they would be too easy to overwhelm and destroy. He decided to place them as far into the forest as he could manage, all together so that they would protect each other. Checking his display, he estimated that he could make it about a third of the way down the trail, near where he was ambushed before. He hoped he had time to set everything up.

Exiting the manor at last, he attempted a short dash. The cacophony of clanging turrets hitting each other stopped him from making another attempt. He ran as fast as he could, removing the leashes from the naginata and holding three tethers in each hand in an attempt to fan them out and keep them from slamming together. This didn't work as well as he thought, until he came upon the idea of connecting them in a long centipede-esque train. The resulting silence was a balm on his weary ears. He found with this configuration he could even use **Dash** again. Constantly checking his minimap, he rapidly approached where he would make his stand.

He was grateful he had the foresight of clearing out the encroaching foliage from the path or he could have been caught up multiple times on his flight. At last, he was there and he began removing the turrets and setting them up, fumbling a bit in his haste. One in the middle of the trail, two more ahead and to the side. Gus spread the turrets six feet apart. He ended up with two staggered rows, hoping the close proximity would allow the turrets to protect each other.

Gus activated the first one; three anchors shot into the ground and secured it. A small display was visible on a tiny panel, along with a red light that winked to green, just as the sensors had. Once green, Gus was accepted as a friendly, and using the display, he dragged a box to designate the attack zone for the turrets.

They would target anything entering that zone, and numerous multicolored lights were fast approaching the area on the minimap. Confirming his choice, the turrets spun to life. Out of the top of the football, two panels slid down, revealing two gun barrels. Everything was happening too fast. He needed more time! Gus wondered what kind of ammunition the turrets used, and how long they would last in the coming onslaught.

Gus again tried to strategize where he would best be placed in relation to the turrets to maximize his efficacy. Was behind better, letting the turrets do most of the work, then he could support them if one, in particular, was attacked? Or was it better to be in front, since the turrets recognized him as friendly and he could take down the less dangerous Shamblers so ammunition would not be wasted on them?

"Nick, can you configure the turrets to aim at heads only and not waste ammunition on other body parts?"

"On it…" Nick said dutifully, "…and done."

"What about selectively focusing on Mantids unless there are Shamblers that get within a certain distance, say, ten feet?"

"Easy peasy."

Gus decided he would head forward, keeping his minimap at its widest scan range. That was probably how the Mantids ambushed him that one time; they circled around from outside the range of his minimap, and then closed in until it was too late. There was a large contingent of yellow dots leading the pack mixed with other colors. He decided to thin the herd a bit and make a calculated retreat to the turrets. He dashed forward and saw the first of the Shamblers, ordering Nick to start one of his fight playlists.

Ass Kicker's Haircut by The Saturday Knights.
Success Rates x 1. (Chain anchor, no bonus)

Gus readied his spear and decapitated two of the lead Shamblers. He spun and thrust into the eye of another. Taking a step back, he repositioned using *Sweep the Leg* on another. "Cobra Kai style!" Gus yelled, sinking the spear into the eye of the downed zombie.

Gus wished he could have squeezed in another training session. He used this new weapon like his old spears, but those techniques ignored the large blade edge fashioned from Razorback. Even still, he felt like he was really getting into the flow of fighting with polearms. The katas made a big difference in positioning and firing some of his counter skills and activated more chain attacks. Oddly, the majority of these first line attackers were Shamblers.

The naginata hummed as it cut through the zombies' flesh with ease. Gus caught a twitch from his perception and noticed Mantids in the trees. He backed up closer to the turrets to get a little coverage behind him.

Bad Seed Rising by Bad Seed Rising. Success Rates x 2. Damage doubled.

Gus stabbed another zombie and felt the jolt of *Wreck-tums* activate. He spun into a **Chained Attack,** decapitating a Mantid in midair. As he fought, he still could manage the Mantids and Shamblers without too much difficulty, thanks to the turrets assisting him. There were just so many! He saw the Mantids spreading out, avoiding the turrets by leaping from tree to tree. They were trying to disable the turrets from behind while they were focused on the oncoming horde!

Gus triggered a *Basic Flight* and jumped to clear the turrets, interposing himself between the eight Mantids approaching from the rear. This many opponents was a different level of challenge, and more than once his new armor stopped a stray talon that made it past his defenses. Gus was a blur of motion, but he had definitely shifted to the defensive. The turrets were tasked to only attack the area in front of them, and Gus' attention was so focused he couldn't access the controls to widen the kill zone.

"Nick! Adjust the second row of turrets to attack this direction!" Gus grunted as he turned a parry into a riposte as his attacker became open.

Hero by The Verve Pipe. Success Rates x 6. Damage increased.

The Mantids were definitely fighting with much more coordination. It was all he could do to maintain attacking, blocking and retreating without letting the Mantids chase him away from the turrets. They fell back as three of the turrets rotated and began peppering them with projectiles. While they were distracted, Gus tried one of his new abilities. He hurried to activate **Wrecks and Parks**. One of the Mantids froze in the air, reminding Gus of a Matrix scene, with it suspended in an attack pose.

The ability was cheap and apparently had no cooldown so he 'parked' three more Mantids. The turrets shredded them to pieces as they were hanging there. He noticed a blue pulse flicker above him when firing **Wrecks and Parks**. He looked up and saw one of the blue creatures that resembled a poop emoji with too many eyes wedged in the nook of a tree. The stupid thing was directing the other Mantids and could sense his powers, the little jerk!

Gus would get to it later. With the herd thinned, he was able to take out two of the remaining attackers. They viciously protected their frozen allies, apparently unaware that they were dead. Or maybe they did and wanted to have the brains readily available to boost any lost HP.

Another chain combo later, the two active Mantids were down, and Gus attacked one of the remaining frozen ones, lopping off its head. Grinning evilly, Gus threw the severed head at the little blue Peeping Tom. Direct hit! With no appendages, it couldn't dodge or move out of the way and it was pushed off of its roost. The squelch as it hit the ground and popped was very satisfying.

Berzerk by Eminem. Success Rates x 24. Damage increased.

Turning around, Gus was shocked to see the carnage that had been delivered while his back was turned. Zombies crawled over piles of bodies, only to become part of the growing mountain as they were picked off by the turrets. The Mantids were better at dodging, but it was difficult for them to dodge every turret. Some stopped to crack open the skulls of fallen Dark Nth and gorged on the neural tissue inside.

Gus wasn't sure if it was some form of psychological warfare tactic, but man… it was incredibly unsettling. The growing pile of bodies allowed the Mantids a higher ground advantage, and Gus moved between the two rows of turrets and sliced at the creatures as they leaped toward him. It was difficult to score kill shots from this angle, but he saw that if he could at least wing them sufficiently, the turrets would do the rest since the Mantids could not flee and their unnatural speed was curtailed by a significant enough wound.

Mr. Hurricane by Beast. Success Rates x 120. Damage increased. Recovery accelerated.

Gus wanted to try firing **T-Wrecks** but he had dipped below 100 MP. He would have liked to see a large dinosaur tear through this mass of enemies. He felt his stamina waning after what felt like constant fighting. It wasn't like the movies, where one guy held off hundreds of ninja warriors, polite enough to attack one at a time. Fighting multiple creatures at a time was *tiring!* The minimap was swathed in color far down the path. *What is happening?*

He retreated behind the turrets to catch his breath. Gus noticed that the green, blue and red bars were refilling at an accelerated rate. He wondered if the labs in the manor could develop some kind of stamina, MP, or HP potion analog. *No use in getting distracted about it now, but man, it would have made a big difference.*

On and on they came, throwing themselves forward, mostly Shamblers now, sacrificing themselves to the turrets. Probably to soak up all the bullets and leave the way clear for the more effective soldiers in the zombie army. Gus wondered why, if they always had this many Dark Nth, they didn't attack all at once.

Before he could work out an answer, all of a sudden, the horde retreated a bit, keeping behind the barrier of bodies, unreachable by the turrets. Even the Mantids in the trees jumped down and hid behind the large mound. Gus did not like what was happening and retreated a bit, unsure what was planned next.

From what Gus could see of the crowd of Dark Nth, they parted to the sides of the path to make way for *something*. It didn't take long to find out what. Large creatures, riddled with muscles, stepped forward through the breach. Their shoulder muscles were grotesquely large and extended up to the sides of their heads, making their whole frame adopt a chevron shape.

"Were those shoulder or neck muscles? How did they even develop like that?" Gus wondered.

Bands of sinew and muscle shone through in torn patches where their growth overtook the skin's capacity to hold it, and Gus could see the tell-tale iridescence of Nth-embedded tissue when the light caught it just right. Gus dashed and triggered **Slide**, gliding quickly toward the huge creature; he chopped upward with the naginata as he got next to it, but instead of the blade slicing neatly through, it was like chopping into a piece of wood. The blade stuck in place.

A huge hand grasped him at his upper back, holding him like a cat by the scruff. Pulling him upward, the giant muscled creature looked at Gus, and he saw a huge dinner plate sized fist punch him square in the face, just as Gus activated **Dodge**. It mitigated some of the damage, but he still absorbed the majority of the force, and it rocked his head as he flew backward.

Darkness set in and Gus was bobbing in and out of consciousness. He began to hear shots, first sporadic as his awareness faded in and out, then more continuous. Gus struggled to regain his senses, but it felt like he was at the bottom of a very deep swimming pool, struggling to swim upward. He would make some progress then would nod off, sinking back into the deep.

Shaking himself to action and struggling to regain his full senses, almost swooning into total unconsciousness. Finally, Gus managed to break through. Opening his eyes and gasping, Gus saw that he lay crumpled amid the turrets. The turrets fired constantly, burning through their ammunition and targeting multiple zombies. Had they not been there, Gus would have been overrun. He noticed with horror that no music was playing. He had lost his song-chain with the hit, and all of its buffs with it.

The turrets were extremely efficient, and the bodies of two of the huge hulks were lying there, large holes chewed through the head and shoulders. Other Shamblers had formed a mound that deflected the other zombies toward the sides. These mounds were starting to get bulldozed away by a second wave of the Juggernauts.

One behemoth pushed forward; its tiny eyes puckered by the bulges of muscle surrounding it. The stare bored into Gus, ordering him to stay there and die. Gus crab-walked backward, slipping and scuttling between the remaining turrets, trying to escape. The large creature interposed its arms in front of its face, forearms acting as literal meat shields, and the turret fire ricocheted off or thudded into them, doing no real damage. A large backhand launched one of the turrets into another before flying off into the jungle.

Gus activated **Wreck-luse**, and the Juggernaut let out a huge bellow. For a second, Gus thought it was a critical failure, but the creature did an about face and barreled through the other creatures, back up the path. All the remaining zombies made way for its wild retreat, with only a few Shamblers too slow to get out of the way and getting flung to the side of the trail as they were tackled by their teammate. A furrow appeared as the zombie plowed through the carnage, rapidly filled with other assorted zombies.

Gus saw his naginata lying there, just a couple feet in front of the turrets, sticking out from underneath a fallen Juggernaut. With the distraction of the fleeing Juggernaut, Gus had just enough time to run forward and grab ahold of the weapon. It took a couple good pulls, all the while another one of the hulks bore down on him, with outstretched hands ready to grab and crush him, or pull him in two. Finally, he pulled it out, his momentum spilling him backward ass over teakettle.

The Dark Nth were close now and as Gus lay on his back, he heard the turrets start to sputter. Whether from running out of ammo or being overwhelmed by the sheer press of bodies, the sound made him panic. The heady scent of rotting flesh made his stomach roil as they came closer and closer. Gus jumped to his feet and swung the naginata around him, trying to make some space from the encircling horde. **Wreck-tums** triggered again and Gus pushed his way out of the gang of zombies in the direction of the weakened opponent, and broke through to freedom. From there he dashed away, not stopping until his stamina and MP were in the red and he was far away.

CHAPTER THIRTY-TWO

My Own Worst Enemy

DAY 9 9:39 AM

1:15:31 remaining

Gus made it to the edge of the clearing, dodging trees in his reckless flight from the zombies. After a bit, he checked his minimap and saw that he was no longer being pursued. He finally allowed himself to stop and collapsed on the ground, his stamina bar exhausted. Just like his very first battle on the island, once he was out of the way, the zombies marched to their goal. Checking his minimap, he saw that the yellow, orange and red dots had continued to pour out of the forest and were everywhere. A pop-up on his display showed that all of his turrets were out of ammunition or inoperable. There was nothing to stop them.

The horde appeared to be congregating near the front entry in a more and more concentrated mass. With so many zombies milling about he would not be able to enter the manor again, and even if he kited them away bit by bit, he doubted he could clear enough of them to get in before the volcano erupted. If Gus never saw another countdown again it would be too soon.

The sheer quantities of mobs made him wonder how there could be so many. There were a couple hundred zombies of different types, probably much more than that, counting those that continued to trickle out of the forest.

Feeling discouraged at his failure, it weighed heavily on him. Then it hit him almost as a wave and he slumped to the ground, leaning back against a tree. How could he have ever thought that he could take on such a teeming mass of deadly creatures? Why did he let himself hope that this time would be different? He felt a familiar despair seep into his core, sapping his hope and motivation. It was like the color was draining out of his world. He cupped his hands over his face, rubbing his eyes as he contemplated what had happened. His father's words haunted him: *Never engage a superior force…*

Even with the Nth, he was still Gus, and somehow life seemed to find a way to ruin things. Couldn't fate finally give him a break? It was so much crueler to dangle the potential of having powers and the manor's capabilities in front of him and, just when he felt he was getting a handle on things, snatch them away. Different emotions battled within him; anger, despair, and sadness, swirling around like waves tossed in a storm. Sadness prevailed though, and Gus could feel the depression swallow him.

They were right. All the people who didn't believe in him were right all along. He had overreached his station. He didn't have what it took to get rid of the Dark Nth and escape the island. The corrupted Nth would eventually find a way in and infect the A.I. and system there. After that, who knew? Turn off the bio-stasis field and infect the world? Gus found it harder to care about the future. Maybe it was for the best that the volcano was going to go off, at least it might prevent the Dark Nth from leaving the island.

"Gus, what are you going to do?" Nick asked quietly.

"I don't know. It probably doesn't even matter now; I blew

it. Just another failure in the life of Gus T. Vannett! I can't get into the manor anymore with all those zombies in the way, but I guess none of that matters because pretty soon the volcano will do its thing and we'll all be dead."

"So that's it, you're done?"

"Might as well be. My father called it. I really am a failure. He must have seen it in me, and I stubbornly refused to believe it. I don't know why, after having so many examples of it blatantly shoved in my face. I really, *really*, wanted him to be wrong. To come back and show him, '*See?* All those years you doubted and underestimated me. No matter how you have chosen to see me, I don't accept your judgment and pity.'"

"Wow. Ok, Gus, I'm sure I'm not the first to tell you to suck it up. But think about how I see things. I've always been an outcast. And I'm great with that. Sometimes I don't play well with others, but I walk my own path—" Nick started to say.

"Yeah, but you do realize that you're not really—" Gus interjected.

"Let me finish! I'm not as patient as the old man, so I'm going to tell you how it is.

"Do you realize how we Nth see things? This construct frames my whole reality, all thanks to you. I am acutely aware of everything that has been recorded about this construct, and it is boiled down into little old me. It *IS* my reality. But let's talk about *you* for a moment. Who are *you*, Gus? Are you a good guy? A bad guy? An anti-hero? Who are you going to be when everything shakes down?"

"Obviously, I'm good—"

"That remains to be seen. It doesn't matter how powerful you get, Gus, life scales in difficulty to match your abilities. Whether you are a super *or* a reg. There's never going to be a magic time when everything is easy and happy. There's always going to be something or someone to blame for your troubles, too. One of my primary purposes and drives is to help you succeed. Are you a quitter?"

Gus pursed his lips closed, not wanting to hear this. Not now. He woodenly shook his head no.

"This way you deal with problems is *not* helping you at all. Running from difficult things never allows you to get past them. Life has a funny way of providing you a different way to learn a lesson if you refuse to learn it the first time. So doesn't it make more sense in the long run to not just *endure* your struggles but *overcome* them?"

"How long do I have to maintain these futile efforts? I'm doubting that I have what it takes to be a super. Even after all I've been through, I've essentially accomplished nothing," Gus said dejectedly.

"You like to think that you're unique in your suffering, but whether you have an interface or not, you need to 'level up' in life. Especially when you don't get positive feedback like XP. More often than not, you'll find that the harder you try to do something good and worthwhile, people will criticize you and curse your name. It's not fair, but people rarely get what they deserve—good or bad. That's why you have to step up, my friend. You can make the difference. But you have to change your perspective. It's all wrong. If you're 'obviously' a good guy, that's what you've signed up for, warts and all."

"Yeah, but—" Gus tried to argue, but Nick forged on.

"Have you ever stopped to think you're not entitled to succeed at everything you do? That's not how things work in the real world. Even with your luck stat being so high. It's probably more of a danger to you now in your current pessimistic state than you can possibly know.

"*YOU* are your own worst enemy. Not your dad, not the system, not anyone. You influence the course of your life by the choices you make. I know part of you doesn't want to accept that, but it is true. You have to stop blaming people, fate, or anyone else for your situation. It's stunting your progress. That is what we Nth have found to make all sentient creatures their happiest. When they are progressing in a path they have chosen."

Gus slumped at the tirade. "Nick, I'm tired of being blamed for all the bad things in the world as if they happened because of me. Regardless of how you say luck works. It's hard to rebound after being smacked down time and again." Gus spat.

"I wish there was a stat for willpower or grit. Something that was measurable that humans could work on to level and improve. That's what seems to separate those who succeed from the 'also-rans.' Don't quit now because you've encountered an obstacle, however insurmountable you currently think it to be. Adapt. Evolve. Overcome. Find your potential and surpass even that. I am on your side." Nick emphasized the last sentence with a gravity out of character for him. This iteration of him, at least.

Gus sat there silently. Nick had kicked out the crutches he had used for so long, and hit him hard with a truth bomb. He couldn't even come up with a valid comeback; all his justifications and excuses seemed hollow and weak. He had not really made any plans as to what he would do if he got back to civilization, other than a vague 'I'll show them all!'

The pressing nature of multiple crises was enough to occupy his whole thought process when he wasn't striving to level some skill, mostly for the thrill of leveling, not to become someone who could actually do something for the world. But isn't that what he always did? Ignore his problems, especially ones involving his inner feelings, when things became too intense. Find a distraction, and use it as a coping mechanism. He resolved to make some changes as Nick finished.

"Figure out who you really are, and what you aspire to be. Forget all your issues, whatever they may be. They occupy far too much of your self-concept, and perceived value. Every species the Nth has ever worked with have family drama. It is universal in any social creature. Are you going to step up and do something about it? Are you a whiner or a winner? A victim or a victor? How much time have you wasted by doing something you didn't really like, with the hope that someone would think differently of you?" Nick exacted, the question not a rhetorical one by his tone.

Gus thought about his ex-girlfriend and all the things she cajoled him to do and he didn't have the balls to resist. He thought of all the jobs he had taken, even being a henchman in the first place, in the vain attempt that his dad would see his resolve and give him the acceptance he felt he deserved. When it came down to it, he had been living a pseudo-life. And he realized that was part of the reason he was so angry. That the people who shaped his life knew so little about him and weren't shaping it to his tastes.

The unpleasant truth of his passive acceptance of this became blatantly clear as well, and the blame rested on *him*, not them. They wanted what they thought was best for him, and since he didn't voice his feelings, they continued behaving as they always did. Encouragement being perceived as nagging. Suggestions perceived as judgments and criticism of his failures.

"Too many," Gus admitted quietly, "but hopefully less, from now on," his voice becoming more determined.

Gus struggled to let go of the feelings of blame and victimization, but it was so hard! They were like comfortable blankets that protected him from the cold truth of responsibility. They gave him an excuse to stay the same as he always was, and justified him when something came a little too close for comfort.

Giving him just enough plausibility to remain in the status quo, changing little and staying unhappy. Not being able to precisely diagnose his own discomfort with life, but knowing that it was not one he had chosen, and cycling through depression, anger, and sadness at how the world had misjudged him.

"Gus, you're the only one who can do anything about this situation. There's no one else to save you. No safety net to catch you if you make a mistake. So unfortunately, the time for excuses and rationalization is over. So I ask you again, what are you going to do?" Nick asked.

Gus stood and walked toward the clearing. Reaching the forest edge, he looked out and wondered what he could do to turn the tables. From his minimap, the Dark Nth were not entering the manor for some reason. Was the manor keeping them out? He couldn't count on them possibly figuring something out in time. He didn't want them contaminating the A.I. that ran the manor, and what havoc that would cause.

Realizing that he wasn't totally defenseless, Gus muttered, "Nothing's ever easy…"

But this time, a determination showed in his demeanor that had not been there before. It wasn't supposed to be easy. And it never would be. But that didn't mean he wouldn't come out on top. To be the person he imagined himself to be, without all the baggage. Or in spite of his baggage. Gus turned his eyes to the manor and set his jaw. Time to get to work.

CHAPTER THIRTY-THREE

The General

SOMETIME THE PREVIOUS DAY...

Methiochos evaluated what his observers had shown him. To be honest, he was expecting... *more*. He evaluated the last skirmish and ordered his Mantids to retreat when the super demonstrated a unique leveling event, allowing the warrior to fight at a much higher level.

It was unexpected to see the increase in martial ability, but one opponent could be managed. All evidence showed that this invader was all alone. Knowing this enemy a little more made him less impressive in Methiochos' eyes. Observers could analyze and detect the use of skills and could determine stat levels, and his nemesis on the island had shown his hand.

There were powers to be sure, odd ones, but they would not be enough to retain the manor. Manticorps must have suffered immensely from his attempted coup if this was all they could muster. Oddly, they had not taken enough control to access its true power. He suspected that Archon knew what made the manor unique. Unique enough for any of the Factions to war against each other to gain control over it.

Time was still difficult to gauge. How long had he been in stasis? What had Manticorps become in that time? Did it matter? The most likely thought was that the interloper was Manticorps' emissary. Had the intruder found it already? If so, then Methiochos had already lost. But if he hadn't, there could be a way to finally overcome the Dark Nth.

Methiochos mentally congratulated himself for deciding to go with the sequential unlocking format for the manor instead of having everything readily available. Initially, he had done it to encourage those he had brought to do their best work, and he would reward them for their diligence by providing benefits and perks that the manor had to offer. Luxury on an island paradise. After their work was done, of course.

That dream was gone now, thanks to some traitor. He would need to clarify his memories by meditating and absorbing more energy, then he could remember who it was. The desire to know burned deep within and drove him to get back to full strength. With each session of meditation, he found that he was regaining both his prior stats, as well as his powers. The many years of hibernation had allowed everything to atrophy. But he would never be unprepared or blindsided again. There was always someone looking for something easy to gain from someone else's work. Just like this invader. *Never again.*

He made plans to end this at their next battle. Methiochos organized his attack methodically. He would use a large phalanx of his infantry to tax the resources of the enemy. Once sufficiently weakened, he would send in his assassins to further harry the super. Then his gladiators would finish him as the other troops surrounded him, cutting off all retreat. With the nuisance dealt with, he could establish contact with the manor. Methiochos knew that if he could access level twenty-three of the manor, there was a chance he could cleanse the taint of the Dark and regain himself.

His army would have to be dealt with before then; the Dark had fully taken them and there was nothing left to save. He could turn them on each other when that time came. They were already willing to consume their fallen; it would be a small step to compel them to attack one another. It would be a shame to lose them, but he would have time once he cleansed himself. He would send them to secure the entrance and after he had regained his full powers, he would at long last leave this tomb of a cave. *Soon.*

Methiochos once again was disturbed by the betrayal that led to him becoming this *thing*. He looked at his ever-expanding body, transformed into what could be best described as a centaur with his lower torso resembling an octopus instead of a horse. He had many more tendrils than eight though, of varying thicknesses and lengths. It was fascinating and repulsive at the same time. A physical embodiment of his power to ensnare and control others.

Someone he had trusted had done this to him. He still did not know who the instigator was; that part of the past was still confusing and out of his grasp. He was glad he had not lost all of himself going into his hibernation; it was a close thing. With his preparations made, Methiochos allowed the tendrils to sink into the magma and he faded back into his memories.

CHAPTER THIRTY-FOUR

Rocky Mountain High

DAY 9 9:59 AM

1:15:11 remaining

Gus looked at himself and it was rough. His newly fabricated armor, despite being durable and functional, was gouged and worn. Much as he hated to do it, he needed to use the Kroutonium for armor. Gus figured that he would need to get into the manor, maybe make some armor of some sort out of the remaining Kroutonium plate and come up with a plan on how to get rid of the Dark Nth. He looked up at the tall building, from the edge of the same field where he saw it for the first time. That seemed like ages ago.

Gus tried to suss out how he could get back into the manor. There were probably multiple ways to enter located around the island, but he hadn't anticipated losing access. You don't know what you don't know, until life hits you with some new problem. Gus hadn't really explored many areas of the manor and the only access to the outside he knew of was from his suite, at the top of the structure. From his hiding spot by the forest edge below, Gus could see the back side of the manor that emerged out of the rock and proceeded upward to the top of the main tower-like structure.

Circling around the field, being careful to stay within the tree line, Gus tried to get a vantage point that would let him plan how he could get up there. He saw that if he could make it to the craggy rock surface above, he could theoretically climb up then across. He would have to circle around since the suite window was on the opposite side of the mountain, facing the ocean. The outer surface of the manor was smooth but if he could use the ledges by the windows as footholds, he hoped he could shimmy around and make it to a balcony and climb up and inside.

Gus hoped he could use **Ether Weaving** to help anchor himself in place and save him in case of falling. He figured he could use his **Basic Flight** skill if there were some short hops between the windows or if he had to climb to another level and there were no handholds. It wasn't a great plan, but it was doable.

However, it seemed like the blob zombies could detect when he activated his skills, and he didn't want to do anything that would make it any easier for the zombies to notice him. He was unsure of their scanning range, but with how adeptly the Mantids moved through the trees, he had no doubt that they could scale the outside of the manor. He wouldn't be able to use his skills as a crutch, and needed to do this on his own as much as possible.

"No safety net indeed," Gus mumbled, remembering Nick's earlier chastisement.

Gus circled farther to the steep cliff that was under the overlook. To the right of the structure, rough igneous rock bulged up and outward like a mushroom cap. The first challenge would be reaching the rock forty feet high, then securing a grip, and climbing upside down over the lip of the rocky bulge to make it on top. Gus had only been rock climbing once or twice on dates, where everything was secure and safe by wearing a harness and having someone below belaying for you.

To be honest, he was never really good at it. The instructor tried to demonstrate some techniques but putting them into practice was a little less intuitive. His arms got tired too fast and he dropped repeatedly off the walls that were studded with grips of various types and colors. He remembered that he was supposed to keep his body as close to the wall as possible, to use his feet to push upward rather than his arms, and to keep his arms straight as possible. There was more, but those were the few pieces of advice he could remember at the moment.

"Time to make the chimi—" Nick said.

Just as Gus said, "Time to make the donuts!"

"Going old school, eh? *I like it!*" Nick exulted.

Gus readied himself for the first part of the plan. If he directed his first **Dash** upward, he found he could run up the rocky cliff wall, but it was hard to go all out with the fear of falling backward if he missed the rocky overhang. Part of his brain rebelled and rejected the idea of running up a wall.

Another problem was that he didn't want to hit the rocky ledge at full speed and knock himself out. Gus found a section of the sheer rock face that had a slight incline that he could slide down if he was short. Attempting a ten-foot dash, he hovered at the apex of the dash and felt the lurch of gravity reasserting itself and he hugged the wall, sliding down. The friction of sliding down the wall slowed him down enough that he didn't hit the ground very hard.

Next was a twenty-foot dash. Gus was more prepared for the sensation, but had dashed straight up and was farther away from the wall than he had expected and panicked for a second, pinwheeling his legs like a cartoon character until he came into contact with the wall and sloppily slid down to the ground again, doing a small roll.

Brushing himself clean, Gus looked back at the cliff face. That time he'd definitely hit harder and had to roll away a bit to bleed off some momentum and spare his poor knees. Gus gave himself a moment to shake out the tension and brace himself for another try. For number three he attempted twenty feet again, but tried to better estimate the angle he would need to stay parallel with the rock face.

Since the dash ability was basically an ether pull, he could direct the vector he travelled if he focused on where he wanted to move. This time he had similar success to his first try. Thirty feet gave him more acceleration by the end of his fall than really felt comfortable and Gus had to roll away again, getting covered in dead leaves and detritus, hitting his head on a small rock as he rolled away. Gus scratched at the itchy painful area on the back of his head. After a couple seconds, the Nth kicked in and removed any inflammation and calmed his pain receptors down.

Gus was at last ready to attempt a full dash that would bring him to the bottom of the rocky overhang. Then the *real* fun would begin. Gus dashed forward and scrambled for purchase but could find no handholds. He began sliding downward, and after ten feet, he tried to dash back up again with a little lateral movement thrown into the push. Gus slid five feet to the left as he again crested up the cliff and was able to secure two handholds. As his momentum petered out again, he felt a sharp jolt to his shoulder sockets as he dropped to supporting himself without assistance.

Gus' increased strength allowed him to pull himself upward but his stamina bar was draining quickly. Gus whipped his leg out onto another rocky protuberance and got his heel anchored there and relieved some of the stress on his arms. Taking a quick breath, Gus pulled and pushed until he could grab two new handholds and was supporting himself by his small foothold. Panting he held there looking for another foothold, his hand patting around the unseen upper edge of the ledge, questing for a handhold. Gus was still fighting gravity by hanging upside down, and realized he had to press on or risk bottoming out his stamina and falling. Losing his progress and hurting himself in the process were good motivators to keep moving.

Gus remembered that he had to rotate his shoulders, not arms, in order to avoid wearing his upper body out. He twisted as he reached for more handholds. Luckily, they were easy to find in the porous rock, but the rock was brutally abrasive and sharp in some areas. Some areas he could fit his fingers in smooth indentations that must have been where there were bubbles when the rock was cooling. They gave him a secure grip while he repositioned and settled his other hand and footholds. Gus reached the lip of the overhang and was at a distinct disadvantage, because he had to remove a hand to quest for another handhold, blind from the lip blocking his view of what was above. He would pat blindly, then have to hurriedly grab back to the handhold until his stamina refilled.

Finally, he found a nice wide groove that he could hang onto with both hands. Gus realized he would have to hook his heel onto another foothold or pull himself up with his arms alone and he was afraid that too much strain would bottom out his stamina mid-attempt, even with his increased strength stats. Gus surged upward with his legs, pulling himself upward, extending his legs to their full length and bracing with one leg secured and one leg to a small recess above the lip.

"Dayum, Dayum, Da-yum!" Gus shouted as he shifted his weight to his upper leg and began trying to pull himself over the edge. Another handhold helped pull enough of his body over the edge that he was supported by the rock, not hanging off of it. A chime sounded as he clung, wrung out on the rocky lip.

You have unlocked the skill: Rock Climbing (Level 1)
Hey, wallcrawler! You are more able to recognize adequate hand and footholds. Level this skill to unlock more functionality.
100 XP awarded

"Really? Now?" Gus panted. "I guess skills are skills…" He realized that there was still a long way to go before reaching his destination. He lay there panting as his stamina bar slowly filled completely. When his heart rate and breathing slowed to a manageable level, he continued on. From atop the overhang, Gus was able to progress with a mixture of an army crawl and rock climbing to continue upward. Ledges and handholds began to show up in the display as red for tiny handholds, orange for medium and yellow for large, easy places to grasp. Following the guided display, he made his way to a flat area atop the outcropping. Sitting down, he let his stamina bar refill, and looked up at the mountain nearby to plan his further ascent.

Luckily, the rise atop the outcropping was gradual and provided multiple larger areas to rest, so he wouldn't be hanging for his life the whole way up. Looking at his hands, he saw that while his gloves were ripped and torn, his fingers weren't bruised or scraped, despite the punishment the initial climb inflicted. Attributing it to Nth assistance, Gus was glad that he wouldn't have to climb on cut, bleeding fingers. This job was difficult enough as it was.

When his stamina bar topped off, he started again. This climb was much easier in comparison, as he was able to simply stand and regain stamina. Gus took a moment to look out at the jungle and forest below as he rose above the canopy. Wisps of smoke were emanating from the volcano now, reminding Gus that the once silent beast was awake now.

From this height, he could see the corner of the lawn and some zombies milling about. He ducked back to face the mountain and kept climbing until he reached the junction where the manor poked out of the rock. There was a sill surrounding the windows and a small two inch ledge that expanded to six inches when in front of one of the large oval windows. Gus was able to grab and transition to the sill and slide to the first window ledge. After sliding to the third window, following the curve of the overlook, he noticed the wind.

Waiting between gusts, Gus timed his movements from window to window when it seemed the calmest. The windows were narrow enough that he could brace himself within with outward pressure, so he was pretty stable while standing directly in front of a window.

The thickness of the divider between each window compartment was only three inches and narrow enough to be gripped and then used as an anchor by his trailing hand as his leading hand crawled across the next window until he could grab the next divider transition. Taking his time, Gus finally made it around the curve of the building to where he saw a familiar view. Looking upward he saw a balcony two stories up. Gus moved until he was in a window recess directly below the balcony. "This one's for all the marbles," Gus said as he prepared himself for one crucial dash. Gus launched himself and caught the edge of the balcony railing. He almost lost his hold with the jolt his already-strained shoulder joints took from the abrupt stop as gravity tried to yank him down after the leap.

Getting a quick heel lock on the edge of the balcony, he pulled himself over the rail to safety. Lying there, he looked to the left and saw his reflection in the dark glass, with the sea behind him. Looking upward, there was no balcony above, but he saw another large structure, octagonal in shape, five stories up. "Always something new about the manor..." Gus panted as he lay there. The cool concrete on his back was nice on his achy muscles, but the naginata he had strung across his back as he climbed was not. Groaning, he rolled over and got to his feet and slid the window open. He thanked his lucky stars that he hadn't had the habit of latching the window shut.

An alarm was sounding as Gus entered the room, and the lights alternated normal illumination with a red flash. Gus quickly changed into a new jumpsuit and picked up his naginata. Running to leave, Gus turned and locked the large sliding window. Now that he was inside, he wanted to be sure nothing could follow him. He looked longingly at the shower but he had no time for that. He had to act quickly before the zombies found a way into the manor.

CHAPTER THIRTY-FIVE

Don't Threaten Me With a Good Time

DAY 9 11:43 AM

1:11:27 remaining

After sprinting up the stairs to the main control room, Gus saw the reason for the alarm. The cameras in the main atrium were focused on the main entry, and the cameras at the main entry just showed a white static. Listening, Gus could hear a loud rhythmic booming echoed every ten seconds.

"What the—" the words dropping off as Gus saw two of the Juggernauts punching the doors in tandem with their enormous fists. Immediately behind them, all sorts of Mantids paced, anxious to make it inside the facility as soon as the smallest breach could be exploited.

Fortunately, the doors were holding, but he could see some significant white discoloration spidering away from the point of impact to the corners of the doors. Right then a small pea-sized piece of glass chipped away and skittered down the entryway.

"Nick, is there any way to reinforce that door?!"

"We could drop the blast doors…"

"Hurry, do it!" Gus yelled.

"Compliance!" A thick metal slab dropped down from the ceiling behind the doors, and an eerie quiet filled the entryway and atrium. Gus doubted the Dark Nth could make their way into the manor through that route, so he flopped down into a chair, shaken by how close a call that had been.

With the blast doors down, the alarms silenced, easing the tension a bit. The lights still pulsed an intermittent red.

"Nick, let me know immediately if any of the zombies move beyond the front doors. I don't want any sneaking in somewhere else."

"Got it," Nick replied, and Gus felt a little more relieved. Only Mantids could climb up to any windows, and they didn't have the strength of the behemoths. If there weren't too many, and he acted quickly, he should be able to hold them off.

Crap. I need to get some defenses in place. Checking his logs, he had 6900 FP to play with, so he began searching the menus to see what he could use. He had also gained some XP from his big battle, but since nothing had leveled, he didn't see the characteristic chimes that urged him to check. He was only 1700 XP from level eleven. He figured he must not have gained any XP from the turret kills, or that number would have been much higher.

"Nick, how many zombies are left out there?"

"Three hundred thirty-one."

Gus blinked; it seemed like there were a lot more. He still had a lot to get rid of, especially the behemoths at the doors. He was unsettled as he accessed the terminal for manor facilities management, and saw that the gold bar representing total energy available for upgrades was much smaller than it was before. Currently he saw basic operations taking up twenty-five units, cafeteria fifteen, training arena seventy-five. He vaguely remembered the bar having 2000 units total, a bit less than a quarter the length of the screen. Now the bar was down to maybe one-fifty points total, and a gauge showed the loss of energy continuing at a slow rate, like a leaky tire.

"Why am I losing energy?" Gus barked.

"Less and less magma is reaching the absorption matrices. This appears to be related to the changes Methiochos made when he first arrived on the island."

Gus growled and tried to come up with a plan, using his FP and energy available. He had found some things, but could tell that it still was incomplete.

He felt a slight tremor and a loud boom outside. Making his way to the smudged windows, he saw that more smoke was roiling out in a large plume from the cinder cone of the volcano. Blacker this time, instead of the gray drizzle it had been. Shaking his head, he went back to the console. After a quick search he found some things he could use but they required Tier 2 of the Foundry. The upgrade was going to be 5000 FP. Wincing at the expense, he unlocked it. There were other goodies he really wanted, but even if he had the FP, he should hold off on them until the power problem was sorted.

Another thirty points of the golden bar were grayed out as more energy was utilized. The gold bar had less than half the available energy remaining. The bar reminded him of a burning fuse on a stick of dynamite. He hoped he could figure out what was happening with the power, whether it was a result of something the zombies were doing, the volcano, or both.

If it got too low, he had no doubt he would lose power to those sections of the manor and they would be inactivated. All the more reason to finish this and see what needed to be done to recalibrate the energy converters that were powering the manor. It was irritating to have yet another problem to deal with, but it didn't bother him as much as it would have before today. Maybe it was because other things were more pressing; he looked again at the countdown. Less than a day and a half. *Get super powers. It'll be fun, right?* Gus sighed and hurried to get the next crucial item on his to-do list: armor.

Gus locked the door to the control room to prevent any Nth

getting inside. He didn't know if it would make any difference, but better not to make it too easy if any got inside. It made him think of any other ways they could infect the manor.

"Nick, can you make steward and any other robots go into a standby mode and hide in storage until we sort the zombies out?"

"Good thinking. You won't be able to access Stuart or any other automated manor systems besides the ones you have unlocked with FP."

"That's fine. It's my next stop."

Gus headed to the Foundry. He checked the screens and tried to enter design mode, but the system apparently had a timeout on how long it retained scans, and he would have to once again stand on the sensor. As he stood to get scanned, the system flashed an alert that there was a hairline fracture down the length of his naginata. Gus was glad that his luck stat was so high or he might have had the weapon splinter in half during a battle. Using Kroutonium only in the blade was a little short-sighted, but he hadn't considered the implications.

A quick check showed minimal time for repairing his naginata. Gus input additional mods for strengthening the shaft. Gus made a core that extended down the entire length of the spear, and connected to the blade. By selecting a reinforcement mod, channels in the core split into a hexagonal meshwork that spread down the shaft, highlighting where the Kroutonium would be placed. Then as the metal was redistributed, the length and width of the blade decreased, but less than Gus expected. The screen directed him to deposit the naginata into a nearby hopper, and a time of one hour with a picture of the weapon showed up in the queue.

Gus swiped through the different types of armor available. Multiple types of items that covered individual parts of the body as well as sets were available, but they had penalties to agility, some severe. Gus needed something that helped with evasion, not slowed him down.

"Gus, would you be open to a suggestion?" Nick asked

tentatively. Thrown off by how different Nick's new persona usually acted, Gus stopped looking at the screen.

"This manor is one of only twenty-six locations worldwide that can synthesize Nth. You now have the ability to make more Nth, which can be utilized in your own body or to create one for me— " Nick started to say.

"Yeah, I remember. Sorry for being selfish; I really should have thought about it more. There's just been so much going on, but that's really no excuse. Here let me see what—"

"Hold on. I have an idea, and just listen to it all before you discount it, can you do that for me?"

"Sure, shoot." Gus cocked his head at Nick's atypical behavior.

"What if you use the remaining Kroutonium to make additional Nth? I could utilize the new Nth and embody it to become a living armor, able to modify according to different needs." Nick suggested.

"You can do that? That sounds awesome!" Gus squinted his eyes knowing that Nick was holding something back. "Wait... what's the catch?"

"There is a little drawback..." Nick said tentatively.

"Spill it."

"Kroutonium is almost always used for weapons and armor. Over the millennia, it has been used like this, then gathered and taken with the Nth if they leave the planet due to an apocalypse event. If you chose to use the Kroutonium to make Nth, it would become part of the Nth as a collective. Forever. It could have large repercussions adding another foreign consciousness in the mix, plus if Earth is lost and I go back to the collective, who knows what happens then? Without a guide, will the consciousness in the Kroutonium take control and a new Nanobot Interface Construct come into being? It could potentially be very bad for the whole cycle and possibly against what the builders intended when they made the Nth." Nick said.

"You're telling me no one in forever has tried this?" Gus said with disbelief.

"Usually most hosts who have access to this amount of Kroutonium are so megalomaniacal that this suggestion would never be considered. I hesitate to even suggest it, but the benefits would be amazing. You would have an armor that would scale with your level, able to be modified on the fly as needed. If the rumors that the quantum server is made out of Kroutonium are true, as well as the rumors that it is unhackable due to its sentience, it could be some of the only armor to withstand a direct Dark Nth attack."

"That seems a little sketchy. You're guessing a lot of that, aren't you?"

"You're right, none of this is tested, so it could offer no protection against the Dark Nth. We could be creating the first Kroutonium-infused Dark Nth if we fail," Nick said ominously.

Overwhelmed, Gus leaned back in his chair and ran his fingers through his hair in indecision.

"I don't know if it's worth the risk. I'm assuming there's no real way to test this beforehand either..."

"No, not really."

Gus was torn again by indecision. He hated how wishy-washy he could be because he was always worried about problems that never happened. *Something has got to change. I can't live in fear forever.* He rubbed his face in his hands and decided.

"You know what? Let's do it. I've lived my life with too much worrying about worst case scenarios, and every time it's been a huge waste of time and a lot of mental anguish playing over the possible bad things that could happen. Bottom line, I can't let these Dark Nth make it off this island. Whether I do or not is immaterial in the long run."

It was discouraging but chances were good he would not make it out of this alive. He would die in ignominy, and no one would ever know that he had become a super or something unique and special when he hit level ten. But with the time limit and the possibility that the volcano erupting would not take out all of the Dark Nth, Gus realized what choice he had to make. While his baser nature wanted to hole up in the manor and hide, and let come what may, he just couldn't bring himself to do it. The world didn't need him any less because it was ignorant of him. And with the bio-stasis field, he was the only one who could.

His gloating seemed so childish now, but it wasn't as important now that everyone knew what he could do. What mattered was what he actually would do. With his new clarity, he replied to Nick.

"I will agree to it if you can put a failsafe that would explode and make us unable to be converted into a Dark Nth. That would keep the Kroutonium out of Dark Nth hands. If the planet goes through an apocalypse event in the future, then it really won't matter to me. It might even help the Nth as a whole evolve more. So, to be clear, you feel you are being hacked or turned, then both of us die immediately. Are you ok with those terms?"

There was a long silence and finally, Nick said, "Yes."

Nick showed Gus the submenus where the Nth modifications and augmentations were stored, and how to program the changes he suggested. He wondered why this menu did not have any cost to unlock. Perhaps they figured in the design that to access the manor, Nth had to be present. Therefore, it wouldn't be a distraction if people used the Foundry to access this functionality.

Nick synced with the control panel, configuring the Nth to be made to link with his consciousness when completed. Gus picked up the unassuming piece of plate from the space suit, took it to the hopper, and put it inside. He thought he would regret using what amounted to a fortune for a handheld weapon and armor, but instead he felt a sense of calm. Of rightness. Within the calm, Gus began to get ideas. Adding some more items to the queue, he began to plan how he would clean up this Dark Nth mess.

"Nick, this whole time I've been here, I've been plagued with carrying things everywhere. Is there some skill or power that will make something like a bag of holding or pocket dimension of some sort? I'm going to need something besides a back-pack for what I've got planned." Gus asked.

"Fiiiiiiinally!" Nick drawled. "How come it took you so long to ask?!" Nick asked. "One of our core protocols restricts revealing certain level information unless it is specifically requested. It was killing me to see you run around like a crazy man, lugging things all over."

"Wait. What?! I didn't have to be carrying those sensors and turrets like I was?" Gus asked.

"You know what the Prime Directive is, right?"

"Like on Star Trek?"

"Yeah. Did I mention Gene got some good ideas from the Nth scouts? Anyway, Nth can't offer some information in an attempt to artificially advance a species. Earthlings have already discovered dimensional folding, but Nth cannot simply give the information until it becomes part of the collective consciousness of the planet's apex lifeforms.

"Besides, you may have not been ready to do what needed to be done to make what you want. We can get started now since we're just waiting for the queue to finish." Nick offered.

Gus bounced his legs in agitation as he sat at the Foundry control center. So much to do, so little time. Gus wanted to hit up another training module, and boost some fighting skills. Maybe that would give him another influx of FP and maybe even a level before confronting the horde. He still felt he had to go back to the main control to see if he could refine the defenses. He was missing something.

"Ok, how much time will that take?"

"It depends, but it isn't complicated. It can be time consuming, depending on how well you learn, though."

"How do I make whatever it is we're making? Something from the Foundry that needs to be unlocked?" Gus sighed, expecting another list of prerequisites before he could begin.

"No. But you'll need a little background so your brain can wrap itself around what needs to be done. Have you ever seen a magician 'disappear' a handkerchief from their hand?"

"Yeah, I think so."

"Typically, they make a show of waving the handkerchief around then cup one hand and start putting the handkerchief in it. The cupped hand has a fake thumb into which the handkerchief is stuffed. For emphasis near the end, the thumb really packs it in there and the fake thumb with the handkerchief inside locks onto the magician's actual thumb. Then, PRESTO! The handkerchief has disappeared."

"Thanks for the entertainment and ruining my sense of childish wonder," Gus snarked.

"I'm getting to the point! Anyway, a pocket dimension can be formed of various sizes and is most easily accomplished by ether folding. You tuck the ether and form a kind of pouch—"

"A seamless pouch?"

"Yeah, I see what you did there. And yes, it IS seamless. Just like those baskets you made, items can be carried without you physically lifting their mass, and their volume can be displaced into the ether. They will remain buoyant there too, like a floating beach ball. The tricky parts are maintaining the opening so you can open and close at will and detaching your pouch from the surrounding ether so that it is portable."

"That does sound complicated."

"You'll get it. Maybe. Ok, let's get started with Trans-dimensional Manipulation 101!"

CHAPTER THIRTY-SIX

Papa's Got a Brand New Bag

DAY 9 12:11 PM

1:10:59 remaining

"Remember that time when you were ten and you tried to blow a bubble out of a full pack of Big League Chew?" Nick asked.

"Vaguely…"

"Well, making a pocket dimension is a lot like that. It's easy to make very tiny ones that have no functionality but as they get bigger, it's a whole lot harder to keep the bubble from popping. If you can get it to the size you want and seal the edges, voila! You have a fully functioning bag of holding. Trust me, it takes a lot of practice, and it's a whole lot harder than it sounds.

"Let's go somewhere open where you have a lot of room to move," Nick suggested. They ended up in the atrium, and Gus' eyes kept drifting to the large bulkhead and the now-muted blows that constantly pealed against it. Blinking and shaking his head, he focused on Nick's explanations.

Nick started to instruct him how pocket dimensions worked,

but Gus was still frazzled and amped up on adrenaline from seeing the Dark Nth almost getting inside, and couldn't concentrate. His mind kept returning to the 'what ifs.' What if the Dark Nth had made it into the manor while he was busy goofing around in the Foundry? What if his preparations took just enough time to allow them to break the door down? *I need to focus and push worry out of my mind,* he told himself.

It was unproductive and he didn't have the time. Gus closed his eyes, taking deep breaths and booting any thoughts from his mind that tried to rile him up or make him worry. After a concerted effort, he could feel the effects of his jittery, agitated state calm and fade. He stopped sweating and the slight tremor in his hands stilled. After five minutes, a chime sounded. Curious, Gus opened his eyes and saw a new skill had unlocked:

Mindfulness (Level 1/42)
You have greater ability to deal with stress and think rationally during a crisis by focusing on the now. Level this skill to better plan and see how to create the future you want.
300 XP awarded
100 FP awarded
1400 XP to level 11

That was a little odd, Gus hadn't seen a skill with a level cap, he just assumed that it would get more and more difficult to increase in levels after a certain time. "Nick, why is the level capped for this skill?"

"Well, from what I can tell, no one has reached the highest level of that particular skill in the history of the Nth. A lot of people guess that it means a type of transcendence or such a deep understanding of fundamental forces that you understand life, the universe, and everything."

That seems familiar for some reason, hmm. But nothing came to Gus. With his mind more centered, he asked Nick to restart his spiel.

"Ok, let's start off small. You know how to shape ether into strands that you weave, right? See if you can use a similar force, but instead of pulling, push using a slight pressure into a sheet of ether, causing it to bulge out. Just like a soap bubble; if you do it too quickly it will pop, too slowly it will collapse. Until you know how to tie off the edge it will collapse anyway, but get a feel for it."

Gus reached out with his hand and could feel something tingle at the very tips of his fingers. It felt like when trying to put two magnets with similar polarities together, and they repelled one another. Moving slowly, Gus could begin to visualize a virtual indentation he was making on his display. Gus had to not only hold his hand still and stable but mentally push MP out of his fingertips to maintain the slowly forming sphere around his hand.

"What's keeping— " Gus started to ask.

"No more questions until you answer that riddle. You've lost your thousand questions privileges. Don't overthink it, most of this is nuance and feel." Gus turned his attention back to the sphere, noticing that his MP gauge was draining at a moderate rate. When the sphere was the size of a beach ball, Gus had difficulty stretching the ether bubble any larger. Holding it in place, he heard a chime.

Ether Warping (Level 1)
Extend a portion of ether into another parallel dimension, creating varying effects depending on design and management of ether constructs.

1000 XP awarded
500 FP awarded
400 XP to level 11

"Whoa! That dropped a lot of XP! Noice!"

"It's a foundational skill for a lot of others, including teleportation, storage, shielding, and stealth. Frankly, I'm surprised you have made a pocket so large. Most supers take years to learn how to make one the size of an orange."

"Really?"

"Yeah, you shouldn't be able to do that as well as you do just yet."

"Maybe it's because I really *am* that awesome…" Gus said, as he took his eyes off the virtual display for just a second. There was a loud pop as the ether bubble collapsed and air ran back into the pocket it had displaced.

"Serves you right. Making the bubble is the easiest part. Then you have to stabilize the edge of the bubble which makes it resistant to collapse. You have to do this quickly, because it requires you to take your attention away from maintaining the bubble's shape and size.

"Kind of like trying to tie a knot in a balloon so the air doesn't gush out. Since you are maintaining the opening, you have to go back and forth, stabilize what I'll call the rim, or lip, of the pocket dimension and then refill the bubble to appropriate size, then stabilize more of the rim until it is fully sealed. Oh, did I mention while you are filling the bubble back up, your work on the rim is unraveling? And you also have to do it all in one shot. The entire thing will unravel if the rim isn't totally tied off and sealed to itself. The tendency of the system is to equilibrate and without that rim locked, your bag will deflate."

"What's the next job after I do the rim, then?" There was a pregnant pause and Gus could tell that Nick was on the verge of dropping a joke that involved the unfortunate combination of the words 'rim' and 'job.' Cutting off any reply, Gus hurriedly amended, "Just tell me what's next…"

"Remember those palm fronds; you are making a braid similar to that, only about a thousand times more complicated. There needs to be stress bearing knots every five weaves or so, like this." Gus saw on his display a complicated movement of ether strands going over and under, then the knot. He'd been a Boy Scout, but this knot was something that would make a hardened sailor whimper. "I know it looks complicated, but the sooner you learn it, the more you can do. Let's get to work."

A while later, Gus had to take a break. The 'simple' knot

was just the first step in an elaborate series of knots that, once completed, would tighten and secure the entire structure, each section supporting the next. His head hurt with the intricate lace-like threading of ether, with its complicated patterns. He made his way to one of the long couches in the atrium and crashed. There were so many new terms as Nick explained the complicated process. He did gain two levels to **Ether Weaving** though, bringing it to three.

"Nick, I need a break…" Gus dropped his focus and watched the small section of his weave unravel, each strand of ether flapping and writhing like an unmanned fire-hose. In a disappointingly short period of time, the entire weave was gone and the bubble deflated back into nothing. A growling stomach urged him to visit the cafeteria, get some more training to finish up the morning, then finish the weaving.

Entering the cafeteria, he was greeted by the Claptrap-esque waiter who acknowledged his presence with a wave of a tiny appendage and disappeared back into the kitchen. Instead of the small robot returning, a large hulking creature with multiple appendages exited the kitchen. Its serial designation of K4-Z was written in blue along its torso, much more noticeable than the other robots.

"Bienvenue to zee master of zee manor!" K4-Z belted out in an exaggerated French accent. "I see zat you now have Energy Absorption, zis is good! I can now prepare infused dishes zat will increase your stats. Instead of only preparing simple food, I can add specialized energy zat your Nth can use."

"Whoa, I was not expecting that. Can you make potions that will raise health or stamina?"

"But of course! You will need to upgrade zee cafeteria with facility points to level two, zough. Zis will also increase zee effects added to meals and zey will last longer. Because zeese drinks all are refined energy, you can only use zem so often, however. You can add more effects in zee lab once you have zat unlocked."

That would be a great addition to his repertoire. Gus had

put many of the manor's facilities on the back burner because he wasn't a scientist, and he didn't think he could get anyone to the island that would have the skills to use it to its full potential. Who knew what he could pick up by trial and error? Maybe he could slowly gain skills like experimentation and research and development, then build upon them. It hadn't occurred to him until just now.

"Let me get you some food." The large robot rotated and returned to the kitchen. While he waited, Gus checked the large backlog of messages that he had neglected since his huge battle in the jungle. He had leveled **Polearms** to six, **Spear Mastery** to six, **Wreck-luse** to level three, increasing the range to fifteen feet. **Sweep the Leg** had leveled to two, and the stun time increased to ten seconds. **Chained Attack** had leveled twice to four. He was just 200 XP away from level eleven, which he could easily make after training. His review was cut short by the waiter bringing a steaming plate of fish with some side that looked like cubed potatoes.

Gus was in heaven after the first bite. It was his first real meal with protein that wasn't cooked over a crude fire and singed at the edges. After savoring the first couple bites, a buff indicator flashed across the display and a countdown timer next to a flexing bicep appeared in the upper left of his display.

+2 strength for 2 hours.

He ate everything, trying not to devour the meal too quickly. Despite it being only one plate, he felt stuffed after eating. Gus wondered if the energy infusion process made the food more filling as well as giving stat increases. Another notice popped as Gus pushed away from the table and reveled in post-feast bliss.

You are Well Fed, increased HP regeneration for 2 hours.

Perfect! He'd have to make sure he ate before training and before fighting the Dark Nth again. He was close enough to another level that he wanted to take out some aggression on some unfortunate pillowbots. His energy had been flagging after the battle and climb, along with the stress of how to protect the manor. After eating, he felt invigorated and his headache had begun to ebb. He was glad for the relief; it was going to be a long day and he had to hurry to get everything done.

CHAPTER THIRTY-SEVEN

I Get By With A Little Help From My Friends

DAY 9 2:01 PM

1:09:09 remaining

Gus excitedly returned to the Foundry and retrieved his finished spear with anticipation. Checking the queue, he noted there was still a little over two hours until the Nth hybrids would be ready. Taking the naginata to the training arena, he stood in the scanner and waited for the computer to analyze him. A ding finally sounded:

Quest Granted: Freak on a Leash
Quest Conditions:
1) Show competence in hitting a target with a spear from over 50 feet
2) Learn the skill **Ether Leash**
Quest Rewards: *500 XP, 300 FP*
Time Requirements: 3 hours
Quest Failure Penalties: Ether Leash skill locked
Do you want to accept this quest? (Y/N)

Gus accepted the quest and instead of seeing Chop Chop, he saw himself on the virtual display. Gus' previous battle footage of throwing his spear was replayed and Chop Chop shook his head and grunted in disapproval.

A target popped up in the distance. The display showed him where to grasp the spear for ideal balance and control when throwing. The spear had a tiny bit of flex in it, and it took a lot of trial and error to improve his aim. Too high and to the left. A slight shift here down and to the right. Too much. And so it went for a while. As the practice became more automatic, Gus started to see improvement.

———

The closest Gus had come to target practice, at least with thrown objects, was playing darts with his buddies after they went to the local pub quiz.

A chime sounded and brought Gus' attention to his practice.

You have leveled up the skill: Polearms to Level 7!
Auto-assist enabled. Can be toggled off/on in the interface.
300 XP awarded
100 FP awarded
LEVEL UP! Congratulations, Level 11 reached!
500 FP awarded
You have (5) additional stat points to assign.
6900 XP to level 12

Taking a break to allocate his points, Gus looked at his stats. He didn't feel a big deficiency anywhere except charisma, and he doubted that would make any difference with the zombies, so he ignored it. He decided on adding two to constitution, two to strength and one to intelligence. He checked his new stat layout.

Gus Vannett
Level 11
Agility: 25
Constitution: 28 (27+1)
Charisma: 18
Strength: 27
Perception: 26
Intelligence: 27
Luck: 27
Fractal core: Level 1
HP: 540
MP: 440
Stamina: 540

Wary of getting hit while fooling around with stat points, Gus focused on the arena again. With the auto-assist enabled, Gus began to see trajectories and angles visible on the display. It was much simpler to consistently hit the center of the target with the assist to help him.

The training had updated at some time and now showed his avatar throwing the spear at the target but always keeping an ether leash threaded to the butt of the spear. After hitting the target, virtual Gus pulled the spear back into his grasp. After three playbacks at different speeds, the virtual display cleared and Gus saw his current position.

Looking at the spear, Gus noticed a small knob at the butt end. Getting ready, he mentally tied an ether weave onto the end of his knob there, and aimed. He threw the spear, but missed the target completely, attention too fixed on the tether. After losing the spear, the tether winked out. Gus tried again, this time weaving three threads into a cord, then attached it to his spear. This tether seemed much more stable. Gus tried again and could focus more on his aim, now that less focus was needed to maintain the tether. The spear hit the outer rim of the target, and Gus was surprised that the tether added no noticeable weight or drag to the spear when thrown. Ether was flipping weird. But he kind of loved it.

Pulling the spear, it plopped out of the target a mere ten feet, due to his hesitation. Gus was afraid of launching his spear toward himself so he pulled with a half-hearted effort. Dragging it back to his grasp he tried again. After pulling a couple times with varying levels of tension, he found the sweet spot so the spear wouldn't fly past him, or approach so fast he was worried of grabbing the blade by mistake.

In no time, the skill became almost second nature, and just like that, Gus had another ranged attack. In addition, he had a way of retrieving his spear if he ever lost it. He had already developed a bad habit of throwing his weapon away; now he could keep it as long as it didn't get stuck into anything. If he had this ability in the last battle, things would have been less dire. He still wouldn't have won, but that was too close a shave after he got separated from his main weapon.

For some reason, the session did not end after a chime and notice indicated he received the ***Ether Leash*** skill. He finished the three-hour practice and the system awarded him his XP and FP rewards. He had hoped to finish early as with other days, but every time one was in a hurry, things seemed to take forever.

CHAPTER THIRTY-EIGHT

Paranoimia

DAY 9 6:14 PM

1:04:56 remaining

The moment of truth with the new hybrid Nth was here. Gus headed back to the Foundry, more eager than scared. If this worked out, there could be some big changes ahead. Following the indicator lights to the conveyor where finished products were delivered, he saw a long flat plastic tray covered with grayish-black dust.

"Big moment Nick, have any final words?" Gus asked.

"No, but my common sense is tingling..." Nick replied.

"That's never stopped us before!" Gus grinned and hit activate on his display controls.

The black and gray grains coalesced together, briefly forming a face contorting in a silent scream. The figure exploded outward, then froze, the jagged edges compressing back into a solid sphere, six inches in diameter. A single string of text froze on the display, with everything else becoming non-responsive.

Uploading...

Gus froze, wondering what had happened. He felt an emptiness and knew that Nick was gone, at least for now. It was like a noise you didn't notice on a conscious level that became apparent when it abruptly stopped.

The silence stretched into an uncomfortable length, and Gus began to pace, cracking his knuckles in worry. Was it supposed to take this long? He doubted he could progress very quickly at all without Nick's assistance. If he had somehow fried his circuits, Gus would have seriously stunted his future possible growth. He regretted being so flippant about Nick's assimilation with the hybrid Nth.

Gus was never very patient at anything, and he would have pushed a reload or reset button if there had been one. He wanted to pick up the ball but worried that it would interfere with the uploading process and really ruin things. Finally, to avoid nervous pacing, he sat down on the metal gangway and waited. He tapped his heel nervously against the metal gangplank, making a *bumpbumpbump.* The metal ridges made the gangway uncomfortable to sit on, but the dread that was building in Gus' core drowned out the physical discomfort. He simultaneously wanted to leave and do *something*, anything, but didn't want to miss it if Nick suddenly came back online. It was maddening.

Nick had kept Gus going, and given him so much information that helped him level skills, and understand his new reality. Besides that, he had been a totally supportive companion. If he admitted it, he was probably one of the best friends he had ever had. One of his dad's old maxims came back to him: *'Good friends make you grow into your best self.'* Tempest usually said it disparagingly, wanting Gus to evaluate his life and see how his current friends were not pushing him to be better.

This had always sparked Gus' rebellious streak and resistance. It made him want to stay just as he was. "They accept me for who I am, not who *you* want me to be," Gus shouted to the empty air. Somehow Nick had motivated Gus without the shame and cajoling. He was tough at times too, but he managed to do it in a way that Gus could totally relate with, and realize and accept his faults.

Not wanting to be away from Nick when the process finally finished, Gus began working on his bag of holding again. He detached his chest plate from his armor and made a serviceable cushion on the hard metal. With his mind fresh, the process of ether weaving was easier this time around. He managed to complete the same weave that had taken him two hours in only about fifteen minutes. A chime sounded, but he barely noticed as time sank away. Gus got into a rhythm and became engrossed in the task. The pressure and worry from the siege faded as he became single-minded in his task.

There was definitely a pattern involved, and it was becoming more intuitive where he had to place his fingers to thread the ether, when to hold and tighten. The tightening step would pull the tiny knots together like beads on a string before the ether threads pulled tight together and interlocked the individual knots. This also condensed the weave incredibly, drastically reducing the finished length of the rim.

The cycle would continue again, forming another length of looser ties and knots, only tightening after reaching the fifth securing knot.

Was that another chime? No matter.

After reaching a length of three feet, he turned his attention to combining the ends together. Fortunately, the end of the weave contained a similar set of picots, or loops, and Gus threaded the last ends of ether through these. Before securing the edges of the rim, Gus pushed to enlarge the internal size of the bag until he felt a strong pushback. Maintaining pressure to keep the bag inflated, he pulled the knots tight.

Looking at the finished product, it resembled a thin loop of black shoelace. Usually, he could not visualize ether at all without the aid of his display, but perhaps due to its condensed nature it was brought into the visible spectrum.

Gus could see that the fifth knots had formed a tiny loop in the chain where the pocket dimension could be attached to a standard bag with a tiny ether knot. It appeared that he made a circle a foot in diameter. Not super large, but it could fit things like the sensors and turrets inside.

Gus reached inside and could put his arm inside up to the shoulder and he pressed against a rubbery stretchy wall on the interior. It was unsettling to see him 'missing' his arm as if he were an amputee. Waving it in front of him and even trying to touch his face, he sensed nothing as the hand failed to contact him as he moved it in the other dimension. He thought it would feel cold inside, but it felt the same as the ambient temperature. Remembering Nick's warning about how living tissues behaved in the pocket dimension, he quickly pulled his arm out and inspected it, but it appeared to be no worse for the wear.

Gus got to his feet and he was achy all over.

How long have I been doing this? His knees popped and he shook his legs to get the circulation back. He did a couple more stretches to loosen up his upper body; he must have been hunched over for a really long time. He looked and saw no changes to the sphere of hybrid Nth on the conveyor belt. Looking at his watch, it was… ***1:23 AM***?! He had been working at it for hours, and did not notice at all. He didn't know how he hadn't run out of MP during the process, but he must have improved to the point that MP expenditure was less than his natural regeneration rate. And he didn't feel tired at all, besides being sore and super hungry. He felt uneasy without the ability to ask Nick for instant status updates on what the zombies were doing. His minimap appeared to be the same, and he couldn't keep running to main control to check the monitors constantly.

Gus wandered into the cafeteria, and the waiter robot saw him and waved him to his usual table.

"Can the chef make food that alters certain stats that I

would like boosted?" The robot nodded in the affirmative. Gus considered that he would try to make another bag while he waited and wondered if it would be more beneficial to boost agility to make the weaving a bit easier or intelligence for more skill stamina. He settled on boosting agility.

This meal was some small grilled meat that tasted vaguely like pork. It was delicious and Gus told himself not to think too much about where the meat came from. This meal gave a three point bonus to agility. As he ate, he pondered why he could still get stat increases, if the meal was engineered to react with his Nth. He still had access to his abilities and skills. The only explanation seemed to be that his Nth must be functional, but the NIC aspect was offline.

As he headed back to the Foundry, Gus reviewed his stats and logs. **Ether Weaving** had leveled to five, dropping MP costs by sixty percent, and **Ether Warping** to two, which reduced its MP cost fifteen percent. That netted him 700 XP and 1400 FP.

Gus felt even more awake after the meal, so he headed back to the Foundry again to make another bag. He was soon in the zone and worked continuously until movement caught his attention from the corner of his eye. Gus was surprised at his progress; the agility boosts had really made a difference! He once again expanded the inside of the bag as much as he could and tied off the ends. An idea began to form in his mind as he looked at the completed rim, a different size than he had initially been intending, but it might just work. He'd have to check out the Foundry controls and queue up some more items.

The Nth-ball that had started at the size of a Bocce ball, began to expand to the size of a volleyball. Gus sat in anticipation of something else happening, but the ball sat there again for five minutes. It felt like at least a half an hour, but checking his watch, Gus noticed that time had barely passed at all. There was no sound or sign that anything was happening, which made the wait that much worse.

Gus decided he had to do something or he would go insane.

He went back to the control room and tried to distract himself looking through the different types of traps and configurations. He could see the ball from where he sat, and every time he looked he saw no change.

There were drones of different types, other classes of turrets, and various traps that could be launched. The higher-grade Tier 2 traps were grayed out. He could read their description though, and these traps seemed to require more extensive installation.

Since the drones and turrets used none of the available energy, he queued everything he needed. He hoped Nick would just come back online already and be ok. He couldn't go into the upcoming battle alone. This was taking entirely too long; he itched to put some of his plans into effect, but he needed Nick.

"Hurry up!" he screamed, his voice echoing impotently among the large machines of the Foundry.

CHAPTER THIRTY-NINE

Glitter Freeze

DAY 10 4:22 AM

0:18:48 remaining

"Guuuuus…" a voice gasped in his head. It sounded like it came from someone who had crawled through the desert, or a dead man's last gasp.

"Nick!" Gus flew out of his seat and made it to the conveyor belt. Grabbing the handrails, he vaulted down the stairways leading to the conveyors where the hybrid Nth were coming to life. The ball fluttered and blinked, winking in and out of activity, each time a different shape. It hurt Gus' eyes to look directly at it, giving him an instant headache and a sense of wrongness.

No, that wasn't the right word, it was just so alien that his mind refused to wrap itself around what it was seeing. Impossible optical illusion shapes formed, but in three dimensions. *No!* Colors and hues, spatial anomalies bent back on themselves in ways that had not been seen before. *No! No! No!* His mind recoiled. He couldn't pull his eyes away though, and slowly, his mind made it past the turbulence like a raft passing the rapids, and everything calmed and smoothed again. The ball dissolved and fell to the tray like grains of sand.

"Did you miss me?" Nick said, from a bald green head that formed from the sand-like particles pushing itself out of the tray and… winking? The tiny head gave a grin and winked. Gus was startled enough he fell flat and barely avoided flipping over the handrails around the gangplank into the machinery below.

"I guess not…" the little head said.

"Nick, is that really you?" Gus asked. In response, the iridium-colored dust fluttered out to create an outline of a human form, and the hue changed to the appearance of purple glitter… It looked like the invisible man after a night at the strip club.

"In the flesh. In the flakes? That's probably more accurate. To calm your fears, the process was a success! And I have a newfound appreciation of what humans and all the other species experienced when they became Nth-assisted. I am undergoing a similar process. With different tabs and gauges much like you have. None of it really applies to you particularly, but it is strange to be on the other side of the process."

"So what can you do?" Gus asked.

"I'm not really sure yet, there isn't exactly a manual, and I can communicate with the Kroutonium but it is… odd. I can direct a question toward it, and I get what appears to be an unrelated image, vibration, or shade of color. It will take some time to connect and communicate. This has never been done before, and I get no responses to my queries to the quantum server. I know you were interested in armor, and that seems to be something it is familiar with, having acted in this capacity before. I can almost say it is *eager* to try out some new things. I can also see that it is talking to your spear. Visible streams of intermittent energy are being sent back and forth, and I know intuitively that they are data packs, but I cannot translate the pulses."

"So you're my new sidekick, huh?"

"Not so much. This form is too insubstantial to be a true functional homunculus, but there is enough to form a triple-ply armor, so we'll start with that for now. I vastly underestimated the amount needed to form a functional Nth body, so this will have to do. You'll need a lot more metal if you want to make that a reality. I'll have my hands full trying to work out communication for the foreseeable future, especially how they can be influenced to function," Nick murmured, obviously fascinated by the turn of events.

"Good, because I don't think we're going to have the luxury of time. When you were gone, the volcano started acting up and we are slowly losing power. We have less than a day, so we have to go as soon as we can. I didn't let the time go to waste though, I did manage to make a large bag of holding," Gus said, proud of himself.

"How big..." Nick said hesitantly.

"Oh, it's huge, you would be proud of me. It's all part of my plan to clean up these zombies."

"Ok, but you should know what happens if a large enough bag gets turned inside out..."

Gus gulped, waiting for the bomb to drop.

"...you create a singularity, Gus. A frelling black hole! Don't go screwing around without guidance again! And I'm sure you didn't store it in any particular way to avoid it getting knotted and wound around itself?"

This reunion wasn't going exactly how Gus would have liked. "Well, come and see it and we'll fix it. From what I could tell, nothing bad has happened yet, right?"

The glittery figure did a facepalm and motioned an arm to indicate 'lead the way.'

CHAPTER FORTY

Below the Surface

Methiochos was frustrated that his minions could do nothing to access the manor now that they had cleared away the opposition. The observers couldn't manage any voice commands, having lost significant amounts of coordination in their conversion. He had even tried having the Mantids squeeze them to see if they could force out enough of a command code to open the manor but the result was as intelligible as a whoopee cushion.

Methiochos could speak, having retained much more of his humanity. He also remembered the key phrases that would activate higher command functions. Saying them out loud, his gravelly voice echoed off the empty chamber. Lead from the front. He would have to go himself once he knew what he needed. It would take just one more cycle, he could feel that, the answers were close. It would be nice to leave this dark prison.

Methiochos sunk his tendrils in the magma for what he believed was the last time. He was almost to full strength. The pain that came after absorbing too much energy would be endured. After he was complete, it would be his time to act.

45 YEARS AGO...

Using his power, Methiochos widened and molded the bone of his left arm into a large plate shield and crawled into the airway, he hardened it into cortical bone, retracting the blood vessels as the hard bone solidified. It wouldn't do to get a bleeding debuff if something hit the shield. He tried to access the ship's computer on his communicator but all he received was a buffering icon. *Dammit!* Without that he couldn't check on ship status or monitor crew locations. *If you want to get anything done, you have to do it yourself!*

His common sense screamed that progressing into the airshaft was the most stupid thing he could do, but he pushed those concerns away, attributing them to watching too many horror movies in his youth. Besides, one must lead from the front.

Dust and clumps of material that could have been the cousins of dryer lint had built up in the corners of the square ducting. Fortunately, the dust showed a clear path for whatever had crawled through here. Methiochos followed the trail in an army-crawl.

A hiss of static and feedback hit his ear. "Do you read me?" a voice buzzed.

"I hear you," he responded, turning down the sensitivity on his cochlear communicator.

"It appears that Dara was last logged in to the infirmary before she went back to her room. I am sending a squad to investigate, and will meet them there. *Holmes out.*"

After a couple more turns, the access panel had burst outward, the wire mesh forming a flower bloom shape. Methiochos climbed out of the walkway, only having a five-foot drop to the floor of the darkened room. From the scant light available, he could tell that this was the general crew barracks. A flash of shifting shadows caught his attention as someone or some*thing* scuttled in front of the band of light leaking under the door. A bunk next to him began to shake as the occupant wriggled and writhed.

Pulling his multitool off his belt and flicking on the flashlight mode, he saw a pallid face of a crewman with a black scratch across one cheek. His eyes were bloodshot and his body vibrated, back arching while his feet kicked back and forth like he was riding a bicycle. His face looked ashen and devoid of expression despite the turmoil his body was enduring.

He heard another scratchy-scratching in the distance and tried to illuminate it with his flashlight. All he succeeded in doing was more fully disclosing his own location. Swinging the light around, he saw that others that were resting had similar scratches on their faces and necks, though they were totally inert.

A screeching noise ripped through the relative quiet of the barrack, as one of the bunks was moved, just the right timbre to give Methiochos a shiver. He backed up toward the lights near the entrance, keeping his own light fanning in a swath in front of him. More sounds and rustling were emanating from the dark. As he reached the bank of switches, he flipped them on with his non-shield forearm.

The harsh white LED overhead lights came on; Methiochos saw multiple figures moving toward him. Some looked like they were sleepwalking, others poised nimbly on the bedposts of the bunk beds. As he fiddled with the door, one of the crew jumped off a bedpost with his blackened fingernails extended, making scratching and clawing motions.

Methiochos barely covered himself in time with his bone shield and returned the attack with a shield bash to the face. The man tripped backward, three fingernails ripped out and still embedded in the bone.

Methiochos retreated out of the barracks doors and hit the control scan pad by the door. "Lock door." The panel outline shifted to red as people, or things that had been people, began to bang and slap against the locked door. Tilting his arm to look at the fingernails embedded in his forearm, he made his way to the infirmary.

Activating his communicator, Methiochos called his security team and advised them of the situation. To cordon off the barracks and block any air ducts in case more of the affected crew were in there.

Methiochos dropped to a knee as he was hit by a headache. It felt like part of his consciousness was being shorn away, attempting to pull him out of the memory. He *had* to get to the bottom of this. Bracing himself, the feeling passed after a tense minute. He shook his head to clear it, then he continued to the infirmary.

His soldiers were there in full tactical gear, surveying the scene outside the infirmary. Holmes reported on what they had found. There had been no changes since they had arrived. The area appeared abandoned, and they had not seen anyone in the halls or surrounding area, which in and of itself was odd.

Methiochos peered into the darkened infirmary. A light fixture had been partially ripped off the ceiling and released occasional sparks as it swung above the chaos, flickering intermittently. Beds had been upturned and bedding torn. Equipment had been knocked to the ground, some spilling their electronic guts onto the floor. Besides the flickering light swinging back and forth, there was no other illumination. It must be on backup power; likely a breaker had tripped. The computers were located at the back of the room, and he needed to get there to check the logs. Fortunately, the breaker panel was right next to the computer banks.

Methiochos stepped into the room, surprised to find the ground wet. Turning on the flashlight of his multitool yet again, he stepped into the room. He lightly kicked an IV stand to move it to the side and shuffled around the debris. It was a shock to see something as clean and austere as the infirmary had devolved to such chaos. He had to highstep over a side-rail to a patient bed that had been bent into an omega shape.

What had happened here? As he approached the breaker panel, he slid the latch and opened the door. Stepping closer to push the master breaker, he extended his hand, reaching out when there was a loud *CRACK!*

CHAPTER FORTY-ONE

Sabotage

"Dammit, Holmes!" someone yelled. Everyone looked back as Holmes sheepishly stepped back, revealing a cracked motherboard from one of the broken pieces of equipment. Methiochos flipped the breaker on and the computers came back to life, taking longer to reboot because of the sudden power loss. The records showed Dara checking in about three hours before, then checking out just a short time afterward.

There should have been nine other people in the infirmary, including staff, those getting routine physicals, and four receiving treatment after minor injuries while training. The communicator vibrated a bit, indicating an incoming message.

"Sir, you wanted us to give you a proximity alert when we were fifty miles from the island. I expect us to be there within the hour," came the notice from the bridge.

"Acknowledged. You haven't noticed anything... off, have you?"

"No, sir. Although, we haven't been receiving status reports as often, which is common when the men are making final preparations for landfall and debarking."

"Noted. Thank you, let me know if there are any changes. Methiochos out." Leaving the infirmary, the quiet in the otherwise busy hallways was unsettling. While trying to formulate his next orders, there was a scuttling in the ductwork above. Gritting his teeth, he yelled, "Follow that noise!"

Whatever was in the ducts had bolted and the men ran recklessly, rushing to overtake whatever was inside. Eventually they ended at the research labs. Humanoid forms dropped in through the ductwork. Their limbs were bent at impossible angles and they leaped around, spilling papers and knocking trays with samples off counters as they attacked the poor scientists within. Before the soldiers could make it inside, some contaminant detector activated and the large white sliding doors went into lockdown mode. White foggy gas sprayed from the ceiling, filling the room with decontaminant, but also obscuring the view.

Methiochos tried to override the door lock but even his clearance would not allow the doors to release a possible pathogen once the lockdown was initiated. The crashing sounds soon stilled, but nothing could be seen in the swirling white mist.

Another hum and someone from the bridge announced, "Sir, you said to contact you if anything irregular happened. There is a little girl here, she says she needs to see you… I was unaware that there were any children on this mission…" he trailed off.

"What the *hell* is going on here?!" Methiochos yelled. Keying his comms, he advised the bridge he'd be right there. He signaled the group to follow as he made his way to the bridge. Had Archon expected his betrayal? Was this some ability affecting his crew, or some engineered creatures attacking them? No, those were all his own men and women in the barracks. Something had changed them. They entered the lift, unsure of what to expect next.

Methiochos stormed out as soon as the doors opened, determined to salvage this mission. He had worked too damned hard to lose it all now. At least on the bridge, he could manage the whole ship's systems, and figure out who this kid belonged to in the process. Mission guidelines were strict, and he had not selected anyone who had extended family ties, knowing that they would not be able to leave the island once they were situated and the shield was in place. Who had broken protocol, bringing a *child* on board?

The bridge crew was managing the final approach, with the first mate standing near a small girl, clutching a small doll close to her face. She looked timid and scared, the way she folded in on herself, holding the doll for dear life.

As he approached, the timid girl turned to face him and recognition flashed in her eyes. She suddenly seemed less timid as she straightened and faced the imposing general.

"Who are you, little girl, and what are you doing on my ship?" Methiochos demanded.

"You've been bad," she said defiantly, "so my friend Basil said you needed to be punished."

"Basil? What does he have to do with anything?"

"He knows what you were doing so he made a surprise for you. Do you want to know the secret? I told the lady at the hospital and she told everyone there."

Methiochos grabbed the little girl by the arms, lifting her roughly off the ground, giving her a little shake. "Tell me what you have done!" In response, she moved her doll as if it was giving him a kiss on one of the arms securing her. Methiochos felt a pinprick and dropped the girl in surprise. She dropped the doll and he could see a tiny needle poking out of its mouth, dripping a purple-black liquid from the tip. The girl grabbed the doll and scrambled under one of the consoles.

"Basil made them and put them in Margaret! He said that they would teach you all a lesson for lying to his daddy!" One of the soldiers attempted to pry the little girl out from under the console and received a poke to the leg from the doll; he cursed savagely at her.

Methiochos started to feel lightheaded. He didn't know

what the needle contained, but it felt like some kind of heavy tranquilizer. The captain, still focusing on maneuvering the large transport asked, "Final approach, should I land?" Methiochos nodded numbly.

For a couple seconds, the stupor waned, and he could see the bridge erupting in chaos. The girl was running around the room with unnatural speed, swinging the doll and hitting anyone she could, crawling in and out of spaces that should not be able to fit a human body. One of the soldiers managed to hit her with a swift punch to the side of the head and the girl crumpled to the floor. His soldiers all had augmented strength, so no doubt the girl had suffered massive brain trauma or had her spine snapped.

Some of the men began shaking uncontrollably. Someone must have had poor trigger discipline because his gun went off, shooting the pilot as the ship was descending.

Pulling the man out of the chair, Methiochos grabbed the controls and attempted to stabilize the large craft. It was much more unwieldy than the small combat transports he had flown in the military, but the controls were the same. He could see the manor, but steered clear. Who knew how many other stowaways were on board? Site B then. He could hit the containment field and sort things out. After they were clear, he activated the bio-stasis field remotely. *That should keep Manticorps out. Nice try, Archon.* The blue green bubble arced past the ship enveloping it and the island.

The grogginess began to kick in again, and Methiochos saw his self-healing skill draining his psi-energy almost completely. It had staved off whatever was trying to infect him, but he knew this landing was not going to be pretty. Site B was built under a large lava-flow. He hoped it would be strong enough to hold the transport. He could barely focus, and the ship crashed into the rock that formed the roof of Site B, slightly on its side. The ship slid on the incline and flipped over, the dome of the ship's bridge puncturing into the structure below, securing it from sliding. The crushed supports securing the dome of the ship were shorn away and fell into the large room below, spilling glass and debris everywhere. Methiochos felt stabs of pain everywhere, and had to grab onto the seat as the cavern gaped below. The cutting sensation, trying to pull him away from the memory grew more intense. He was almost done, he just needed to…

Something grabbed him in a bear hug and pulled him away from the chair, twisting backward as if trying to perform a wrestling move. The attacker slipped as it lost its foothold and they both fell out of the ship onto the unforgiving ground. Unfortunately for the attacker, he was the first to hit and braced Methiochos' fall. Still, he had hit awkwardly and his left ankle bent at an unnatural angle. Coughing as he rolled away from the now-inert attacker, he saw one of his soldiers, muscles swollen and continuing to writhe like there were angry worms crawling under his skin.

More bodies began to fall and jump to the chamber below. Methiochos crawled to the control panel on the far side of the cavern. Pressing his bloody hand on the panel, he brought up the site defenses on the console and turned on the perimeter containment fields. Now, whatever or whoever was on the ship was trapped in here with him, for better or worse. Better to sacrifice himself to keep people free. From what he had seen it resembled only one thing… but that couldn't be. That was just a myth to scare recruits…

He sat down, his back leaning against the console, looking at his broken ankle. Dark particles swarmed over it, dissolving the broken limb to a stump. Oddly, it didn't hurt like it did when Methiochos had to use his self-healing to reset a bone. Focusing the last of his mental reserves, he tried to refashion the altered appendage. As if in retaliation, more of the dark particles swarmed his lower body. He noticed that as this happened, his mind became much clearer, and the grogginess eased.

As the particles swarmed over his legs, he could see that he was changing and that his efforts to control his healing were met with a barrier. So be it. He marshalled his attention, abandoning his legs and set to making a bulwark of his mind, shoring up his defenses for when the Dark returned. He knew how to fight, and the general knew when to abandon a position that was overrun. This… *thing*… would not defeat him. Let the battle begin.

CHAPTER FORTY-TWO

Payback

DAY 10 4:43 AM

0:18:27 remaining

Gus sighed in relief that he hadn't inadvertently messed up his latest project too badly. There were no knots, and he learned how to make tiny ether hooks that suspended the rim, much like a shower curtain. From there, he easily made the transition for his first part of the plan.

Nick had guided the glitter-like framework to overlay Gus' current suit to gain some information on how he moved as a precursor to functioning as an armor.

"How well are you integrating so far, Nick?"

"Still synchronizing basic movement. It'll be a while before the hybrid Nth can function as an armor adjunct just yet, so try to stay out of sight for now, and keep moving."

"I'll admit I'm underwhelmed so far," Gus griped, "and we need to hurry! That whole process took way too long." Gus made some final preparations to some drones as he complained.

"Yeah, yeah. It'll be soon; distract yourself kicking some zombie butt in the meantime."

Not a bad idea. Gus opened the window to the room he had found closest to the courtyard below. He wanted to be in range to use his abilities, and this was a lucky find. This floor was mostly office suites located two stories above the lawn, with a view of the ocean. He didn't know how anyone could work here; he would've been too distracted to get much done, staring at the tropical bay and the waves rolling in below.

Using his controller, he activated the programmed routine and sent out the drones with their payload. After the small contraptions cleared the window, Gus sealed it again. He didn't want any curious Mantids climbing up to discover where the drones had come from. The controller had a strong enough signal that he didn't lose any bars with the window closed, and Gus selected one and viewed the teeming masses below the drone's camera.

When they were in position, Gus used the drone's cameras to tweak their position so they were over the most populated area of zombies as possible. He found where all the observers were clustered together, trying to access the voice command pylons. Shamblers swayed in place around them as Mantids weaved through the crowd. The Juggernauts were not to be seen, and Gus suspected they were taking shifts banging on the doors.

On his command, the drones all plunged toward the ground together. A circular swath a hundred feet across enveloped the largest density of the horde and swallowed them up into the large rim of an enormous bag of holding. The drones dropped to ground level then began to converge inward toward each other in the center. The Shamblers who had not been caught up stared onward dumbly. Hearing the high-pitched whine of propellers, Mantids and Juggernauts turned to see what had happened, but not seeing past the Shamblers crowding immediately around the drones, they turned back to their work of trying to bash in the front doors.

Once the drones had met in the center, they began to fly upward, then inverted their arrangement to keep gravity pulling any of the zombies out of the opening. Seeing that the zombies had made no retaliation, he opened the window again, and stepped out onto the sill, to ensure he didn't lose the signal.

Gus directed the drones to take their payload out to sea. From his vantage he could see the drones fly past Atlantis Beach and off to the ocean. Gus was worried the distance would be a problem but the signal bars remained strong even when the drones reached their prescribed destination. Gus reversed the flying formation so the enormous bag of holding was again open underneath and instructed the drones to spread out.

Zombies of different shapes and forms began spilling out of the opening, tumbling end over end until they splashed into the water a hundred feet below. Gus wasn't sure if this would kill the zombies, but Nick had assured him that the inside of a pocket dimension was not conducive to life of any kind if the bag was sealed for as short as five minutes, probably less. He wasn't sure, but he didn't see any of the bodies flailing about in his magnified display. He expected this of the Shamblers, but wanted to see if any of the more active Mantids were affected.

Gus ordered the drones to return and surveyed the lawn area. While they returned he zoomed in with his augmented vision and looked at the water. Nothing moved of its own power, it must have worked! There were a couple zombies that had drifted back onto the circular area of cut grass where it had been sheared away from the bag's displacement. The numbers seemed much more manageable, but Gus wanted to try to scoop up as many as he could.

Unfortunately, with significantly fewer Shamblers moaning and banging around, the whirl of the drones was more noticeable to the Mantids, who began to congregate to view this electronic interloper. After finding they could not reach the drones by jumping from the ground, some Mantids began to climb the manor and leap outward, tumbling and falling as they missed.

None of them seemed to be damaged by the huge falls though, to Gus' disappointment.

Gus tried for a second drop and some of the Mantids leaped out of the way, but a fair number hit roaming Shamblers and could not dodge the edge of the descending bag. After it fell, Mantids fell upon the drones and shredded the fragile devices. Some jumped in the circular ring of fabric tearing it to shreds. The thin rim of the bag of holding remained on the ground inconspicuously. The creatures did not appear to have enough understanding to mess with the thin strand lying on the ground, and fortunately did not invert it.

Time to move to phase two. Gus grabbed another set of controllers and turrets supported by four drones were deployed to the area in front of the manor. Gus maintained the drones above the jump range of the Mantids and let the carnage begin. Mantids and Shamblers began falling in waves. Gus' happiness was short-lived, as the Mantids began tearing body parts off of the fallen and throwing them at the drones. Before he could change their altitude, more than half of the turret-drones were hit and came crashing down. Loss of even one drone meant the rest were insufficient to keep the turret aloft, and the turrets were torn apart either by the fall or Mantid attack. Still, they were able to selectively target around twenty Mantids before they had to retreat.

The turrets were much less deadly at the greater height, with their accuracy dropping off rapidly. Gus chose to recall them before they wasted their power. Juggernauts had come away from the front door to investigate the fracas. Gus had been waiting for this, and tried out his **T-Wrecks** skill for the first time. A fifteen-foot creature materialized, formed out of ether condensed into typical matter and directed by the Nth. The dinosaur bellowed and Gus mentally commanded it to target the Juggernauts. The dinosaur easily snapped through the head and shoulders of a Juggernaut, and a well-placed tail swish knocked three approaching Juggernauts back, staggering one and breaking the legs of the other two.

As more Juggernauts approached, the dinosaur would bite and scratch with a clawed foot. The creature's larger mass and strength overcame Nth-reinforced muscle and tore through the zombie tanks. Once in a while, one would slip past and land a solid punch on a leg or the chest as the monster was turned and fighting other enemies, but a quick bite or kick ended these attacks with extreme prejudice.

While the Juggernauts were no match for the T-Wrecks, the Mantids were what brought it down. They managed to leap onto its back and began to bite and tear. The construct made an effort to shake them off, but the Mantids held on like ticks. The damage added up and the dinosaur dissolved into nothingness. Gus checked his logs, but unfortunately, he gained no XP from the drone or T-Wrecks' kills. *When I have time, I'll need to ask Nick about that...*

Gus caught the one Juggernaut closest to him with **Wreck-luse**, and he stampeded over a couple Shamblers and a Mantid who were not expecting him to turn and run. Another Mantid was stiff-armed by the Juggernaut and flew back into a wall of the manor, falling boneless to the ground after its spine was snapped.

Gus surveyed the remaining zombies and their number had been reduced to fifty or less, with only Shamblers and a dozen Mantids in the mix. Gus could not see any remaining Juggernauts, but the relentless banging had stopped so he hoped there were few to none of the beefy zombies left.

A Mantid climbed onto the roof, facing the courtyard, looking for attackers. Gus threw his naginata, severing its spine, and then retracted the weapon with Ether Leash. There was enough chaos in the zombie ranks that he was not noticed.

He edged out farther on the balcony and was able to pick off four more Shamblers in the same way, but after that, the remaining zombies remained out of a direct line of sight.

Time to move to the final phase. Following the map Nick had provided, Gus made his way to floor twenty-three. As he made his way down the hallways to the external exit, the floor looked unfinished compared to others. He had to confirm first generation access again to stop on the floor.

Gus' footsteps echoed down the long concrete tunnel. This level didn't have finished flooring of any type. Gus activated **Dash** and sped down the long hallways that smelled of cement and dust. Each **Dash** kicked up plumes of grit and dust behind him and he soon reached the final destination marker on his minimap. Gus stood before a simple door with a keypad access code, instead of the usual hand scanners.

"Nick, what is the password?"

"040815162342," came the reply.

"Can I change it? I'm never going to remember that," Gus asked.

"Even if you typed it repeatedly for a while?" Nick teased.

"Pretty sure that's a no," Gus said resolutely.

"Alright. Just enter it and then give me the new numeric code." Gus entered the code with Nick repeating the obscure numbers a couple times until Gus got them correct. The panel's outline shifted to green.

"Ok, hold the pound key for three seconds," the green outline began to flash, "Now enter the new code."

Gus pushed in 8-6-7-5-3-0-9.

"That's not long enough, needs to be at least 12 digits," Nick advised.

Gus added 8-5-3-5-9-3-7 to the string of numbers. "Now hit the pound key again and it's reset. Not just for this panel, but for any panel of this type on this floor."

Gus didn't think there was anything else to see down here, so he opened the door, which revealed a small nine by nine foot room. There was a ladder leading upward, and he began to climb. Reaching the top, Gus encountered another of the circular submarine-style hatches. This lock was easy to spin loose, surprising him.

He had to push hard with his one free hand, elbowing the side of the ladder to get enough leverage to pry the hatch open. Detritus and plant roots had grown over the hatch and had to be torn free or uprooted, bit by bit. Gus had to spit out bits of dirt that spilled in around the edges of the hatch, falling on his head and in his mouth and eyes.

At last, the hatch flopped open, somewhere along the forest path, a hundred feet to one side if the map was accurate. Gus climbed out and shook himself like a wet dog, brushing his hair and face to remove the dirt and leaves there.

Closing the hatch, Gus saw the small button release on the top that would read his fingerprint and unlock. Gus cleaned the sensor and checked that it worked before sealing the opening. He placed a marker on his minimap to save the location for the future.

Looking upward, Gus saw on a nearby branch the top of a telltale blue blob facing away from him. Keeping quiet, Gus inched forward and readied his spear. He launched it before it could get sight of him and the poor little guy deflated on his branch, a bright blue cottage-cheese-like discharge dripping down the tree trunk. He examined the creature and his ***Wreck-ognize*** skill let him analyze the creatures' remains:

Level 3 Observer

HP 0/10

This creature is the result of a hacked Nth to maximize intelligence. The original host usually was a specialist in a field requiring a large intelligence stat, such as a researcher or engineer. Basic strength and constitution are bottomed out to boost the intelligence of this creature, resulting in the loss of any protective physical structures, including a skeleton. Observers do have increased stealth and mental misdirection abilities as a compensation. Observers can share information they accumulate with fellow Dark Nth to help them direct external activities of others and mobilize.

Gus realized that this must have been how the creatures were able to coordinate their attacks against him when he was routed so badly. After scanning the remains, blue dots began to wink on in his minimap. Knowing what to look for, Gus began hunting for the other observers. He found three others, spaced roughly two hundred feet apart on the trail. Working backward, he cleared the path back to the manor.

Before entering the field, Gus asked, "Any change in that shielding functionality, Nick?" Gus inquired.

"I believe that the hybrid Nth can provide a small increase in resistance at the moment. We… I mean I am attempting to develop predictive shielding that would allow reallocation of the Nth to be more concentrated at the site of an attack, providing increased protection. By mapping your movements these last hours, it has improved the algorithm, but what would speed the process is to practice some battle maneuvers. Just don't rely on them providing much protection yet, and you should be fine. This dual consciousness is totally messing with me. The Kroutonium aspect is super analytical and I really have to work to translate the concepts into something understandable."

"Sounds good. I think I can clean up the remainder of these Dark Nth and we'll see where we end up."

Creeping up the incline to the manor, Gus saw the last group of zombies, which consisted of mostly Shamblers and some Mantids. If he targeted the Mantids, the Shamblers would be easy to finish with his naginata and ether leash.

Staying hidden, Gus stabbed a Mantid facing the manor in the back of the head. It unfortunately screeched as it was hit and the battle was on. Gus dashed forward and used an ether leash to grab a Mantid and pull it closer as another leash propelled his spear forward.

The creature met the weapon in flight which struck dead center in the chest, then flipped upward, slicing the neck and head into two neat slices which fell to either side. Gus pulled the spear back and settled into his katas, fending off the few Mantids who remained, staying on the lawn so they could not flee or climb to evade his attacks. They became wary and attempted to circle him, but Gus would grab one and attack it before he could be flanked. They were no longer safe with their usual tactics, as one by one they were snared by a limb and the spear killed them while immobile.

Gus had been dodging Shamblers by instinct, their slow speed and lack of aggression making them practically a non-issue when it came to fighting. Ridiculous how these things had given him a run for his money less than half a month ago. He really had been a mess.

For the next hour, Gus was on cleanup duty. The remaining Shamblers were easily taken down as Gus manipulated the naginata with **Ether Leash.** He gained a level and the exercise reminded him of Yondu's telepathically-controlled arrow from Guardians of the Galaxy. He wasn't that good yet, but he began to be able to use the leashes to guide the weapon to a specific target. Without the Juggernauts and Mantids to support the Shamblers, they posed no threat to Gus' current skills. Finished at last, Gus let out an exhausted sigh. He could see no more enemies on the minimap, even at widest zoom. The silence was a relief in and of itself. He couldn't resist a peek at his stats and he had gained 2600 XP and 5400 FP total from the cleanup.

Gus fist pumped and made his way up to the lawn.

"Nick, can you tell Stuart and manor A.I. to resume normal functions?"

"Hold on," Nick said distractedly, "Ok, they should be back online."

Gus summoned Stuart and a pylon slid out of the grass.

"Yes, Master Gus?" Stuart purred.

"Can you send some staff to clean up the remains of these zombies so I can feel comfortable in this area again? And are there any droids that could do maintenance on the front doors?"

"Of course. Anything else you may need at this time?"

"Lift the blast doors and that should be it. Thanks, Stuart," Gus said.

"My pleasure," Stuart said and went quiet. Gus trotted to the remains of the bag of holding and severed the weave of the rim. While it was functional for his plan, he didn't like the risk the large bag had and as soon as he had untied the knots, he watched as the rim unraveled, like fuses fizzling as they raced around the edge of the rim until they met and the whole construct evaporated. Gus watched entranced as the weave degraded. Gus wondered if there were zombie bodies floating through the void somewhere. Soon thereafter, the big brothers of the beach cleaners rolled out of a service door that was practically invisible halfway to the beach.

The large robots functioned much the same way as their beach brethren and removed the black decaying corpses and body bits of the zombies. Even the decaying smell was gone, replaced by the faint hint of ozone. Gus marveled that just a short time ago, the area was a zombie apocalypse and now the only evidence that anything had happened was the circular patch on the grass where the bag of holding had scooped up the zombies.

Not long after the bag had totally disappeared, one of the large balls cleaned up the drone remnants, and evened out the trim of the grass, and the circle from his initial attack was barely visible.

Gus headed inside to clean up and get ready to see what was beyond the forest. Thinking back, he realized that he hadn't slept in a long time. He hadn't felt the usual effects of exhaustion and fatigue that he had while pulling night shifts as a henchman.

"It's thanks to your **Energy Absorption** Nth ability. They can utilize energy that would be wasted, like heat, and absorb solar energy as the sun hits your skin and transfer that directly to your cells. They also have a greater capacity for constant cellular repair, so you need to sleep less. Your brain will need to recharge and dream, but typical fatigue for you is one less thing you have to worry about as long as you take care of yourself," Nick answered before Gus could ask. "That was a freebie. You still haven't answered the riddle."

Gus checked his watch and the countdown timer. 1:49 PM. Nine hours and change to fix the volcano. He looked over and saw that some lava was just beginning to seep down one side of the crater. The smoke and ash had increased noticeably. His body craved sleep but he knew he had to press on. He tried to focus on the riddle and ignore his weariness.

Gus tried to guess. "An astronaut? An alien? The moon? A werewolf? A vampire? Frankenstein? A worm? The sun?"

After each guess, Glitter Nick would shake his head.

"I don't know," Gus finally admitted defeat.

What loses its head in the morning and gains it again after it gets dark? Gus turned the question over and over in his head as he went back into the manor. He would grab some food to gain a final buff and then see what was at the end of the path. He had no doubts that Methiochos was probably there, waiting for him.

"Keep at it," was Nick's only reply.

Gus imagined his bed calling to him as he ate mechanically. *Ah damn, it's a pillow!* He realized, sitting up and smiling. Nick was right, it did feel better to figure it out by yourself.

+1 intelligence

Gus' grin grew even wider. *Even better!*

CHAPTER FORTY-THREE

The Final Countdown

Methiochos finally had his answer, Basileus! He would have to exact his revenge if the boy still lived. Anger welled up the more he thought of it and planned the myriad ways he would get justice. In the midst of his plotting, he became aware that he was receiving nothing from his mental links. Absolutely nothing. His mind remembered the pains he felt during his reminiscence but couldn't be distracted. He had left his troops without guidance! His anger surged again. *Always someone trying to take what was his! Never again!* Methiochos flexed his tentacles and rose to his full height. This would end now.

DAY 10 2:24 PM

0:08:46 remaining

Gus felt satiated by what would probably be his last meal. He was decidedly not excited about what the day had in store. It was time to reset whatever had happened with the lava flows and see if he could sort out this mess with the volcano. It was a good bet that Methiochos was there, along with the answer to what had happened to him way back when. Gus hoped he was done with Dark Nth, but he'd have to prepare some goodies just in case.

"Gus, if you are going off to meet Methiochos, he's got regeneration skills, and I can tell you, they're super handy. Unless you're fighting against someone who has them, then they suuuuck! He may have gained some other abilities too, so be on your guard. Just FYI." Nick warned.

"Nothing's ever easy, right?" Gus replied as he got to finishing his preparations.

"If it's any consolation, the sync has been completed! The hybrid-Nth are interlaced over your existing armor, providing an adaptive shielding. They're synced with your abilities as well, so as you level defensive skills, you will improve the armor as well. I would recommend a short training in the arena just to familiarize yourself with how it works."

"That's a good idea, but I don't think I have the time."

"Then *make* the time. It should only take thirty minutes or so if you hurry. It could mean the difference between life or death, but your call," Nick urged.

"Fine. Can you remotely queue things at the Foundry Nick?"

"Of course."

Gus mentally kicked himself. *How much time could I have saved if—No. No use in getting upset about it now.* "Put some stealth mapping drones into the queue."

"They should be ready by the time you finish training."

"That'll do, pig," Gus mocked.

"Insulting bacon? Just get to training before you pull down the wrath of The Beard on you." Gus furrowed his brow in confusion. "Never mind. Just go!"

As Gus entered the training arena, he stopped and looked at the quiet room. He was a total noob when he first started here, and now was getting pretty confident with fighting. He still felt like it may not be enough, but tried to not go down that rabbit-hole and the self-doubt that lurked there. Gus stood on the scanner, and waited. And then he waited some more. Just as he was about to step off the scanner, a quest dropped:

Quest Granted: The Final Countdown
Quest Conditions:
1) Familiarize yourself with your new armor's capabilities
Quest Rewards*: 300 XP, 100 FP*
Time Requirements: None
Do you want to accept this quest? (Y/N)

That was simple. Gus accepted and three pillow-Mantids assembled to battle him. Gus got in his usual stance to start fighting. The pillow-Mantids began attacking like they were berserkers. The fury of their attack had Gus retreating and misplacing his steps. He fended one or two off with his naginata, but one got in a swipe from the side. As the holographic claw scraped at his face, Gus saw the padded arm blade under the projection getting closer through his peripheral vision.

Gus braced for the impact, when a surge of heat occurred, accompanied with a slight tickle on his skin. The final impact, if it could be called that, was like getting hit with a paddle shaped balloon, noticeable but harmless. Gus saw a crackling silver sheen flare at the site of impact as his eyes panned down by his cheek. A tiny bit of his MP and stamina were used in the process but to avoid getting slapped like Charlie Murphy, *definitely* worth it. Gus retreated out of the arena, and began to ask questions.

Instead of simply answering, Gus' vision suddenly went black. His point-of-view shifted, and he was seeing the world as if through an insect's eye. Well, not exactly like an insect, but the effect reminded him of how their eyes worked. There were many tiny hexagonal areas that were stitched together to create a mosaic of the world around him.

The motion in there was a discrepancy; he could feel more Nth moving to this area. The resolution of the view sharply increased as more Nth got in position and gave more feedback on the attack.

Without knowing exactly how, Gus felt the Nth adopt a honeycomb arrangement of multiple layers around the projected site of impact. As the padded blade of the pillowbot began to make contact, the hybrid-Nth began converting the kinetic energy into other forms of energy, then dissipating the remainder as heat. Gus could understand as he shared this consciousness briefly that the full brunt of the attack was not only absorbed, but redirected as in Judo or Aikido, allowing a portion of the force to glance and pass over, causing the enemy to overshoot as this slip occurred and providing an exposed overextension. As quickly as it assembled, the honeycomb structure disassembled to reposition itself in a consistent lattice around his whole body.

Gus' vision winked black again and then he was back to normal. The experience was more than just seeing what was being done, he understood how and why it was being done. Just like a dream though, aspects of the experience that made sense to him and that he knew on an intuitive level and didn't question just seconds ago began to fade and leave his consciousness. He tried to grasp at them but gave up when they retreated.

Gus strode back into the arena and the fighting resumed. Gus took a couple more risks, but was able to get more critical strikes as he expanded his style past the defensive style he had acquired to avoid getting scratched or infected by the Dark Nth. Occasionally, he found that he had the tendency to retreat and overprotect himself when he could have ended the fight.

After a bit of sparring, he became freer with taking more chances when he was facing the last pillow-Mantid alone. Once they were all defeated, they would reset and he would start again. Before he realized it, a half hour had passed and he completed the quest. The arena went dark.

Gus found he was hungry again and grabbed a snack to go

so he would be buffed for the longest time possible. At his request this one delivered a five-point bonus to intelligence. As he began to eat, he saw that it stacked with his previous buff. Gus knew he was going to have to rely heavily on abilities and the increase to his MP pool, even if temporary, could get him out of a clutch situation when fighting Methiochos. The effects only lasted two hours, so it was time to grab his drones and get going.

Gus sent the drones ahead of him to scout the cave, and began running down the path.

CHAPTER FORTY-FOUR

Final Boss

DAY 10 3:54 PM

0:07:16 remaining

Gus arrived at the cave entrance. The drones had done a good job and mapped the inside of the cave. He entered the first chamber. The sulfurous scent of rotten eggs was more obnoxious the deeper he progressed into the chamber. As the light faded, yellow lines and textures illuminated the walls and areas ahead. Gus' display also enhanced what he could see, but everything had a green tint as the display shifted to night-vision mode.

Meaty undertones tainted the smell of the chamber as well, and Gus couldn't tell if they were from some prey the zombies had eaten, or remnants of their own decomposition. He struggled to breathe in the cloying, sulfur-rich gases. After a half-coughing, half-gagging fit, the silver cracking centralized over his face. A bubble formed over his mouth, nose and eyes. Somehow the hybrid-Nth was able to filter out most of the fumes. It was like breathing through a thick cloth but it was clean.

Taking a moment to clear the tears that had welled up with the coughing and irritating gasses, Gus saw that the mask allowed his hand to pass through but it maintained its shape. Once he was ready, he continued his descent.

The path descended downward until it opened into a large dome-shaped alcove. As the light diminished, Gus' display clicked and the darker areas farther away were highlighted with a green tint, revealing the contours underneath. Gus was glad he had so many stat points allocated into perception.

Looking upward, Gus could see the remains of something large and man-made upended and wedged into the rock. It was entrenched so tightly that no light filtered in from around the edges. With his augmented vision, Gus could make out panels and some seats along one end of the cavern. The drones were inside and the yellow paths on Gus' display showed their journey as they crawled like little spiders along the roof of the chamber, having shifted from their flying mode to this quieter stealth mode.

Irregular rough walls of porous lava-rock were illuminated by the hellish orange light of a roiling magma pool along the right edge of the alcove. An ominous shadow played across the far wall, writhing and snapping like Scylla from Homer's Odyssey. The majority of the creature making the shadow was enshrouded by the dark, and Gus felt a deep sense of dread. He wasn't sure what he was expecting, but it sure as hell wasn't this.

He crouched and sought to hide behind something, but the layout of the cavern offered no real cover. Only the general darkness appeared to have masked his arrival. Gus felt sweat slick the surface of his spear as his hands reacted to the adrenaline pumping through his veins. This... *thing* was something different altogether. Gus sensed that this monster was the driving force behind the zombies and their attack on the Manor, and was glad that they had all been cleared away.

Gus stared at the black mass, trying to activate **Wreck-ognize**. The only information he received was a name:

The One.
Level: ??
HP: ??/??
Description: ??

So helpful. Gus had no idea what weaknesses this thing had. Gus gave the mental command for Nick to roll the playlist.

You have created a song-chain!
RE: Your Brains by Jonathan Coulton

Damage vs zombies/Dark Nth increased x 1.

"YOU!!!" The One shouted mentally.

Before he could react, Gus felt something like greasy tentacles wrenching his mind open. A voice in his head rasped like heavy stone scraping across the floor, low and grating. He dropped to his knees from the intensity of the mental attack. The attack felt like tentacles probing deep into his brain and Gus felt his muscles turn to mush.

Before he totally fell on his face, dark whips emanated from the being and lashed his upper arms and hung him there.

"I do not know how you have come this far. But you saved me the trouble of finding you. Come, puppet, let us claim my domain!" the voice commanded, and Gus was hoisted to his feet by the black tendrils. Gus could not tell what the tentacles were made of but they supported him without gripping him tightly.

The figure elongated, stretching and sliding like a slug up the incline, carrying Gus ahead of it. The movement was painfully slow, and Gus could not budge against the tentacles that kept each limb secured. His soundtrack continued to play as he hung helplessly.

Vegan Zombie by Zach Selwyn

Damage vs zombies/Dark Nth increased x 2.

Gus struggled internally against the tendrils in his mind. He began to get angry at the powerlessness he had felt the majority of his life. His brow began to furrow in fury, and he clenched his jaw in both determination and rage. The thing calling him a puppet had triggered something inside of him. He had felt like that was accurate for his past life; other people pulling the strings, and him dancing along at their whims. No more. With a surge of emotion, he shouted back mentally, *"GET OUT!"*

The resistance must have caught the creature by surprise because it lost its hold and Gus pushed the influence out and away from him. With control of his faculties again, he activated **Dodge** and slid free of the jelly-like appendages holding him.

He landed nearby along the cavern wall. Gus removed his naginata and readied it in front of him. The tendrils attempted to bat at him, but they lacked substance, like getting hit by a gelatinous wiffleball bat. Gus sheared off some nearby tendrils with his spear, and they fell away, splattering against the cavern floor. The writhing mass undulated and more tendrils extended and formed. They braided in a manner Gus recognized from using **Ether Weaving**. Gus jumped just in time as a braided tendril slammed into the cavern wall, blasting chunks of the soft porous stone from the impact. The thicker tendrils were going to be packing much more of a punch.

Gus had to survive long enough for the playlist to ramp up damage modifiers. He stabbed out at the tentacles, slicing some that came close. More often, he was forced to hop around the bumpy surface near the wall, evading attacks and trying not to twist an ankle. His attacks were doing practically no damage. He would have to figure out something different. He would run out of stamina long before this thing did. His pathetic slices at tentacles didn't move the red health bar to show even the slightest of slivers. He needed to do more damage!

Monitoring his stamina and MP bars, he began dodging and ducking. He had to hold out as long as possible before using an ability to escape. Tentacles jabbed into the rock around him like black lightning strikes. Gus dodged and evaded partly on instinct, trying to avoid being hit. There wasn't time to consciously process the motions, and he relied on his agility and used some of the moves from his naginata katas to move along the uneven ground.

Some powdery debris from a nearby strike momentarily blinded him and slowed him enough to be bashed by a tentacle. His armor tightened in response to the strike. The sharp tip of the tentacle flattened, not able to break skin. It did not absorb the entire force of the blow though. The rapid successive attacks appeared to overwhelm the armor. Good to know. Gus grunted as he hit the wall like he'd been kicked by a horse. Coughing to regain his breath, he barely rolled away from a huge tentacle swinging down to pound him into the ground.

Who Do You Voodoo by Josef "J7" & Christopher H. Knight

Damage vs zombies/Dark Nth increased x 4.

The distraction also allowed The One to ooze out tentacles on either side of Gus. They were slowly enlarging, like huge black waves ready to crash down and envelop him. Gus sent his weapon to the left with **Ether Leash**, trying to carve out an escape hatch. The damage was quickly repaired as more black material flowed into the tear. Losing room to move, Gus ran toward one wall and planted the tip in the ground. He then dashed, using Ether Leash to push up and away, imagining he was pole vaulting. Whether it was his adrenaline or fear, it worked! Gus sailed over the black wall as it began to crash downward to smother him, the polearm following him with a tug to avoid being buried in the tar-like material.

Gus turned and attempted to activate **Wreck-luse**, but the skill failed against the boss' high level.

The One remained near the center of the room. Gus couldn't get close enough to engage anything besides tentacles. Gus jabbed at the tentacles and by another stroke of luck he hit **Wreck-tums!**

The distraction was just enough for the Dark Nth to make its move on Methiochos. Clouded by anger, and weakened by the critical hit, Methiochos lost the battle he had maintained for so long. The Dark Nth took control, and Methiochos was no more, there was only The One.

Before Gus could reach it and get in a killing blow, The One sunk two thick tentacles into the magma pool, which were somehow unaffected by the heat. They pulsed as if drinking from the pool and the HP drain abruptly stopped and began to quickly reverse. The magma was sustaining it somehow.

Those tentacles have got to go.

Gus dropped a **T-Wrecks** right next to the magma pool, and it went to town on the feeder tentacles. One of its taloned feet compressed one of the feeders, which seemed to impede its ability to regenerate HP. Magma spewed in large arcs as the dinosaur ripped flesh, causing a breach in the living pipeline. The heat quickly sapped the construct's HP, but the tentacles succumbed to the carnage before the **T-Wrecks** started to dissolve. The mass of tentacles probed at the magma but they were thinner and were burned as they tried to mimic the function of the feeders. The One had regenerated to about 80% of full health, however.

Zombie Me (Apoca-Mix) by No More Kings

Damage vs zombies/Dark Nth increased x 8.

This song-chain is taking too long to power up! Gus desperately slashed at tentacles by swinging his weapon in front of him like he was chopping wood with his naginata. He attacked any tentacle within his reach with abandon. So focused on his task, Gus did not notice that the hybrid-Nth around him had begun to emanate a crackling field of energy. Attacking tendrils were repelled by vicious shocks that caused them to lose cohesion. Nor did Gus notice the magma starting to cool as energy was leached from it, and the stone began to lose its orange amber hue.

All Gus could see were the tentacles. He hacked and hacked and they regenerated. The lighting in the chamber changed to a pale blue-white as the energy ball around Gus expanded. He continued to chop and slash at the tentacles. After losing the ability to suction energy and convert it into tendrils, combined with Gus' wild abandon, he must have hit a critical point, because The One shook. Without the supplemental energy to sustain them, masses of tentacles dropped to the cavern floor.

Living Dead Girl by Rob Zombie

Damage vs zombies/Dark Nth increased x 16.

With the start of the next song, Gus' arms began to move even faster. He felt like he was rowing with the back and forth slashing of his polearm. By the time he had completely severed the two large tentacles with sucker-like paddles on the ends, the magma had cooled to a solid surface behind him as his Nth pulled energy away from it using **Energy Absorption**. If he would have taken a mere one or two steps backward he would have fallen through the thin wafer of solidified stone covering the magma.

Gus felt like his muscles were humming with pent up energy. He pushed forward and the sparking electric bubble followed him, burning away tentacles and the slime that composed them. Gus noticed the size of the energy bubble shrinking as its energy was used up.

Sitting there, blanched by the crackling blue-white light, Gus got his first clear view of The One. His upper torso was strong and muscular, while his other half morphed into some inbred octopus-spider baby. A large segmented abdomen was supported by wriggling villiform legs underneath. Larger wriggling tentacles lined the sides and four long segmented spider legs crouched in a recess in the center of the room.

Zombies Ate My Neighbors by Single File

Damage vs zombies/Dark Nth increased x 32.

"Ya nasty!" Gus shouted as he charged the abomination. A chitinous leg deflected the naginata to one side and Gus flowed into a kata, blocking incoming attacks from multiple legs. The blade severed the jagged sharp edge of an attacking leg, spurting ichor as if it were a lost limb in a Tarantino film. Gus whipped the naginata around with **Ether Leash**, managing to separate another leg at the joint near the torso. A rebound swing hit another leg and triggered **Wreck-tums!** Gus hit it again and it hung limp. The leg with the severed tip was moving much slower, so Gus could focus on attacking the last leg. Waiting for it to attack, Gus blocked and activated **Counter Attack**. He chopped the leg off at the first segment, leaving a tiny stub, waving ineffectually. Screaming in pain and anger, The One lifted his body up by tentacles and heaved himself away from the center of the room. "Anyone tell you that you've got them moves like Jabba?!" Gus taunted.

Don't Stop Me Now by Queen

Damage vs zombies/Dark Nth increased x 64.

Gus smiled as the beginning words of the song began. "Tonight I'm gonna have myself a real good time..." Good times *indeed*. Dashing forward, Gus threw the naginata straight at The One's chest. Instead of dodging, The One brought his hands together and caught the blade between his pressed palms. Gus yanked as hard as he could with the **Ether Leash,** which barely slid the naginata out of The One's grasp, but he also pulled himself forward unintentionally as well. Tentacles lashed out and wrapped around his arms and legs, pressing them to his side. The One lifted Gus to his level, exaggerated dark bulbous eyes visible under greasy unkempt hair.

"Have you wondered how I have sustained myself, little worm? I have the abilities of all the Dark Nth… because I would consume them and incorporate them into myself." A tentacle came up to Gus' face, thin as a razor, and gouged into his chest, tearing his suit and into his skin below. Gus watched in horror as black particles dripped off the tentacle, crawling in the wound.

He flung Gus into the corner. "Now I'll let you get nice and tenderized, we'll have a nice bite to eat, and then I will take the manor." The One had only one ambition; to get off the island and feed. Regaining his brood and consuming everything. With Methiochos' memories, it knew exactly what to do. The floor resonated as The One laughed deep and low. Gus lay coughing in a pool of his own blood, which rippled from the vibration of the laughter, mocking him, face down and gasping.

The area he had been stabbed began to heat up like he was being branded. Gus finally pulled in a breath only to let it out in an agonized scream and the vibrations increased. *So close! I almost did it.* Liquid fire flowed through his veins and Gus began to seize on the cavern floor. All too soon the process was over. A tendril grasped his leg and lifted him high above the cavern floor, drawing him closer.

The One lifted the tentacle above him and unhinged his jaw, retracting it like a snake and preparing to devour Gus whole. When Gus' head was right at the opening of the gaping maw, Gus popped his head up and yelled "Surprise!" and jammed the naginata he had been loosely holding down the gullet of the monster. The blade began to spin more and more as the two ether leashes Gus had wrapped around it over and over again were pulled, turning the weapon into a whirling drill of death.

The blade of the polearm shot out and bore into the soft

throat lining of The One, shredding, slicing, and tearing—hitting the spine after chewing up the back of the throat and continuing to burrow downward. Gus felt the tentacles spasm tighter, then slacken, dropping him to the hard floor. The One slumped there, the very tip of the naginata protruding from his mouth, slowly spinning to a stop, while black slime bubbled and oozed out around it.

Gus lay there while his log filled with a multitude of messages. It was over.

"Your hybrid-Nth say, 'You're welcome,'" Nick quipped.

Really? Snarky now? Gus looked down to his chest and saw the pristine skin exposed by the jagged tear in his suit. Apparently, Nick was right. Hybrid-Nth were resistant to hacking. They had surrounded the infectious Dark Nth particles and burned them out. Painful as hell, but better than the alternative.

Gus looked back at the remains of The One, and with an **Ether Leash**, he lifted the naginata out of the gore. It was almost totally black with the sticky ichor coating it. Instead of having to clean it with his hands, he was able to manipulate the ether to clean the naginata completely of the black slime. A chime sounded.

Due to its composition of Kroutonium, your naginata has obtained a new ability from having vanquished a boss!
Vampire's Kiss (Level 1)
Upon critical hit, transfer damage dealt into health for the wielder of the weapon. Higher levels deal more damage and higher rates of transfer.

The shaft of the weapon had acquired an ebony tone to it, glinting like polished obsidian, having absorbed something from the boss it had just killed. It spun there and glistened with a menacing black sheen. Gus had a name for the naginata pop into his mind. *Jet.* Referring both to its speed and color. Gus pulled the weapon to him. As he grabbed it, he felt a tingle in his hands, as if locking in the special ability to him specifically.

"Gus, reset those settings at Site B," Nick yelled.

Climbing to his feet, he swung the naginata, gathered the limp hand of The One and made his way to the console. He pressed Methiochos' hand to a sensor panel on the far side of the room, and reset the magma channels. He couldn't see under the hardened magma to know if it had worked, but hoped that whatever had diverted power away from the manor was restored, and that it would be enough to keep the volcano from erupting.

He was ready to make the climb out of the cave.

"I know you haven't found anything good from those other zombies, but I'd recommend checking the boss. Sometimes they have a little somethin' somethin'."

Gus looked at the remains and wrinkled his nose. He remembered mucking about in the fat zombie for Razorback.

"It'll be worth it, trust me. Just use **Wreck-ognize** if you don't believe me."

He focused on the corpse of The One and thought about what he wanted. After three seconds, a message dropped:

Loot available

Gus used an ether leash to pull the ten-foot creature on its side. The force of the impact dislodged a silvery, metallic, crystalline ball out of the overstretched mouth. The outside was jagged and rough like the inside of a geode.

Gus picked up the ball and found that checking The One, there were no other items to be had. Gus reviewed his logs as he walked home.

CHAPTER FORTY-FIVE

Runnin' From the Devil

Gus checked his logs as he tossed the crystalline ball back and forth.

You have leveled up the skill: Wreck-tums! to Level 3!
+5% chance to trigger (15% total)
500 XP awarded
300 FP awarded
You have leveled up the skill: T-Wrecks to Level 2!
500 XP awarded
200 FP awarded
LEVEL UP! Congratulations, Level 12 reached!
500 FP awarded
LEVEL UP! Congratulations, Level 13 reached!
500 FP awarded
LEVEL UP! Congratulations, Level 14 reached!
500 FP awarded
You have (15) additional stat points to assign.

You have obtained a Mandrite shard. Mandrite shards are precipitates of pure intelligence and can confer new abilities when absorbed and integrated by your Nth.

Gus focused on the crystal and ***Wreck-ognize*** triggered, showing him some more information:

This Mandrite shard contains:
Psi-link (skill): *Once integrated, allows the user's interface to display other Nth within the vicinity, even if not visible by line of sight.*

Leech (skill): *Once integrated, allows the user to extract data from the target's Nth, and copy the information and abilities to their own Nth. Users can disable temporarily or erase this information once extracted.*

Gus stopped walking as he read the shard's properties. This could be HUGE!

"Gus!!!" Nick yelled, startling him. "You need to get back to the manor control room, now! You have to reset the flows there too; the magma channels are backing up even faster now that they're reset."

Gus began to ***Dash***, and made it back in record time. Sirens blared and red lights were flashing all along the halls. A female voice kept warning, "Please evacuate, situation critical. Destruction imminent." The message kept repeating as Gus ran through the entry and entered the elevator. The doors slid shut painfully slow, as elevators always do. It crawled up floor by floor, leisurely taking its relaxed trip to the command center. As the doors slowly opened, Gus burst forth from the elevator and ran to the command center. Throwing the door open he pulled up the access to the main command console. Red alert windows flashed along multiple screens. Gus frantically looked around, the flashing lights making it harder to navigate.

He tried to access the menu that controlled the flows, but was denied because he didn't have access to the Alpha Protocols. Gus rushed to the scanner and almost slipped in his haste. He placed the severed hand on the scanner. The green line scanned up and down, obviously having difficulty reading the corrupted sample.

"Hurry up, dammit!" Gus said through gritted teeth, as the line slowly repeated scanning, Gus looked over at one screen, which showed that there was already lava spilling down multiple sides of the volcano. Gus pushed the back of the hand into the screen to see if it would elicit a better imprint. A nearby pressure gauge showed that the volcano was already past predictions for eruption. His countdown said he had a couple hours left. The inaccuracy made him even more irritated.

Finally, there were enough data points to trigger the system to recognize Methiochos' hand.

Recognized: Methiochos, DNA and handprint recognized. Alpha Protocols unlocked.

Gus quickly opened the menu and finally found the appropriate window to give him admin privileges.

Reset root access? (Y/N)

A prompt directed him to use the scanner to finalize the process. Placing his hand on the scanner, he felt the characteristic green scan line pass up and down his hand, then a sharp prick as the machine collected a DNA sample from a drop of blood. A pop-up on the display showed the anticlimactic change.

Confirmed. New Master of the Manor: Gus Vannett

Gus saw that all references to Methiochos were being erased line by line from command options in the directories as the change was made.

The computer displayed the prompt: Alpha commands transferred.

"What now, Nick! Hurry, what do I do?"

"Open tunnels 1A and 1B, then 2B, after that you should be fine," Nick advised.

Gus opened the tab with Alpha commands. Where was it? Under the 'Diagnostics' tab there was a warning that showed there were blockage errors on tunnels 1A and 1B, and 2B. Entering the command to open the channels, Gus let out a long sigh, slumping in his chair now that he had finally dealt with the crisis at hand. The sirens continued their grating cadence and the lights did not shut off, but Gus assumed it would take time for the pressure to equalize.

After a minute, Gus reexamined the screens, and all the alerts were still in effect. In fact, the pressure continued to rise.

"Uh, Nick? Why are the pressure levels not leveling out!?"

"Let me check… That should not be happening.

"Oh boy. It appears that the door seals are not responding to the signal to open. I can't tell if it's because the wires are just too old, or that the heat has melted them, but I've got some bad news for you, boss. You're going to have to go down there and open those channels manually."

"Wait, what?! Opening a barrier sealing off molten magma, by hand? What kind of idiot design is that?"

"Actually, there are three channels you need to open. Two are to divert the flow to energy converters. Then, you'll have to open the main conduit. Finally, you'll have to dash like you did around the island. Except without the help of your playlist, sorry. Cooldown and all. You can access the channels through the jungle exit tunnel. I'll update the map. But hurry!"

"Grmmmmm! Nothing's ever easy!" Gus yelled as he alternatively ran and used **Dash** to get to the accessway as quickly as possible. Opening the manhole-sized entry port, he slid down the ladder, holding the sides with his feet and hands. Reaching the tunnel, Nick auto-updated his minimap to show where to go.

A nondescript side tunnel led to a dead end with a hand-scan panel. Gus slammed his hand down and waited for the agonizingly slow green light to scan up and down. He'd have to look into upgrading these, they were horrendously slow, and he always had to access them when time was scarce. After an eternity, the system recognized him and the large door buzzed and electromagnetic locks disengaged. Gus pulled hard on the door and could not budge the large slab of metal. Even with his higher strength stats, he struggled to pull with all his might. This door probably had all kinds of rust and grime locking the hinges in place.

"Umm, boss? Doors that push reduce the speed of those who pull before they read…"

Gus stopped pulling and looked to the side to see where Nick had placed a flashing yellow box on his display around a small panel that simply stated, 'PUSH.' Gus rolled his eyes in exasperation and pushed on the door. It easily and silently slid forward. Gus almost tripped, stepping into a groove just behind the door. Looking up, he saw a large slab of rock suspended beyond the door in an alcove.

"Dude!" Nick mentally shouted at Gus, who shook his head to focus and began running down the passageway, mad at himself for always being so easily distracted. The walls appeared to be bored straight out of the rock, being perfectly cylindrical except for the floor, which was thankfully level. The passageway beyond was long and straight, and Gus began spamming **Dash**. He wasn't sure if the uncertainty of when the volcano would erupt was more or less nerve-wracking than a countdown would be.

Occasional tremors and an ominous resonating rumble would shake the tunnels, spurring him to push his limits and move even faster. The grating noise got so loud that Gus was worried something would shift and the tunnel would be filled with molten rock, but fortunately, it held.

Coming to a T-intersection, he jogged through a series of twists and turns. Gus came to the first door Nick had marked. Instead of a scanner, this door resembled a submarine door with a large handwheel.

Gus grabbed and wrenched the wheel. After a tense second

where Gus wondered if he was turning it the wrong way, the wheel shifted and began to turn. The door opened and Gus was off again to the second door. The pathway to the next door was even more convoluted, and the inability to dash in the narrow curving passages made Gus all the more anxious. Stinging sweat dripped into his eyes and he swiped it away with his sleeve. Was it hotter or was it just because he was exerting himself so much?

Before he could ask, Nick responded, "It's a little of both. Hurry, you don't have much time, Gus."

Gus pushed on, slamming into the second door and began yanking on the wheel to open it. A tremor knocked Gus off his feet, and he scrambled back up, pulling on the wheel. After a loud screech that sounded like nails on a chalkboard, the door relented and opened.

It was definitely getting hotter, Gus realized. Following the minimap, he headed for the last marker. Gus thanked his luck stat that this last passageway was straight. Irising the minimap out, he could see his escape path once he opened the last chamber. Three straight hallways and then he would be out. He just hoped the pressure wouldn't be so high that he couldn't outrun the magma once he opened the release valve.

As Gus neared the end of the hallway, it became harder and harder to breathe. The air was becoming hotter and it was quickly becoming uncomfortable to move. He was two hundred feet from the end of the hallway, and the heat became an almost physical barrier he had to push against. The super-heated air began to make him cough, lungs already burning from his extended run. Gus blinked as he began to get lightheaded.

He stumbled drunkenly and fell to his knees. The floor of the chamber was hot and singed his hand as he reached his hand forward to brace himself from falling onto his face. He yanked the hand to his chest; the pain of the burn gave him a moment of clarity. He tried to force his brain to think. He began to have a coughing fit, as if his lungs were rejecting the hot air, but his brain was trying to override them as it became more starved of oxygen.

Gus looked at his burned hand, squinting from the heat. A red welt was already starting to rise. A silvery sheen floated over it, like heat waves on a hot desert road. He stared for a bit as the shimmer played across his skin, watching the red welt shrink like a pool of water drying up in the desert, being slowly absorbed. Absorbed. His mind perked up for some reason at the word.

Blinking, he recognized the shimmer as his Nth. Nth that had the **Energy Absorption** skill. Holding his hands out, he tried to imagine the heat flowing into the shimmering Nth. It was so difficult to focus amid the coughing fits and his delirious state. He closed his eyes, and pulled on the heat.

Instantly, his mind clarified. Still coughing, Gus envisioned a web of Nth in front of his mouth. He gasped in air that was much easier to breathe, stripped of the suffocating heat. Gus pushed forward, absorbing energy from all around his body. It felt like he was walking into a strong wind with how the heat whipped around him, ever intensifying.

Gus began to feel supercharged with the excess energy that the Nth directed into his entire being. His lungs stopped burning, and he could actually feel them recovering from the damage of the scalding air.

All his senses seemed amplified, as if his whole life had been in black and white and low volume, then suddenly burst into full IMAX glory of sound and color. Currents of energy became visible to him, and he could see them bleeding some of the excess energy off into the ether. His muscles thrummed with energy with each step forward.

Gus approached the end of the hallway and saw a shimmering bubble surrounding the access panel. It crackled and sparkled with purplish energy; apparently it was some kind of force field that protected the interface. Gus tentatively reached toward it and it enveloped his hand as he accessed the scanning panel beneath. Placing his hand on the surprisingly cool panel, he waited for the scanner to do its thing. A message popped up on the display:

Authorize tunnel 1A opening?

Gus readied himself to run and pushed the button. He exploded away, activating **Dash** as a loud creak occurred. Looking over his shoulder, he saw the wall at the end of the hallway began to slide into the roof. Bright magma began shooting into the rift below the door and Gus turned and focused on his escape. Seeing the first turn up ahead, Gus improvised attaching an ether tether along the corner of the hallway to slingshot him into the next hall without losing too much momentum.

It worked! He kept dashing, keeping an eye on his MP gauge, but the extra energy absorbed from the heat must have been supplementing his skill expenditures as it was not nearly as depleted as it should have been from all his skill usage. Gus was approaching the next turn, and then it would be straight on until the end. Gus could hear a rushing noise behind him, but refused to look as he progressed closer to the end of the tunnel.

He took the fact that he didn't feel any heat behind him as a good sign and continued to the end of the hallway. Instead of climbing, Gus slingshot himself to the top of the ladder using two ether leashes.

Gus grasped the rungs of the ladder and encountered another hand wheel. Opening these wheels one handed was difficult. Unsure if it was the energy boost or just adrenaline, Gus managed to loosen the wheel, open the door, and slide out. Slamming the door shut he twisted the handwheel on the other side and tightened it until it was securely shut.

Woof to the woof! Gus sat there for a bit, mentally exhausted.

"We're golden," Nick said. "Power levels are stabilizing and pressure levels dropping. Good work!"

The longer he stayed sitting down, the more his body was powering down and yearning for sleep. Gus stood, stretched, and shuffled to the elevator. Even though it was only mid-after-noon, it was time for some shut-eye. Gus looked at the crystalline sphere and got the prompt to absorb the skills and consume the Mandrite.

"Gus, I'd recommend you wait until you are in bed before doing that; it can take a while to assimilate a new skill, especially a powerful one."

Gus nodded, then numbly made it to his suite. He took a long enough shower to get clean. Grabbed a robe and crashed into bed. He activated the crystal and accepted the prompt to absorb both skills. He was asleep in less than a minute. He didn't hear the crash of chimes and notices that filled his log.

EPILOGUE

Gus had a lazy day, enjoying the chance to just do nothing for a change. Eventually he made his way to the control room to see what he would plan next to develop the manor. For once, he ignored his logs and just existed. Nick repeatedly reassured him everything was normalizing and Gus ate, napped, and took a relaxing swim.

With the magma rerouted, his available energy bar was significantly larger. He would run out of FP long before he exhausted the energy capacity of the manor now. The bio-stasis field, unfortunately, was non-functional. Diagnostics showed that the capacitors to initiate the field's creation had been essentially fried due to maintaining the field for so long.

He took a well-deserved break, and occasionally he worked on improving skills. Eventually he checked his logs and experience gains. For the first time in a while, Gus got to relax and enjoy himself.

Unbeknownst to him, a red light began to flash, indicating a message had been received.

The control panel was dusty, because he had not used them at all during his stay at the manor. The display read:

One (1) message received.
Play now? (Y/N)

    The unanswered message carried a warning. On it, a sinister voice that would have sounded vaguely familiar whispered, "Thank you, whoever you are. We have been looking for the manor for *sooo* long. Now that we know where you are, we will be seeing you soon to reclaim what is ours!"

ABOUT CARL STUBBLEFIELD

The author began his plans for world domination by first becoming a dentist. It is a well-known fact that dentists have unearthed the ancient secrets of how to crush the hearts of men and to hear the lamentations of women and children. When this was insufficient, he created worlds where he could torment the good guys before moving to the next phase of his plans. Known for nefarious accomplishments that involve crippling dad-jokes and debilitating puns.

From his secret lair hidden in the Pacific Northwest, he lives with his wife and three children. They haven't left yet, but the mountain is covered with genetically altered wolves and other creatures. I'm sure that's just a coincidence, though.

Connect with Carl:
HenchmenUnite.com
Patreon.com/Henchmen_Unite
Twitter.com/ouroboros999
Facebook.com/groups/CarlStubblefield

ABOUT MOUNTAINDALE PRESS

Dakota and Danielle Krout, a husband and wife team, strive to create as well as publish excellent fantasy and science fiction novels. Self-publishing *The Divine Dungeon: Dungeon Born* in 2016 transformed their careers from Dakota's military and programming background and Danielle's Ph.D. in pharmacology to President and CEO, respectively, of a small press. Their goal is to share their success with other authors and provide captivating fiction to readers with the purpose of solidifying Mountaindale Press as the place 'Where Fantasy Transforms Reality.'

Connect with Mountaindale Press:
MountaindalePress.com
Facebook.com/MountaindalePress
Twitter.com/_Mountaindale
Instagram.com/MountaindalePress

MOUNTAINDALE PRESS TITLES

GameLit and LitRPG

The Completionist Chronicles,
The Divine Dungeon, and
Full Murderhobo by Dakota Krout

King's League by Jason Anspach and J.N. Chaney

A Touch of Power by Jay Boyce

Red Mage by Xander Boyce

Space Seasons by Dawn Chapman

Ether Collapse and
Ether Flows by Ryan DeBruyn

Bloodgames by Christian J. Gilliland

Wolfman Warlock by James Hunter and Dakota Krout

Axe Druid and
Mephisto's Magic Online by Christopher Johns

Skeleton in Space by Andries Louws

Chronicles of Ethan by John L. Monk

Pixel Dust by David Petrie

Henchman by Carl Stubblefield

Artorian's Archives by Dennis Vanderkerken and Dakota Krout